SIGNAL OF GUILT

VAL CONRAD

Black Rose Writing | Texas

ISBN: 978-1-68433-744-6
PUBLISHED BY BLACK ROSE WRITING
www.blackrosewriting.com

Printed in the United States of America
Suggested Retail Price (SRP) $21.95

Signal of Guilt is printed in Book Antiqua

*As a planet-friendly publisher, Black Rose Writing does its best to eliminate unnecessary waste to reduce paper usage and energy costs, while never compromising the reading experience. As a result, the final word count vs. page count may not meet common expectations.

To the ones we couldn't save.

To Sgt. Jessica Brittain, for having the heart to do what you do.

And to all those who fight the monsters.

SIGNAL OF GUILT

PROLOGUE I
September 15, 2001

Like others desperate to find their loved ones in the days after 9/11, Zach and Julie Samualson had gone to New York, looking for his daughter.

Air travel had been shut down on 9/11, leaving Zach to drive from their home east of Portland, Oregon, detouring to Albuquerque to be with Julie when her mother died after a second stroke. Then they drove on to New York.

Because of their delay, Julie had asked Brandan Callaghan, a deputy in Michigan, if he would go search. He got to New York late on the 12th, but he couldn't get to Manhattan until the next day.

Julie and Zach joined him on the 14th, but the day's search was unsuccessful.

"Time to call in my favor," Zach explained to Brandan, trying to be heard over the loud voices in the fast-food line. "A guy I worked with in Houston is friends with someone who works for our cell company. Harper explained years ago how they locate a phone's general location. Maybe they can do more now, but even that would be a start. I read that eventually, a phone could be tracked as it travels between towers. Theoretically."

Brandan nodded. "Right now, theoretically would be phenomenal and appreciated. We could walk all of Mid-Manhattan and have passed her on the opposite side of the street in every block without knowing."

Zach dialed a number, but the call failed to complete the first time. He hit redial, prepared to do so dozens of times, but the second attempt connected and rang twice.

A snippy curt voice answered, "Sullivan."

"Harper? Hey, it's Zach Samualson. I didn't catch you sleeping, did I?" he said into the cell phone that suddenly felt small in his hand. Time zones bounced in Zach's head — was Harper one hour or two earlier? He'd been in all four continental time zones, having driven from Washington to Manhattan in the last week.

"No, I'm on duty, but I'm free at the moment," Harper Sullivan replied. "Where are you these days? You're not in New York, are you?"

"Actually, I am," Zach said, surprised.

"I warned you the damned DEA would send you to hell one day," Sullivan remarked. "Is it as bad as what we see on television?"

"Not sure it's not worse, but I'm not with the DEA anymore. I'm here trying to find my daughter. She was in Manhattan when the planes hit the World Trade Center."

"Son of a bitch! You have a kid?"

Not the take-away point Zach was trying to make.

"We have years to catch up on, but right now I need your help," Zach said, frustrated. "I'm here with another deputy from Michigan, walking Manhattan for several days, looking for her. The hotel manager where she'd been staying kicked her out, so we have no idea where she is now. She's diabetic, Harper. I've got to find her."

"I understand. How can I help?"

"You once mentioned a friend who works at a cell phone company."

"Oh, yeah, Brady. We've been friends since grade school."

"Cell companies are able to locate a cell phone in real-time, triangulate it from towers, right? I've read enough to believe in other possibilities."

"Probably," Harper said, pulling the phone away from his ear, giving it a worrisome look. "I don't think much about that stuff. Wouldn't have a phone if I didn't have to."

"I'm desperate. Can you put me in touch with this guy, Brady? I've got to find her. You can imagine that nothing in New York is working in our favor. It's crazy."

Harper sighed. "I'll call him. If he's able and willing to help, I'll give him your number."

"Thanks. Next time I get to your neighborhood, the beer's on me."

"For the record, I'm not in Houston anymore either," Harper explained. "I'm a deputy with Benton County, back in Brighton where I grew up."

"Glad you didn't catch us speeding through there a few nights ago then," Zach mused. "I'd have introduced you to my wife, though."

Before he answered, Harper paused to listen, then responded to his dispatcher that he would be responding to a 10-50 with injuries. "I'll get in touch with Brady. Gotta run, Z'. Hope you find her."

The call went dead.

"Yeah, Harp. Me, too," Zach said to himself.

September 14, 2001, 4:48 p.m. EDT

"Zach? It's Brady Cayson again."

"Thanks again for offering to help. Did you find anything?"

"Probably not as much as you'd hoped," Brady answered. "Let me explain how this works. The network recognizes the difference between a phone that powers off intentionally or the battery dies versus when the battery is removed or the phone is terminally damaged. Your daughter's phone disconnected abruptly from the system before noon yesterday. Normally I could get closer, but with all the disruptions there, well. I triangulated its last known location to a six-block area in Manhattan."

"I'll take what I can get, Mr. Cayson," Zach replied, writing down the street perimeters Brady gave him. "Thank you."

"Hope it helps."

PROLOGUE II
April 5, 2007

Pale blue silk curtains swayed lazily in the breeze of a ceiling fan, making the late afternoon sunshine ripple shadows on the bedroom walls. A woman lay in a dreamy, erotic pose in the bed, head turned slightly to the left. Lips parted seductively. Her right arm extended almost to the edge of the mattress, beckoning. The shimmering blue satin sheet draped over her trim stomach and hips then cascaded to the floor, leaving bare her firm, tanned breasts with dark nipples.

The scene suggested a 1970s poster, tipping far past the edge of an R rating, in an evocative scene any man would dream of coming home to find.

An almost perfect image, except . . .

Except for a black mark and trickle of dried blood from her right temple to her ear.

Except for the almost-black stains splattered on the blue satin pillowcase on her left side and maybe white shards of bone disrupting the smoothness of the pool of congealed blood.

In the two decades of his law enforcement career, Harper Sullivan had seen dead people. That this woman was dead wasn't the shock miring his muscles and his thoughts as though he stood knee-deep in drying concrete in a room where the oxygen had been sucked out.

He stood at the side of the bed, head tilted, intrigued by the woman's slightly milky blue eyes. The eerie, unblinking stare trapped the breath in his chest, refusing to let go. The idiotic incongruous impossibility of her death slowed his comprehension of the obvious, even seeing the pistol on the floor where it had tumbled from her hand.

The silverish metal and black grip wavered against the cream-colored carpet. He blinked, hoping the vision was a dream.

A hallucination?

No. Definitely a nightmare.

That is my wife! his brain announced. Repeated. Kept repeating like an irritating jingle stuck in his head until he realized the words came from him. Until his voice became a hoarse whispering shriek. Then his brain stopped processing what he saw altogether. His vision faded to a gray mist. His knees trembled.

No! He shook his head to make his brain re-engage, took a deep breath. The icy reality of her death squeezed his chest harder.

None of this makes any sense!

A deep voice echoed in his head. *Harper, you know it all makes perfect sense.*

Like the flowing lava oozing toward houses in Hawaii, the truth crept toward him, trapped him. Prevented his escape. Threatened to consume him in flames.

She was dead.

His wife.

Lilah Dawn Gentry Sullivan.

Dead.

The visible evidence implied she had shot herself.

Looking at the gun again smashed his guts in a vindictive punch, as he realized that she'd chosen to use a gun dear to him. Not just any of the other eight pistols he owned, but the one meaningful gift from his father when he graduated college in 1987 — a Smith & Wesson Model 5903 9 mm with an aluminum alloy frame and 4-inch stainless steel slide, black wrap-around grip. He'd carried it when he traveled and kept it in his bedside table most of his adult life.

Lilah had asked him to teach her to shoot it when they were dating, and he had, but then she felt it was too big for her. He offered to find her a pistol she liked, but she declined. After she got pregnant, she insisted that Harper buy a gun safe to make sure their child would be safe. And he had. After Hurricane Katrina, he'd heard about enough transient crime from his previous coworkers in Houston that he moved the gun back to his bedside table, assuring Lilah that Meredith was old enough to understand it was not a toy. That had become another major argument.

Again, he wanted to scream that she had used *that* gun. Angry at her disrespect, her lack of consideration! She had the combination to the safe, had access to every other gun he owned.

Why this gun?

His heart skipped a beat.

The question of why rose in his throat again.

In a searing flash, all the reasons why splashed from his memory to his stomach, causing a wave of nausea that bent him over and threatened again to drop him to his knees. The question wasn't so much *why* she would kill herself, but why did she think shooting herself with this gun would be the ultimate way to hurt him.

The answer was simple. She was *that* angry.

Over the fourteen years they'd been together, she'd built a wall of ire, brick by brick. Argument after argument. Lilah had accumulated thousands of reasons to be mad at him, as though she categorized and rated them based on severity. She never forgot a single one.

The Pissed-Off-Lilah Scale of Angry.

Usually, her irritation was about his job. But he had been in law enforcement long before they met, so his dedication to the badge was no secret. They weren't living together when she got pregnant, which had been the only reason he'd ever been truly mad at her. He intentionally delayed marrying her until a month before their daughter was born in 1994, which made her permanently angry, he figured.

Their most recent fight began three months ago when he missed their daughter's performance in "Little Shop of Horrors." Even though his absence had been an unavoidable situation — a semi-truck versus car head-on crash that killed three adults and a toddler — his wife had made it clear he'd put his job first for the last time. Since then, he'd had to make his own coffee in the morning before work because Lilah was still asleep in the guest bedroom. He came home to cold leftovers, if there were any at all.

And once, six weeks ago, he had come home at noon to change shirts and discovered another car in the driveway.

Lilah's best friend's *husband's* car.

While there might have been an easy, ordinary explanation why Ellanie was driving her husband's car, Harper knew Ellanie Thomas was working because he'd seen her ten minutes earlier in the emergency room, where he'd gotten his uniform shirt bloody. Unable to convince himself of any innocent reason for Eddy Thomas to be there, and unwilling to face the possibilities, Harper simply drove past his own house and went to the cleaners to see if he had any clean uniforms ready, then returned to the office to change.

Then there was a conversation he'd overheard a few weeks ago at a friend's birthday party when Ellanie had told Lilah she thought Eddy was having an affair.

Bet you didn't think he was screwing your best friend, huh, Ell'?

Harper opened his eyes again, although he'd hoped the bedroom scene scorched into his memory had been imaginary, but Lilah was still dead on their bed. He leaned far enough to touch her shoulder with the backs of his fingers, finding her body cool. There was mottled blood pooling — he couldn't remember the words for it — on the back of her arm and chest in strange contrast to the blue satin sheet beneath.

Though most of Harper's thoughts remained sluggish, one immediate plan of action formed in his head, unbidden. Irrational.

Solid and logical.

Standing in their bedroom, trying to remember to breathe, the idea congealed like the dark bloodstain on the pillowcase.

How simple would it be to take the gun and let the investigators believe someone else had shot her? Maybe they would find evidence someone else had been in his bed with his wife today — hair fibers, DNA. Semen, as much as *that* thought stirred fiery red-hot coals of rage in his chest.

Maybe, even if Lilah had killed herself, Eddy Thomas would have to confess to adultery to save himself from a murder charge. Who would believe *him* if he — a minister! — was having an affair with a married woman?

A shiver shook Harper, a mix of shock at the idea and shame at his contemplation of it, stunned at the enormity of the temptation to do something so raw and horrifying.

Something he would find deeply satisfying.

Something he had little doubt he'd get away with.

Something so wrong. And yet, so right.

None of the men he worked with would suspect him, gun or not.

Either way, removing the gun would not change the fact she was dead.

Lilah was dead.

Without another thought, he opened the dresser and chose an old black T-shirt, used it to pick up the pistol and wipe away the fingerprints — he'd clean it thoroughly later — wrapped it loosely in the shirt.

Carrying it as if it were explosive, Harper walked to the closet and dropped to his knees to pull the carpeted block panel allowing access to the house's crawlspace. Leaning his upper body into the hole, he felt around until he found a shelf on the far side of one of the joists. Meant for hiding things. He tucked the wrapped gun on it and made sure it was not visible.

The dank smell of untouched dirt lingered in his nostrils after he replaced the panel and tossed a few pairs of her shoes over it.

Then he stood, straightened his uniform, pulled his cell phone out of his pocket, and dialed 911.

The agony in his voice was real.

He heard the first siren within minutes. Within the hour, he'd lost count of how many people had entered the house.

Two years later, two things from that day hadn't been cleared — the case of Lilah Sullivan's murder, and Harper Sullivan's conscience.

Part 1

CHAPTER 1
October 2007

"Dad, you haven't changed. Mom died months ago, and you still just go to work and leave me by myself. I get on the school bus alone. I come back to this dump alone. I can't stand being in the same house where someone killed her anymore, all by myself every fucking day!" his 13-year-old daughter hissed.

"I tried to get someone to pick you up and — " he shouted, ignoring her language.

"Someone else, yeah. You don't give a shit about me. I want to go live with Grandmother Reba in Florida."

"You want your grandparents to run your life?"

"Can't be any worse than you ignoring me."

"Ignoring you?" he repeated. "What would you like me to do, Meredith? Sit home with you and mope? If you think me going to work to make the money you insist on spending on every whim is *ignoring you,* then maybe you should get your ass on a bus and go to Florida," he said, never believing she could, or would.

But it was the last thing he got to say to her.

He came home two days later to find her gone.

That night lasted forever to him. First his wife, now his daughter, choosing to leave.

To leave *him.*

"What the hell is wrong with me?" he yelled. His voice vibrated through the sheetrock and echoed around him in the empty house, followed by a scream so loud it left him hoarse. "I gave you everything I had. A dependable income. Insurance. Stability in a safe community. That wasn't enough, but I don't know what more you want from me."

He had no one else. Tears blurred his vision but would not roll down his cheeks.

Lilah was gone. It didn't matter how. Her death left a hole in his heart he didn't know how to fill. Now Meredith left, too, because they couldn't find common ground to help each other through the grief.

Pulling himself together a little, he called Lilah's parents, Oscar and Ruth Gentry. Admitting he didn't know where Meredith was burned in his gut.

His mother-in-law didn't make his confession any less shameful, but that had been her way of dealing with him since before he married Lilah. With him sitting at the table, Ruth had made it perfectly clear to her daughter at dinner one night that Harper would not be a suitable husband: He'd been married before, and he was a policeman. And, if that wasn't enough, he was Baptist, not Catholic.

Being Caucasian and male were the only two qualities that she *didn't* disapprove of, though she probably doubted one of them, if he had to guess.

"He'll either cheat and then divorce you or get killed at work," she told Lilah that night over pot roast and gravy, unperturbed as though she were mentioning a sale on ground beef.

The fact that he'd done neither still earned him no grace. Instead, she blamed him for not being able to protect or save her daughter.

Now blame would extend to her only grandchild as well.

In desperation, he called to ask if she knew anything about Meredith leaving.

"Yes," Ruth replied, not needing to say out loud the rest of her thought, that *of course, she did*. "Oscar drove over and picked her up this morning. She told us it was your idea. I'm sure she will be better off with us, Harper. We're happy to have her."

Harper wasn't fooled when Ruth's polite charm failed to cover the bitterness in her voice.

Ruth was raised in the era when a Southern lady could tell you to go to hell and rot with such charisma that you'd believe you'd been offered a glass of sweet tea for the trip.

"For the record, Meredith going to live with you was not my idea, Mrs. Gentry," he had replied, knowing better than to call her by her first name. "I know she's unhappy here."

"She's welcome in our home, Harper. Her mother died at an awful time in her childhood. Meredith needs time."

Time away from you, the woman didn't need to say out loud.

After their goodbye, Harper put the receiver back in the cradle on the kitchen counter.

Tears dripped from his chin as he emptied the last of a bottle of vodka into his coffee cup.

CHAPTER 2
Thursday, September 24, 2009

A woman in a white Tyvek jumpsuit crouched, head tilted, studying the rear driver's side wheel of a dark blue sedan struck broadside by a train.

The tire had shredded from the wheel as the car skidded off the paved crossing as the locomotive bounced it along the track at over 45 miles per hour. What was left of the aluminum rims had ragged scrapes from contact with the steel track, gravel, and wooden ties, until the car finally swung free over the embankment.

Her job at the scene had nothing to do with the crash, but the primary detective had specifically requested her to collect and analyze data from a cell phone, the Engine Control Module, and a laptop found in the car. She had collected those three things, each now in signed and sealed evidence bags she held against her chest, yet something about the car itself had drawn her closer to look.

Never having seen a train versus car collision, she was curious about the mechanics of the crash and its evidence, hoping to expand her knowledge in her first year at a real job after six years of college and a year's internship as a computer evidence technician with Tarrant County Sheriff's Office Crime Lab. Complicated scenes like this, a train striking a car at a functional gated crossing, impact on the driver's side, were uncommon. Interesting, but not her job, she told herself, still mentally connecting the car's damage to the obvious cause of it. The bigger question, of course, was why the car was on the tracks. Not her job, either.

Collisions such as this were usually caused by one of three reasons: Suicide, homicide, or stupidity.

No witnesses had been found.

A sole occupant was male, fifties, she'd been told. Car was a rental. No luggage was found, just the laptop and a cell phone.

A smooth baritone voice behind her spoke loudly, perhaps trying to startle her. "What the hell do you think you're doing?"

Although she hadn't been listening for someone to approach, she didn't visibly flinch or look over her shoulder.

"I'm — "

"I don't care *who* you are. I asked you what you were doing."

"No, sir. You asked me what the hell I *think* I am doing," she answered, standing and turning to face the challenger, "and I *think* I'm observing the displacement of the metal edge of the car's left rear wheel where it contacted the pavement, railroad ties and tracks after the tire tore away but before the vehicle left the impact area of the train, *sir*."

His eyes widened at her answer, obviously not what he was expecting.

Pale, blue-gray eyes that didn't quite match, like shades of a storm cloud, she thought. So intense she expected the storm behind them.

"And what is your deduction from your *observation*?" he asked.

"I believe before answering your question, I should know who is seeking my opinion, *sir*." She thought better of crossing her arms, but the defiance was hard on her face.

Each time she said the word *sir*, her tone intentionally became more condescending and sarcastic. Her stepmother had once told her that addressing someone as sir or ma'am was always proper etiquette, but it didn't have to be a sign of respect if not earned or reciprocated.

He yanked off his cap and took two steps forward, putting them inches apart, surprised to discover she stood eye to eye with him at his smidge over six feet tall.

"Accident Reconstruction Specialist, Deputy Kelly Morgan," he said, frowning, which created a crease between his eyebrows.

Except he didn't *have* eyebrows. Nor did he have any hair on his head, which was the same fair complexion as his face except the red skin imprint of his cap. And the mottled flush of irritation on his cheeks.

"Okay, Accident Reconstruction Specialist Deputy Kelly Morgan," she replied. "My *opinion* of my *observation* is that the tire was sheared from the rim by the lateral torque during an approximately sixty-two-foot skid before the car was pushed off the tracks, but the bare edges of the 18-inch five-lug aluminum wheel show diagonal scraping, *sir*."

She keeps calling me *sir* even though we're close to the same age, he thought, and it's pissing me off. Which is exactly why she keeps doing it.

"And what do you conclude from this *observation*?" he snarked.

"My conclusion is that the accident reconstruction specialist should draw conclusions from his own interpretations, sir. I was simply observing for my personal interest." She took one step back and walked around him, leaving him standing beside the wreckage.

After a dozen light steps, she glanced over her shoulder to see him watching her walk away. Near her vehicle, she reached into her pocket and clicked a button on the fob to open the hatch of the plain white SUV and placed the three pieces of evidence she'd been carrying into a lockbox, closing it, and pulling the key from it. Then she pulled her long blond braid from the collar of her white Tyvek suit before she unzipped and stepped out of it, folding it neatly and tucking it next to the evidence box.

After she pulled the hatch closed, she saw in the glass reflection that he was still looking, so she turned and gave him a playful wink as she walked to the driver's door, mumbling to herself as she got inside, what an arrogant ass he was, slamming closed the door. She put on her sunglasses and started the vehicle, backing up to pull away. From behind the mirrored lenses, when she peeked one last time, he was still staring at her as she drove away.

Kelly Morgan muttered something similar about that insolent woman who'd traipsed through his scene. "Who does she think she is?" he asked, pointing in frustration to the air where she'd just left.

Another deputy nearby followed Morgan's stare, then chuckled. "That is Digital Forensics Specialist Deputy Amber Samualson.

Probably collecting the Engine Control Module and the laptop and cell found in the car," he said with a wide smile he tried to hide.

Morgan shot the older man a look of irritation. "What's so damned funny?"

"You two. Already looks like a divorce in the making."

"I didn't even know her name!"

"That's how it always starts."

CHAPTER 3
Thursday, September 24, 2009

Harper Sullivan pulled his patrol car into the reserved parking at the hospital, taking a moment to gather his wits and get his notebook before stepping out into the afternoon heat where he'd already spent an hour, trying to keep a few motivated cows inside the pasture where the ATV had knocked down the barbed wire fence.

"Grass isn't any greener on this side," he'd said as he shooed them away for the fifteenth time. "No wonder we eat you."

He opened the car door and stood, wiping the top of each boot on the back of the other leg, and then dusting off his pant legs again. A trickle of sweat snaked down his neck till it met his shirt collar as he walked to the emergency department ambulance bay doors and finally into some shade.

Taking off his sunglasses first, he punched the door code to access the much-appreciated air conditioning amid the chaos that had arrived fifteen minutes ago in the ambulances.

The madness was reminiscent of the classic Emergency Room on Prom Night on a Friday the Thirteenth During a Full Moon superstition, when a car crash yields multiple teens, involving speed, alcohol and/or a broken heart, and one or more fatalities. This was three teenage girls in a four-wheel off-road vehicle that rolled down a hill. No alcohol. No high speeds. Just bad luck when the driver got too close to the edge, and the dirt gave way.

A doctor exiting one of the trauma rooms caught Harper's eye, shaking his head as the finale to another life.

Fatality number two. The first had been at the scene of the accident.

"The other one went straight on to surgery for the arm and hand injuries. Hoping she doesn't lose it altogether," he said as he walked on by.

Not much more information than that was necessary from him. Harper only needed identification of the dead child by distraught parents whose world had just shattered.

"Hey, Harp," Ellanie Thomas said in a solemn, respectful voice, having come from the same room the doctor had. "What a tragedy. Will you need her clothes?"

Harper shook his head.

"We'll have her cleaned up in a few minutes for the family."

"Thanks, Ell'," he said.

Harper was always dismayed how the heroic efforts of the emergency room staff altered a patient's appearance. Shocked how many tubes could be inserted into a body. And why nurses like Ellanie took the time to make a family's first encounter with a deceased loved one a smidgen better.

As distraught as her death had left him, Harper was glad his last memories of Lilah were not here in the emergency department. After the law enforcement investigators had released her body to be taken for autopsy, Harper refused to see her in the casket, even though he understood morticians had made her look as if she were sleeping.

Innocent. Peaceful. Beautiful.

No, he hadn't wanted to see that either — he'd seen plenty more than enough. While not pleasant, he chose to keep the memory of her, lying in their bed, with a bullet entrance at her temple, blood on her head and hair, dripping on the pillow.

No matter how long it had been, that memory fueled his anger at her and at the man who'd been in their bed. As outraged at Eddy Thomas for screwing his wife made him, Harper felt sorry for Ellanie Thomas. She wasn't responsible for what her cheating, hypocritical husband had done. Harper was most pissed how Eddy could stand in front of a church congregation and preach fidelity, honesty, and integrity, when he failed to exemplify any of those qualities.

In Harper's imagination, if Eddy confessed, he would be a quintessential model of imperfection to his church by admitting his human sin of adultery. Uplifted, praised for his confession and repentance. That was the most unacceptable part of this. Eddy would be forgiven by everyone else. Maybe even Ellanie.

Sweeping his anger back into its worn and warped mental box, Harper readied himself to meet the parents of this girl, on their way from where they both worked at a fiberglass tank company on the other side of town. For the last ten minutes, the father had probably been speeding, cutting off cars in their way, knowing in his heart that bad news waited on this side of the glass doors.

Harper considered this, for he couldn't decide which might be worse for a parent: to open the door to a deputy or trooper and hear that news, or be called and told little before having to drive to the hospital. As much as he didn't like making death notifications, he believed it might be kinder to parents to fear the truth before driving instead of hoping for a mistake or a miracle.

He took his paperwork to an empty desk in the back of the department. Ellanie would let him know when the parents arrived and were ready to talk to him. The doctor would speak to them first, let them see the body of their daughter. Ellanie would probably drape her arm around the mother's shoulders if the father had not already done so. Or she might help him off his knees where he'd dropped, begging God to let it be him instead.

Things she did for families were not skills taught in nursing school; they came from both personal and professional experience. Before marrying Eddy Thomas, Ellanie had lost her seven-year-old son to a fast-growing brain cancer that had taken his life in four months, then lost her husband when he couldn't stand to look at her because she signed the do-not-resuscitate order when the boy had become comatose.

Yes, beyond providing medical care to patients, Ellanie understood how useless words were and how a genuine tear or a simple touch could help someone to hold on to the shreds of sanity when nothing made sense.

She did so with such honest compassion, Harper thought. *How could she live with a man who made a joke of their marriage?*

He turned his thoughts to the narrative of his report.

Car crash reports. He must have written a thousand in his career. Most weren't fatalities of kids his daughter's age.

Wait, how old was Meredith again? Fifteen. No doubt her grandparents would buy her first car or give her one of theirs instead of trading it in every two years as they'd done for as long as he'd known Lilah.

Stop thinking about her! He chided himself back to his job.

He began writing in his backhanded capital letters. *Dispatched Code 3 for 10-50 at 8542 Rabbit Foot Lane on an ATV rollover. EMS responded times two for three reported occupants. Arrived to find a four-wheel all-terrain vehicle that appeared to have skidded off the rocky trail toward the driver's side, then rolled down an embankment, coming to rest on its passenger side against a pile of broken cement. Three occupants were present:*

Occupant #1 – Driver, uphill from vehicle approximately twelve feet, determined by EMS to have suffered unsurvivable head/brain injury. Three-point seatbelt found retracted and unbuckled as if not in use at time of crash. Patient pronounced dead at scene by JP Tom Haggerty at 1529.

Occupant #2 – Front-seat passenger was in the three-point seatbelt harness, conscious but in distress, with her right arm pinned between the upper frame of the vehicle and the ground surface; transported by EMS to Benton County Hospital.

Occupant #3 – Backseat driver's side passenger, also in a three-point seatbelt harness, was unconscious, with severe bleeding from several wounds, including the head. EMS was removing this patient first on my arrival; transported by EMS to Benton County Hospital, where she was pronounced dead shortly after arrival.

The four-person / four-wheel-drive all-terrain vehicle appeared to be traveling north/northeast on a dirt path. Observation of the tire tracks shows the vehicle had been operating parallel to a caliche pit for approximately 75 yards, then swerved left possibly to avoid a cactus or yucca. It then appears the left-side tires lost traction on the loose rock and/or caliche, and the front wheels began sliding downhill. When forward momentum had ceased, the vehicle rolled to the driver's side, down approximately thirty-five feet 1.75 times, rolling over a three-strand barbed wire fence into a pasture being grazed by approximately three dozen head of black cows and calves.

No rancher himself, Harper couldn't tell a Hereford cow from a Longhorn bull most days, but the breed and gender were immaterial. He and a volunteer firefighter had taken turns turning the cattle back from the scene while everyone was working.

The rancher, a neighbor of the driver's family, arrived to mend the fence before Harper left. The man felt horrible that the girls had lost control on the hill.

"Years ago, I rolled an old pickup down yonder," he said, pointing, "where the pit veers onto my land. I bet they were out looking at the new calves."

Harper recorded the man's words.

The anguished howl of a man echoed through the hall, no doubt the girl's father. Other voices, some sobbing from those facing that overwhelming wall of new agonizing grief.

When Lilah had died, Ian had quietly urged Harper to come to the ED, and Ellanie offered her genuine comfort, even while suffering the loss of her best friend. The two of them sat in a seldom-used treatment room, crying together.

"Seeing her like that," he'd sobbed, "tore my heart out. She was so beautiful. Why?"

"We can't understand the choices people make. Maybe we'll learn after we die," she'd told him. "She knew you loved her, Harper. What she did isn't your fault."

"How do I tell Meredith? She and Lilah are so close," he'd said, then corrected himself for the first time of many, he figured. "*Were* so close. I don't know how to do this, Ellanie."

"One breath at a time. You've seen others in this same spot. The only way to go forward is the same way you do every day. One breath. One step. I won't lie and say it ever gets easier, because if it does, I don't know the secret," she'd replied.

They put their heads together and cried harder.

One step. One breath.

Harper didn't remember if her words were helpful that day or any since, but he hadn't forgotten them.

He stood and gathered his notebook and report, slowly making his way to the nurses' station for when the girl's parents came out of the trauma room.

A paramedic came through the ambulance bay doors. "Cool. I was hoping I didn't have to chase you down tonight," she said, handing Harper a cell phone in a sparkly pink case. "One of the firefighters found it under the ATV after you left. It's broken, but it belongs to one of them."

Harper took it. "If these things could tell us what happened."

CHAPTER 4
Friday, September 25, 2009

The halls beyond his office door were dark and had been empty for hours on a Friday evening. Even the cleaning staff had finished, leaving Brady Cayson working at his computer in silence. He seldom worked this late, but his wife had taken the kids to a church supper benefitting a mission trip to Mexico the coming summer.

While waiting for a lengthy document to print, Brady swiveled his chair toward his credenza and leaned back. Because the flickering fluorescent ceiling lights bothered him worse at night, his office was lit by a standing lamp in the corner and a desk lamp once used by his grandfather.

After rubbing them with the heels of both hands, his tired eyes focused on a poorly lit framed photo almost hidden behind a stack of reports. Not that he needed light to spark that memory of him and four friends, but the photo had caught them in a perfect moment on a white-water rafting adventure twenty-five years ago — their graduation trip. The recollection was as vivid in his mind as in the photograph, but the five friends would take no more trips or photos together.

His memories were interrupted by a phone call, a coworker with a question that might have waited until Monday morning, but everyone Brady worked with knew he would have an answer and be available to offer it if he were at work. Even at nearly midnight on a Friday night. If someone dared call his cell phone after hours, it had better be news that the building was on fire, because he'd worked his way up in the company past where his family time could not be compromised for anything less.

He checked his watch. It was now Saturday morning.

Tonight's project was a teaching outline and slide presentation for a group of network engineers in the Philippines. Fifteen years ago, he would have been expected to fly to Timbuktu and give it himself.

No longer traveling seven months out of the year, he kept several projects going simultaneously, something between those that rose to the top of his priority lists. Now that he was through with this task, he needed to spend time on a court case evaluating the phone signal of an indicted criminal.

Cellular networks record any phone's location as it connects to towers during a call, but new phones stayed connected to exchange data in real-time, even if not connected by a voice call. The so-called "smartphone" was a single handheld device performing dozens of computerized functions previously accessed separately — newspaper, camera and photo albums, alarm clock, calculator, note pad, music player, map, library, calendar, email, and Internet access.

Locating a phone's current location based on GPS was a closely monitored tool for cell phone companies, and some 911 centers had incorporated that ability for emergency calls made by cell phone when other means of locating the caller failed. This could narrow a location down to 5 meters in a live view only. However, records provided as latitude and longitude could be assembled to track historical locations of the phone by plotting multiple triangulation points.

In one prosecution case Brady had worked on, he provided evidence that the system showed the perpetrator's and the victim's phones had been near the location and at the time of the murder. But after his girlfriend was beaten to death with a bat, the suspect took her phone with him as he traveled from Texas to Florida. Along the way, he texted her from his phone, and he replied from her phone to his for several hours, thinking that the conversation on his phone would be a perfect alibi, and he would get rid of her phone somewhere along the way. He entered what was to be her last text, "Help someons brking in heyv got bats and . . . "

Meanwhile, the woman's body had been found less than 45 minutes after the murder, and police learned her cell phone was missing. A court order was obtained to begin recording text message content from her phone when Brady discovered text messages were being exchanged to and from her phone in real-time.

Law enforcement then got a warrant for the cell company to locate both phones and subsequently arrested the boyfriend/killer in a hotel in Shreveport, Louisiana, where he'd been drunk and high for six hours, starting at the bar next door. Both phones were in his car. The murder was less than 24 hours old.

His defense attorney, while likely a poor excuse for a lawyer in the first place, didn't understand the overwhelming weight of these cellular records or the expert witness armed with detailed maps, copies of call records, and texts that led the prosecutor to a quick first-degree homicide guilty verdict.

Though Brady had been that expert witness in this and other trials, documents he prepared for prosecutors were usually historic, showing a relationship between parties through reciprocal calls and texts if it had existed, and the geolocation of the users' phones before and during the crimes. That had been the first time active phone location was used to find a suspect's phone in a live situation.

The ability to track the movement of someone's cell phone live, even when it wasn't making a call, was pure gold, Harper Sullivan pointed out at a weekend get-together a year ago. Brady agreed.

The same friends in the rafting photo discussed the ideas over a pitcher of beer and pizza. These were guys Brady had graduated high school with before going their not-so-separate ways.

All but one of them lived within a fifty-mile radius of the Dallas-Fort Worth area after college. Four had ended up in careers in the world of computers, sprung from their high school days of programming in Basic and Nerd Nights as they had called dedicated nights spent with Brady's first computer, an Altair 8800. Bruce worked for an IT department in one of the biggest hospitals in Dallas. Jeff had worked with Mike for a networking company. Pancreatic cancer had taken Jeff's life at a much-too-early age a few months ago.

Only Harper's profession, the others had teased him, dealt with people who sometimes shot at him. Law enforcement had been his life since their college graduation, and his computerese had stagnated since that time, too. He was also the only one of the group who had been married twice already, though his first divorce was no surprise to his friends. His second wife had been murdered in their home, something that the others never discussed in his presence because he hadn't dealt with her death well.

As if anyone really could.

Brady, however, hadn't married until he was in his thirties, and although his job was sometimes demanding, he knew his marriage was rock solid because he made it a much higher priority than work, especially since the kids came along. Before that, work had sent him worldwide — and it still did occasionally — but now his time at home with Elizabeth and his family was seldom interrupted by either of their professions.

CHAPTER 5
Wednesday, September 30, 2009

Having met only three vehicles in the last ten miles, the Honda Accord zipped down the highway at six miles per hour over the posted speed limit, hugging the occasional curves with ease. Its tan color with weeks of dust and road grime would have camouflaged it against the water-starved Texas Panhandle grasslands that stretched to the horizon in all directions, had the sun risen yet.

The driver, an experienced registered nurse, now worked nights in the region's largest hospital cardiac care unit. However, as a fresh graduate six years ago, her husband had insisted she work in the small hospital in their hometown so he could keep an eye on her — although he'd told her it was so she wouldn't be on the highway at all hours. But she had made friends there. After separating from him and moving to Amarillo for a new job, she'd continued working at the smaller hospital in Harris four days a month and on-call, for both financial and social reasons. So, when the nursing supervisor called her at 4 a.m. and begged her to work the day shift, she agreed.

On her way this morning, she was thankful to be driving in the dark at 5 a.m. instead of being blinded by sunrise — the autumn sun wouldn't peak over the horizon until she arrived to work.

But yesterday had been her day off, and she'd run errands all day then stayed up till eleven, watching a movie, so she hadn't had nearly enough sleep. With an occasional yawn as she drove, she sipped a double-caff cappuccino from a coffee hut, transferred into a dull aluminum travel cup to stay hot, occasionally singing out loud and off-key to a couple of songs on a CD she'd burned for road trips. She'd never sing where anyone heard, only alone in the car. The tunes got her energized for a day at work, and she'd need it.

The supervisor told her that the intensive care unit was full, with two patients on ventilators. Her shift would be busy, she thought, but she might bump into one of the radiology techs. She'd made it clear she was interested in him last time they worked together, so maybe he'd finally ask her out now that her divorce was final.

Final. *Finally final*, she said, repeating singsong, smiling at the redundancy of the phrase. She had waited seven frustrating months for a judge to declare her "I do" to be a "You don't anymore." Still, the separation and divorce proceedings had been an ugly, too-public mud-slinging fight echoing to a large degree the tone of their marriage, but it was over. Shaking her head, she declared at the top of her lungs that, "Never again!" would she allow someone so much power over her as the ex-husband had taken: isolation from her family and friends, financial limitations to her social life, and sometimes physical violence but more often sheer intimidation through fear.

Maybe someday, she'd even quit having nightmares of the things he'd done to her.

Yep, she thought, today was going to be a fantastic day.

She stretched toward her bag on the floorboard of the passenger side, unable to reach deep enough for the granola bar she wanted. Unbuckling the seatbelt allowed her to lean the necessary few inches more, and she was feeling around in the clutter when the steering wheel jerked, and it sounded like a blowout . . .

***

The report written by the deputy who had responded to the scene stated only facts, but had it read what was really on his mind, it would have said: *The car swerved slightly to the left, only to be over-corrected so hard that it veered off the pavement, the backend spinning clockwise around the front on loose gravel and dirt off the shoulder. The skidding wheels appeared to have caught on something that caused the car to roll several times until it went through a fence and down approximately 200 yards into the ravine. The seatbelt was not in use at the time of the accident. The driver was ejected about halfway down the slope.*

Rescuers would later debate whether being ejected was a blessing or a curse for the driver as the car had continued its tumble to the bottom of the canyon. Because it was dark, passing motorists didn't notice the skid marks or the fence destruction. Neither the driver nor the car had been visible from the road except through a small canyon. Her bright orange scrub top had caught the eye of a passing helicopter pilot three hours later. She was barely alive when the ambulance and rescue units arrived.

On initial investigation, the skid marks and other evidence pointed to the roll-over being an accident, the proverbial one-car-off-the-road-and-speed-was-likely-a-factor sort of crash. One of a fraction of crashes where the ejected occupant survived.

The driver, 32-year-old Caitlyn Parker, had been flown from the scene by medical helicopter to the closest trauma hospital where she remained unconscious for four days, undergoing three major surgeries, including repair of internal bleeding from her liver and spleen, the removal and stabilization of a completely crushed cervical vertebra, and trephination — removal of a small piece of her skull to allow relief of the brain swelling.

The intensive care nurses in that regional hospital were her coworkers. They had been quiet when discussing whether she would want to live as she was, now believing she was a paraplegic, but they did their best to save her.

On the fifth day, she opened her eyes and reached to touch the surprised nurse changing an IV bag. He asked if she could understand him, and she squeezed his arm. Two days later, she was breathing on her own, off the ventilator, and able to move her left arm and fingers.

The next morning, she made a statement to the Benton County Deputy who came to see her. Just four words.

"My ex-husband did this."

Then she closed her eyes, and her heart stopped beating.

***

Watching the sudden, and at least to him, quite unexpected cardiac arrest of Caitlyn Parker shook Deputy Harper Sullivan to the bone. Not so much that she died, but that had he waited until after lunch, or even stopped for a cup of coffee, the woman's last words might have gone unheard.

But what had she meant? he wondered as he walked out into the sunlight. According to the staff, Caitlyn had no visitors. Divorced, childless, her parents dead, they said. *What* did she think her ex-husband did? Was she even lucid? The charge nurse had told Sullivan that Caitlyn didn't remember the accident though she was oriented to herself and her location; however, amnesia after such a traumatic event or a coma was not unusual.

Now that the accident had become a fatality, the accident investigation would change course, but only slightly. After days in the hospital and surgeries, he doubted an autopsy would yield anything useful now. He stopped in the lab to see if her original blood samples from the ER were available for toxicology testing, and he filled out a requisition for them to be sent to the state lab.

His duties complete, Sullivan walked out to his patrol car in the emergency department parking lot. Like countless times before, he reached to open the door, bringing into focus the dent and chipped paint below the handle. The metal had buckled where he had kicked it during a blind rage of anger and grief as his wife's body was wheeled out of the house.

For the last time. Ever.

Although the shop had touched up the damage, the dent and scar of the chipped paint remained. The department would have given him a different vehicle if he'd asked, but he preferred to keep it as another reminder.

That memory still threatened to drown him in moments like now. During the first year, if he let down his emotional wall, he only found solace deep in a bottle of vodka. He was better now. He didn't look away from the door or cringe at its memories most days.

But watching Caitlyn Parker die unwound the knots Sullivan had tied up his emotions with. Grief oozed out, wrapped its slimy stinging tentacles around his chest and squeezed till he could hardly catch his breath. He yanked open the door and slid into the seat, slamming the door before starting the engine. Wishing he could drive fast enough to leave his past behind him.

He'd screwed up Lilah's death with his selfishness. He owed it to this woman to investigate the cause of her death.

CHAPTER 6
Wednesday, September 30, 2009

"G'morning, Mrs. Preston."

"You're late, Mom," the second of the boys announced as they scrambled into the back seat of her car.

"Funny. You didn't call last night either," Dierdra replied.

"Sorry," twelve-year-old Blaine told his mother when he slammed the car door closed. "I can't find my phone."

Blaine and his friend Drake smelled faintly of Drake's father's cigars. The sharp odor made her nose twitch.

"Again? I suppose the Lawrences don't have a phone you could use?" Dierdra asked, irritated they would be stuck in the crowd of cars dropping off students, which meant she'd probably be late for work, too. If Drake hadn't been with him, she'd have dumped her son out two blocks away from the school and let him walk. "Look under the seat."

Blaine bent over like a spaghetti noodle to look beneath the front seat. "Wow, how did you know?" he asked, sitting up and grabbing for his seatbelt, barely clicking it before falling under the electronic gizmo's spell.

What an addictive mind-control device the smartphone has become, she thought. *Even adults have difficulty putting one down nowadays.*

She pulled away from the curb at the Lawrence's house and started toward the school, letting her mind wander back to last night, enjoying a twelve-minute daydream in silence, thanks to those very phones.

Because Blaine had stayed at Drake's house last night to work on a school project, Dierdra had spent the night with the man she had been seeing over the last year. Hooking up was a much closer euphemism to their relationship than words like dating or seeing each other. Stephen called it something else entirely too profane to repeat. An occasional night in a hotel insinuated an illicit twist to their relationship, perhaps adulterous, but she had been divorced for four years. Stephen had been separated for two years, finally divorced eight months ago, but he seldom discussed that.

Come to think of it, we seldom discuss anything.

Blushing, she looked in the mirror to make sure Blaine hadn't been watching her.

She'd known Stephen long enough to understand why he was single. Again. While he was intelligent, his personality was brash, demanding, and lacking emotional connection to most of his peers or any of the public. Even with her, he showed a limited amount of overt affection with absolutely no signs of commitment. Somehow though, despite their curt, often antagonistic professional interactions in court, they'd found a comfortable physical connection. No way could they live in the same house or develop a permanent relationship, but dinner and a night in a hotel occasionally provided all the elements either of them wanted from a partner.

Dierdra yawned, even though she had slept well after a couple of glasses of wine and great sex. *Twice. And this morning, too.* She smiled. Part of the attraction was that neither of them wished to make their business public, thus keeping the secret took a little planning, which built anticipation.

Although the sky was now shades of blue and white, had Dierdra Preston been awake for it, the sunrise had been a wild blend of gold and red clouds on the horizon, Stephen had told her this morning. "Almost as pretty as you," he'd said, a rare compliment from him.

Dierdra remembered blushing. Years had passed since a man had told her anything of the sort.

"Shit," Blaine muttered, interrupting her thoughts. "My phone died."

"Blaine, watch your language," she reprimanded him as she turned the car into the school parking lot.

"Sorry," he said, his backpack in his arm, ready to make a quick getaway as soon as the car stopped so he wouldn't get a lecture.

At least Drake thanked her for the ride as they scrambled out the doors.

Then they were off in a burst of energy Dierdra might have envied twenty years ago.

She drove on to the office. After she parked, she checked her mileage log and realized she was almost out of gas. Her gas gauge was stuck at half a tank, so she had to keep track of the mileage after every fill-up. The odometer was higher than she recalled.

Then she remembered how her morning had begun in the hotel, awakened to the sound of the lock mechanism, startled out of a crazy dream. Stephen was letting himself in, two sacks in one hand, and a carrier with two steaming cups in the other.

"I brought breakfast," he said with an easy smile. "Then maybe we'll have dessert."

"Coffee?" she said, sitting up and pulling the sheet over her naked body.

"Of course," he replied, handing her a cup after he'd set the bags down. "I had to take your car, though. I have a flat tire. Hope you don't mind."

So, he'd driven her car when he went for breakfast, she thought as she got out and went inside the courthouse. Big deal. That explained the extra miles, but oh, had coffee and fresh croissants, and more sex made it a fabulous morning, whether or not she'd seen the sunrise.

CHAPTER 7
Friday, October 2, 2009

The sun had dropped its last ten minutes above the horizon behind a bank of orangish clouds, leaving a fading light on the crash on I-30 West. Drivers jostled for the lead in the Friday race home until at least six cars tangled, starting with one harried woman from Childress, who already felt trapped in the second of four lanes when her car had a flat. Panicked and unsure in the heavy traffic which shoulder to move to, she guessed wrong to move to the left. A driver in the fast lane slammed on his brakes to avoid hitting her car from behind. A third car, also speeding and tailgating, slammed into the second, which then hit the first. The first car spun to the right into the second lane, colliding with a fourth car, pushing it to the right in front of car number five. That driver tried to avoid being pushed into the lane to his right by steering left, which caused his car to turn crossways, and the sixth vehicle struck it broadside on the driver's door.

The other northbound drivers had avoided the chaos in the same miraculous way NASCAR drivers drive through a track crash obscured by smoke — with a little luck, a few expletive phrases, and maybe one or two closed their eyes and hoped for the best.

The driver of car six was not the only occupant injured, but he was the only one pinned in the wreckage with a grill buried in his door. He'd probably have freaked out at the smell of gasoline and antifreeze, had he been conscious before the firefighters pulled a hose to wash down the spill before pulling the cars apart to extricate him from his crushed car.

Fifteen minutes later, the last ambulance pulled away without the driver of car six, whose heart had run out of blood to pump before rescuers had gained access. Had he not bled out before the firefighters and paramedics lost the race to reach him, the accident wouldn't have even made the 10 o'clock news. The transition to a fatal crash raised its newsworthiness to a 20-second blurb without footage if there was time.

Predicting the fatality and knowing from experience that traffic reduced to one lane would cause a significant delay, the patrol sergeant requested a crash scene investigator as soon as she arrived.

An hour into the incident, Deputy Morgan had fought his way through miles of backed-up traffic, finally reaching the three closed lanes a mile away. He parked his white county SUV near the divider behind the wreckage.

Morgan made his preliminary walk-around the crash, now in dusk with wildly flashing reds and blues of the six or seven other emergency vehicles and four wreckers, like a disco of decades before. Even the traffic noise had a syncopated rhythm. He liked older music from the *Saturday Night Fever* era, and some song by The Bee Gees was playing in his head as he took notes.

In the second lane, a newly licensed teenage driver somehow got through the flares and emergency vehicles unscathed, scattering a dozen cops and medics, plowing into the middle of the crash scene.

She later told the arresting deputy that she'd been blinded by all the red and blue lights, and she was confused where to go as she came barreling down the freeway, three lanes of which had been closed for more than a mile. A deputy, following her with the intention of ticketing her for disobeying warning signs, noted he could see the conglomeration and directional arrows clearly at least a mile away. The report also noted that her skid marks began 22.4 feet from the point of impact with an estimated speed of 50 miles per hour. Save a bloody nose from the airbag smashing her glasses, she was unharmed from the crash.

Kelly Morgan was not so lucky. Whether he heard the vehicle coming or the yells of emergency workers, he looked back before impact then turned sideways to the pickup coming at him. Ironically, in that instant, he remembered an instructor's lecture point that adult pedestrians turn sideways to the impact, but children turn to face the vehicle about to hit them. That difference changed the mechanism of injury as much as the size difference.

The bumper of the full-size pickup first struck his leg two inches above his right knee. In what seemed like a slow-motion movie to him, he heard his femur snap, felt the ligaments and tendons rip apart as the knee dislocated in a nauseating crunch. His body twisted as the leg gave way. Ribs cracked when his right chest crashed into the grill and hood, his feet left the roadway, then his head slammed into the hood. He didn't remember being knocked clear of the crash instead of being pinned between vehicles. He didn't remember falling to the pavement. He wasn't aware that one of the splintered ends of his fractured femur punched through his skin and his navy-blue cargo pants with a sound he might have compared to a watermelon being cracked open like an egg, had he been considering such things.

Given those individual facts, Kelly was lucky to have survived long enough to hit the ground. Had rescue crews not been on scene, at his side within seconds of the crash, his body would have been transported to the morgue with Driver 6.

Three Fort Worth Fire Department paramedics worked on him while the ambulance that had left empty was requested. Police closed all westbound traffic to create a landing zone for the helicopter or to allow the ambulance to access the scene. Responders discussed calling for air transport, but the estimated ground transfer time to a Level I Trauma Center was less than the ETA to the scene of a helicopter, so police prepared for the ambulance to approach from the nearest off-ramp going the wrong way.

Medics immobilized Kelly's cervical spine, placing a rigid collar on him while holding pressure on the femoral artery at his groin to slow the bleeding from a four-inch ragged rip across the midshaft open angulated fracture. They placed a long backboard next to him, ready to roll his body to the side after a splint was placed on the leg, although one paramedic interrupted that process to intubate him.

By the time the ambulance arrived back at the scene, Kelly was packaged for transport, with an ET tube in place to protect his airway, a collar to protect his neck in case he had a cervical spine fracture, a long backboard with head blocks to keep his body in a flat position and support the fractured femur, and two IVs of normal saline running to replace the blood he'd left on the asphalt. Without invitation, three fire paramedics joined the one on the ambulance after the gurney was loaded into the back doors and locked into place. Even if unnecessary, eight hands were better than two.

Kelly was one of the family of blue. Two police units escorted the ambulance to the hospital while others blocked intersections.

The ambulance arrived, putting Kelly in the trauma bay less than nine minutes after he was loaded, seventeen minutes after the crash, with a third IV running on blood tubing, awaiting the first unit of O-negative blood. Within half an hour of arrival, before his next of kin got there, he had been to CT scan then whisked down a brightly lit hallway to a surgical suite.

Too bad cameras weren't recording, because the whole scenario ran like a Hollywood script, perfect on the first take.

CHAPTER 8
Friday, October 2, 2009

"Mom, where were you the other night?" Blaine asked, feigning innocence as he poured milk over a mixing bowl-sized serving of Cheerios he was having for dinner. "I did try calling from Drake's house."

Dierdra raised her head from the newspaper, a twenty-four-page waste of wood pulp. "It's none of your business."

"I think I'm old enough to know what's going on when I can't reach you."

"I think you're *not* old enough when I can't reach you," she replied. "You first."

"I was at Drake's house," he said, his voice jumping almost an octave, a betrayal that his adolescence had not yet overcome.

"Umhmm," she said, turning her attention back to the paper and her cup of tea.

"Really," he said, trying again for a more adult range of vocals, but seeing that she had already dismissed his lie. "I mean, we went over to Seth's house to play video games for a couple of hours, but I was back by nine."

"By nine?" Her eyebrow raised, but she didn't look up.

"Maybe it was closer to ten, I wasn't keeping track. We were done with our project." He ate in silence, thankful she wasn't going to have kittens over the curfew breach. Almost finished eating, he asked again. "So how about you?"

"No, sir, you lost your right to ask when you didn't tell me the truth to start with," she replied. "How did you get to and from Seth's house?"

"We walked." He stood, still scooping the last few bites into his mouth on the way to the sink before he turned the bowl up and drank the remaining milk, which he knew irritated her even more than pouring it down the drain. When that didn't get a reaction, he rinsed the bowl and the spoon, then put them in the dishwasher before heading to his bathroom to brush his teeth.

When he was out of her sight, she shook her head. The back-and-forth between them was a lot less angry these days than it had been a few years before, when Blaine still blamed her for his dad leaving.

Though not part of their formal agreement to separate, Dierdra and Grant Preston had agreed not to discuss the grounds for the divorce with Blaine or to talk badly about each other. Grant hadn't been guilty of adultery or domestic violence, but he had issues with gambling and financial irresponsibility, jumping from one scheme to another without having the income to match it.

They had lived in Austin while Dierdra put herself through law school, struggling to keep them above water despite Grant's increasing lack of motivation to keep a job. He had come up with every justification imaginable why he skipped from one job to another, becoming more like a stepchild she had to support than the son she had carried for nine months. She couldn't even count on Grant to pry his ass from bed to care for their child while she worked, so she had to pay for and deliver the child to daycare and preschool most days.

She got an offer as a county assistant prosecutor right out of school, so they moved to Benton County. When Grant wouldn't look for a job, she filed for divorce and was awarded primary custody of Blaine.

The biggest insult from the divorce was having to pay another attorney to represent her.

"Get the meanest dog in the pack, Dee," her father had told her, slipping her an envelope with a thousand dollars in it. "Get the best you can for you and the boy."

The boy.

Dierdra tried to remember a time that her father referred to Blaine as anything but "the boy." To Blaine's face, he called his grandson by name, but never when talking about him.

She feared it was a subconscious method of distancing himself from the child, which stemmed from the death of her brother, three-year-old Trey, who'd drowned in a pond behind their house when she was eight. Nearly thirty years later, a decade after he died of cancer, Dierdra wondered if her father blamed her for not watching Trey more closely.

Lord knows she still blamed herself. She'd spent the year that Blaine turned three obsessively smothering him, unable to escape the irrational fear that he might also die as punishment because of her childhood inattentions.

Blaine came back into the kitchen, carrying his sneakers.

"I need another pair," he announced, breaking her concentration.

"Really? We just bought those a month ago!"

He shrugged, but they both knew he was in a rapid growth spurt. These were size 11.

"Maybe Thursday night I can take you to the mall for new shoes. I have a big case that should be finished by then."

CHAPTER 9
Monday, October 5, 2009

As if beginning her Monday morning with a lukewarm shower because the pilot light on her water heater went out wasn't bad enough, a gossipy coworker in the hallway to the locker room accosted Amber.

"Did you hear what happened to Kelly Morgan?" Debby asked in a harsh whisper, leaning forward as Amber pulled off her jacket. "You know, that gorgeous guy who does the car crashes? He was at a big freeway wreck Friday night and got hit by a drunk driver who crashed through the scene!"

"You mean the accident reconstruction guy?" Amber asked, her voice suggesting she didn't find the news juicy. She opened her locker and hung her jacket on the hook, then grabbed a white lab coat.

"Yeah! I heard he was unconscious when he got to the hospital. Had to have surgery, something about his leg."

"That's too bad."

"That's all you have to say?"

"Yes, Deb. I don't know him," Amber stated, thinking her reply should have included the words *arrogant* and *jerk*. "I mean, I hope he's okay, but we're not friends." In her head, she added, *Kinda like you and me, Deb.*

Appalled that her gossip had not incited a similar junior-high-school reaction from Amber, Debby turned to the next unwitting and likely unwilling recipient who came into the locker room.

Amber closed her eyes before she rolled them, clipped her ID badge to her collar, and headed to her cubicle in the computer lab.

She liked her job. Computer evidence differed from other types of evidence the crime lab techs worked with. Digital data didn't decompose or stink, although sometimes it required decryption or reconstruction of files, but she worked on copies of the devices, allowing her to manipulate data for use without destroying the evidence like running DNA did. She was free to browse folders and files without fear of tripping a self-destruct command or deleting something by accident. Even if she completely screwed everything up, she simply started over.

She also liked that her cubicle sat in a spotless air-conditioned office, with all the tools she needed to do her work, though she sometimes missed being outside. No, maybe not working outside, but having the freedom to be outdoors. To be horseback in the wilderness, with no one around for miles. That daydream was for another time, she thought.

She couldn't be an expert in every facet of criminal forensics, as much as she might enjoy learning.

She lacked experience in specialties like DNA, dental forensics, or crash reconstruction, for example, but she took every opportunity to learn, like the day she met Kelly at the train crash. Hundreds of manufacturer model performance and engineering details affected crashes as much as environmental factors. Interesting, but computers were where she felt the magic.

Her father had once told her she could do anything, she just couldn't do everything.

Yet she was thinking about Kelly Morgan again when she sat at her workstation.

Deb had called him gorgeous, but Amber didn't recall him that way. He wasn't bad looking, and the bald head suited him. But the lack of eyebrows and eyelashes around his gray eyes made him look a little spooky. Some sort of genetic condition, she thought. *Figures.*

Thoughts of him vanished as she unlocked her evidence locker and gathered her laptop and an external drive copy — the working copy of the computer that had come from the crash where she'd first met . . . The thought of him crossing her mind again irritated her.

Her first task from the crash had been the cell phone. However, it was an unregistered device with no history of calls or texts, no GPS. Short of being set up to work, it had not been used.

She had passed the Engine Control Module to another technician.

The deceased driver had been under investigation for possession of child pornography. On initial scan through the files with low-level encryption, she'd concluded that hundreds of images were saved. He had been in possession of it, but the laptop might not have belonged to him. That was the first item on her list of questions to answer. While the main user had good computer skills, he was no match for her. The encryption she'd encountered so far was basic commercial software-based, so it was easy to crack. The biggest challenge to Amber was the lack of folder and file organization.

After working for two days on files with harder encryption, she'd decrypted a spreadsheet with columns listing ID number, age, gender, other characteristics. Unsure what kind of list this was, she decrypted three subfolders holding hundreds of digital pictures of children matching the ID numbers. Dates ranged back eighteen months, but the most recent she found was two days before the train killed the man in possession of the laptop.

One folder was named *Active*. One was *Completed*. One was named *Dead*.

She forwarded these spreadsheets to a contact with the National Center for Missing and Exploited Children.

The spreadsheet made more sense now. It was an inventory for buyers to shop. Children, sortable by age and appearance, race, sexual experience, even Tanner physical development score, which she had to look up. Specifics someone who wished to purchase might designate.

You could choose a four-year-old Hispanic boy. Or a 12-year-old prepubescent girl with blond hair and green eyes.

Amber had almost puked, realizing how she would have met those criteria and how easy a target she could have been as the child of a single parent. She rarely thought of what could have happened to her before her grandmother died and her mother was murdered, but her biological father and his wife, Zach and Julie Samualson, had saved her from her mother's killer and from being lost in the system of foster care.

There, but for the grace of God, go I.

Friday before she left, Amber had also determined that one coded column in that spreadsheet was a list of pseudonyms though not all children had one, making her think these were buyers. She'd stayed late, looking for a file with names to match the pseudonyms with no success. It was useless to investigators until she found real names. A second column was made of symbols, but she suspected it might be the chat sites where each child had been located.

Today's goal was to find the list of buyers.

"Amber," a woman said from the doorway, "come to my office."

She nodded. Following protocol for evidence, she placed the laptop with its piggy-backed hard drive copy into the evidence box and locked it before going down the hall to the office of her boss, Tarrant County Sheriff's Department Director of Criminal Evidence Analysis, Dr. Bonnie Goldsmith.

"Yes, Ma'am?" she said from the door.

"Come in," the woman said, waving from behind her desk. "Shut the door, please."

"Am I in trouble?"

"No, not at all," Dr. Goldsmith said. She was a slightly heavy but well-dressed woman, always with one heavy piece of turquoise jewelry or another. Today, she wore a pendant of heavy silver with scalloped edging surrounding a two-inch disc of the stone, hanging from a double linked chain, falling a few inches below the hollow of her neck against the background of a red silk sweater. "Do sit. What have you found on the laptop so far?"

"The most significant thing so far appears to be an inventory list of children," Amber explained, "and code names of either the people looking to provide or those who will buy them."

"Those people are pure evil," Dr. Goldsmith said, shaking her head. "Commerce of children like they were, maybe cattle?"

"I was thinking like cars, you know, with available options." The analogy seemed accurate yet malevolent.

Dr. Goldsmith nodded, looking at something in the corner behind Amber for a few moments more. "You're okay working on this? It must be heartbreaking. I don't know if it's any less disturbing if you don't have children."

Amber shrugged. "I wish I could do more than hack the computer in this case."

"You do?" Dr. Goldsmith said, tapping her pen against her chin as though the concept fascinated her.

"Sure. I'd love to put these sleazy people away in general population in a maximum-security prison for the rest of their brief lives," Amber answered. It was true pedophiles seldom lived long around other criminals, like there was honor among thieves.

If you're convicted of having sex with a child, a serial murderer who beat his adult victims to death with a rock will happily face an additional life sentence to do the same to you.

"Maybe I can help you be a part of that, Amber. But I have a huge favor to ask first."

Amber nodded, realizing that the hook had been set.

"You heard about Deputy Morgan?" Dr. Goldsmith asked. "A car hit him at the scene of an accident Friday night?"

"Deb told me before I even clocked in. Is he okay?" Amber asked, trying to be polite since her boss had brought it up.

"The doctors think so, but he has a rod and screws in his femur, a severe knee dislocation, a few cracked ribs, and a concussion."

"I can identify with that. I was the pedestrian hit by a vehicle in New York City after 9/11."

"Really? I didn't know you were from New York."

"Oh, I'm not! I was a freshman in college and flew from Seattle to meet a guy there the day before 9/11. I watched the airliners hit the buildings from a hotel window. It's a long story, but two days later, I was chasing some punk who'd grabbed my backpack and ran in front of a car. I don't remember being hit, or much else the next few days. They put a rod through my femur. Lots of PT and misery with a walker, but that was because I had also broken my arm."

"The biggest problem with Kelly's recovery is the femur and knee injury because he lives in a three-story unit that doesn't have an elevator."

"Stairs were my biggest obstacle, too," Amber agreed.

Bonnie Goldsmith leaned back in her chair, considering whether to trust the young woman who had been hired a year ago after a twelve-month internship. Thoughts fell onto her mental scales, tipping the balance to one side then the other until she must have approved, nodded to herself, then explained. "Few people know that Kelly is my son, for obvious reasons. I took my maiden name back after my divorce. But I live in a two-story one-bedroom condo, so staying with me isn't realistic either. His father lives in Colorado," she said, waving her hand to dismiss that thought as if it were a pesky mosquito. "It's an enormous favor to ask, but you're the only single person in the department who lives in a house. Could I persuade you to let him stay with you until he can maneuver the stairs at his apartment again?"

"Deputy Morgan? At my house?" Amber stammered, realizing that she should have seen where the conversation was going a full minute sooner.

"I understand if you say no, of course," Dr. Goldsmith said, but her voice was saying that Amber shouldn't say no. Not to her boss. "It would help Kelly. And I'd make sure you're paid rent and expenses."

Amber had a three-bedroom house in the South Edgewood neighborhood southeast of downtown Fort Worth. Her previous years in dorms or small apartments had cultivated her hatred of lack of privacy, loud noises, and sometimes smells of others living around her. She loved having her own space — the house, garage, and the backyard with an enclosed pool. Keeping the place up after the major renovation was more work than an apartment, but it was hers. No roommate who didn't do chores or pitch in for rent this month. No one to stomp around upstairs all night and keep her awake.

"I understand his situation, Dr. Goldsmith, but I don't see how . . . I mean, I can't take care of someone and work."

Dr. Goldsmith smiled. "That's what Kelly said about living somewhere besides his place. Maybe a month, six weeks. He won't need you to take care of him. All he needs is somewhere without stairs, maybe a ride to work when he's ready to come back until he's cleared to drive. Will two thousand dollars make the offer more satisfactory?"

"It's not the money. We've only met once and — " Amber held her tongue.

"And Kelly is arrogant and egotistical, I know. He got that from his father, much to my embarrassment. But he is smart, like you."

Amber blew out her breath, making her wispy bangs flutter. "Do I have a choice, Ma'am?"

"Of course. I don't want this to sound like a bribe, but honestly, it's a tiny bit one. They have asked me to suggest a computer specialist from this department. Someone who would be a dependable team member working on a project addressing child porn, pedophiles, and human trafficking."

While Amber might have a valid argument about the offer being more extortion than bribery, she also recognized the opportunity to stop the most heinous of crimes. Still, she hesitated to answer.

"I'll make it three grand a month, plus cover food, utilities, entertainment," Dr. Goldsmith said, an imaginary push of all her chips to the middle of the table.

Amber held her tongue.

"StarData Cellular is lending an engineer who volunteered in a similar group, bringing experience with him from Atlanta, I believe. Kelly, when he can get around in a few weeks will provide the law enforcement coordination. You would be the computer expert who can worm into chat programs, hack encrypted files, and interact with the suspects."

Amber's eyebrows rose without her realization.

"We may add a fourth person in the future for adult trafficking, dark web investigations, and such. To get started, it's the two of you until Kelly's released to work."

"Why a cellular engineer?"

"I'm afraid Paul will have to explain that to both of us." Bonnie smiled. "You like to learn. I've seen that fire in you, to investigate new things. To seek justice. To protect the children. This project is perfect for you."

Amber closed her eyes and took a deep breath, then nodded. "Yes, I'd like to do it."

Dr. Goldsmith smiled again. "Make a list of resources you think you'll need. Outline your ideas for me. We'll meet with Paul after lunch."

"Thank you." Amber stood.

"Kelly was not a choice I made, by the way. When the sheriff asked directors to assemble a team, that position was offered to another officer. Unfortunately, his sixteen-year-old son died last week. He has three younger children, so I don't expect him to return to service, much less to this task force. Kelly was their alternate. He'll be a week or so late, though it's a perfect desk-duty recovery position for him, too. From what I understand, it won't delay your duties. You'll be working with Paul Keegan to set up how the team will work. He'll be here this afternoon."

"I look forward to doing something to make a big difference," Amber said, her eyes brightening.

"The project will require some evening work, when predators are more likely to be contacting children."

"Understood. What about the evidence I'm working on from — "

"Work the next few days to transfer your cases to Debby. This project will take more time than you might believe."

"I don't mind. Thank you!"

CHAPTER 10
Monday, October 5, 2009

"I need to go out to the scene of that crash again," he explained to the sheriff. "And to inspect that car, too."

As Sullivan had expected, Ian Molina shook his head and sighed. "Like you don't have enough to do that you want to go dig around for things that won't make any difference?"

"We shouldn't investigate a murder because it won't change anything? What if she was right? What if her ex-husband did something to cause her crash? He could have forced her off the road."

"Do you know who her ex-husband is, Harp? He's the ranking deputy in Marshal County. His father is a district judge. Lots of family money and clout." Molina picked up a stack of paper from one side of his desk, tapped it on its edge to neaten it, then added it to a pile on the other side. "We can't accuse him of something without undeniable proof, now can we?"

The proverbial "we" that Molina used was a pointed substitute for "you," both men knew. Molina had been elected sheriff. He was better at the political games associated with law enforcement and the legal system. Sullivan, who had four years of seniority, lacked the skill, diplomacy, or interest necessary to balance the political influences of the department.

"We won't *find* undeniable proof if *we* don't look for it, Sir. I don't wish to accuse him or anyone else without evidence, but we should investigate her statement — " He wasn't surprised when the sheriff's booming voice interrupted him.

"They divorced, and it was messy. You assume her words were some accusation regarding the crash and that you can find some evidence to prove it? What if it was nothing more than vengeance on her part?"

"And what if it wasn't?" Sullivan countered, standing up. "It's our obligation to at least investigate, not just write it off. That's part of our job, last time I looked."

"Fine, do what you want," Molina said, ending the argument like Sullivan's wife had done throughout their later marriage, though the statement meant that things were neither fine nor that he had permission to do anything. The unspoken continuation of the sentence was a curse: *See what happens to you next, because I'm not willing to back you up when this shit comes down around your ears.*

"I want to do my job," Sullivan replied, speaking as he got to the door. "It's my responsibility. She's dead, and I owe her that."

Molina's face softened a fraction. "This isn't about Lilah, Harp."

"No, it's not about her," he said, "but wouldn't you have investigated her death if you'd heard Lilah say it was me? If there's no evidence, fine. If it is a murder, maybe I can solve hers." He refrained from slamming the office door on his way out, but his heavy footsteps echoed down the hall and out the door.

Both men knew the words Harp hadn't said: *Because you never solved Lilah's.*

Halfway across the parking lot, the dispatcher sent him and another unit to back up a DPS trooper on a traffic stop on the freeway after a drug dog for a search was requested, putting an end for the rest of his shift his intentions to investigate the crash that killed Caitlyn Parker.

CHAPTER 11
Monday, October 5, 2009

Although she was studying a case file for a presentation to a judge the next day, Dierdra answered her cell phone because it showed Stephen was the caller.

"Hey," she said, flipping the page before she gave him her attention.

"They approved me time off next weekend for a conference in San Antonio," he said without a greeting or small talk, which was his norm. "Let's get away Thursday for a long weekend."

Not an invitation. Not even a question of whether she'd like to go.

That didn't go unnoticed by the woman who'd graced his bed occasionally for the last eleven months.

"I'll have to see if the Lawrences can keep Blaine," she replied, wondering if she really wanted to be committed to being with him for four days halfway across the state. "When do you need an answer?"

"I want one now," he said bluntly.

She flipped through her daily calendar. "I doubt I can get away. There's a court case that probably won't be finished for two weeks."

"Fine." He hung up.

Offended by his lack of courtesy, Dierdra was certain she'd made the right decision. The sex was wonderful, but she had been the recipient of too much rudeness recently to make it worthwhile.

Maybe it was time to break it off, she thought, going back to her review for trial.

CHAPTER 12
Wednesday, October 7, 2009

Harper's phone rang. It was still dark outside.

Caller ID showed the sheriff's office main number, so the extension placing the call was not made public. Harper was sure that only Sheriff Molina would call him this early. He answered reluctantly.

"Harper," Molina said. "You asked to investigate that rollover fatality? You got it, courtesy of the Marshal County Sheriff. However, for the record, he states that the deputy in question has an alibi for the night before and the morning of the crash."

"I want a state mechanic to examine the car, so can we make sure it's still available?"

"You can do whatever you want," Molina stated. "But I'd like it to be completed in 24 hours."

"It's my day off, Ian," Harper complained. "Give me two days."

Molina sighed. "Okay. I'll call the wrecker company."

Why would a sheriff want an investigation of a crash that might involve one of his own men?

Why would he have to?

Had that been the sole reason Sheriff Molina surrendered to Harper's request?

Ian Molina hadn't been one of Harper's "work friends." He offered time off and administrative support after Lilah died, but he made sure Harper remained outside the investigation of her murder.

Harper had to admit that his supervising officer had done everything by the book in the case, leaving no stone unturned, as the saying went, but the investigation had not produced a suspect. Harper stayed out of the case, offering nothing to direct suspicion toward Edward Thomas. The fewer details Harper provided, the fewer lies he had to keep straight in his head. If Molina had made any connection to Thomas, Harper supposed he would have gone along with it, but that had not happened.

The thought of Eddy Thomas being charged with the murder of Lilah Sullivan was the singular hope that kept Harper going some days. While it might never happen, Harper was satisfied that Thomas had caused Lilah's death, regardless of whether she had pulled the trigger.

Before her funeral, though Harper's anger hopefully looked enough like grief no one else noticed, he couldn't help but stare down Edward Thomas in the few moments of eye contact they'd made. If Eddy felt any responsibility for her death, or if he knew it had been a suicide, he never brought it up. Any clarification he might offer about her death would have required confession of the affair.

But after Lilah's funeral, when Eddy Thomas had offered his hand in condolence, Harper had pulled him close and whispered, "I want you to know that her affair wasn't a secret."

CHAPTER 13
Wednesday, October 7, 2009

Amber spent the rest of the morning with Debby, going over the evidence collections from several other cases she was working. Only two of them were urgent, meaning there might be prosecution within thirty days. She decided, however, she would keep working on the laptop she'd retrieved from the car vs. train wreck.

The detective was working on the premise that the driver was involved somehow in a child trafficking ring, but no fingerprints or facial recognition matches had been made to identify him. DNA was pending, though the way the system was backlogged, results could take several months. This case, without an obvious violent crime connection and with a dead suspect, was low on the priority list. Although the driver had died with the laptop in the vehicle, he might have been a courier, not the owner. The files Amber'd accessed so far were encrypted, but she needed to keep going.

Though the security used wasn't the most difficult she'd encountered, the problem was that *each* individual folder and file was encrypted differently, so she had to try multiple programs to crack the new password on each. It made sense to have a master list for this mess, she thought, but she hadn't found it. She cut into the files, layer by layer. Like an onion, cutting it sometimes caused tears each time she found a new document with more instances of child exploitation.

Then she began finding files that had extensions that indicated the wrong file type, starting with a file named M2002.dll in the system files, when it was really an MPEG file. If she renamed it correctly, the file was a four-minute video. By renaming files, they were hidden in plain sight unless the user could determine their content without the extension. This revealed a whole new problem to address, meaning she would have to review every single file on the hard drive if she couldn't isolate these intentionally misnamed files some other way.

At lunch, she measured her blood sugar then grabbed the chicken salad, celery sticks and peanut butter, and yogurt from her lunch cooler in her locker, then she ate by herself in the breakroom, thinking of the man Dr. Goldsmith had told her about. Chewing, she pulled a notepad from her jacket pocket.

What is the difference between an internet-contact pedophile, a child abuser, and a kidnapper/trafficker? Which does this project focus on? she wrote.

How will this team catch the target predator?

A childhood riddle came to her: *How do you catch a rabbit? You sound like a carrot.*

She jotted down a few ideas, but she had no clue how to start or what questions she needed answered, which left her fearing she had nothing to offer as she cleaned up her table and went back to work.

Instead of getting out the hard drive, she queued a set of documents to share with Debby. She'd finished as Dr. Goldsmith brought Paul Keegan by the evidence suite and introduced them.

"I'm glad you two can move forward with this without a deputy for a short time," she told them, leading them to a conference room with an oak table large enough to seat twenty people. "Paul, I'm sure you'll find Amber an exceptional computer expert, but she also has a serious dedication to stopping child predators."

"I've heard a lot about you from your peers," Paul said as they took their seats. "You can make a big impact on this."

"That's how you move a mountain," Amber replied. "One grain of sand at a time."

"I like the analogy, but I prefer to think of it as filling a wheelbarrow with manure to move to a burn pit, one pile at a time."

They laughed.

"Okay, so that's the goal. How do we do it?" Amber asked. "I don't understand how this works."

"First, my only actual value to this team is to keep it up to date with the evolving cellular technology, to have a cutting edge, and to provide instant access to location in the event of an emergency. I'm not a law enforcement officer, so I cannot do more than that, but predators have changed tactics, which affects how they are caught."

Amber nodded.

"Let me start with some history first," he said. "Several organizations have done something similar, outside a law enforcement setting. You might have heard of Perverted Justice, which has been successful by being a non-law enforcement team of volunteers who engage with pedophiles online until sufficient information is gained to either identify or entice him — predominantly men, yes, but not all — to show up at the sting location."

"Didn't one of the television networks participate, using television footage of these guys showing up to meet their victims?" Dr. Goldsmith asked.

"Yes, and it brought national notice to the problem, but I worry attention has moved on to the next media target — scandal, election, war. But the laws have changed, requiring law enforcement to be involved. I volunteered with a similar task force in Atlanta, again providing tech support," Paul explained. "When we moved here, I met Sheriff Ray George, who's my neighbor. He thought something similar might work in the DFW area."

"Explain the technology support," Amber requested.

"You have a cellular phone, right?" he said, taking a folder from his briefcase for each of them.

"Doesn't everyone these days? I just bought the newest iPhone," she said, placing her phone on the table.

"Unfortunately, some people don't have cell phones yet, especially the new smartphones, but it's booming, with most using one of the four or five main cell carriers," he said. "You were off over the weekend, I presume?"

"Yeah," she replied.

"If you are a StarData Cell Customer, when a prosecutor subpoenas such historic information, all I need is a name or phone number to pull records from which I can build a report of where you were, numbers you called or texted or that called or texted you, and whether you used any of the applications."

Amber frowned.

"We've always been able to triangulate the location of a phone based on direction from, and signal strength and thus proximity to a tower, or better yet multiple towers, like in a large city. Now, smartphones stay in touch with the network all the time, to get messages and alerts in some programs. As long as the power is on, it exchanges information."

Amber wrinkled her nose.

"In an emergency, we can isolate and tag a particular phone, so that no matter where it goes, we can get a location in real-time through the network. Historical tracking takes time because the report, a Mobility Usage with Cell Location, provides a numerical string of about thirty digits of latitude and longitude, which has to be interpreted for use by humans," he said, turning to Amber. "You'd think writing software to translate the data to map points would be simple, but we haven't been successful doing it yet because the format is not quite perfect."

Amber nodded.

"Another problem is tower ownership. If you drive from here to Houston, you cross areas not covered by our towers, though connectivity is available from one major company to another, although some smaller regional companies still charge users for roaming, when their phones connect to a tower their companies don't own. The third problem is that the languages of the networks are not universal, making access to the data as a phone passes from one cell company to the next difficult to obtain. Going across town, that's not so much a problem as cities are well covered by the major companies."

"How does that help?" Amber asked, getting frustrated. "I mean, I understand what you're saying, but you're teaching me how to cook filet mignon when I need to buy a leather belt. How does this help find a pedophile?"

"You have wonderful metaphors, Amber. When the internet first became a venue for criminals of all kinds, the only choice was to use a computer."

"I remember my mother had an account that used a dial-up modem," Amber said. "Connection seems hundreds of times faster now."

"Thousands, actually," Paul said. "Those first social programs allowed people to chat privately — a perfect hunting ground for child exploitation. Then advancing technology became about speed. DSL, then cable and satellite internet, all using stationary connections. Criminals, especially these predators, learned how easy it is for law enforcement to locate IP-4 addresses at fixed locations. Then came the wireless modems, so pedophiles connected via laptop through Wi-Fi at a library or fast-food restaurant, making them semi-mobile. Now, cellular technology supports chat programs heavily used by kids and their predators, using an IPV-6 address, which is difficult if not impossible to trace. That has changed the way law enforcement catches them."

"Now they use cell phones."

"Current programs like Smiley or StayInTouch feature both group and private conversations. Private chat allows the exchange of information necessary for the predator to assess that the child has the qualities desired, regardless of what they are."

"I've learned a little about some of those choices recently," Amber said, thinking of the laptop she was working on. "That still doesn't tell me what I'll be doing," she said, looking back and forth from Dr. Goldsmith to Paul Keegan.

"Simply put, your job is to lure them into providing any identification, get them to commit the felony crime without entrapment."

Dr. Goldsmith added, "Amber, I'm sure you know, but in Texas, someone who solicits a minor to have sex commits a third-degree felony. If you get him to arrive in person, intending to have sex with a minor, it becomes a second-degree felony. Prosecution is near 100% because confession is more common than a trial and all its publicity."

"Victims bond with their predators, who provide the illusion of love, acceptance, boosted self-esteem. Trust must be established both ways. The first test might be whether the child will provide a photograph or be willing to commit to doing something against the rules, like sneaking out. At some point, the predator has to provide something that will identify him — a phone number, a real email. With those, the assigned deputy uses his resources for identification. Your job is to act like the kid the predator wants and get that information."

"I don't know anything about acting like a kid!" Amber exclaimed.

Paul laughed. "Most normal adults don't. I've got a couple of wonderful coaches for you. My daughters are eleven and fourteen. They are thrilled to help. In fact, they instructed me to invite you to dinner Friday night so they can meet you. We're having pizza, if that's acceptable."

"Absolutely! I'm looking forward to it."

He slid a business card toward where her phone still sat on the table. "We'll see you at six, then."

Dr. Goldsmith stood and gathered her papers, tapping them into a neat pile. "Very well, you two. Keep in touch with your plans. Let's meet again soon." She nodded and left them at the table, though Paul had stood when she did.

"Is she always that serious?" he asked Amber in a whisper when they were alone. He sat again.

"No. Sometimes she's worse."

They chuckled.

"You talked about predators, like getting him to meet a child for sex. Are there trafficking bounties set for children meeting certain criteria? I'm working on a laptop, though I haven't cracked it far, and I found what I think is a list of buyers or sellers."

"I don't know much about that, but it would make sense there are bonuses for delivery of a child with particular characteristics, but that's a completely different side of trafficking from what we're going to do."

"I want to do this," she said. "I just didn't think it could get any worse than what I've seen on this laptop."

"Unfortunately, Amber, you're very wrong."

CHAPTER 14
Friday, October 9, 2009

"Thanks for coming down, Harp," Tim Strickland said, pulling a greasy red rag from his hip pocket to wipe his hands. "I found something interesting in that car you asked me to check out." He extended his right hand, which was still no cleaner than before, but Harper shook it anyway.

"Interesting?" he echoed.

"Odd," Strickland offered in clarification.

The two men squeezed between cars and equipment in the shop to go out a back door into bright noon sunlight.

The Honda Civic lay heaped in a corner of the lot, barely recognizable as a car.

"Even if the wrecker crew didn't cause any more damage when they dragged the car up the hill and onto a sled, it had to be a mess," Harper said. "Probably missing a lot of pieces."

"Yup, but none I needed to scratch my head about except this," he said, squatting by the front wheel. Or where it had been. "The wheel was knocked off the axle as the vehicle skidded on the gravel, it looks like."

"Probably so," Harper agreed.

"Oh, I don't question it. See the scrapes here, and here," he said, pointing with the flashlight beam. "But the question is, why? Tie rods, two for each wheel, keep it roughly parallel to the other. While a tie rod's not a simple piece to replace, it's usually not damaged in a wreck."

Harper wanted to say *If you say so*. Instead, he nodded.

"There's supposed to be a nut that holds this," Strickland pointed with a flathead screwdriver he'd pulled from the other hip pocket, "onto this bolt. The nut is castellated, slotted. Held in place by a cotter pin. The nut was missing."

"Which means what, Tim? I'm not a mechanic."

Tim stood and dug in his pocket. "I figured you'd ask." He screwed a castellated nut onto a bolt he'd already drilled a hole through the threaded area a quarter of an inch from the end. "This is the same kind of nut, with these dips that look like castle parapets. They get lined up with the holes in the bolt so that a cotter pin," he said, pulling one from his pocket, "goes through like this, and then the pin's ends are split and wrapped around the nut each direction to lock it in place, and this keeps the nut from loosening."

"And this is important because…?"

Strickland gave him an insulted expression. "How did you even get to work today, Harper?" He shook his head and continued, demonstrating with the pieces in his hands. "It means the pin was missing from here. The nut came off the bolt. Then the tie rod became unhooked so the front connection failed, which would let the wheel turn with no control, causing the skid."

"Interesting," Harper said, thinking. "As in, this is the cause of the accident?"

"No, what's interesting is that she'd picked up the car from the mechanic the afternoon before the wreck. The car had new tires, a wheel alignment, brakes, etc."

"Could the nut thingy have been left off then?"

Tim laughed. "The receipt was in what's left of the console, so I called the shop. They keep an itemized list of everything done and anything that might need repair soon. Says the tie rods were in good shape. Even the boots looked okay."

Harper knew he'd regret it, but he asked anyway. "What are boots?"

"The rubber expandable covers," he said, pointing, "here."

"How far could the car be driven if the pin came out of the nut?"

"Depends, maybe a hundred miles, maybe more. But the cotter pin wouldn't come out or break. There's no stress or load on it to speak of."

"How do you remove it?" Harper asked, his mind speeding away with a scenario.

"Use pliers to grab the loop and pry it out."

"No fingerprints?"

"No, fingers wouldn't get enough grip," he said, demonstrating on his example parts. "You won't find any for a conviction in this mess after it has been outside and dozens of people have touched it."

CHAPTER 15
Friday, October 9, 2009

"What a pleasant surprise, Sergeant Sullivan," Dierdra Preston said, standing behind her desk when the uniformed deputy entered, offering her hand to shake. "How's law enforcement these days? Please, have a seat. Can I get you something to drink? Coffee? Water?"

"No, I'm fine, thanks," Harper said, moving to sit after she did.

Some manners were so engrained he didn't even consider not doing them, thanks to his mother.

"I have what may become a problem," he said, pulling a stack of photos from an envelope in his clipboard. "Accident occurred out north of town. Appeared to be a typical loss of control and rollover/ejection. The victim died several days later. Her statement directly was 'My ex-husband did this,' which she said directly to me."

"How did she explain that accusation?" Dierdra asked, making notes.

"She didn't. She died." When he saw her head tilt, he continued, "I mean, she closed her eyes and her heart stopped, right then."

"Wow," she said, twirling her pen. "Nothing to anyone else?"

"Not that the nurses admitted. When I first asked for the car to be brought to the county yard for further investigation, the sheriff was a little hesitant. Seems the ex-husband of the victim is Stephen Royce, a deputy from Marshal County."

"Ahhh, I see. No one wanted to step on those toes, I suppose." She tossed her heavy silver pen down on the blotter, trying not to show her surprise. Or nausea that wiggled in her stomach.

"Apparently not, but then the Marshal County Sheriff asked that we *do* an investigation, along with a proffered alibi for the time of the accident and the day before, though without details."

She pondered this a moment. "Do you think he had anything to do with the accident?"

Harper looked over his shoulder to make sure they were alone. "Look, I know you're seeing Royce, so I'm trying to tread lightly."

Dierdra's face flushed, and she nodded. She took a sip from her water bottle. "I appreciate that, though I believe the relationship has begun to die off."

What she was thinking was how tiresome his "my-way" attitude had become in the last few months. Initially a man who made most of the decisions felt like relief, but lately, he was more a man making demands.

"The mechanic says the car had recently had work done on the front end — brakes, alignment. Reputable place, he assures me. Yet the right forward tie rod had come loose, which could cause the accident."

"Harper, I know nothing more about cars than where to put the gas and which direction to turn the key."

"Me either, but I got the lesson." He gave a half-smile. "The mechanic who did the work on her car covers his bases. He takes digital photos of every job he does, before and after. The pins that keep the nut on the bolt were there on both sides, front and rear, before and after service. No disassembly or work was done on the tie rods." He set a pair of photos on her desk, followed by the photo of the disconnected tie rod in the wreckage.

"You think it was sabotage?"

"The mechanic says 99-1, that the pin was removed, which allowed the nut to loosen. He doesn't think it could be an accidental occurrence," he said. "I don't know who to suspect or how to prove it. But as they say, the spouse is always a suspect."

"Stephen is still angry about the divorce," she said. "And you didn't hear me say this, but I could imagine him being *that* angry."

"What would Royce have to gain? They're already divorced. She didn't ask for anything from him — no spousal support, house, etc. The car she was driving was the one she owned when they got married."

"I don't know, Harper, but keep digging."

"Yes, Ma'am."

CHAPTER 16
Friday, October 9, 2009

Paul answered the door to invite Amber into their home and introduced her to his wife, Vanessa.

"We've ordered pizza, so it ought to be here in twenty minutes," Vanessa told them, waving to the patio. "Why don't you two grab a drink? I'll be out in a minute."

Amber followed him through the kitchen, where he pulled out a couple of colas from the refrigerator. "Or we have beer or wine," he offered.

"Do you have water?" she asked.

He nodded, exchanged one bottle for another and handed it to her.

They went out through the sliding glass door onto a covered patio to a picnic table and assorted outdoor furniture.

"What did you think of the process we talked about?" he asked as they settled in wicker chairs.

"I still don't know what to say to a pedophile," Amber said. "That concerns me."

"Your goal is to access the hot sites — and there are plenty of them. I suggested the task force needed someone who can get *inside* the programs, not just pretend to be a child a predator would be interested in. You are providing bait to gain his trust. "

"Like what?"

"Predators look for kids who are isolated, neglected, angry, with low self-esteem. Those with school problems such as reading
58

difficulty. Social bullying or home neglect when the child doesn't fit in. Divorced parents with custody problems. A recent relocation away from friends. Current or previous abuse. Thoughts of running away or other teenage angst. When desperate and standing on the edge of a cliff, a child desperately wants to believe in the acceptance and attention a pedophile offers. You signal distress, and he offers what looks like love. Praise. Interest. Options and safety."

Could she pretend to be a gullible preteen or teen whose parents didn't keep track of her online activities — or his? Could she act like a boy?

"What if I screw something up?"

"Ever been fishing?"

She shook her head.

"The theme is easy. Bait a hook, throw it in the water, wait for a fish to bite, reel it in. But crazy fishermen buy a hundred choices of bait or lures, study where certain species of fish hang out, what time of day and weather they eat, lots of other things that complicate fishing," he said. "Fish get hungry, so they gobble what is available if it interests them. They don't care what color the fisherman is wearing or what brand of rod he uses. Don't care if he screws up and casts into the brush a hundred times before, only if he presents them something they like when they are looking."

"I'm making this too hard?"

He nodded. "I won't lie to you, this is disgusting and enraging. Remember though, while you have a predator's attention, no one is being harmed in what you're doing. Hopefully, you'll go to bed knowing in your heart that you did something that really makes a difference. Something that 99% of the country approves of. That tomorrow, one less monster can hurt a child."

How had Paul gained the trust of his daughters to get them to take part in helping her? Wouldn't involving them be a dangerous thing to do? Maybe not the older one, but eleven seemed awfully young to be flirting with the world of predators, like taking your kids to a zoo with no fences. *Look at the tiger, Sweetie. Doesn't he have gigantic teeth? He's dangerous, but you can scratch his ears. Listen to him purr.*

"I'm astonished how much information you can obtain from a cell phone through its network," Amber said. "But if it provides information to the police, I'm all in."

Paul smiled. "That's the first step."

"How do we get what we need then?"

"We start with your impersonation. If you get a name, email, or a phone number through the interaction, the law enforcement liaison can use that information to match identification with other existing records, including cell carrier databases. I can just make that easier."

"How do I pretend to be one of those children?"

"You'll build several personae," he said. "Don't think of it as work or you'll overthink it as an educated adult. You pretend to be a 13-year-old who has an older guy who likes her and tells her she's smart and beautiful. Or a nine-year-old who wishes someone would listen to him because his father abuses him after his mother died. You make mistakes because a kid would. Poor confidence, desperate for someone to pay attention. Bad grammar or spelling."

"That makes me nuts! I can't misspell something intentionally," Amber exclaimed.

"Think of it as acting. Rehearsal without make-up," Paul suggested. "Most of these people are not at the far right side of the bell curve in intelligence. Lacking morality but not necessarily stupid."

"Maybe not stupid, definitely evil. Just so I'm clear on this, if we somehow determine a predator is going after a real child, we can still act, right?" Amber asked.

"Yes." Paul cleared his throat, but his eyes twinkled. "As a parent, I understand your concern. The serendipitous finding of a crime in progress against a child shall be handled as any other crime. Hopefully with extreme prejudice."

Amber laughed. "My father is a federal agent. I introduced him to a boyfriend I brought to dinner once, and Dad casually mentioned while cutting his steak that he had a gun, a shovel, and an airtight alibi. He is a huge believer in doing the right thing."

"I have three daughters. I'll have to write that one down," he said. "Mackenzie and Neela are jazzed about teaching you how to, as my middle daughter put it, act like a vulnerable and weak child."

"You said you have three?" she asked.

"Calista is seventeen months old. I don't think she can help you much."

"She's the one I'm most prepared to act like!" Amber said, laughing. "I can babble endlessly, cry and scream when things don't go my way."

"Cal is learning from her sisters at an alarming rate. I suspect she'll be reading *War and Peace* before kindergarten," Vanessa said as she joined them. "But she may not be walking until junior high, the way Mac and Neela carry her everywhere."

"I'd've loved to have had siblings," Amber commented.

"Where did you grow up?" Vanessa asked, taking a sip of Paul's drink.

"Until I was a teenager, we lived in New Mexico," she said. "Then I lived with my dad and step-mom in Washington till I started college."

"Your parents are divorced?" Paul incorrectly concluded.

"No, my mom got pregnant in high school in Albuquerque and moved to Tucumcari for a few years then back to Albuquerque. Dad didn't know about me until my mother was murdered."

"Oh, I'm so sorry to bring it up," Vanessa said. "We didn't know."

"No need to be sorry for asking. That was a big part of why I went into forensics and why I am eager to work on this project. And I'm happy that I got to know my real father."

"You said he was a federal agent?" Paul continued.

"He was DEA when I went to live with them," she explained. "Then he quit that. After they moved back to Albuquerque in 2002, he eventually went to the FBI in a terrorist task force."

A distant doorbell chimed, followed by squeals from their kids.

"Pizza's here. Be right back," Paul said, hopping up to go pay for dinner delivery.

"Your poor stepmother, having to deal with two cops," Vanessa said.

"Oh, don't feel sorry for her. She was in the New Mexico State Police long before my dad began as a cop in Houston. Julie's older than

Dad." Amber smiled. "One or both of them has worn a badge since I went to live with them."

"Pizza!" two high-pitched chants echoed through the house. Giggly jabbers joined them.

"Girls, bring the plates, please, and grab yourselves a drink. We're eating outside," Paul told them, doubting anyone heard him over the squeals. "Mac! Stop swinging Calista around in circles before you both puke!"

"You were saying about siblings?" Vanessa asked. "We'll loan you all three of them for the weekend so you can see what you missed."

"I have a swimming pool," Amber whispered as the blur of girls came into view. "I'd be the favorite aunt, hands-down."

Paul set two pizza boxes on the table, took the plates and napkins away from Neela, who was dancing around the table, making Calista laugh. "Who wants pepperoni?" he yelled over the chaos.

Both girls' hands shot up as they kept swirling until Paul whistled between his teeth. "Females! Sit or go to bed hungry!"

"Looks like herding cats," Vanessa said. "But they always come for their favorite food."

"After a few threats," he added.

Everyone settled down and Paul dealt out paper plates like poker cards. Chaos was broken with a moment of silence as Paul said grace, then the boxes flew open and pizza seemed to explode into hungry hands around the table.

"Dad says we get to teach — " Mackenzie began, stopped when Vanessa interrupted her with a snap of her fingers.

"Do not talk to our guest with your mouth full!"

Mac made an outrageous show of swallowing before she continued. "Dad says we're going to teach you how to act like a kid," she said, then took another huge bite.

"That's what he tells me. What's my first lesson?" Amber asked.

"That kids talk with food in their mouths," Neela said under her breath.

"What else?" Amber persisted, taking a bite and chewing.

"We've told them that the goal is to engage online characters who hunt children to harm," Vanessa said.

Mackenzie made a spectacle of swallowing first again. "Dad told us how some guys want to lure kids away from parents and then sell them. I want to help with that."

She sounds like she's 31 not eleven, Amber thought. "Then your help is most welcome."

After dinner, Amber, Paul, and the girls sat in the den. He pulled up an older transcript that he'd edited to discuss the best responses Amber could make to certain questions for particular ages.

"What do you look like?" was the first question they discussed.

"Hair color, length, eyes," Neela said.

"No!" Mac argued. "Perverts want to know if you have boobs!"

Amber had to bite her lip to keep from laughing.

"I think Amber needs to see some of your language. You two go get your tablets," Paul said. "We'll do it live."

The girls scrambled out of the room.

"Their input can help you with this," Paul said. "Keyboard shorthand, slang, timing. You'll see. We did this a few months ago to show them how predators hook kids, so they can identify someone paying too much attention to them online, like when they're out in public. But we keep close eyes on their online chats."

In a practice chatroom, Amber and the girls practiced girl-talk. After an hour, Neela's attention had waned, so she was playing a game on her computer. Amber began watching her interactions with the characters, although it was for a single player. "Tell me more about the game," Amber asked. "How do you learn where to go and what to do?"

"Mostly by getting killed," Mackenzie said.

Neela leaned forward and stuck her tongue out at her sister. "You go so far, explore, do something right and go on, or you die and start over," Neela said.

"See? You get killed!"

"That doesn't sound like fun," Amber observed.

"In some games, you save your place as you go along, so you don't have to start back to the beginning. In others, you only get so many lives to live before you have to begin over."

"Which is better?"

"I'd rather save as I go," Neela said. "We only have one game where we can play at the same time. We can either work together or work separately. In some, you take turns and compete, like an arcade game."

Mac picked up several video games. "In this one, it works better to go through the forest and work as a team, so you're always in the same location. If we race cars, we compete against each other, and we see our own location on half the screen."

"In some games, all you do is shoot everything in sight. That's kinda boring," Neela continued. "I've heard of a few games that people play online against everyone else in a very large game world."

"Where'd you hear that," Paul asked.

"Wendy's brother told her," she said without looking away from her screen. "Wendy's my best friend. Her older brother lives in California. He's in the Marines."

Amber looked at Paul, who rolled his eyes.

"This evening has been an overwhelming look at the life of a teenager," Amber said, looking at her watch, surprised to see it was after ten already.

Amber had learned the most from Mackenzie, who had cozied up next to her on a loveseat to type and explain things.

"You have terrific kids," Amber told Paul as he walked her to her car. "When I grow up, I want to be as smart as they are."

CHAPTER 17
Saturday, October 10, 2009

"Staying with you wasn't my idea, you know," Kelly said as he crutched his way into Amber's living room through the glass storm door that she held open for him. "I told my mother that I'd be fine at my place."

"To be clear, this wasn't *my* idea, either. I'm not happy someone dumped you on my doorstep on my day off," Amber retorted. "What if I hadn't been home?"

"Dumped me?" he asked, insulted, and aggravated that she was so miffed at him. "I tried to call an hour ago, but you didn't answer."

No, she had been in the pool, then the shower.

"You just came over anyway?" Amber asked, frustrated. "Look, it doesn't matter. I'll show you around, then I have errands to do."

"The friend who *dumped me* at your house, as you so eloquently described it, will be bringing over some of my things later," he said, looking around the house.

"Great. Your bedroom and bathroom are to the left through that hall. House rules: No visitors unless I know in advance, and no one stays overnight. I'm not here to entertain or clean up after you or your friends. You make a mess, you clean up. The garbage day is Thursday. If you want something from the grocery store, write it on the list on the fridge. Hot water lasts exactly nine minutes; I'll leave you hot water if you do the same."

"I was afraid I'd be banished to the doghouse, but you don't have a dog," he said, stepping toward her kitchen as she snatched up a leather hobo bag and keys, obviously angry. "Wait. I'm sorry. I suspect you had little more choice than I did. My mother is a force of nature, used to the world being under her control."

"She is that," Amber said, her voice softening.

"I promise not to get in your way or ruin your life. Let's not be enemies. I don't want to butt heads the whole time. Give me a few days to get back on my feet, then I'll be ready to work on the child exploitation project," he said, moving toward the patio doors. His eyes widened in surprise. "You have a swimming pool?"

"Yes, and you are not to use it when I'm not here," she replied. "That's a safety thing, until you are back to using both feet."

"Yes, Ma'am. Anything else?"

"Don't call me Ma'am."

"Habit," he said. "Blame my mother for that, too."

CHAPTER 18
Saturday, October 17, 2009

Neela Keegan and Wendy Barton planned to be at the mall all day. Neela had saved money for them to go to a movie, and she'd told her parents they were going to see *Where the Wild Things Are.*

Wendy had other ideas.

Teenagers filled the mall, congregating like clumps of sticky rice. Some hoped to see a pre-release of *Saw VI* later that afternoon. As a mall-wide marketing tactic, the theater hid secret employees in various stores to give away free tickets to several different movies showing that day, a strategy to bring shoppers to anchor stores not typically browsed by teenagers buying for back to school. The marketing strategy targeted kids with money, even if it was parental bribes for good behavior, grades, or just to get out of the house.

Wendy Barton had spent Friday night with Neela Keegan, BFFs since first grade. Vanessa had dropped them off after one o'clock at the mall for the movie. Now the girls were on the prowl for these tickets to the R-rated movie. If they could score tickets, it would save Neela's money, not that she was interested in a gory show.

They bounced through store after store, fueled by a food court supply of carbohydrates and the hope of seeing the newest teenage horror flick.

"I hate that we only get one class together this year," Wendy complained about their junior high courses. "We could have so much more fun."

Best friends for years, Neela had begun to see that the merits of making grades acceptable for college and being an all-around decent kid were lost on Wendy, who'd begun stealing cigarettes and cash, and she'd swiped a bottle of her dad's vodka for them last night. Worse, Wendy had started a few arguments when Neela wouldn't take part in the misconduct.

Today, though, they were friends on a single mission, if Neela could keep them out of trouble.

"Have you seen Mark this year? Like, he's got a bod' now!" Wendy said in what only pretended to be a whisper, her voice carrying to a crowd of boys walking twenty feet ahead of them. "I'd like to get my hands on that."

Neela elbowed her. "Stop it! You can chase boys on your own time." But when Wendy stuck out her bottom lip in a fake pout that portended a future fight, Neela relented. "If we follow them, we won't find the tickets. Let's try Macy's!"

And they peeled off to the left, argument averted.

"We haven't got to do this since school started," Wendy told her. "How long were you grounded?"

"A whole month," Neela said, not wanting to confess something Wendy would find an unworthy offense.

"For what? Taking your mom's car or something? Geez, your folks had to be really mad to ground you for a month," Wendy replied, reverting to her conspiratorial low voice. "While you were MIA, I've been talking to this older guy in CommStock, that new chat program I showed you last night. He thinks I'm cute, like maybe I could be a movie star."

"I'm sure you could, when you grow up."

"No, like now. He lives in California, and he says there are curtain calls all the time for teenagers for movies. Like *our* age. He likes my long hair."

"How does he know about your hair," Neela asked.

"I sent him some pictures."

"That's dumb, Wendy! You — "

"Dumb? Someone who wants to make me rich and famous isn't dumb."

"No, it's BS," Neela said. "My dad's working with the police to arrest people who are child predators."

"Then it's a good thing I'm not a child," Wendy said in defiance. "He's not a predator, and besides, I told you, he lives in California."

Neela pointed to a girl with green hair, hanging around the perfume counter, not looking at anything but her phone. "I bet that's one!"

Green hair and special tickets indeed. What a super afternoon it would be, Neela thought, as they scurried out of the department store toward the theater to get the best seats.

CHAPTER 19
Sunday, October 18, 2009

Amber returned home at five-thirty, finding her new temporary roommate standing in the kitchen, crutches tucked under his arms, tearing lettuce into a bowl.

A guy, she thought, *tearing lettuce* instead of cutting it.

"Have a nice day?" Amber asked, setting her bag on the foyer table, and then putting a sack of groceries on the counter.

"I did. I had a quick nap while I waited for a load of laundry, but as wonderful as sleep sounds, I don't want to be awake all night. The hospital schedule screwed up my internal clock." He finished with the lettuce and started cutting cherry tomatoes in halves, tossing them in the big bowl a handful at a time. "Your pantry is a little skimpy, but I managed baked spaghetti, if that's okay."

"Okay? It smells amazing!"

Their eyes met, and they spoke at the same time. Amber insisted he go first.

"My mother told me you were hesitant to have me stay, which I understand. If our previous work run-in caused any animosity, I apologize for that," he said, finishing the salad with parmesan cheese he grated fresh, then he pushed the bowl to the other side of the island. "Could you put that on the table, please?"

She did. "I'm going to go change," she said, going around the island toward her bedroom. Not that she needed to change clothes, but she didn't want to explain that she was an insulin-dependent diabetic. Or that that terrific-smelling spaghetti he'd cooked was 99 percent carbohydrates and bound to make her blood sugar skyrocket. She would adapt for one night.

Truth was, Amber didn't want to have to explain her diabetes to anyone. She'd thought of getting an insulin pump so she didn't have to do two injections a day, but it would not work well with her choice to swim daily for exercise. She had found a physician in Fort Worth who worked to reduce her insulin doses from four injections a day to two, a long-acting solution at bedtime and an intermediate-acting dose before her largest meal of the day, which was usually her lunch.

Amber wiped her fingertip with an alcohol prep, then stuck it with the spring-loaded lancet, squeezed out a droplet of blood against the strip she'd stuck in the meter. While it processed, she wiped the blood off her finger, then went to her closet to find a slouchy sweatshirt and jeans. It beeped in fifteen seconds. She recorded the readout in her workbook, then joined Kelly again in the kitchen.

"First, I realize I'm an ass most of the time," Kelly began, "but when I came to Tarrant County, most of the department thought of me as a spoiled kid, especially taking the accident investigation position. I'd only worked a couple of years in Abilene. Being a division director's son didn't sit well with some people either, which irritated me. I don't answer to her," he said, turning off the oven.

"I suspect you were the kind of kid who never did," Amber replied with a smirk.

"You know what I mean. I'm first-rate at what I do, but the bad attitude lingered because I still work harder to prove myself. I'm sorry you were the recipient of something you didn't deserve."

"You were a little, um," she paused, finger tapping her chin as if she were deep in thought, "a little harsh to the stranger at the train crash."

He laughed. "I was, but I was awed by your answer. And pissed off that you kept calling me sir."

"I have a mom, too," she said.

"You had everything right about the car. Saw things I hadn't been looking for. The diagonal grinding marks of the wheel edges indicated something important to the investigation."

"I'm not well versed on automobiles and crashes, but I'm interested," she replied. "You can tell me about it over supper."

She finished putting away the groceries she'd bought, then she set the table for two.

He opened the oven to remove breadsticks glistening with butter and chopped garlic, sliding them into a large bowl. "How about some wine?"

She put the bread on the table next to the bowl of salad. "You shouldn't be drinking alcohol with the painkillers, Kelly."

"Haven't had any in four days. That stuff's bad for you."

He opened the oven again and moved a covered casserole dish to a rack to cool. "You're not a wine illiterate, are you?"

"What's that supposed to mean?"

"You don't have any wine in a box, right?"

"Aren't you the wine snob?" she asked. "No boxes." She leaned to open the glass door of the cooler built into a cabinet and pulled out a green bottle with an off-white label in a grip that made it a suitable weapon to hit him in the head, she thought. "Chablis?"

"No, what else do you have?"

"I have a white Merlot, Shiraz, Moscato, Pinot Grigio, or maybe Pinot Noir — I can't remember."

"One's white, the other's red. Really?" He shook his head. "Noir, meaning dark?"

"Got it. And white Zinfandel in the fridge."

"Put that up," he said, pointing to the bottle she held. "Get the Shiraz. That should go with baked spaghetti."

Amber put the bottle back and grabbed another. "The corkscrew is in the second — " She stopped when he held it up. "Why not a white wine? Isn't it supposed to match the meal? Pasta should have white?"

"If you carry the wine and glasses to the table for me," he said, "I'd be happy to explain it to you."

"Who *are* you?" she asked, taking the bottle and two wine glasses from the rack to the table and sat.

He made his way on his crutches to her right side and picked up the bottle, "May I introduce you to the real Kelly Nathanial Morgan." Presenting the bottle, label toward her, he then cut the seal, inserted and whirled the corkscrew with the flourish of a professional sommelier in a five-star restaurant. He eased the cork out of the bottle and showed it to her.

"Why is the cork presented when a bottle is opened?" she asked.

"To show that the cork hasn't dried out, Madam; that the bottle has been stored properly on its side."

Amber nodded, watching him pour a few ounces into the glass and present it to her.

"Once uncorked, the aroma, color, and taste are evaluated by the head of the table to assure it is to his or her satisfaction. If the server is familiar with the wine, he may offer qualities specific to it."

"Do you know this one?"

"Not this particular vintner," he said, without looking, "but Shiraz is most often from Australia, and a similar wine, Syrah, from northern France. Typically, these are dry, full-bodied, opaque wines with hints of red, blue and black fruits, sometimes violet flower notes. The grape skin offers the hue to wine, which in this case is a deep, rich reddish-purple."

She swirled the garnet-colored wine in the glass, held it up to the light, then took a sip. "I see. Quite a show." She nodded with approval.

He filled her glass, then his own, and then sat next to her. "I paid for college working at Chef Michel's."

"In Houston?" she asked, taking a guess where the restaurant might be.

"No, in Boston," he said, pronouncing the city with the strong *ah* of the area. "My graduate degree in engineering is from MIT."

"Wow."

"Are you impressed? I've always wanted a woman to be really impressed by that, you know? I worked so hard for it." His voice sounded needy, but he grinned.

"The wine or the degree?" she said, laughing. "We should toast. To impressive schools, degrees, and working hard." She raised her glass.

"To new friends and great wine."

They touched glasses and sipped. He served salad to them each.

For most of the course, they moved with formality worthy of a fine restaurant, with small bites, sips of wine, quiet snippets of polite conversation.

"So, you've heard my confession. Tell me something about you," he said.

"Okay," she said, not sure what to reveal. "I'm the only child of an unwed teenage mom who married when I was four, and we lived in Albuquerque until my early teen years. After my mother died, I met my biological father and his new wife, and I lived with them. Dad was DEA. Julie, my stepmom, had once been New Mexico State Police, but when she moved to Michigan, she became a medical examiner investigator. When they got married, they moved to Washington, and she became a deputy with the MEI duties. The year I started college, they moved back to Albuquerque."

"I'm sorry to hear about your mom. What does your father do now?"

"He's in the FBI, to Julie's mortification." Amber made a wicked smile.

"Why did you pick forensic computer science? I can't imagine how you managed to not be a homicide detective or something."

"I found out I like some of the same things Julie was doing — processing and interpreting evidence — but I was fantastic at computer stuff. They moved during my first year in college, but I stayed in Seattle to finish my undergrad, then I did my graduate degree here." She took a bigger bite of salad to give her an excuse to stop talking.

He nodded, also chewing, motioning for her to go on. When she took another bite, he said, "You have some horse things around your house. You don't look like a cowgirl."

"Thanks to my dad, I am. We competed in team roping and penning."

"You can rope?"

She nodded. "I also worked as a trail guide two summers. Went on a couple of searches, too. I still have my Stetson and spurs." She broke a breadstick in two, and he took half. "What else must you know about me?"

"Why such a big house for one person? Is it a divorce winning?"

"No!" she said, frowning at the idea. "It was a foreclosure, had a lot of damage but nothing structural. It was a steal, especially with the enclosed pool. Originally, I intended to flip it, but I worked so hard on it, I thought I'd keep it a while."

"You did all this?" he asked in amazement.

"Not all of it, but I can swing a hammer as well as a rope." She took another sip of wine. "What would be something unusual about you that most people don't know?"

"The restaurant thing, probably. I'll think of another answer if you'll bring the baked spaghetti to the table," he said, making a half shrug and nod to his crutches, leaning against the kitchen island.

"The least I could do for dinner," she said, bringing the dish to the table and removing the glass top.

Steam billowed from the spaghetti, which appeared to be deep with cheese. Amber served them each a generous helping before sitting again.

I may need more insulin for this, she thought, considering again all the carbohydrates the meal held. She reached for the wine bottle to refill their glasses.

"Allow me," he said. "This wine will be perfect with the spaghetti. I hope you have another bottle."

Amber waited for him to pour for them both, then spun her fork in the cheesy spaghetti.

Kelly picked up his fork, then paused. "Although it's not unusual, most people don't know that I'm also an only child of parents who divorced when I was fifteen. Looking back, they shouldn't have tried so long to make things work on my account." He broke another breadstick, giving her half, then swirled his in the spaghetti sauce on his plate, took a bite and chewed, swallowed, and continued. "My mother grew up in DFW. After a bad car crash a few years out of college, she couldn't tolerate being on her feet all day, so she found a job with the crime lab. Married. Had me. Got divorced. My father moved to Colorado, last I heard."

"What did he do, last you heard?" she asked, repeating his caveat, then taking another sip of wine.

"He was a cop," Kelly said, shrugging. "He's probably retired now. Or dead."

"You're a little bitter, I'd say."

"I told you, I worked hard at MIT. When I graduated summa cum laude with master's degrees in both criminal science and mechanical engineering, he couldn't be bothered to come to Boston because his ten-year-old daughter had a dance recital that week. He'd been divorced from my mother for eight years. So yeah, I'm a little pissed at him and his other family," he said with a sneer. "Catch the math?"

"Got it."

"I haven't spoken to him since. I came back to Texas, worked as a police officer in Abilene for a few years." Then he stopped talking. Stopped eating, like he was lost in an unpleasant memory.

"Kelly?"

He shook away whatever had stolen his attention. "This new task force reminds me of a case I worked."

"I'm sorry," she said. "From what Paul tells me, we're working to prevent things like that, to catch predators before they can target a kid. But I'm all in. Like the story of the man who saw a little boy carrying newly hatched sea turtles to the ocean's edge to put them in the water. The man said, 'You can't possibly save them all, so what difference does it make?' and the little boy said, 'It makes all the difference in the world to the ones I save.'"

PART II

CHAPTER 20
Monday, October 26, 2009

"Being a 13-year-old is damned hard work," Amber complained as she thumbed through transcript printouts from her first night of chat she'd spent, engaging two potential predators.

Their goal, using social sites to troll for pedophiles who were scoping out vulnerable kids, had been slow to start. First, Amber had to learn each new program as she went. With adequate time, she'd accessed the operations of both chat programs. Last night, they agreed that Amber should graduate to her first trial at being a kid.

Kids who were in jeopardy, they agreed, were most often those living in a split household with major dysfunctions or those with emotional holes needing to be filled by anyone who'd pay attention to them and provide praise or acceptance, then love.

"Remember, kids like that eventually will do whatever is asked by the person who meets those basic emotional needs," he said. "Even when what's being asked of them progresses to actions that are grossly inappropriate or dangerous, a desperate kid will do anything to feel special to someone," Paul had told her. "Try to remember that when these tests of loyalty are presented."

"Like what?" she asked.

Paul rolled his chair back and pulled a stack of paper from his briefcase, browsed through several, and pulled one page from it. He slid it across the table to Amber.

As she read an excerpt from a transcript, her face went slack, then pale.

"Oh my God!" she whispered. "How ... how could anyone tell a kid to do that?"

"In that case, the boy wasn't a sex crime victim. He was the victim of a serial killer. The point is, we never really know the true intention of a predator's next confrontation."

Amber nodded, then turned back to the monitor, which was also projected onto a large screen at the edge of the table.

"I hope we don't find that. I'm not sure I could go through with it."

"This guy you've been talking to tonight is going down in an enormous ball of flames soon," Kelly replied.

The conversation with this man who called himself "Robby" had become their primary focus when he became interested in the young teenage girl Amber named "Erin," who voiced to anyone who would listen how her parents were divorced, how her mother expected her to be a happy kid who made average grades but insisted she babysit her four-year-old half-brother a lot while her mom went out. Erin had gained a bit of comradery from others close to her age. But then came Robby.

Robby told her how much he admired her ability to hold it together like an adult. "Most adults can't do that."

She had made a grand show of gratuity for this recognition, stating she wished her parents would notice.

He invited her to a private chat room, which Amber accepted.

She whined a little that she was old enough to stay home with her little brother alone when the adults wanted to go out, but she wasn't old enough to take the city bus to get a job at the mall. "I want to have money that I don't have to work for," she said, seemingly unaware of the incongruity.

Robby also chose to ignore it and asked what kind of job she really wanted.

"I think I'm pretty enough to be a model," she said.

He asked for a picture, and Amber balked a little, saying she didn't have a camera. Besides, she told him, she thought all the pictures she had made her look like she was twelve, when she felt she looked more like she was sixteen when she wore make-up, but her mom wouldn't let her. She agreed to take one over the next weekend she spent at her dad's.

"I can ask him to take one," she told him, "so it will be really good for you."

"You shouldn't tell him about me," Robby cautioned her. "Fathers can be very protective of first boyfriends."

"Am I your girlfriend?" Amber asked.

"Do you want to be?"

"OF COURSE!!!!" she wrote.

"Does your dad ever leave you home alone? I'm hoping we can talk on the phone for a few minutes. I want to hear your voice."

"Sometimes he has to leave for work on Saturdays. He works for the electric company."

"We can talk online, but if he leaves, then you can give me the phone number."

"Okay."

"Maybe I can send you a picture?"

"surr!!!" she replied.

"And when we talk, I'll tell you what I would like to do to show you how much I admire you."

After Amber ended the conversation, saying that her mother had told her twice to turn off the lights and go to sleep, Amber, Paul, and Kelly set back in their chairs, as if they'd finished sweating over a major exam.

"That was icky," she said.

"Yes, but we're getting close," Kelly added. He rubbed his leg, aching as the fractures healed. "Remember, you can't ask him his identity, but like the photo, the offer has to be his idea. Same with discussing sex. You can't entrap him."

"What about pictures of me?"

"We'll get something set up. The photo has to be you, an actual person, but we can alter it to an age-appropriate shot."

She nodded. "I can't believe how fast he moved. Is that normal?"

"He's either done this several times," Paul offered, "or he's an absolute first-timer who doesn't know enough to be cautious."

Kelly leaned back to stretch.

"How much longer will you be on crutches?" Paul asked.

"I had an appointment yesterday. The surgeon says the bone is healing well, but it isn't as fast as I'd hoped, of course. Once it's mended, they'll evaluate the knee for replacement," Kelly said, wincing at the glare that Amber gave him. "But he thinks swimming is great exercise."

"Then off you go to exercise," Paul said. "See you tomorrow evening."

CHAPTER 21
Friday, October 30, 2009

"I think we've got him," Paul said of "Robby" after four more nights of work. "He's committed to this trip to meet her."

"You think so?" she asked. "It seems so unreal. And slimy."

"This guy is sleazy, but he's hooked big time," Kelly agreed. "Reel 'em in."

They agreed they had ample evidence to seek an arrest and search warrant and chat records subpoena for the conversations he had been having with "Erin," pending the definite date to meet.

"I'll contact our judge first thing in the morning so we can set up a stake-out," Kelly said.

"You did incredible, Amber," Paul said.

She had played her part well, even with a few hiccups.

"It's difficult to keep track of everything with two targets," she told them.

"I suggest you take a few minutes after each session to log your notes," he said. "That does two things for you. First, you record stuff that is stuck in your head. Things you'd remember if you were that kid. Second, it lets you get those details out of your head."

"What's that supposed to do?" she asked.

"Let you sleep, hopefully. Consider a long list of errands you'd have to accomplish before catching a flight to Hawaii at noon tomorrow."

"Hawaii. That sounds like something I'd make a list for," Kelly quipped.

"If you go to bed and think of something else for the list but you haven't written it down, your brain worries all night it will forget. Lack of quality sleep makes forgetting something a self-fulfilling prophecy. Write it down, your brain realizes it's off the hook for remembering, so you sleep better."

"Notepad by the bed," she said. "Got it."

"Make your notes before you start another session, even if we," he said, pointing to himself and Kelly, "are impatient to move on. Then the next day, review the prior night's transcripts and add to your notes if you need to. Keep a list of things like appearance, family history, and important things that your character told the target, or that target says."

"Sounds like a lot of work."

"You set up the list the way you like it, and I'll keep notes for you during sessions once I see how you want it to look."

Amber found the idea useful, so she worked on her thoughts while Paul and Kelly reviewed details for a warrant. When she was through, the men joined her.

"That really does take my mind off it," she announced. "Thanks!"

"Then go try it out. See how you sleep," Paul told her. "Let's meet at one tomorrow afternoon at my office. I've gotta see if the kids are ready for Halloween."

***

Before going to Paul's office the next day, Amber and Kelly spent two hours of their Saturday morning at the crime lab, using the computer program investigators used to "age" missing kids, only in reverse, to create a picture of "Erin."

"I wish we could use a missing child's photo," she said. "I hate being photographed."

"You can say without lying that it is you in the photo. And you can refer to this photo as proof you aren't a cop because you look 14. You're not *denying* you're a cop; you're offering altered proof someone believes," Kelly said. "Besides, do you want to be the one apologizing to parents of a missing kid because we used a photo of their child?"

"As a parent, I'd be delighted someone was still looking at a photo of my missing kid, I think," she replied. "I guess there's a one-planet-in-the-universe chance we picked a photo of a missing child that a target would recognize."

The original images of Amber had been regressed to her young teens. With that photo and incredible editing software, the tech created an impressive picture for Robby of a young teenage girl with makeup and a t-shirt pulled off one shoulder, sitting on a barstool in an imaginary cluttered house with a few random toys and part of a television screen commercial in the background.

"Give me a few more hours, and I'll have a dozen more with other clothes, backgrounds, aging," the tech said. "If you need more later, let me know."

Fortunately, not all kids would be able to take photos on demand, and uploading was a tedious task. This would give Amber time to edit an image if she were asked to provide one that would prove it was up to date, like holding a current newspaper, wearing a certain color, or a piece of paper with something written on it.

When Robby came online to chat that afternoon, their conversation eventually transitioned to her having the photo. He gave her an email address, and Erin sent the picture.

Kelly went to work trying to find the identity of the user and anything else the application might save, though it wasn't a well-known email program.

Robby was pleased, he told her. "You are so beautiful!" and ten minutes of further cooing and gushy praise. "Could I get a picture of you in your underwear? Something sexy. Lacy?"

"I don't know how I could take it," she confessed. "And I don't have any lacy underwear."

"Oh, baby! We'll have to get you some! A face that lovely deserves lovely lingerie."

"What's that?"

"Pronounced lawn-jer-ay, my Sweet. Like really fancy pajamas and stuff."

"Oh, it's spelled weerd."

"What color do you think you'd like? Black and silky? Hot shiny red?"

"You pick."

"I have a friend who does professional portraits — headshots for models. I bet he could take some fabulous photos of you that would make you look seventeen or older. That would make modeling agents take notice."

"I can't afford that," she said. "Remember, I don't have a job."

"You are a natural, Erin, and I think you can be a star. I'll loan you some money, but he'll give us a discount, okay? He knows all the right people to get a beautiful young woman onto the runway, or even into Hollywood. Have you ever considered acting?"

"No."

"Get me a picture with a little more skin today, something that makes you look willing to pose. Or why don't I come take a few? You could pose for me. I've got the evening off today and tomorrow," he suggested.

"I dunno."

"Maybe we can go to a park to shoot some pictures."

Amber looked at Kelly.

"We can have a team at the house in an hour. It's perfect."

Amber turned back to the keyboard. "My dad's working today," she typed. "I'm not supose to leave."

"If he's not there, it will be our secret."

"Secret?"

"If he wanted you to be a model, he'd already have pictures of you."

She hesitated. "okay but it has to be while he's gone." The hesitation to the request was, the team believed, a realistic reaction. They didn't want the character to be too eager, but not too resistant, either.

"Perfect. I'll call my friend and see if he can come, invite him over to take the portraits, save some time?"

She made a keyboard smiley face.

With a few more negotiations about time, the pair agreed he would come to her house at four o'clock. But he gave her his cell phone number, in case something happened.

Paul reached for a keyboard to log in to his work computer and find the account identification for that number.

His real name was Warren Robert Swanson. The phone was a new smartphone with GPS, not a burner. The account went to a post office box, but Kelly ran the name through the law enforcement database to find a home address, then through state and national crime databases for criminal warrants and history.

With that, he was off to make final arrangements for the search warrant of Swanson's house and the arrest warrant for the safe house. Kelly sported a big grin when he returned.

Amber began making notes and printing the day's transcripts of her conversation with "Robby" and made notes for the team that would be arresting the alleged pedophile at a house they had rented for this purpose.

The clock ticked away the slow minutes as they waited.

"Wonder if someone's with him," Amber asked. "Or what he's driving. I can imagine a sleazy van with carpeted walls and . . ."

Kelly sat at a computer station. "Let's see." He logged into a surveillance system that included the house's front-door view from a car parked down the street, conveniently a cul-de-sac. Inside the house were three officers, with two more outside, behind bushes on either side of the building. Two more would be in place at the entrance to the cul-de-sac, blocking the exit by vehicle, should something go wrong.

"Based on prior cases, he might even stop a few houses away to send a message and make sure you're home alone," Paul said. "With that, I'm going to excuse myself. You two and them," he said, pointing at the monitors, "do not need me tonight. Let's meet at Ronna's Café tomorrow for brunch and wrap-up?"

They nodded and agreed on ten o'clock.

"Everyone's in place," Kelly confirmed. "As soon as they get a definite identity, they'll execute the search warrant on his house and work, if he has a job. We'll go to the residence."

Amber shivered. "Goosebumps," she explained, getting up to pace the room.

"He's probably a low-level molester with a pile of child pornography that he — " Kelly stopped himself from finishing this thought. "Never mind." He tapped more keys. "A real triumph will be to identify and catch a group who monitors these chats so they can nab kids when they are in vulnerable situations, like shopping or restaurants. Like the ones on the laptop from the train wreck."

"How do you know that?" she turned and demanded.

"I investigated the crash, so I followed the evidence, too, once I found out he was involved in child trafficking."

"But I haven't finished with the hard drive!"

"You left the file on the table one morning while you were swimming. I was eating a grapefruit, reached over and browsed it for something to do." He studied her scowl. "We *are* on the same team here. Literally."

She blinked away her annoyance and sat to work on the report summary.

Forty-two minutes later, Kelly nudged her to come watch the video stream showing a white delivery van had turned down the street, idled past the surveillance car two doors away, then made the circle turnaround before parking on the street in front of the house. He spent a minute doing something in the space next to his driver's seat, then stepped out, holding what looked like a small flower bouquet, headed toward the door. He rang the doorbell, which did not make a sound he could hear, pushed the button one more time, then he opened the glass storm door and knocked softly on the wooden door before trying the knob.

As planned, it was not locked.

When it turned, he looked both ways to see if anyone was watching, then pushed the door open slowly.

Inside, the house was furnished, but before he could mentally compare it to the background in the photo the girl had shared, five armed officers surrounded him, yelling orders for him to drop the flowers and to put his hands on his head.

"I must be in the wrong house," he cried, surprised at the gunpoint reception his entry earned. He danced around a bit but didn't resist. "I'm supposed to pick up a date who is house-sitting!"

At least he'd prepared a story of a misunderstanding.

The next man, the photographer, arrived and knocked fifteen minutes later, let himself in to the same greeting party. He hadn't been prepared with an elaborate story, just that he was booked to come to this address to take family photos for holiday cards. He was too upset to remember the man's name who had contracted him for these photos, but he had camera and lighting equipment in his vehicle.

"I get referrals from the website I use," he whined. "I take pictures, get paid, go home, email the pictures back."

Obviously, the stories didn't match, making the situation even more suspicious. The men were kept apart.

Within five minutes, officers had driver's license data and matching vehicle registration addresses for both men's residences.

"Let's go!" Kelly said, "it's our turn. We'll start with the primary suspect."

Duty officers met the duo there, having waited to enter the house. Inside, Amber took into evidence two laptops, a PC tower, dozens of unmarked CDs, and a portable hard drive storage unit. Kelly found boxes of VCR tapes with vague titles and a stack of magazines that would make *Playboy* or *Penthouse* look like first-grade picture books, he said.

"I doubt there's any value for prosecution in the mags as evidence. I'll leave it for his wife."

The most disturbing find was a cheap digital camera with two extra memory cards in a canvas case and a pair of size 4 toddler panties stuffed in the compartment beneath a slave flash.

"That'll be hard to explain to a judge," Kelly noted.

Two hours later, evidence had been packed and transported to the crime lab, the house searched, two other vehicles impounded, and one freaked out executive from a security company had been transferred to a county jail cell to face interrogation.

"He had the balls to ask if we could maybe keep this from his wife," one detective told them. "She's coming home tomorrow from a business trip to Chicago to that," he said, thumbing over his shoulder to the house they were leaving. "We left her a copy of the search warrant."

"That was nice of you to explain why her home was flipped like a pancake," another said. "I give her an hour till she finds something we missed."

"She'll have a divorce lawyer on the phone before lunch, I bet."

Amber and Kelly thanked them, then she drove to the second suspect's house, where officers had not waited for them to start the search.

"We don't find any evidence of child photography, much less kiddie porn," a sergeant detective who'd introduced himself as James Pierce told them. "He appears to run a legit photograph business, portraits, family shots, some travel magazines and stuff."

"No hidden drawers, walls? Attic? Under the house?" she asked.

"Nothing above. The foundation is pier and beam construction. We haven't looked there," he said with a shrug. "Hey, Bateman!" he yelled, walking away from them, giving instructions.

"I've got to sit down for a while," Kelly said. "I'll be on the porch."

The surrounding activity didn't require her, either so she followed him outside to wait while someone crawled around under the house. The break had barely been long enough for Kelly's tired leg and arms to rest.

"Y'all need to see this," James said from the screened door. "We found what you were looking for."

They followed him inside to the kitchen.

He stopped six feet short of the table where a dusty gray plastic tote sat. "I took the top off, didn't touch a thing after seeing that first picture," he said, his slightly sunburned complexion looked like dough.

Amber, tall enough to peer over the top easily, turned to look.

Then she covered her mouth and ran for the front door, her stomach heaving up the candy bar and juice she'd eaten on their way over from the rental house.

Kelly nodded for Pierce to put the lid back on it. "Seal it. Take it directly to the evidence locker. We'll go through it tomorrow. Did anyone else see this?"

The sergeant shook his head. "Only me, and I wish to God I hadn't, but I'm glad no one else did."

When Kelly looked out the bay window facing the street, his partner was still throwing up in front of her vehicle. "Anyone have a bottle of water?"

CHAPTER 22
Friday, October 30, 2009

An hour late, Harper came around the side of Ian Molina's home into an oasis. A pair of hundred-year-old oak trees cornered the lush yard, looming over a stone path winding from a patio seating area to a covered six-person hot tub, a koi pond and gently bubbling fountain, and two dozen people.

Several of his coworkers greeted him when he entered the cooking area, looking for the usual cooler of drinks.

Ian stood as grill master, flipping burgers, cobs of corn wrapped in bacon, and his signature steaks.

"Hey, Harp! Glad you could make it. Grab a drink. Steak or burger?"

Harper made a *Pfththth* sound. "Who wouldn't show up for one of your steaks?"

Belinda, Ian's wife, brought him a plate and utensils. "Great to see you, Harper. Potatoes are ready, if you want to butter up. Grab a drink."

Harper leaned over and brushed a kiss on her cheek.

Although Ian had kept a professional distance, Belinda had fed him for weeks after Lilah's funeral, dropping a meal by the station near his end of shift time each evening. His favorite had been her meatloaf with roasted corn like Ian was grilling.

"How's Meredith doing?" she asked, following him to the buffet-style table of food.

"She's doing good, working on Advanced Placement courses in science for college."

"And how are you, Harper?" she asked, using a pair of tongs to serve him a foil-wrapped potato the diameter of a softball. "Really."

"It's a little easier this year. I got past most of the big firsts. Her birthday was tough. I've stopped drinking. Getting a little more exercise."

He was lying to her, and they both knew it.

"I still pray for you every morning, Harp. You'll get through this."

"Thank you, Belinda. I appreciate everything," he said. "I'll get through, but then I don't have a choice, do I?" He unwrapped the potato and split it in half, smashed it a little then scooped a heaping spoonful of soft butter onto each side.

She gave him a solemn look, wondering if he'd sat at the edge of suicide, like other police officers whose widows she had met.

Harper shook his head as if he read her mind. "No shortcuts in grief. With her murder still open, there may be worse to come."

She nodded and left him to dress his potato, off to greet the next couple who arrived.

He took his plate and drink over to a picnic table and sat opposite Dennis Caldwell, another deputy, who worked the night shift.

"Hey, Harp. How's things?"

"Nothing different, you?"

"I hear you caught that wreck with Royce's ex-wife."

Ian brought over a platter of steaks. "Medium, medium-rare, or rare?"

Both men took medium-rare and an ear of corn.

"Yeah, she might have lived if they'd found her sooner. She was on her way to work."

"Nurse, right?"

Harper nodded, slicing off the first bite of his steak and putting it in his mouth. He chewed a few times and made a sound of approval.

Ian came back around to check, got a thumbs-up from Harper and Dennis, who didn't interrupt their meal again through most of the beef.

"Car was so smashed up, hard to tell which side is up, someone said."

"Yeah, it's a heap. The driver wasn't able to tell me what had happened before she died," Harper replied, not repeating what she had said or what he'd learned from the mechanic.

"It really doesn't matter, does it?"

"Only if it was an accident."

As if the planets aligned over his head in a malignant constellation, the Thomases came around into the back yard, greeting everyone jovially as they went. Eddy veered off to speak to Ian. Ellanie waved at Belinda on her way over to where Harper and Dennis sat.

"Hey, guys! That," she said, pointing at what was left of their steaks, "looks scrumptious! Where's the beer?"

Dennis pointed over his shoulder toward the cooler.

"Can I bring either of you something?" she asked, gliding on by in jeans perhaps a little too snug for a woman her age, but way too tight for a preacher's wife.

"Damn, I wish she wasn't married," Dennis whispered when she was out of earshot.

"Really?" Harper hissed. "Last I heard, you were married, too, Hotshot." He grabbed his plate and headed to get a burger on his way to an empty table on the other side of the yard. His path took him past Eddy, who'd been handed a steak and an ear of corn at the grill.

"Mind if I join you?" he asked as Harper took the burger and stomped on by, but Eddy followed without an answer. He swung a leg over the picnic table bench at the same time as Harper. "Haven't seen you at church lately."

"You know something, Eddy, you won't, either."

"I understand if you're still bitter at God because of your wife's death — "

"I'm not mad at God. I'm angry at the man she'd been screwing. I'm angry at whoever pulled the trigger that fired a bullet through her brain. Me going to church will not change that, will it, Eddy?" He glared across the wooden table, clenching his jaw to keep from saying more. Clenching his fist to keep from pummeling the man's face.

Eddy kept a calm expression. "It is said that confession is good for the soul."

"Interesting words. Do you live by them? Are *you* going to confess, because *I* don't need to tell God *anything*," Harper whispered. He stood and leaned closer. "Your God can't change the anger I feel, but He knows the truth."

CHAPTER 23
Friday, October 30, 2009

Kelly rode with Amber to her house in silence. He'd have driven if he could.

He suspected her response to the photo on the top of the box embarrassed her, and to be honest, he'd almost been beside her, puking up their last snack together.

She'd returned to the porch, rinsed her mouth with the bottled water he handed her, and they went back inside.

The tote lid had been replaced; two techs were working to seal it for transport. They were solemn, but they didn't have the pale ashen expression Pierce still wore.

Amber had followed Pierce to the crime lab to deliver the tote, keeping the van in view. Pierce was responsible for the chain of evidence until it was behind the locked reinforced door of the evidence room, but being able to back this up in court herself made her feel a tad better.

Inside, Kelly and Pierce warned the evidence tech not to open it.

If the contents below it were any fraction of the incomprehensible revulsion of the top photo, anyone seeing it without some emotional preparation, if there were such a thing, would need a barf bag.

Or need psychiatric admission, Kelly had muttered to himself as he locked the box away. "We'll come to do inventory on it this week."

With that, Amber drove home in silence. She pulled into her driveway, turned off the engine, then she sat, eyes closed.

"Come on," Kelly said after a minute. "Let's go."

She nodded, still they sat in the near darkness for several more minutes.

Finally she sighed, pulled the key from the ignition, and opened the door. The feet she swung out to the dry surface were heavy, like she had slogged through knee-deep freshly poured concrete.

Neighbors might have thought zombies walked from the car to the house and unlocked the door.

"How 'bout a beer," she said after ditching her bag on the foyer table.

"No, beer without pizza makes me feel bloated at night. I'll open a bottle of wine. You go take a shower."

She nodded but didn't take a step.

"Then go change. I'll find unbreakable glasses, then we can go sit by the pool," he said, going around her to the kitchen.

When she didn't move, he turned to see a tear rolling down her cheek.

He rambled back to her on the crutches, touched her arm to gauge her response, then embraced her.

"This is harder than I ever imagined. How could someone *do that* to a baby?" she whispered as the tears distorted her voice.

Kelly didn't answer. No answer existed. He held her as she cried.

"You don't have to keep doing this," he said.

"Yes, I do," she said, pulling away and wiping the tears away with her palms. "There's no reason I can't do this. It's just acting."

"This is no more acting than sitting in a wading pool is swimming away from the sinking Titanic." He crutched over to the kitchen area. "But in your first case, your work got *two* of those bastards off the street with a significant amount of evidence. *You* made that happen. That's badass."

He chose a bottle of wine, opened it, and poured them each a glass.

She picked them up with one hand and walked to the back door, opening it for them.

"Grab the bottle," he suggested. "We'll need it."

Outside, they each sat on a chaise. Kelly helped lift his leg.

"Hurting?"

"Just tired."

Amber turned up her glass, taking several gulps.

"Glad I didn't open an expensive wine," he said as if talking to himself.

"Yeah, me too. Would'a been a waste." She took a more civilized sip. "Tell me about this wine."

"This is a California Pinot Noir, a balanced and somewhat lighter red wine, between a Zinfandel and a merlot. It pairs nicely to both red meats and fish, making it quite versatile."

"I thought Zin's were light," she said.

"Typically, wine gets its color from the skin of the grape. However, because rosé had become so popular, California winemakers found a way to produce an alternative to rosé that previously had been a blend of red and white grapes or sometimes, a blend of finished wines. The two rosé wines you have are exclusively from Zinfandel or Merlot grapes, not a blend. The lighter shades of these two are created by removing the dark grape skins from the juice earlier."

"This is nice," she said after taking a sip. "Wine is more complicated than I'd ever imagined. Thank you for educating me. It's a welcome mental change of direction."

"I understand a great deal about wine, but when it comes to what's in the glass, I believe you should drink what you like. I'm not a wine snob. Some of my favorite casual wines come in a box. I simply know more of the chemistry of it." He reached over to refill her glass and topped off his own, which he held up to the dim lights. "Some wines, you probably do not want to know, are even more fantastic because of a fungus, causing what they call Noble Rot. It is from the same family of fungi that cause bleu cheese, and penicillinase."

"Oh yuck!"

"Sounds bad, but it can impart a much grander complexity and sweetness because of the dehydration of the grapes, so it requires more of them to make wine, and it adds an aroma reminiscent of honey or ginger. It's an extraordinary stroke of silver lining in a hurricane," he said, turning up his glass and draining it. "Tonight, we needed a social serving of alcohol to erase the day."

"Tomorrow, we do it again."

"Nope. Tomorrow, we set out Halloween stuff and get costumes and tons of candy for the trick-or-treaters." He smiled. "We've got to have some fun or we'll go crazy."

CHAPTER 24
Monday, November 2, 2009

"We've been baiting this guy for eons with no nibble," Amber said, leaning back in an office chair she'd rolled in from the garage to her kitchen table. Although they found it easy to work at her house, she couldn't relax on the sofa or recliners. Feeling that casual made her unfocused. "I'm beginning to think he won't ever bite."

"It's Monday. Let's let him cool a few days, then. I still think he's waiting on something specific. Or it's his first time, and he's afraid to commit," Paul said. "We've given him high cards to play: the big fight with her divorced parents, a hint of abuse by the mom's boyfriend. We can explain her absence as being grounded for a week from her computer. If he thinks she's angry enough, maybe he'll play on that."

"What does a 12-year-old girl get grounded for?" she asked, writing in the notebook where she kept notes about her characters and the data being exchanged.

"Mmm, maybe drinking when her parents aren't home?" Paul offered. "Or maybe while she's at someone else's house."

"Personal experience?"

"We grounded Neela for drinking when her friend brought a bottle of vodka when she spent the night," he said, wrinkling his face. "She says she only had a little. Initially, it was two weeks, but she argued being grounded wasn't fair, so I increased it to four. She'd been grounded during the summer for sneaking out to a party when she was at another friend's house."

"Your girls aren't supposed to experiment with how to teach me to be a teenager," Amber said. "Sorry."

He waved off her apology. "Not your fault. She knew what she was doing wasn't right. Mackenzie is our golden child for now — no misbehaving, no chasing boys, no hiding to use the computer."

"Does Neela hide to do this?"

"No, but I'm never sure what she gets into at other kids' houses. We've had the *talks* about sex and the black hole of the Internet, and such. It's a scary time to be a kid."

Kelly yawned then apologized.

"I agree. Let's call it a night," Paul said, standing and stretching, grabbing another green grape from the bowl they'd been snacking from. "I think we should skip tomorrow night. It doesn't seem realistic to be online every night, and I think we've hit all the target chats at least twice this week. We all need a break."

Kelly agreed, getting to his feet and situating his crutches. "I need to do the inventory from the photographer's house tomorrow."

"How much longer till you're back on duty?" Paul asked him.

"Much too long. I'm going bonkers with these crutches, but the swimming exercises help. I'm trying to sweet-talk my way to another month here so I can keep using the pool," he said, speaking behind his hand as if Amber couldn't hear them.

"We should get your family over this weekend for a pool party and barbeque," Amber suggested.

"That'd be great, but if I mention it now, they'll drive *me* bonkers about it all week," Paul said, putting his laptop into its neoprene case. "I'll check with Van and confirm. It will be a surprise for the girls."

Amber walked him to the door, and they exchanged goodbyes.

Kelly slumped back into the recliner where he'd spent the evening. "This is harder work than chasing bad guys."

"My dad would say it's like fishing."

"Really? Fishing isn't hard."

"You spend the day baiting hooks and casting, a few minutes reeling in a fish, an hour cleaning and cooking it, ten minutes eating it, and a week smelling it in the house," Amber said, picking up the bowls from the table.

Kelly laughed. "That, I'd agree with. I'd like your dad."

"You would."

"I agree. Monsters are snatching kids off the streets or their homes, and we're fishing in the swimming pool," he said. "Patrols respond to failed grabbings or the cases where a mom feels threatened or freaks out because some slimeball is following her around a store, or when someone crowds her in the parking lot. We seldom catch anyone committing a crime."

"I like the philosophy of the single father who caught a guy leading his four-year-old daughter away at a rest stop restroom. Beat him to death with his bare hands," she said.

"Kudos to him. I'd like to catch guys like that, too."

She waved at Kelly. "Come on." She crossed her arms to yank a loose t-shirt over her head, revealing the black swimsuit top beneath. "Let's take a swim and exercise your leg."

"Yes, Ma'am!" Kelly got up and went to change.

Before he went out the door, he stopped to watch her.

She was wearing the bikini bottoms that matched her top. Not too skimpy but accentuated her curves.

Kelly tried not to stare as she went to the far side of the enclosure to open a few windows for a breeze. Realizing he really liked watching her, he crutched outside while she was still across the pool, tossed his towel on a chair, his crutches beside it, and took two hops to the pool edge, where he dropped into the water in a splash. He surfaced, shook off his hairless head, and laughed. "I like my place, but this seals the deal. Will you marry me?"

"I bet you say that to all the girls with pools."

"Only the single ones," he said, leaning back to float. "I've got morals, you know."

"I see," she said, then took a two-step lead to an almost splashless racing dive that powered her the length of the pool without moving a muscle, breaking the surface in time to take a breath before she made the underwater turn and kicked off, coasting to near where Kelly floated on his back before she surfaced.

"You were a swimmer, too?" he asked.

"Nope. Just graceful."

Kelly rolled his eyes. "Tell me more about your dad."

"Like what?"

"Is he really as big as he looks?"

"And then some. Every bit of six-and-a-half feet tall. You've seen the pictures," she said, thinking of a photo of him standing beside her at her high school graduation, dressed in a gray Stetson and white long-sleeve shirt and blue jeans with gray boots — his perfect idea of formal attire. "He's been a cop most of his life, but the cowboy part I think he was born with."

"Poor girl. You never had a chance, did you?"

"What? Cowgirl?"

"No, cop."

"You've never seen me on a horse."

"You'll never see me on one, either," he responded.

"Why not?"

"My idea of an adventurous ride is a Ford Mustang on a racetrack, not a wild mustang dragging me through a field."

"That's too bad. On horseback, you're that much closer to Heaven."

"And that much further from the ground."

CHAPTER 25
Tuesday, November 3, 2009

Dierdra and Blaine had finished supper. He was in the living room playing a video game. She'd retired to her bedroom to a big snuggly chair to read Diana Gabaldon's newest release, *An Echo in the Bone*. Something not for work, which was a rare occurrence.

When her cell phone rang, she saw the caller ID and hesitated to answer.

Stephen Royce hadn't called her since his invitation to San Antonio a month ago, so Dierdra assumed he was pissed she hadn't taken time off to join him.

A fifth ring did not follow. She waited to see if he left a message. He did not.

If he called back and if she answered, a big if, she could say she'd been in the bathroom. Or that she'd left her phone on the kitchen counter. Maybe she should go run a bubble bath — that would be a good excuse, if she decided she wanted to give one.

She made up her mind, wiggled out of the chair to go to the master bathroom.

When she flipped on the light, she remembered why taking a relaxing bath wasn't on her list of favorite things — the bathroom walls were still the deep blue that her ex-husband had chosen, making the room feel smaller. Aggravated that she hadn't removed the last of the marine theme to make the room something she would enjoy, she worried the apricot color she liked wouldn't cover the dark blue. She'd removed all his trinkets, including a large piece of coral and the fishing net shower curtain, replacing them with beach-themed décor, including a sawgrass basket of seashells.

The difference had been water.

Her phone rang again. She didn't look.

Why did she need a reason for not answering after he'd gone for weeks without calling her? Let him be mad.

Except, she thought, *what if he did something to his ex-wife's car?*

He wouldn't do anything like that.

Would he?

Her phone rang a third time in ten minutes.

She gave in and looked. This time, the caller ID showed a blocked number.

Oh, isn't that clever?

"Hello?" she said.

"Are you avoiding me?" Stephen asked, his voice dull and cold.

"Avoiding you? You haven't called me since you went to San Antonio."

There was a long silence, and she thought about hanging up.

"Are you free this weekend? Either night."

"No, I'm sorry," she said. "I've already made plans."

"You're lying," he replied in a dead growling whisper.

"I will not tolerate you calling me a liar, Stephen. I don't think we should see each other again." She pulled the phone away from her ear to push the disconnect button. She wasn't sure, but she thought she heard him reply.

"But I do."

She tossed her phone onto the counter, realizing that she was trembling.

He had sabotaged his ex-wife's car; she was sure of it now. But she had no idea how to prove it.

CHAPTER 26
Friday, November 6, 2009

Another solitary Friday night nearing midnight, Brady Cayson didn't go home to his family tonight because Liz had taken their three kids to her parents' cottage at Lake Texoma for a late autumn weekend getaway. He had missed a few of their short trips like this one because of work. Sometimes it was good for Liz to get them away from home without him. Or sometimes he took them skiing and she stayed home. He suspected the winner was the spouse left alone and not the one with the kids, but it was always enjoyable for everyone.

As a family, they always made time for special events for the kids, taking two annual weeklong trips to locations chosen from the "vacation jar." Each kid put in two destination choices on New Year's Day each year, a summer and a winter choice. They drew for the winter trip in January, the summer trip in May.

Brady's friends and coworkers warned him that when the kids got into their teenage years, they might be too embarrassed by the mere existence of parents to enjoy such family vacations. He doubted that because they were involved in so many activities together. For now, though, he and Liz were happy to plan for trips they could all enjoy.

The ringtone of his cell phone startled him from his daze, loud even from its location under a stack of paper. After the five-minute conversation, he pushed the button to end the call and collapsed back in his chair, deflated as the words played back in his head.

Missing. Ultimately, that's what Vanessa had told him, that his friend and coworker Paul Keegan and their eleven-year-old daughter were missing.

"Sometime after 6:30, he called to tell me he was on his way to pick up Mackenzie from a friend's," Vanessa had explained. "They say he stopped there a little after seven, chatted fifteen minutes, and left. I haven't heard from him since."

Brady looked at his watch. It was a quarter after ten.

"Maybe he came back by the office for something and got sidetracked," Brady had offered, trying to defuse her anxiety.

"Why wouldn't he call me?" she countered. "I've tried calling him like a hundred times," she'd said, which probably translated to seven or seventy. "At first it was a no-answer ring, four times then to his voice mail. At nine, it started going directly to the message. When I called 911, I was told that because of the circumstance, I should give it another few hours."

The skin of Brady's scalp tightened. "I'll go check his office. It's probably nothing."

"Don't brush me off, too, Brady. Please? Something isn't right." She took a deep breath. "Paul told me about his project at work, this locating a phone thing. Can you do it? Can you find him?"

A dozen scenarios ran through Brady's head — an affair, gambling, drinking. None of these seemed within Paul's stable husband and father character. But if he were going to do something he didn't want Vanessa to know about, he wouldn't take Mackenzie along with him.

Brady agreed to locate the phone.

After he hung up, he dialed Paul's number one more time. One ring then voice mail, which meant the phone was turned off. Or dead.

The phone, or Paul?

CHAPTER 27
Friday, November 6, 2009

"I'm a little surprised you agreed to have dinner with me," Kelly told her as they walked along the sidewalk toward the theater.

"I figured you were tired of cooking for me. I believe I'm getting the better end of the deal," Amber replied.

"Dinner and a movie, to boot."

"Maybe I'm celebrating you leaving," Amber replied. "Looking forward to swimming without a bathing suit."

"For the record, I never required that you wore one on my account." He glanced at her and grinned. "I accept your wardrobe choices. Heck, I'd have been happy to swim nude, too. Your pool, your rules."

"Aren't you the accommodating gentleman."

"I also let you pick the movie," he answered. "Makes this a perfect date."

"You — this is a — a date?" she stammered, stopping to look at him.

He shrugged. "I didn't want to scare you, but I was afraid you'd say no if I called it a date, and maybe it isn't. I want to get to know you — the real you, not the one who shows up for work."

"I didn't think I was a different person."

"You are, though. When you work, you're completely dedicated. No one at work gets to see that cowgirl, the woman with dreams or tears. In fact, the only time I recall you deviating from that practical, no-nonsense role at work was at the car versus train, when you winked at me."

"I did not!" she huffed.

"Maybe it was dust in the air." He turned to face her, as close as they had been that day when she'd stood up. "But dinner and a movie don't have to imply anything more than becoming better friends. Calling this a date has no further implication than two people intentionally scheduling an event together."

She shrugged.

"I like you, Amber. You agreed to let me invade your space despite knowing I can be an ass. You cut me a break from the nepotism issue. But you like my cooking. And we work together pretty well."

"You've grown on me a bit," she finally said, not backing up despite being able to feel the heat from his body. "Kinda like a bad haircut."

"Good pun."

"I like you, too, but I don't want to mess up what we're doing at work."

"Promise. I'm exceptional at keeping secrets," he said as they broke the stare and resumed the walk. "I'm curious about your 9/11 escape."

"See? How do you know about that?" she demanded.

"I said I was great at keeping secrets, but I'm even better at learning them."

She slugged his arm, hard enough it hurt, but not too hard. "I'm going to have to have drinks with your mother. I'm sure she has baby pictures or old movies with interesting stories about you to share."

He ignored her threat and explained. "You have a scar like mine on your leg, but you didn't explain it, so I didn't ask. I mentioned it to my mother one day at lunch, and she said you'd been injured while in Manhattan during the September 11 terrorist attacks."

Amber's stride lengthened a few inches, making it harder for him to keep up.

"I take it you don't wish to discuss it?" he asked.

"Not really. Do you want to tell me why they call you Taz?"

"Nope. Changing the subject. Did you enjoy the fettuccini tonight?"

"Very much. And the wine was perfect," she said, slowing again. "A German Riesling, you said, right?"

Kelly nodded.

"I've had some German white wine before, nothing like that."

"You probably had a *Liebfraumilch,* a semisweet wine that is mostly exported. The translation is 'beloved lady's milk' referring to the Virgin Mary," he explained. "I don't like it. I much prefer German red wines."

"We'll have to try some next time," she said.

"I promise to keep expanding your wine experience if you promise there will be a next time," he said. "But what I have in mind I'll serve at home. The best German red wines, when you find them, are crazy expensive in restaurants."

"Why?"

"Supply is much smaller. The wineries in Germany do not make red wine for Americans like they do the whites. One extremely popular vintner there grows his crop on twenty acres, which is microscopic compared to Napa Valley."

"What's your favorite?"

He tilted his head, thinking. "I would choose a late harvest Spätburgunder, which is a similar wine to Pinot Noir except it is a darker garnet shade with aromas of black cherry, raspberry and strawberry, clove, cinnamon. It's kinda earthy."

"Sounds lovely. Julie had some wines from Michigan," she offered. "She had a cherry wine I liked."

"Cherry? Interesting. Haven't had anything like that. I've been to a few wine shops that serve locally pressed wines that aren't fermented. It's like drinking fruit juice with a pint of plain ethanol in it."

"That sounds disgusting."

"It's worse than disgusting."

At the theater, they stood in line for tickets, which Amber insisted on buying for them. Inside, she also paid for a giant bucket of popcorn, extra butter, and two extra-large drinks. Then she realized she'd have to carry it all.

"I think you like being on crutches," she observed.

"That's what I like about you — your dedication to blatant honesty, even when you're wrong."

In the dim lights of the coming-soon movie trailers, they found seats and settled in.

"I still want to know why they call you Taz," she whispered as the lights went out and the sound boomed.

"Maybe someday I'll tell you."

CHAPTER 28
Friday, November 6, 2009

Brady's concern grew, though he believed there had to be a logical, reasonable explanation why his friend didn't answer his phone. Calling Paul's cell, Brady listened to his friend's usual boring voice mail announcement, left a message after the beep. "Hey, Paul, it's Brady. I had a question about a project at work. Call me when you get a minute." The message sounded benign and unalarmed, should someone else access the voice mail. Although Brady didn't have a rational reason, not sounding panicked seemed prudent.

He dialed Paul's extension in the building, but there was no answer.

Brady grabbed his keys and took the stairs down one flight to check Paul's office, which he found dark and empty. Then he took the elevator up three floors to a hallway leading past closed offices to a double-locked doorway requiring a physical key and an ID/keycard.

He had a choice of two methods. One he could do in about fifteen minutes, but it would only provide the current location. The other could take more than an hour to run and another to process, but the result would provide a detailed location history over a longer span. He could not run them simultaneously on one computer. Inside, he sat at a terminal and booted the software that would allow him to locate the signal of Paul's phone. Setting his fingers on the keyboard, he decided to spend the extra time to gain the optional information.

Then he went back to his office to find the current phone location, which showed Paul's phone was inactive, as he'd suspected. He'd made the right choice to obtain the phone's location history. By the time the computer assimilated data and he interpreted it, the conclusion left a burning ache in his stomach.

Paul's phone had left work at 1836; been to a location he assumed was Mackenzie's friend's house in Grapevine from 1910 to 1925. From the mall, it traveled to an area near Grapevine Station Mall, where it stayed from 1942 to 2026, then it went north, pinging its last tower at 2054. Then, according to the system, it disconnected at 2056 without notice, meaning the battery was removed. Or the phone had been destroyed.

A dozen possibilities ran through Brady's head, with contradictions abounding for each. Stopping at a mall with a young daughter wouldn't have been unusual, he supposed. He'd have to ask Vanessa if there was a birthday or other occasion for which Paul or Mackenzie might have wanted to buy a present. Yes, Paul might have driven north from the mall, but why? What would take him *farther* from his house without calling Vanessa? That was a long way to go by accident.

Perhaps his cell phone had been lost or stolen at the mall, so Paul himself didn't go north but the phone did. But if that was the case, where was he now, and why hadn't he called home?

No matter what possibilities Brady thought up, they concluded with Paul not contacting Vanessa, which was grossly out of character. He called her three or four times a day from work.

Brady went back to his office and packed his laptop, grabbed his jacket from the rack, and headed to his car. The obvious choice was to follow the only track available, from the office to Mackenzie's friend's house to where the phone ping was last recorded.

Climbing into his vehicle, Brady headed to the first location, where Paul had picked up Mackenzie after seven. Vanessa had confirmed this, so Brady made it his first waypoint. From there, Paul's phone signal created a path of overlapping cell towers that put him at a mall. Not to a particular entrance but most likely on the east side.

The parking lot on this side was deserted, only a half dozen cars spread out over five acres, he figured. The sodium vapor lights cast orange puddles of light.

After circling the massive building, Brady parked his car at the outer edge of striped asphalt. He'd had a childish hope he'd find Paul, sheepishly looking for his phone or watching his car being pulled onto a wrecker. That disappointment, however irrational, made Brady realize he didn't know how to find his friend in the real world, regardless of how good his computer abilities were.

But he had a friend with those skills he lacked.

He picked up his cell phone and scrolled to the speed-dial number for the one friend he hoped could spend a little time to help him, even from two hundred miles away.

A voice of someone who didn't hide annoyance at being awakened delivered the grumbled greeting.

"Harper, it's Brady. Wake up, man, I need a big favor," he said.

"Brady, you know it's after midnight," the gruff reply announced.

"I didn't call to find out what time it is," Brady said, trying to sound as if he were smiling. "Go nuke a cup of coffee. I need you to walk me through something. It's important."

Brady heard a rustling in the background, and he wasn't sure if maybe there wasn't a little swearing, too, then the sound of a door opening, but no direct response to the request.

It *was* only fair, Brady thought to himself.

After Lilah's death, Harper had called Brady and the others in their circle of friends late at night, occasionally drunk. Mostly Brady. A lot.

Though Brady hadn't minded the calls, he often returned to bed to his lovely wife with a whole new appreciation for her in his life. He couldn't grasp trying to be a father without Elizabeth, who wrangled the bunch to meals she both shopped for and cooked, to coordinated trips to school and sports and church and everything else she did. He couldn't imagine life without her, so he stayed up talking to Harper without regret.

"Okay, Brady," Harper broke into the memory. "Coffee's brewing. What's up?"

"I got a call from a coworker's wife a few hours ago. Paul hasn't returned home or called."

"Maybe his car broke down," Harper offered, trying to stifle a yawn.

"No," Brady said. "Even if it did, he hasn't called his wife to come get him and that was hours ago."

"What do you want me to do from Brighton, Brady?" Harper asked, running his fingers through his hair, waiting less patiently for the coffee.

"Before I left the office, I pulled the data and plotted the location of Paul's cell phone movements tonight," Brady admitted. "There is no current location."

Harper sighed. "Shall I come arrest you for doing something illegal, because honestly I don't know what that's supposed to mean."

"I'll explain it over a beer sometime. Remember what I did for that friend of yours right after 9/11. Zach? I got the last location for his daughter's phone in New York City? Sorta like that," he said.

"Worked for him," Harper admitted, "so what's the problem."

Brady hadn't known whether what he'd done had been helpful or not. "After Paul picked up his daughter, they stopped at a mall. I'm there now. The place closed at nine. But then the mapping shows the phone, and presumably the Keegans, traveling north from here some five to eight miles. As of 8:54, it pinged a tower then went dead. The last contact it made to a tower was some 20 miles north of his house."

"Okay, I still don't understand. You mean he drove further away from home?"

"The log only proves that the phone went that direction, not that Paul went with it," Brady explained, supposing it had only been obvious to him. "But yes, it was further away from his house than the mall."

"He probably has one of those damned intelligent phones with all the flippin' pictures of stuff for things you — "

"Harper!" Brady stopped the diatribe he'd heard several times already regarding the functions of a smartphone that his friend would never use, mostly for lack of interest. "Paul and lots of people have smartphones and don't hate them. With a phone like that, it's always communicating with the closest tower. It sends data back and forth all the time."

"Even when I'm not making a phone call?" Harper cringed.

"Yes, the network keeps track of where you are in relation to its towers, even when you aren't talking. By plotting that data, I can get the general location of the phone by triangulating its directions from two or more towers. With more data, I can deduce a location change. That's how I knew where it was going. With me so far?

"I'm gonna need a bigger cup."

"A few phones have built-in GPS, but his doesn't."

"Okay," Harper said, hoping Brady's story would begin to make sense after coffee.

"The phone disconnected from the network at 8:56, meaning either the battery was removed or the phone was destroyed. By triangulation, that is an area about 400 square feet, near Grapevine Lake on the west side."

There was silence on the phone.

"Harper," Brady stated emphatically. "I need you to help me find Paul and Mackenzie. I have the technology, but I don't know the rest. I don't want to screw this up for the cops. For Paul."

"How can I help you?"

"I'm not exactly sure. Vanessa told me the police took a report, but because Paul is a healthy adult, they are not actively looking. She's certain that he'd have contacted her by now," Brady said. "I'm driving from the mall to the last location the phone pinged."

"You're alone. Is that such a good idea? What if you find something?"

"I don't know, Harp. That's why I called you. What am I supposed to do? No one else is looking, and his phone stopped working somewhere near the west side of the lake around the county line."

"Any reason to think that he dropped his phone in a stranger's bag and then went to the airport and left the country?" Harper asked, waiting for the coffeemaker to spit out its last drops. "Something about custody, divorce?"

"Not likely. He and Vanessa have three kids, stable jobs, go to church. No reason he's ever let on that he would want to leave."

"Threw the phone into the lake? Something I often want to do," he muttered. Too impatient to keep waiting, he took the carafe out before the coffeemaker had finished, filling his stained cup, and then rattling the glass pot back under the drip. He dumped in a spoonful of sugar, the stirring making a dull twinkly sound. "Dropped it on the side of the road, in a toilet? Hell, let the battery die. I forget to charge mine all the time."

"If the battery died, the system would know the phone separated intentionally as it powered down. In this case, the phone abruptly disconnected from the network. Paul would know that."

"Okay. Then what's your conclusion?"

"Something happened to the phone, sure. But Paul disappearing makes no sense." Brady thumped the steering wheel with the heel of his hand.

"That's my point. Worst-case-scenario, they were abducted by aliens, car and all."

"Harper," Brady threatened in a single word, making it two tones.

"Okay, not aliens. Maybe the phone fell out of his pocket in the mall, someone took it, found it useless, and threw it in the lake."

"Still, he'd have gone home or called by now."

"What if it was his wife who was cheating. . ." His voice faded to silence.

Brady recognized Harper's slide into personal history, but he refused to let this become a conversation about Harper's past. "He never mentioned he thought his wife was cheating or wanting to leave her for any other reason," Brady stated, then considered a moment. "But if that *were* the case, he would have taken all three kids."

"Or none of them. Just eliminating possibilities. Would the wife have wanted him dead for some reason?"

"Even if she did, he had his daughter with him. And why would she have called me? She asked me to track his phone. To find him," Brady replied. "Calling me makes little sense if she planned to kill him."

"Confirming her alibi for this evening is someone else's job, but for now we'll assume you're right about her," Harper countered. "From what you're saying, if this was an intentional job, it would make sense that at least two people were involved."

"Maybe coming out here alone wasn't such a bright idea," Brady admitted, looking around at the decreasing signs of life. "I can't narrow down the area any smaller, so unless he's standing beside the road with his thumb out, I won't find anything helpful."

"We don't know that, so keep driving. I'm trying to find out where you're going, but all I have is a state map. Not much detail."

"You could log in to the mapping program on your computer," Brady suggested, chuckling.

"Maybe next decade, I'll learn what that means," Harper replied. "I never envy your gadgets. Besides, Meredith took the PC with her when she went to the Gentry's," Harper said, his voice getting even more solemn. "Not like I was using it."

"You'll have to trust me then. Not much except the lake and some parks, according to the map I'm using. I even took a quick look at the satellite images before I left the office, but it looked pretty covered in trees." Brady turned right toward the lake. "Okay, I'm at the parking area leading to a boat ramp. Looks deserted. There's a public restroom with lights around it."

"Don't park near the building," Harper told him. "As far away as you can."

"Why?"

"Now you get to walk in my world, Brady. You are going to scan the lot for evidence."

Brady parked and got out, looking around at the surrounding trees.

"First, are any cars left in the lot?"

"No," Brady told him.

"Take your flashlight."

"What makes you think I have one?"

"Because you're a Boy Scout," Harper answered. "Let's suppose your friend intended to go inside when he got there. Where would he have parked?"

Brady looked around. "The men's and women's entrances are on opposite ends of the building. If the lot were empty, he'd park close to the entrance, but not in one of the four handicapped spaces."

"Which side of his desk is the phone on?"

"Why?" Brady thought for a second. "He's right-handed, but the phone sits on the left."

"It would already have been dark when he got there, so I'm guessing he parked so his daughter's side was closest to the entrance. Stay off the grass but walk to the door of the women's side on the sidewalk. Look at the concrete and the right side in the grass as you go for fresh gum, trash, blood."

"Blood, great." Twenty seconds later, Brady said he was there.

"Do not touch the door. Can you see inside?"

"No, it's a solid door."

"Walk back down the sidewalk toward the parking lot, looking at the grass on the other side," Harper coached.

"Okay, hang on." There was a pause. "Back to the asphalt."

"Now do the same thing on the men's side. Take your time."

"I don't see anything, Harp." He made a frustrated sound. "I'm at the door. Same, no way to look in."

"Use your shoulder and push the door, see if it's locked."

"Yeah."

"Someone closes things up at night. What time?"

"Sign near the entrance said the park closes at 10."

"Way past that. Walk back," he said. "Is the parking lot paved?"

"Yeah."

"Now walk around the edges, where cars park. Does the lot have a curb all the way around or bumper things to keep cars off the grass?"

"Is that what they're called?"

"Hell, I don't know, but you get what I meant, right?"

"Yep, bumper things, it is."

"Walk the asphalt along where the engine would be if the cars were parked against the bumper things. Tire marks, fluids that might have leaked from a car recently, drops of blood," Harper instructed. "Do you have any paper towels, leftover napkins in your car?"

"No. The kids cleaned it."

"Meredith never cleaned mine," Harper muttered. "Is his a newer car?"

"Yeah, about two years. There's hundreds of stains out here."

"Fresh stains." Harper heard Brady's steps. "Antifreeze should be a neon yellowish-green or orange. Transmission fluid is reddish."

"I know what color fluids for a car are, Harp, though I'm surprised you do," he replied with increasing irritation.

"Car crashes leave puddles. See anything?"

"Nope, nothing in the spaces along the front opposite the restrooms."

"Do the same all the way around."

"In these streetlights, nothing is the right color, but I don't see any fresh drops or puddles," Brady was saying, then he hesitated. "Wait. This one looks new."

"If it doesn't look like blood, smell it," Harper said.

"I'm not touching it!"

"Take pictures, close up, with maybe your shoe next to it for size comparison, then a wider shot to show where it is in the lot. Then put your finger into the middle, so you don't ruin its shape, and smell it."

He waited while Brady took the photos.

"Smells sorta sweet," he announced. "It's reddish clear. Not oily."

"Not blood, that's good," Harper concluded. "Now look around where that car parked, then along the edge of the pavement. Buttons, trash, other puddles or smears, tire tracks — anything."

The coffee maker hissed out its last drops before Brady spoke again.

"I found a ring, Harp," he said, his voice strained. "Plain gold, man's size. Now what do I do?"

"Don't touch it. Hang up and call the police. Explain that your friend called his wife hours ago to say he was on his way home but never showed up. You followed the phone signal, found nothing except the ring."

"What if they don't believe me? I mean, they might think I have something to do with their disappearance."

"Where have you been for the last fifteen hours?" Harper asked.

"Working."

"Then I'm sure your company has plenty of video surveillance showing that's where you've been, Brady. See if finding his ring will get the ball rolling. Be persistent but polite. When you're done, call me back."

"I didn't sign up for this, Harp. Sorry to get you involved, too," he said. "I'll call you in a while. You might need to come bail me out."

"Which I would do. Either way, it'll be fine."

The two disconnected, and Brady immediately dialed 911, tried to explain why he needed an officer to respond, but the dispatcher wasn't listening after he said it was not an emergency, putting him on hold mid-sentence.

Finally, another voice came on the line, and to Brady, it sounded like his father.

"This is Deputy Bailey. Just so we're clear," the man began, "dispatch transferred your call to me, and I'm in no mood for bullshit about some man who didn't go home last night."

"You can come arrest me but at least hear me out," Brady said. "Earlier, Vanessa Keegan called to report her husband had not come home, and she was told to wait. Hours later, she called me because I work with him at StarData Cellular. I tracked the location of Paul's cell phone's last few hours. After he left work, the phone's final location was near the west side of Lake Grapevine. The battery was removed or the phone destroyed."

"Maybe he ran over it," the deputy said. "I'm still listening for something earth-shattering."

"I'm here at this park. At the edge of the pavement, I found Paul's wedding band. I haven't touched it, but I shot a picture of it with my phone and enlarged it enough to see the engraving. I'm sure it's his."

"Maybe he lost it," Bailey offered.

"Maybe, but there's a whole string of maybe's that make little sense, from maybe he got lost to maybe he was abducted by aliens. But how many maybe's have to exist before someone considers this serious enough to investigate?"

"You make a fair argument, but a lost wedding ring, a dead cell phone, and a missing husband and his car do not add up to a crime," the deputy concluded. "Is there anything else I can do for you tonight?"

"How long?" Brady cleared his throat in frustration. "How long until authorities will accept him as being missing and do something?"

"Contrary to what you see on television, Mr. Cayson, there is no mandatory waiting period to report someone as missing. A report was taken, and there is an area-wide BOLO for him. However, since he is a healthy and mentally stable adult traveling in his own vehicle, the Department of Public Safety and this sheriff's department will not prioritize him as a missing person because he will most likely be home by sunrise as husbands often change their minds and go home."

"Did his wife make it clear to you that Paul Keegan had his eleven-year-old daughter with him? That she is also missing?"

There was a silent pause on the line, long enough that Brady took his cell phone from his ear to look and make sure the officer hadn't hung up on him.

"I wasn't aware of that fact, no. That changes the situation," he finally said. "I'll call the wife and get the details. Give me your exact location. I'll send a unit out to where you are. Stay put."

"Thank you," Brady said, taking a breath. "I'll be waiting at the restrooms near the boat launch at Meadowmere Park." Brady pushed the button on his phone and growled before calling Harper back.

"What's the scoop?"

"Harper, they weren't going to do anything until I mentioned the kid," Brady complained. "Vanessa didn't tell them that Mackenzie was with Paul."

"But they are listening now. That's what matters."

"What do I tell his wife? What if something bad has happened? The deputy or whoever I spoke to told me to wait here for an officer, but shouldn't I go look for Paul?"

"Not now. I doubt that anything you do will change the outcome. You don't want the same thing to happen to you. Plus, you can do something the cops can't do for themselves with that phone tracking stuff."

Brady sighed. "Should I have told the authorities about tracking the phone? I mean, it's not exactly legal."

"If it's not exactly *illegal*, worry about it later. Prove it's useful to them in plain English."

"Very funny, Harp," he said.

"I'm serious. I told you a long time ago that law enforcement would love having a tool like that, if they knew what information was available and how to get it, right?"

"Yeah but — " Brady leaned against his car and massaged his temple with the heel of his free hand.

"They may not know it exists," Harper continued, "how it's done, or how it can be useful right away. That's what you need to tell them."

"I didn't bring the details."

"That information showed them where to look next. Knowing where that phone went saved them a lot of steps looking in the wrong places. That led to the ring, giving more weight to the presumption he was really at the location, not just his phone."

A patrol car turned into the parking lot, and despite the three glaring streetlamps illuminating Brady, the deputy turned on his spotlight.

"Deputy's here, Harp, I gotta go."

CHAPTER 29
Friday, November 6, 2009

"Thank you for a nice evening," Amber said, as she put the key into the lock.

"You're slamming the door in my face, are you?"

"I'm still deciding," she said as the deadbolt slid. "Nightcap?"

"You don't intend to get me drunk and sleep with me on our first date?" Kelly asked as if she had besmirched his honor.

"I thought we decided it wasn't a date." She stepped back to let him go in first, so she could lock the door behind them.

"Did we? I can't remember."

"Why do we keep doing this?" she asked, slipping off her vest. The evening hadn't been cool, but the pockets kept her from needing a purse. And it covered her weapon. "My dad and Julie used to pick at each other all the time, but I never understood."

"We could stop, but then what would we talk about?" he replied.

She went to the cabinet and opened a door to a complete rearrangement of wine and liquor glasses. "What would you like?"

"Amaretto, please?"

"I don't have any am — " she began, opening the cabinet door to her liquor, finding several more bottles than the last time she'd looked.

"Excuse me?" he said, pretending he had misunderstood her.

"How do you do that?" she muttered. "Let me guess. Two shots over ice?"

"Nope, I like amaretto straight. But make it three shots. I'm not driving tonight," he said, pulling out a barstool at the island and sitting.

"That will be twenty bucks," she said, pouring the caramel-colored liquid into a snifter. The liqueur smell was strong but sweet, and she took a sip before handing it to him. "Mmm, that's nice." She poured herself a shot.

"Probably twenty-four. Put it on my tab," he said with an easy smile. "Let my mother pay for it."

They went out onto the patio and swapped secrets under stars lost in the city glare and an occasional jet plane out of DFW until after three in the morning.

"We're supposed to meet Paul later," he finally said. "We ought to get some sleep."

"Yeah, I know." She stood and offered him a hand.

"Do I get a kiss?" he asked.

"Do you want one?" she asked, finding them face to face again.

"Amber, I've wanted to kiss you," he said, leaning forward as if she were a wild rabbit he wanted to touch, "since the moment you stood up to me at the train crash."

CHAPTER 30
Saturday, November 7, 2009

Harper Sullivan was left with a dead connection, a jittery stomach sloshing coffee and uneasiness.

Brady Cayson was his best friend. Had been since Harper's family moved to Brighton in grade school. They were neighbors. Their friendship circle had grown and had brought all five of them through puberty, girlfriends, graduation, wives, children, a couple of divorces, Lilah's death, and most recently the death of their friend Jeff.

The four friends had been bearers at the funeral, along with Jeff's two brothers. Later, sitting at a table in Brady's back yard, Harper could see that Jeff's death affected them, but they were too reserved.

"You guys were there for me when Lilah died, but this hurts us all. We gotta have each other to lean on," Harper had told them. "Stop being careful what you say because of me."

After a few beers and shots of tequila, celebrating the life and mourning the loss of their friend became more honest. Reminiscing lasted past midnight.

All of them, Jeff included, had lent a shoulder and later an ear to Harper's grief over Lilah, but mostly it had been Brady.

Although he was never certain, Harper feared he'd been so drunk one night when he called Brady that he might have confessed what really happened when he found Lilah.

Brady had never mentioned it, so neither had he.

Sipping his coffee, Harper went to the recliner that faced a television in the living area of the small two-bedroom apartment he'd rented after selling the house where he'd lived with Lilah and Meredith. Had it not been for his daughter's potential visits, he'd have settled for a tiny studio instead — what need did he have for more space? A bed, the recliner, a microwave and fridge, and a shower were all he needed. Most of the time, he didn't even use the bed — he preferred to sleep in his recliner.

Lilah's death and the subsequent investigation had taken a huge toll on Harper, as expected. He'd struggled with raising a teenage girl, juggling work hours to accommodate her school activities. When she began having problems in her classes, the school counselor called him in.

"Your wife died, Mr. Sullivan, but Meredith's *mother* died. It's different," the woman told him. "You must understand that Meredith is at the age where she is neither a child nor an adult when it comes to emotionally processing this enormous crisis in her life."

I must? Is that supposed to mean I already should or that I need to learn?

Although he did not answer aloud, the voice in Harper's head screamed. His wife had been screwing around, but he had protected Meredith from *that* fact.

Mustn't someone understand how hard it is on me?

Dealing with Lilah's death *had* been rough on him. He had withdrawn from society in general, especially after Meredith left to go live with her grandparents in Florida. He no longer bothered to go to church, didn't eat out unless he was on duty, and he had no real friends in town anymore. Having a badge made sure that was true, but he didn't socialize with anyone from work, either.

Reclining the chair, which faced the forty-two-inch television he'd bought Lilah and Meredith for Christmas the winter before . . .

Before. After. Everything in his life now got categorized as either before or after Lilah's death.

He squeezed his eyes shut, wishing the day that separated the before and the after could be erased from his mind. Still, those moments jangled in his brain like keys on a ring, often when he least expected them.

When his phone rang, it startled him enough that his half cup of coffee dropped out of his hand to the floor, spilling dark liquid on the light beige pile carpet.

Still cursing, he threw a couple of used napkins to the floor and answered.

"Sorry to wake you," Brady said, no doubt grinning. "Again."

"I bet you are," Harper replied. "What happened?"

"Honestly, I'm not sure. The deputy took my information. Asked how I came to be involved in all this, tossed the wedding ring into a plastic bag, took a quick walk around the parking lot, then he drove away." He blew out a long sigh of exasperation. "No interest at all in how tracking the phone led me here or even looking around for the phone. I dunno, Harp. This doesn't feel right."

"It isn't." Harper had finished stepping on the napkins soaking up the lukewarm coffee. "I'm guessing this has already crossed county lines, right?"

"When I checked the map, I'm standing on the county line between Denton and Tarrant County. The Denton County Sheriff put out an Amber Alert. That's good news. Hey, I gotta go."

Harper hung up and sighed, muttering to himself. "The bad news, Brady, is that I don't think this is going to have a happy ending."

CHAPTER 31
Saturday, November 7, 2009

Harper slumped back in his recliner.

He was certain Brady had no clue what he'd gotten himself into by offering to help his coworker's wife. While this guy being missing might be nothing more than an awkward miscommunication between spouses, Harper could only think of worst-case scenarios. Imagining a dead man didn't affect him much, but the thought of finding a little girl's body made his jaw muscles twitch.

The two cups of coffee he'd drunk were certain to keep him from going back to sleep, even when he couldn't suppress a yawn. There was no sense in trying. Brady would call again, no doubt. Helpless and only offering long-distance advice, Harper knew that if anyone had the tools to help law enforcement with this case, it was Brady.

If the LEOs would listen.

Kinda like the FBI showing up. Great tools and experience were an asset if one would put agency competition aside to use them.

Harper leaned back and closed his eyes, letting his mind wander through his childhood when he'd first met Brady. Moving from Houston to Brighton, Texas, late in the year during second grade, Harper'd suffered the rest of the school year being the new kid, alone. He became friends with Brady during the summer, riding their bikes through the neighborhood. They became best friends when Brady snuck them each a can of beer from his uncle's refrigerator. After being in the same classroom in third grade, their teacher saw that there was little way to control their shenanigans when they were together and passed along the advice to separate them in the coming years. Then came Mike the following year, Jeff the next. Bruce didn't move to town until they were freshmen in high school, but he was the perfect fit. Eventually, the high school couldn't separate them completely, but they had matured.

Before becoming teenagers, wild imaginations and fearlessness made them invincible. They did things like catching frogs and snakes for science class and then set them loose when the teacher didn't want them, causing twenty kids to scatter to the screams of panicked girls. Whose fault was it they were studying dumb old rocks instead of something useful, Harper remembered saying in his own defense to a principal who found it impossible to keep a straight face.

"It's fall, and frogs will be gone by the time she gets around to teaching about them," Brady had jumped into the argument.

It had been Mike who suggested the idea of gluing all of Mrs. Morrison's pencils into her desk drawer, but it had been Harper she'd accused of that prank. She'd called him by his full name, which is how the world learned that his middle name was Lee. In eighth grade English, when reading *To Kill a Mockingbird*, someone put together his name with the author, which led to more teasing.

Almost fifteen years after that frog incident in grade school, while pacing in the church hallway before the wedding to his first wife, Marcy Johnson, Harper's mother made a confession. Although she had named her son in honor of the author of her favorite book, she hadn't known Harper Lee was a woman. And Brady, who had been standing beside Harper, had been laughing about it ever since.

Harper hadn't thought of Marcy in years. Last he'd heard, she'd married a judge and was raising three kids in Olympia, Washington. She was one of the many people from his past who'd moved on to more successful lives.

Despite job offers from other jurisdictions or agencies when he was ready to leave Houston with ten years of big city experience under his belt, he'd chosen to return to Brighton. His second marriage had begun in the backyard of that same house in 1994. And they moved into that house after his parents died within a few months of each other a year after their only grandchild was born. Lilah had died there. He and Meredith continued to live there a while, even though he still dreamed of Lilah sprawled on their bed. He'd wanted to keep the house after she died until Meredith left and living there alone broke the rest of his heart.

All his dreams had been in that house.

And then his nightmares.

He sold the house on the edge of town. Not much had changed except his address. He still had nightmares, sometimes waking in a cold sweat after dreaming Lilah opened her eyes and screamed at him.

Occasionally, he wished he had a new patrol car, too, he thought, but the dent was really in his mind, not in the door.

After his friend's funeral, he envied Jeff Riker's cancer, imagining that being dead would be an improvement over the life he was barely living. He regretted such stupid, self-loathing jealousy, the misery that left him with secrets now he struggled to keep to himself.

Wishing he had something to pour in his coffee to dull that pain, he shook his head and stood up. "Brady was always there for me," he said, stretching his arms toward the ceiling. "Least I can do is return the favor and help him find his coworker."

In half an hour, he'd showered and dressed, packed a change of clothes into an overnight bag, put that and a large travel cup of coffee in his pickup and hit the road, guided by a ten-year-old state map unfolded to the area north of Dallas-Fort Worth. He even plugged in his cell phone to charge, in case his next conversation with Brady was important and lengthy.

He had made it to Highway 287 and stopped for a refill when his phone rang.

"All sorts of people are involved in this now, Harp," Brady said without a greeting. "What did you do?"

"Wasn't me. It's what should have happened the first time your friend's wife called in," he answered, pulling back onto the highway. "Who is there and what are they doing?"

"Everyone, it looks like. Deputies from Tarrant and Denton County and DPS officers. They've begun a search, put out a radio description of the car and plates, and I've been working with one deputy to plot out the map closer to find where the phone was when it went off," Brady said.

"I'll be in Decatur in about three hours. I'll get back with you before then so we can pick a place to meet."

"You're coming?" Brady asked in surprise. "That's the best news I've heard all day."

"It's just past midnight, so you probably don't have much to compare it to," Harper said with a chuckle. "Hopefully, it's the worst. Call me if you find anything useful."

"I wouldn't know it's useful unless I tripped over it. Any hints?"

"Sure, find the phone. With any luck, your pal will be holding it, sitting on a tree stump, cursing that he tripped and twisted his ankle and broke them both."

"I don't think that's what happened," Brady said.

Harper shook his head. "Me, either, Brady. Me, either."

CHAPTER 32
Saturday, November 7, 2009

Driving at night, miles felt slower than daytime. Deer were still moving, crossing highways, as carcasses occasionally confirmed.

Not the reason or the manner Harper wanted to get a new truck, although the thought of buying one had crossed his mind.

Harper tapped the button on his phone that would pull up the contact list, chose a number for a man he hadn't spoken to in eight years.

"Hey, Harp, what's up?" Zach Samualson said in a cheery voice that belied it being well past midnight.

"Oh, you know, protecting the citizens, writing speeding tickets," he said evasively. "Can I bend your ear a bit?"

"Sure," he said. "Give me a second."

Harper heard some rustling around, a car door slamming, maybe a building door opening and closing, then a refrigerator door doing the same. A carbonated drink can tab popping. And finally, the sound of a body settling into a recliner, the foot extending.

"Better. Just got home," Zach told him. "Tell me what's on your mind, Harper."

"You remember Brady, the guy who helped you locate your daughter's phone in New York?"

"Of course."

"One of his coworkers went missing several hours ago, along with a pre-teen daughter."

"Where did this happen?" Zach asked.

"In Fort Worth, north in the smaller cities. Brady's friend's wife called asked him for help, so he tracked Paul's phone's movements to a lakeside park, then the phone disconnected from the system," Harper explained. "Brady called me, and I talked him through a walk-around of the parking lot. He found Paul's wedding ring. When he called the sheriff's department, they finally did something when he mentioned the little girl."

"Everyone is doing their thing, I suppose?"

"Finally."

"Okay, so what can I do for you?"

"Your daughter. You said you found her. How?" Harper asked.

"You want the short version or the long one?"

"I got hours to drive. Make it the long one."

"Okay, you asked," Zach said. "My daughter met a guy in Michigan during our summer trip, before she started college in August 2001. Once she was at school in Seattle, he talked her into making a two-day trip to New York to meet him. If the kid weren't dead now, I'd still be beating the truth out of him. Different story.

"The first night, September 10th, they went to dinner and she put her wallet in his jacket. The next morning, he left the hotel with her wallet and without his phone, to go to some sort of appointment with a lawyer, we think. Never found out," Zach said, stopping to take a drink. "Alone in the hotel, everything was fine at first. She was looking out the window at the city, saw the planes hit the Twin Towers. He didn't come back. She stayed until they kicked her out for not being able to pay, because she had no ID or credit cards without her wallet. If she'd only been able to convince them to call one of us to pay, things would have been vastly different, but she didn't. By then she was having trouble making calls on her cell phone."

"Yeah, I remember kidding when I asked if you were there. Big shock."

"On the streets, she ate at a church soup line that evening, then they offered her a place to stay for the night. The next day, some jerk swiped her backpack, and she was struck by a car while chasing him, somehow losing her phone. She ended up in the hospital with some serious fractures, didn't know her name."

"Where were you and her mother?" Harper asked, slowing down in a small town for its famous speed trap.

"Her biological mother was murdered five years before. I was at home in Washington."

"Single dad?"

"No, I'm married. In fact, we'd gotten married a few weeks before her mom was killed."

"Married and a father? That warps my bachelor image of you, Z'."

"You'd like her, Harp. Julie's worn a badge longer than either of us," Zach said. "And my kid has become a powerhouse of her own. She's a computer forensic specialist with the Tarrant County Sheriff Department now. Anyway, Brady triangulated the location of her phone's last position, and we found it. We eventually tracked her down in a hospital by calling around, so what he did really didn't help, but it could have."

CHAPTER 33
Saturday, November 7, 2009

After a long chat with Zach, Harper cringed at the hum of tires on the road as he followed his headlights through the darkness, his head swimming in doubts. What was he doing, going down there? Harper thought.

But the answer settled into his chest with ease. He wasn't going as a cop. He was going to offer support to a lifelong friend, someone who had listened to him many rough nights, both before and after Lilah died. A friend who didn't speak *cop* any better than he spoke *tech*. He intended to be as dependable a backup as anyone could ask for.

Letting his mind focus on the music that blared through his speakers from a cassette player, he covered the next two hours without worrying about his life or Brady's.

Or Paul's.

Eventually, he entered the endless city of the metroplex, following an outdated map. He pulled into a drive-through to get more coffee.

His phone rang. He tapped the green phone icon and raised the phone to his ear.

"Hey, Harp," the voice on the other end answered, sounding flat.

"I'm in Rhome. Where can I meet you?"

"I'm still out near that park. They found Paul's body, but not the car. They asked me not to leave yet, whatever that means."

Honestly, Harper thought, that request could mean anything from 'you're our prime suspect' to 'we're hoping you can save our asses.'

However, he realized that saying it out loud would not be as funny as when he thought it. "Give me directions."

Brady told him then hung up.

The next forty minutes seemed to take longer than the previous hours to Harper. Traffic was still light. Finally, flashing lights came into view through his bug-splattered windshield.

Stopped by a deputy before he could make the last turn, Harper had to identify himself and explain why he was there. He parked next to Brady's car and opened the door to the chaos of a dozen men and women talking around him.

Ahead, near an ambulance, Brady leaned against a patrol car, so Harper headed that direction, only to be stopped again. Although he had intended specifically not to show his badge, he finally had to do so to extricate himself from further questioning, and he was still explaining as Brady approached.

"He's with me," Brady announced as if that were supposed to explain things to the deputy.

Apparently, it did, because the deputy shrugged and walked away, leaving the two men amidst the commotion.

"Paul's dead," Brady said in a low voice.

Harper bit his lip, thinking that finding a body meant someone was dead. But he realized Brady was rehearsing the words for later. "I'm sorry."

"I just wish — " Brady's voice broke.

Harper interrupted his friend. "Wishing won't change the outcome for Paul. Let's focus on finding that little girl and the bastards who did this. That is what we can do to help."

Brady nodded. "What do we do?"

"You found Paul's phone?"

Brady nodded. "Crushed, like someone drove over it intentionally. It was near where they found his . . . him."

Harper understood choosing not to call his friend just a body.

"Sir?" a voice called, so he paused and waited for a deputy to approach. "Sorry about before, I didn't know you were a cop, too. I'm Deputy Jan Turner, Denton County."

Harper extended his hand to shake. "No problem, Deputy. Nice to meet you. I'm here for Brady Cayson's moral support, not as law enforcement."

"About that," the deputy began. "The sheriff heard you were here and wanted someone to ask if you *would* help."

The smile on Harper's face was crooked. "You got volunteered to ask me, right?"

Shrugging, the deputy chuckled. "Was either that or go get more coffee."

"I don't know what I can do to help, but if he thinks so, I'm happy to lend a hand."

"She, sir. Our sheriff is a woman."

Harper's eyebrows raised, one higher than the other. "Just the same, *she* ought to know who she's getting, I suspect."

"A quick hello, then you two can go about your business," the deputy said, waving the pair to follow her to a white SUV with a lightbar on top.

A short woman with a wavy blonde pixie cut and wide blue eyes looked up when the men came around the front of the vehicle.

"You must be Sergeant Sullivan," the woman said without offering to shake hands. She smoothed a map flat on the hood, though she was barely tall enough to do so.

"Yes, Ma'am," Harper replied. "Not intending to interfere, I came to offer support to my friend."

"Sarah Webb," she said as a curt introduction, confident that her uniform and badge stated the rest for her. "And your friend is Mr. Cayson, I presume?" She made a quick size-up of the two men, then perched her reading glasses in her curls. "So, Sergeant, have you ever worked a case using cell phone data like Mr. Cayson tells us a cell company can provide?"

"Not a live case like this," he told her. "It's miles above my head technologically."

"But you think it can give us something helpful?" she pressed with a frown.

"It's my understanding that Brady's information brought you to this park, which led to the discovery of the body of one of the two victims, and the phone. That should speak for itself, Ma'am," Harper told her. "He believes — "

"Sullivan, you both can believe in fairy dust and jolly green giants," she said, sniffling in sarcasm, "but if you have information helpful in finding that little girl, I'd like to use it. What is it, how can we get it, and what can we do with it?"

Harper shrugged at Brady. "You tell her. It's your fairy dust."

Brady explained that they were where they stood because the phone data had placed the last known location in this area until going black.

Webb nodded her head. "Is there any chance this child has a phone?"

"I'd have to go back to my office to find out," Brady said.

"Then do it. Get us more we can use. We're looking for that little girl by whatever means we can employ, gentlemen, and honestly, I'll deal with legalities later." She took business cards out of her shirt pocket, one for each man. "Call me directly if you find anything."

She lowered her head back to the map, effectively dismissing the two.

"Your truck or my car?" Brady asked.

"Let's get them both back to your office for now," Harper replied. "No sense in leaving them in the way here."

CHAPTER 34
Saturday, November 7, 2009

In an empty parking lot, Brady pulled into a space near the building where he worked, and Harper parked his 14-year-old pickup next to it.

Looking at Brady's coupe, Harper envied the smaller vehicle for its better fuel efficiency, what with the price of gasoline these days. Then again, he didn't have a family of five to cart around in the eight-passenger vehicle Brady's wife usually drove. This led him to miss his only child, who had abandoned him for Lilah's parents when he failed at being a father.

He slid out and was standing behind his truck, waiting on Brady, when a dark red mid-sized SUV parked in front of the main doors. A tall woman dressed in black cargo pants and boots, a bright yellow shirt under a dark windbreaker, stepped out, then stood by her door, waiting for them.

When Brady finally opened his door and stood, he began explaining, "I called my wife to check on her and the kids, then I got a call — "

Harper made a slight nod toward the building, silently questioning whether Brady knew the woman who was obviously expecting them. He was answered with a slight nod.

As the men walked toward the building, the woman took a few steps toward them. Harper saw a man in dark clothes on the other side of her vehicle stand up then reach inside the back door for something.

By instinct, Harper thumbed back his jacket for access to his firearm.

Kelly Morgan, who had been reaching into the back seat for his crutches, recognized Harper's movements as possibly hostile, and came around the back of the SUV with one crutch and his hand on his sidearm.

Seeing the silent and near-instant escalation, she held out her arms. "Stop!" the woman yelled. "We are both Tarrant County deputies, here to see Brady Cayson."

Both men froze, hands on guns still in their holsters.

"Gentlemen?" Brady said, walking intentionally between them to break the spell that looked like two dogs sizing each other up before the blur of teeth and fur.

"Harper Sullivan, Benton County Deputy," he replied, withdrawing his hand from the holstered gun first, reaching for a badge.

"Deputy Kelly Morgan," the other man said, not moving from where he stood, but reaching for his other crutch.

"Deputy Samualson."

"That makes me Brady," he said in a sigh of relief. "You cops are too intense for me."

"Like I told Mr. Cayson on the phone, we've been working with Paul Keegan in an internet child exploitation project," she said. "When he didn't show for a meeting this morning, we called his house. Vanessa told us he was missing."

Brady stepped closer, explaining to completion to Harper that Amber had called him on the way to the office. "Let's go inside." He led them to the doors, slid his ID card and entered a six-digit number on the electronic pad, then pulled the door open for them.

Inside, the commons area was wide open with a central check-in desk, and he signed himself and the others in. They followed him to the left to elevators, to the third floor, and around the corner to a conference room.

The others sat, but Brady went to the far cabinets and grabbed them each a bottle of water then joined them.

"Let's start with you guys," he said, rolling his chair closer to the table. "Explain this project Paul was involved in?"

Amber spoke first. "Several months ago, the sheriff's office organized a task force to address online exploitation. My job was to handle the computer stuff, hardware, software, and for me to impersonate children on known online hunting sites. We were using Paul's experience having done this before in Atlanta. He believed more predators were using mobile sites, and if the first piece of identification we got was a cell number, he could access account information for the owner's name."

"And you?" Brady asked, turning to Kelly.

"Sir, I'm the deputy liaison, to coordinate warrants and arrest teams. But we'd been working together, learning."

"Getting the user's real name allowed us to browse histories for priors, employment that might put him in contact with kids, such as a teacher. It was a sign that he had reached the point of trust with our 'child' and would be looking for information about her, too," Amber finished.

"Now you," Kelly demanded. "Where's Paul?"

Brady took a deep breath. "One statement first: Paul and I have been friends since he got here. Family outings, work trips. But he never told me about this task force thing."

Kelly exchanged looks with Amber.

"I didn't consider it a secret," she said.

Brady nodded. "Last night, Paul picked up his middle daughter at a friend's house. Vanessa expected him home around eight, but when he was late, she called. And kept calling and calling, but he never answered. Before midnight, she called me and asked if I could locate the phone, so I did."

"He had shown me how that works," Amber said. "What did you find?"

"He picked up Mac, then they stopped at a nearby mall. Then the phone signal went north, not south toward their house. Vanessa told me the police were hesitant to investigate the matter at first, so I followed its path to a park by the Grapevine Lake area. I'd called Harper for his help on what to do, and with his instructions, I found

Paul's wedding ring," he said, sighing again. "The police got involved when I mentioned that Paul's daughter was with him, so when they came to the park and began a search, they found . . . well, Paul's dead."

"And Mac?" Amber asked, her voice weaker than before.

"She and the car were gone. They found Paul's phone, smashed. Cops are working on it."

"Why are you back here, then?" Kelly asked. "Why aren't you helping to look for her?"

"We came to see if Mac might have had some device with her that we could track. Do you know?"

"I don't think so. Paul was cautious about the girls," Amber said, her composure regained. "How can I help?"

Brady made a motion that she should follow. "You guys," he said, pointing to Kelly and Harper, "go do something that cops do. I don't have a clue what that might be."

"Let's check security footage from the mall," Kelly suggested. "You'll have to drive, though."

"Take mine," Amber said, tossing Harper her keys. "I'll send you the location."

CHAPTER 35
Saturday, November 7, 2009

Harper didn't understand how the other deputy could send an address to Kelly's phone, nor how Kelly could navigate them through the conglomeration of roads under construction in the metroplex, but he followed directions that took them straight to a large white mall.

"Food court is on the other end," Kelly said, pointing for him to go around the circle drive to the north. "Security is just inside the mall from there."

"Glad you know that. I have an odd question," Harper said, as he was parking where Kelly indicated. "How well do you know Miss Samualson? It is miss, right?"

Kelly chuckled. "Yeah, she's a miss. She's been in the crime lab doing digital evidence for more than a year now, I guess. She's a first-class computer geek, but don't tell her I said that."

"Deal. Do you know where she's from? Anything about her family?" he persisted after they got out, and he tried several times to hit the right button on the key fob to lock the vehicle.

"Grew up in New Mexico, went to college in Seattle."

Harper hummed, thinking. "Nah, it couldn't be."

"What's got you in mental overdrive?"

Inside, they dodged the weekend crowds looking for early lunch. "Hey, let's grab a bite. I didn't get breakfast this morning," Kelly said. "Crutches take a lot of energy."

Harper hadn't eaten either, so they each bought a drink and a pretzel, then found a table.

"What happened to you?" Harper asked.

"An idiot teenager drove her way into a six-car freeway crash I was investigating." Kelly took a huge bite and chewed almost a minute before taking a drink. "What's your thing with Amber? She's a little young for you, isn't she?"

"Amber?" he repeated, trying to recall if Zach had said her name. "Way too young. I think I used to work with her father." He wadded the pretzel wrapper and wiped his mouth. "Have you met him?"

Kelly shook his head. "But she said he's a cop, too. So's her stepmother. Let's get going."

"Gotta be her. Small world."

Footage from the mall was easy to browse, having a time frame. The delay was finding the entrance Paul and Mackenzie used. Harper stood beside the deputy sitting at the console, scanning through six screens of video, hoping to identify Paul and Mackenzie more quickly than Harper could by pictures from Vanessa.

Within half an hour, they learned that the father and daughter had entered through Macy's and gone straight through to the StarData Cellular store. He must have bought something that she was carrying when they came out. Video inside was color with higher resolution, and it showed them chatting, laughing, Mac skipping and swinging a medium-sized white plastic bag as they headed to the same exit they came in.

The security guard changed back to footage from outside, which was in black and white almost three hours after sunset, fast-forwarding to the time Paul and Mac left.

"Can we find out what they bought?" Harper asked, still thinking about the bag.

"Sure," said the guard. "I'll call the manager — "

"Stop there. Can you enlarge that?" Kelly asked, pointing to the images from the parking lot.

"Sure, a little." What was gained with making the picture larger was lost in black and white graininess.

Harper grumbled. "Just once I'd like to be blessed with crystal clear footage of what I needed to see."

Kelly nodded, and the video advanced frame by frame. "That's them." They watched closely. "Is that a nurse?" he asked, leaning closer toward the screen and squinting.

"Someone in scrubs," Harper agreed. "The picture is better from back here, if you'd move your head."

Kelly scooted the rolling chair back a few feet. "Yeah, wow. Okay."

They watched a woman in dark scrubs, with what was probably an ID card hanging around her neck, stop Paul and point to a car a few spaces away from his. Because of the angle, the camera couldn't see the side of it when they paraded to look. More waving and looking. The woman checked her watch, talked more. And apparently, she asked for a ride.

"Paul's a gentleman. He'd offer to help change a tire, which looks like the problem. Maybe she didn't have a spare, so he offered to take her somewhere. The timestamp shows this took place after 2120." Kelly looked at his watch. "That can't be right."

"Camera time didn't get changed back from Daylight Saving Time," the guard explained.

"So 8:20 p.m., okay. If she's really a nurse, she wasn't going to work unless it was at 10:30, but few places work eight-hour shifts now. Maybe she was late getting off work at 7 p.m. Where would Paul be taking her?" Kelly wondered aloud as the three then went back to Paul's car, the woman insisting on sitting in the back seat.

The car backed out, left the view of the camera.

They all let out a sigh.

"All right," Kelly said. "Let's get this back to the lab and see if they can enhance this woman's face or ID. Can you guys watch to see if someone comes for that car, maybe get a license plate?"

The security crew was happy to help, took a business card from Kelly in case they found something else.

"Then we should go to traffic control and see if they can find his car and see where he went. Maybe we'll get lucky and find out where he dropped her off."

CHAPTER 36
Saturday, November 7, 2009

"She has a tablet," Amber said as Brady booted the computer.

"That makes sense," he said, typing in a lengthy password. "My kids have tablets, so I figured Paul's did, too."

"Vanessa's a mess right now," Amber said. "But her sister came to stay with her today. I can't imagine losing a husband and not knowing where my child is."

"I'm glad she has someone with her, but gladder you are here." He finished setting up software Amber had never seen Paul use. "Maybe you could call her and ask if Mac had that tablet with her."

"I can, but I doubt it. It's Wi-Fi only, and she told me she and Neela weren't allowed to take them to other people's houses."

"Only three devices are registered for the family. The company gives us all the cell service we want, but we have to buy the phones or tablets," he explained.

"That's a sweet deal," she replied.

"Paul, Vanessa, and Neela, they each have phones," Amber confirmed. "Paul said Mackenzie had to wait another year."

"What other devices could a kid have?"

"E-readers? Kindle recently came out with a second-generation device," she offered.

"My kids are voracious readers, but they want paper books. Would Mac want a reader?"

Amber shrugged. "I haven't spent that much time around them, but she was really helpful in teaching me how kids talk so I can act like one."

"Why?"

"I scouted a dozen social chatting sites, pretending to be different kids, trying to attract an adult who is a little too interested in meeting a child. These guys make promises of whatever attention lures the child to them, something to entice a child to commit to some inappropriate behavior, like nude photos, things that can be held as leverage for keeping secrets. Maybe the predator promises a job or a modeling contract," she said. "Some offer that seems like a better deal than the child has at home. As a predator grooms the child I pretend to be, I try to obtain information for identification, such as an email or phone number. Once he commits a criminal act, like asking the child for nude photos, says he wants to have sex with someone he believes is a minor, or he arranges to show up, we get arrest warrants, search and seizure warrants, and permission to track the phone if necessary."

"What if he wasn't using a cell phone, or it wasn't our network?"

"Paul had some connection to another cell company, but he never said which one."

"Why use the cell network at all?" Brady asked.

"He said these people had figured out that static IP addresses were easy to locate, so they were using cells more often. Second, he said he'd solved how to track some newer cell phones." She frowned. "That if we really needed to track or locate a phone, he was able to do it quickly."

"We were too late to help Paul," he said, rubbing his temples. "We've got to find that little girl."

CHAPTER 37
Saturday, November 7, 2009

"I've been trying to call you for half an hour," Kelly complained when Brady let them into the building.

"Sorry, I forgot to mention that the room we're in is shielded to prevent calls or transmission in or out," Brady explained as they walked back to a breakroom. "I couldn't find another trackable device on Paul's account."

"Maybe we aren't looking for the right thing," Harper said, carrying a box of food. "Let's eat and talk."

Despite the urgency of the situation, they were hungry enough to follow Harper like he was the Pied Piper to the conference room. They sat while he passed out burgers, fries, and drinks.

Anxious to hear the news, Amber was bouncing her lower legs on the balls of her feet, which caused the table to vibrate.

Kelly reached under the table, resting his hand on her knee to stop the motion.

"Video at the mall showed Paul and Mackenzie walking out to their vehicle, stopping to speak to a woman dressed as a nurse, then giving her a ride," Kelly began. "After seeing that, we went to the traffic control division to check cameras in hopes we could see if he dropped her somewhere in the same cell tower covering the mall, but the timing doesn't make it seem likely. They are working on it. We stopped for food." He stopped and took a bite.

"After we left the traffic division, the manager of the store where Paul and Mac went in the mall called. It was a StarData phone store," Harper continued. "Paul was buying Vanessa a present, he told the salesperson, although he didn't mention a special occasion. But the salesperson remembered Mackenzie telling him she was excited about the new phone because it meant that her mom's phone would pass down to her sister, which meant she would get her sister's phone."

"A new phone?" Amber and Brady said at the same time.

"Yeah," Kelly said with his mouth full. "But it was still in the box. They said the phone would be operational within an hour of the purchase. But they provided the phone number and an IM number, I think he said." He pulled a piece of paper out of his jeans pocket and held it out.

"IMEI number!" Brady said, snatching the paper. "Yes!"

"Even if it isn't turned on?" Harper asked. "I'm confused."

"Mac would have had a new phone out and running before they got out of the parking lot, I bet," Amber said. "She's very computer capable. With those numbers, Brady can find it, can't you?"

Brady's mind was displaying necessary commands into an imaginary screen above their heads. but he nodded.

"Brady, go. Get the program started, then come back to eat." Amber said.

He scrambled to his feet and swung around the door in a jog.

"Will this work?" Harper asked Amber. "Do you really think we can find her with that?"

"Mac turned on that phone, I'm sure of it." Amber stopped and said a brief prayer. "If she remembers what we were doing, even if she hadn't before, she will find a way to turn that phone on."

The three interspersed conversation with chewing.

"We know she has the new phone, and you're sure she'd have gotten it out of the box in the car," Harper said. "If this nurse hurt Paul or made threats, how would this young girl hide it so we can use it?"

"I don't have the answer to that, but I have absolute faith that she did," Amber replied.

"She soaked in everything we were doing like a sponge," Kelly added. "But I have to wonder about the coincidence of her becoming a victim of one of the very monstrosities we were chasing."

"There's no way anything we were doing could trace back to her," Amber replied.

Harper wiped his mouth with a brown napkin. "You're sure?"

"Positive. She said she hadn't even heard of most of the sites we were accessing, but she denied ever using any of them," Amber said. "She was teaching me lingo and chat shortcuts to help me fit in."

Kelly shook his head. "I don't doubt she kept our gig a secret, but what about Neela?"

"Vanessa told me Neela is a goody-two-shoes who recently had gotten into trouble a few times, but that she hardly uses their computer except for writing school stuff," Amber said. "I don't see how she could have messed this up."

"But if the new phone were for mom, who would give the older kid her phone so that Mackenzie would get a hand-me-down, the older kid already had one. What does she do with it?" Harper asked.

Amber and Kelly exchanged a look that transitioned from concern to worry.

"No idea," Amber confessed. "She didn't get as involved in my learning session. What, maybe an hour that evening when I was there. She lost interest in what we were doing, but she was playing a video game on her tablet."

"Maybe someone on the arrest team mentioned it to someone who might be one of the targets. You hear of a coach or some big-wig who's around kids all the time getting busted for child porn."

"I think you use all the tools you have to find this kid, then figure out where the hole is."

"You don't think finding the hole could lead us to her?" Kelly asked.

"No, at least not as fast." Harper's cell phone rang, and he pulled it out of his vest pocket. "'Lo?"

"Sergeant? It's Dierdra Preston," a woman's voice said in his ear a bit too loudly. "I think we have a problem."

CHAPTER 38
Saturday, November 7, 2009

"I gotta get back to work," Harper said when he finished his call from the assistant prosecuting attorney. "I've been jumping up and down to investigate a one-car fatality accident, but it's got some serious politics involved in it."

"I'm a crash reconstruction specialist," Kelly offered. "Can I help?"

"Anything official would drag you into court, I'm afraid," Harper said. "I suspect someone sabotaged the car. The last words the driver said before she died were 'my ex- did this.' And the ex-husband happens to be a deputy in a neighboring county."

"Ouch!"

"If I swing a bat and don't get a home run on this, I may end up here working security in this building."

"All the more reason to have an expert," Kelly said, "even unofficially." He finished the last bite of his burger and wadded the wrapper into a tight ball, making an easy hook shot to the large bin in the room's corner, then swiped two fingers in the air for the score. "Tell me, what did the accident look like."

"Ten-year-old Honda Civic on a dry rural two-lane highway, before sunrise. Sole occupant, a nurse on her way to a part-time job starting at 6:30 a.m., not wearing a seatbelt. Loss of control, short skid to the driver's side, correction to the right with a subsequent clockwise spin on the shoulder, then flipped, also toward the driver's side.

Estimated the driver wasn't ejected for approximately three rolls down the hill, a thirty-degree slope, I'd guess."

"Not bad off the top of your head. What evidence makes you think sabotage?" Kelly asked.

"It was a week till I got the wreckage to our shop. Mechanic says the nut on the tie rod bolt was missing. Vehicle'd had some front-end work a few days prior — brakes, alignment, but not those. The shop owner had some cover-my-ass photography for the work, and that nut and the cotton, um, cott — "

"Cotter pin," Kelly supplied.

"Yeah, that. It was in place when the car left the shop on September 29, the afternoon before the crash. My mechanic said the vehicle could have driven ten miles or several hundred miles until that nut came off if the pin was missing, depending on how much turning was done. I need to rebuild her work schedule and travel log."

"Are you sure he did it?"

"He's my unofficial prime suspect, but I can't even say that until I have some proof that he could have done it, because of the politics. He lives in Marshal County; she was in Frederick County. The accident was in Benton County, where I live."

Amber joined the discussion. "What do you need to prove first?"

"Motive isn't a problem. He's still angry that she divorced him. Then I must show that he had access to the vehicle. She picked it up the same day they completed the work, so it didn't sit out for a night at the shop, which is only two miles from her house. She lived 34 miles from the ex-husband's house. There is one main highway between the towns." He stood and stretched, leaving a few bites of his burger. "I asked our county assistant prosecutor what she'd need to indict this guy in a criminal case. She's all in, but guess who she's been sleeping with."

"That is seriously screwed up," Kelly concluded, shaking his head. "Let me know how that turns out for you. And if she needs an expert witness, tell her I'm interested."

"I'll do that. Now what I need is for someone to draw me a map to get out of town." Harper said. "I've been following Brady around or following directions till I don't have a clue where I am."

"Not a problem. Hey, while I'm doing a map, maybe you can figure out about Amber's dad."

"My dad?" she asked, looking up from some papers. "What about him?"

"I used to work with this big guy, Zach, when I was in Houston. Hadn't heard from him in a long time, till right after 9/11, when he was looking for his daughter in New York. He asked me to ask Brady if he could do his thing and find her phone."

Amber beamed, "Yep, that's my dad. I wasn't sure who had helped, but I knew it wasn't Paul because he wasn't here in 2001."

"I called and talked to Zach on my drive last night to get some advice about finding Paul."

"How is he?" she asked with a laugh. "Still with the FBI?"

"He said he was, why?"

"Dad's been threatening to quit for years. He misses the ranch."

"Fine and still employed. He's proud of you."

Kelly stood and handed Harper a brown napkin with a series of roads on it.

"Thanks. You two keep up the outstanding work. Some kid you save could be the one who saves the world someday," Harper said. "Tell Brady to keep me posted."

CHAPTER 39
Saturday, November 7, 2009

"Let's go find Brady and see what he's found," Kelly said. "I sure hope this works."

Amber nodded. "I can't imagine what Vanessa's going through."

They made their way to the locked room where Brady worked, knocked on the heavy door and waited. After several seconds, Kelly rapped harder.

"Coming," Brady called from inside. "Just a second."

A minute later, he opened the door. "Sorry. I'm done. She did it," he said, turning away from them to hurry back to his chair. "She turned on the phone."

"Why doesn't she call 911?" Kelly asked.

"They couldn't find her unless she knew where she was," Brady responded, returning to his map and printed list. "It looks like the signal went southwest from the park, stopped for half an hour, then resumed until its near Junction on I-10."

Amber walked around the table to look at the map. "These are the towers you plotted?"

Brady nodded.

"They've stayed off the freeway?" She followed the angle southwest until she got to Del Rio. "I doubt that's where they're going specifically, but it's close."

"You mean you think they will cross the border to Mexico?" Brady asked.

"I do. And it wouldn't make much sense to be transporting one child if the intention is trafficking. There may be others with her."

"Can we call the phone?" Kelly asked.

"No!" Amber said, way too loudly for the room. "She may not have it muted, and we don't want to give away that she has it since it's the only tracking we have."

"It makes sense to me not to call it. Or text it." Brady made a humming noise of indecision. "Presuming the phone was fully charged, which I doubt, the battery might last 48 hours if it's not being used for voice. It shouldn't have a bunch of apps on it though, which will help."

"Do we know for sure it's her? What if her kidnapper found it and tossed it onto a southbound truck somewhere along the line?" Kelly asked.

"We can't, but I believe it is," Amber replied. "Call whoever is in charge of the investigation. Tell him — "

"Her," Brady corrected without thinking.

"Okay, her. Tell *her* we know Mac has a phone that appears to be moving toward the Mexican border around Del Rio." Amber pointed at the map. "If we can isolate the signal to one of these highways, she can coordinate a law enforcement response for a roadblock search on both ends, both directions," she said, trying to remember how it had been done in a manhunt in Oregon years back. "Even if we don't know what kind of vehicle it is, they stop everything going both directions. Maybe you can even tell when the signal stops moving."

Brady handed her the card. "You make that happen; I'll do what I can."

She handed the map and card to Kelly. "You do this. I need to go visit Vanessa, let her know what's happening."

CHAPTER 40
Saturday, November 7, 2009

Kelly's directions out of the mess of highway construction had him free in half an hour.

Once out of heavy traffic, Harper's thoughts returned to Brady's ability to place a cell phone in a particular place and time.

The Sullivan house was three miles outside of the city limits of Brighton, and the Thomases lived on the far side of town. Tracking Eddy's phone location that day could show he had been at Sullivan's house around the time that Lilah died.

Harper wasn't concerned that the data would show he was home earlier than his call to 911. Not like he'd been home for an hour. Ten minutes tops, which was easy to explain — he'd stopped in the kitchen first, reading the mail or something. He hadn't been near the area of the house during the day shift.

A thought smashed through his head like a sledgehammer on a snowball. So jolting, he almost slammed on the brakes, which would have caused an accident, he saw when he checked his rearview mirror. The concept was so obvious, he was stunned that he hadn't realized it till then.

Because he was her spouse, he hadn't been told specific details of the autopsy or investigation. He didn't *know* the caliber bullet used, so he couldn't be certain it had been from his pistol.

He had assumed that Lilah had committed suicide because he found his gun on the floor beside her. But what if . . . what if . . . what if she really had been murdered?

CHAPTER 41
Saturday, November 7, 2009

Amber rang the doorbell, but a woman she didn't recognize opened the door.

"I'm a friend of the Keegans," she said. "I need to speak to Vanessa."

The woman looked her over, then nodded. "She's in the kitchen."

Amber went straight there, and when Vanessa stood, they hugged.

"I'm so sorry, Van."

"Tell me what's going on, Amber. Have they found my baby?"

"Paul and Mac stopped on their way home and bought a new phone we presume was for you. Mac was able to keep it with her when she was kidnapped. Brady's been able to locate the phone, and Brady and Kelly are working with the police to find Mac."

Vanessa nodded, and they went into the den area to sit.

"What we were doing wasn't a big secret," Amber began, "but I have to wonder if this entire operation was specifically to target Paul."

"I don't understand."

"It's possible that someone, even me, could have mentioned this to someone who told someone else that we were working on catching child predators. I'm not saying that's definitely what happened, but we need to look at the possibility."

"I don't talk to anyone about Paul's work. Frankly, most people would think it's boring or too political."

A shadow peeked around the doorway as her oldest daughter looked in, having heard the conversation.

Vanessa motioned to Neela to sit beside her on the sofa.

"Amber thinks they can find Mackenzie," she said.

"I heard. It was me!" She turned to her mother's arms and began crying. "I did it. I got Dad killed and maybe Mac, too!"

Vanessa started to pull away, to ask more questions, but Amber shook her head slightly. "Hold on to her," she whispered.

Neela finally cried herself down until she could talk, though her face was still blotchy red and puffy.

"Tell me what you mean, Neela," Amber coached.

"Weeks ago, the weekend Wendy stayed over, and we went to the movies. She was acting all slutty and stuff in the mall, and she started telling me about this guy she'd met on the computer. That he was going to help her become an actress or some crazy shit," she said, waiting for the scolding for cursing, but her mother didn't flinch, "so I said Dad was trying to catch slimeballs like that."

"What did she say when you told her that?"

"Nothing then, but that night, she got on my tablet and talked to him a long time, laughing, and making me take pictures of her for him. She probably told him what I'd said," she said. "That's why I haven't been friends with her since. He was creepy."

"Tell me more about Wendy. Is she a good student? Does she get in trouble?" Amber asked.

Neela frowned as she thought of her friend and the questions. "Wendy doesn't do much in school, but she's pretty smart so she gets okay grades. She's been drinking, stealing her dad's liquor, money. When we were at the mall, she stole some makeup."

"Is her family stable? Her parents still together, that sort of thing."

"Her mom died five years ago. She has an older brother in the Marines, and a younger brother at home, and her dad spoils him with stuff. Buys him toys and takes him places. He kinda ignores Wendy."

Vanessa added, "Yeah, I took her to Macy's to help her buy bras a few years ago. I also talked to her when her periods started."

"Mom!" Neela whined, embarrassed.

"Honey, we're women. We all have them," she said.

"No step-mother in the picture?"

Vanessa shook her head.

"I need to go talk to Wendy and her father," Amber said. "But I'd like to see if we can find anything on your tablet, if I may?"

"She broke it. When I told her she had to stop, she smashed it on my cedar chest."

"Why didn't you tell us, honey?"

"I was afraid you'd think I was doing it, too," Neela said, more tears falling. "Is she in trouble?"

"Neela, what happens between her father and her isn't up to me, but he needs to know she's been talking to strangers, sending pictures, and so on."

"Serves her right," Neela muttered.

"Neela Darlene! No matter our own troubles, we should not wish them on others!"

That might be true, but I agree with Neela, Amber thought.

CHAPTER 42
Saturday, November 7, 2009

The man who answered the door looked like he'd been sleeping after a week-long bender. Hair, what he had, stood out in a frizz on the left, matted flat on the right. A sheet wrinkle crossed his neck up to his jaw then across his cheek, resembling a worn ant trail.

Amber would have bet his breath would peel paint if he exhaled hard enough.

"Mr. Barton," she said with a kind smile that was not what she felt. "I'm Deputy Amber Samualson, Tarrant County Sheriff's Office. May we speak for a moment?"

He looked around behind her, saw she was not in an official vehicle. By the time his gaze came back to her, she was holding out her ID and badge. He nodded and unlocked the screen door, but he didn't bother to open it. Instead, he turned and walked away.

"Sure, Deputy, please come on in," she muttered to herself in a deep falsetto voice as she reached for the handle and entered, trying to figure out which direction he'd gone.

She *hoped* he'd gone to change clothes.

From the back of the house, she heard music blaring, only muffled by distance and four thin walls, she'd guessed. Probably Wendy.

She found Frank Barton sitting at the kitchen table, in what used to be slick black basketball shorts and the wrinkled, dull whitish plain t-shirt she'd seen through the half-screened door.

His first word to her was, "What?"

Thankfully, he didn't offer her coffee as he poured some dark liquid from a coffeemaker into a cup. Neither looked like it had been washed in months, much like everything else she saw around her.

"Mr. Barton, I need to speak to you about Wendy."

"What's she done now?" he asked without interest as he poured three teaspoons of clumped sugar into whatever he was drinking.

"Her friend Neela told her about a project that Mr. Keegan and I were working on for the sheriff's department, a program to identify and catch child predators — men and women who lure children from their homes, away from the safety of their parents. Who assault them. Kidnap them. Sell them for sex trafficking." She paused when he showed no interest. "Your daughter has been talking to a man online who meets our criteria as a predator. He's been asking her for nude photographs."

"Says who?"

"Says Neela."

"Bullshit! Little rich girl."

"Maybe we should ask Wendy?"

"Yeah, sure," he replied with grouchy indignation. He took a big swallow of his coffee, then yelled, "Wendy! Come out here!"

Nothing in the house changed.

"Damn that kid," he grunted, clambering up and stomping around the corner and down a hallway toward the music, pounding on a hollow wooden door. "Wendy!" he bellowed, then wiggled the doorknob. "Open the fucking door!"

No answer.

Amber entered the dimly lit hall in time to see him try to shoulder the door open, an uncoordinated and ineffective effort that probably would leave a bruise on his upper arm. The thin wooden door bowed when he hit it, but how it hadn't splintered was beyond her comprehension.

"Move," she said, frustrated that he appeared to be regrouping to try again. Hearing how hollow the door was, it would give before the cheap lock.

She stepped around him and landed a well-placed kick inside the knob, and the bolt cracked through the jamb, but the door hardly opened. "It's blocked," she said, pushing against it. The dresser or whatever was on the other side moved with moderate effort, but the carpet peeled off the floor with it. She was trying to squeeze into the room, but the broken jamb caught on her clothes.

"Wendy!" he screamed again in her ear, sticking his head inside before Amber could get out of his way.

A younger boy stuck his head out from a room behind Frank. "What's going on, Dad?"

"Get back in your room!"

"She's not in here," Amber barked back. "She went out the window. Have any idea how long ago?"

The alcohol and angry crimson staining Frank's face faded to worry and shame. "No. I got fired a month ago, so I wasn't. . . been drinking ever since."

"She left in the morning yesterday, Dad," the boy said, peeking out of his door. "I tried to tell you."

"Do you know where she went?" Amber asked the boy, wiggling back out of the bedroom, pushing Frank Barton away from her as she moved toward the boy's door.

"No, but she was up all night, talking to some guy on the phone."

"Does she have a cell phone, or was she using a landline?"

"She was using Dad's cell phone. The house phone got shut off." The kid cowered from his father, who'd said nothing.

"Is the phone here?" Amber asked.

"She said she was going to take it with her," the kid said.

She turned to Frank Barton. "Write down your phone number. Maybe we can still find her."

CHAPTER 43
Saturday, November 7, 2009

"Kelly, I'm on my way back. I think I found out how this started," Amber said into the speaker of her phone as she drove to the cellular company. The news had left her out of breath. "I have another phone number for Brady to locate. I think it's right with Mac's." She repeated the number from the paper Frank Barton had given her. "A friend of Neela's might also have been kidnapped. I'm almost there. Come let me in."

She disconnected before he said a word, parked and jogged to the glass doors, where Kelly met her.

"We've got to get Brady to locate this phone," she said, headed to the elevators.

"Wait, Amber, we can't justify that in court."

As the elevator opened, she said, "Don't worry. I got Frank Barton's written permission to locate his cell phone on this carrier. We don't need any sort of warrant." She had to wait for him, then pushed the button six or seven times, as it that would make the doors close faster.

"Good thinking, I think," he said. "Slow down, Amber!"

The stainless-steel doors opened, and she burst out and down the hall, swinging into Brady's office with Kelly still twenty feet behind.

"I went to see Vanessa. Neela said she'd told one of her friends what we were doing because this friend mentioned using one of the programs we haven't gotten to yet, and she bragged about having an 'older boyfriend.' Then I went to the girl's house, and she's missing, too. Her brother said she'd left yesterday with her dad's cell phone."

"You think they're together?" Brady asked as Kelly came in. "Wouldn't it make more sense to have taken Neela?"

"Maybe they thought it was Neela. Doesn't matter. You need to find this phone."

Brady looked at Kelly for agreement then took the paper. "Let's try it."

They went back to the secure room. Brady sat at a keyboard, logged in to a different program, and searched for a current location where that cell phone was in the network.

Kelly looked up from the screen and saw Amber pacing behind them. He nudged a chair out and nodded for her to sit.

She did, but within seconds, she reached for a paperclip and began fidgeting with it.

"Amber, stop," Kelly whispered, not having seen her so anxious. "He's working as fast as he can."

"We've got to find Mac, we just have to," she said.

"I've got it!" Brady finally shouted. He raced past them out to the hall, running to the closest office with an open door, swung around the desk and sat to use the phone.

Kelly and Amber caught up as he began dialing.

"Sheriff Webb? It's Brady Cayson, from the park this morning? We've found where Mackenzie Keegan and another girl are."

Sarah Webb took notes, asked questions, and thanked him, but when Brady began to tell her how the information had been obtained, she simply said, "I don't want to know," and hung up.

He replaced the receiver in the cradle and leaned back, realizing how uncomfortable the chair was, not even sure whose office they were in.

"What?" Amber demanded. "What now?"

Kelly, still on crutches, pushed her toward a chair facing the desk.

"We wait. She'll call local authorities to locate them."

"If you know what highway, they can block it and stop everyone, right? RV's, trucks, ambulances. Everything."

"That's pretty much what she said."

"They have to stop everything," Amber repeated, remembering how state police had done that when someone tried to kill them in Washington eight years ago. The woman had beaten the roadblocks and burned down their house.

Kelly took her hand as she made the next lap. "They will find her, Amber. Take a breath."

Tears crept over her lashes and slipped down her cheeks.

"Let's go back to my house," Brady suggested. "This could take several hours."

***

By sundown, Brady had served them homemade teppanyaki on fried rice, a six-pack of Löwenbräu Dark, and they were halfway through a movie his kids had rented when the sheriff called. He put the call on speaker so they could all hear.

"I wanted to let you know that DPS and local authorities in south Texas have arrested two men for kidnapping for trafficking sixteen female minors, including Mackenzie Keegan and the other girl you told me about. They were taken to a local hospital and are being treated for dehydration and some minor injuries. I have a deputy on the way to get them, so they should be home by mid-morning," she announced from the phone on the table.

"You can't return Wendy Barton to her father," Amber blurted. "I think she's being neglected, maybe even abused. I went there today to talk to her father, and he's a train wreck drunk whose wife died and who lost his job."

"I'll check on that then," the sheriff said. "I've already called Mrs. Keegan. She said to tell you thanks."

"I appreciate you letting us know."

CHAPTER 44
Monday, November 9, 2009

"Harper, it's Brady. Got a minute?"

"Yeah, I'm headed home from work. I hope you have good news."

"I do. They found Mackenzie and fifteen other girls stashed in a locked shipping container on a flatbed near Del Rio. They're okay."

Harper let out a hoot.

"And we found out how the whole thing was aimed at Paul. It wasn't so much what they were doing. Kinda complicated but his oldest daughter told a friend about this project, and this girl had a 'boyfriend' online. When she told him, he thought Paul was spying on her and thus him, too. He'd intended to kidnap her anyway, so he solved the spy problem and got a bonus kid."

"Damn," Harper said. "This guy, was he arrested when they found the girls?"

"Um, no." Brady hesitated, looking for the right phrase. "I think you call it suicide by cop?"

"A waste of paperwork for firing a weapon," he muttered. "How'd you do it?"

"We had a fair track on that new phone Paul had purchased, thanks to you and Kelly, but when Amber found out that Neela's friend might be involved, she went to her house. The father was on a long drunk and had no idea his daughter wasn't home, but the son knew. She had taken her dad's phone, so we located it, too, and found them together."

"Wow, that's amazing, Brady." He raised his arms to stretch. "I wish you could solve Lilah's murder that easily."

"Maybe we could. You've never asked, Harp."

Harper Sullivan realized he'd probably crossed a huge line, not to mention almost hanging himself with his poorly thought-out statement.

"Harper?"

"It, uh, geez, Brady, it never even occurred to me," he stammered, pulling into the sad apartment complex where he'd lived for a year. "So how do I get you to do that for a case?" he said, thinking of something besides Lilah.

"If you want to do this, suggest it to whoever's in charge of the case and let him do the work on this. Stay out of it."

"Yeah, of course." He hesitated, trying to think through the ramifications. "But that's not what I meant. How do I request help for a current case?"

"Describe what you're looking for."

"I'm trying to find out if a man could have sabotaged his ex-wife's car. They live nowhere near each other. Could it possibly show that he went near the car at her house the night before the crash that killed her?"

"Tracking could only show his phone was there," Brady said, "but even if the phone wasn't, it doesn't prove he didn't go without it."

"Not a slam dunk either way," Harper said, still sitting in his car. "I'll have to think on it. I'd like Ian, my boss, to see how it works and suggest it about Lilah himself. That's what I meant."

"Gotcha."

Harper heard Brady's car slow.

"I'm home, and I haven't seen the kids in what seems like a week. I could use a hug, you know? Catch you in a few days."

"See ya."

They disconnected.

Harper looked back at the dreary building, where no one waited for him.

Use a hug, indeed.

PART III

CHAPTER 45
Monday, November 9, 2009

"Hello, Mrs. Gentry. It's Harper. How are you?"

"I'm doing well, Harper. And you?" Her voice was formal, icy.

"I'd complain, but no one listens. Is it finally cooling off?"

"Yes, but it's getting crowded. It's worse every year. In the spring, the part-timers leave to go north where it's cooler, and the tourists show up. In autumn, they must pass on the highway in Tennessee."

"You're probably right. How's Meredith?"

"She's doing well in school. She made honor roll again, and she's looking at colleges."

"I was hoping to talk to her. She's not around, I guess."

"No, she's at the library, studying with a couple of friends."

"Listen, Mrs. Gentry. I know you and Oscar take great care of Meredith, but I've recently run into a case where kids are being kidnapped and sold into — "

"Stop it, Harper! I'll have none of that nonsense. I will not let you make her worry every time she steps out into the fresh air. We live in a wonderful community."

"I want her to be safe."

"She's safer here than she was staying home alone with you, so don't you — "

There was a rustling sound, and a different voice replaced Harper's mother-in-law's.

"Harper Sullivan, I don't know what you've been saying to my wife, but I won't stand for you upsetting her or Meredith," the older man said in a hard, flat voice. "Don't bother calling back."

With that, Oscar Gentry hung up on him.

Harper sighed. He hadn't meant to upset anyone, only to tell *his daughter* she needed to be careful with the information she made available and the strangers she spoke to on the internet. He ought to have the right to speak to her about whatever he felt a father should tell his child.

No, he thought, she's not a child anymore. Her sophomore photos, and the bill for them, had been sent to him several months ago.

His daughter had inherited a haunting resemblance to her mother, especially her eyes. She had a beauty he feared would make her a perfect target for sex trafficking, and he didn't think he could ever forgive himself if something happened to her.

CHAPTER 46
Monday, November 9, 2009

"I hate funerals," Amber said, walking into the living room. "And I feel responsible for Paul's death."

"Neither of us is responsible for what happened to Paul. In fact," Kelly said, checking his tie in the reflection of the framed photo on the wall, "if we hadn't been doing what we were doing, Brady couldn't have gotten the pieces of the puzzle that helped find Mackenzie."

"I still hate them."

"May I say that you look, um," he frowned. "I guess it would be in poor taste to say you look dressed to kill, wouldn't it? You are stunning in that dress. And heels. Why don't you like funerals, I mean, besides the obvious reason?"

She sighed. "I've been to funerals for a lot of people I was close to. First my mother and her mother. Nana had lung cancer. Then going to my father's was impossibly hard because I'd just begun building our relationship and — "

"Wait, your father? I thought you went to live with him after your mother died," Kelly said, forehead crinkling in confusion. "He's a cop, right?"

"Oh, yeah. I guess that wouldn't make any sense to you. Dad was working on a DEA case that crossed over to the FBI's investigation of a financial thing, and Dad got shot. To solve their case, they let everyone believe he was dead. Funeral and all. It was horrible."

"How long did it go on?"

"Several months. Finally, Grandmom Vera invited me to come back to Albuquerque and stay with her, and I found out Dad was alive, but we still couldn't tell Julie."

"Why not?" he asked. "That's cruel."

"Exponentially cruel, when she was part of the case and didn't know it until the one guy intended to kill her. I'll explain it some other time."

"Then I understand why you hate funerals," Kelly said. "There is so much about you I don't know."

"Why would you want to hear about that stuff?"

Kelly, having transitioned to a cane and a locking knee brace, reached for her arm and stopped her, stepped close. "I want to know what makes you who you are."

Her cheeks flushed to a dusty rose, not the brash splotchy red her face turned when she was embarrassed.

Kelly noticed this and nudged her toward the door. "Let's get going. You can drive," he added, kidding. "I love having a chauffeur."

She closed the door firmly behind them. "One of these days you'll go back to your life and your third-story apartment, and your own car," she said, locking the deadbolt behind them and stepping around him to go to her car.

He watched her first few steps before following. "You wear another dress like that, I may go jump off a bridge just to break the other leg," he mumbled to himself.

The church was not yet full, but they were half an hour early, expecting a crowd. Even had he been on crutches, no way could Kelly stand for an hour. Nor could Amber have managed it on the heels that matched her black pinstriped skirt and jacket.

Mackenzie met them at the door, waiting for them.

"Mom asked if you would come sit with us," she said after hugging each of them.

"No, there's plenty of family," Kelly argued.

"Please?" she begged in a three-second whine.

From behind her, Vanessa spoke. "You both had become part of our family before Paul died. Because of the two of you, Mackenzie is home safe." She also hugged each of them in a long embrace, not the brief, casual partial hug of those barely acquainted.

They accepted her invitation and followed her and Mac back through a doorway to the family room.

Vanessa introduced them to her sister and to Paul's parents, his father in a wheelchair with oxygen. They had heard who Kelly and Amber were, and each one offered sincere gratitude for bringing Mackenzie home safe.

Amber noticed that Neela was standing alone in a corner of the room, so she went to her.

"It's my fault. Everyone is whispering about it," she said, trying to sound angry, which did nothing to hide the fact she'd been crying.

"No, Neela. It's not your fault any more than it's mine. I felt guilty this morning, but Kelly pointed out that the man who took your friend might have meant to grab you, too. Mac wouldn't have had the information that you did that helped find her. Because you told me about Wendy, we had another great clue to finding them." She wrapped her arms around the girl. "You are as much a hero in this as anybody, but losing your dad is still hard."

"How would you know?" the girl said, making a wimpy effort to pull away.

"My mother was murdered when I was 13. My grandmother died near the same time of lung cancer. I'm not saying I know how you feel, because it's not the same, but I understand it's hard."

CHAPTER 47
Wednesday, November 11, 2009

"Dispatch, Benton County 289. I'm eastbound on I-40 at mile marker 190, in a high-speed pursuit of an early model white Chevy sedan, occupied times two. Arizona license but I can't read."

"Benton 289, 10-4. Will dispatch units from Shamrock to intercept. Stand by."

Radio traffic continued, but Harper concentrated on keeping his distance from the swerving vehicle that had gone four miles now since he'd turned on his lights to pull it over for speeding. He'd clocked the car at 85 miles per hour by radar initially, but it sped up now that he was chasing it.

"Benton 289, Shamrock 412 is unable to intercept from his location. I have a deputy westbound, returning from a transport in an unmarked. He can intercept from the east. DPS Units 1262 and 1268 are en route from the west."

The four units swapped details for several minutes. Harper could see the flashing lights of one DPS unit behind him as he topped a hill. When he looked a second time, he was amazed at how much the vehicle had gained on him.

His speedometer showed 95 mph, so the trooper must be haulin' ass to catch up, he thought.

Probably a tenth of a mile back from the Chevy, Harper hoped the driver would choose to slow down, but hadn't appeared to do so yet.

Then the car swerved again, this time into the median, which had a post-and-cable divider.

Harper wasn't close enough to see the car hit the divider, but there was no question about the ejection of a body into the air when the car rolled. After that, a cloud of dirt obscured the crash.

"10-50," he said into the microphone. "Benton 289, on scene of 10-50 with ejection. Roll EMS."

He pulled to the median a hundred feet from the vehicle, which was now upside-down, tilted with the front-end touching the ground.

The dispatcher did her job as Harper jumped out, hurrying through the thick dry grass toward the car.

Both DPS units from west of him pulled in at the same time a county sheriff's car stopped on the other side of the cable divider.

The first victim Harper came to was unquestionably dead, but he knelt to feel for a pulse anyway.

DPS trooper Jerry Reitano jogged to the vehicle to look for the other occupant, peering into the passenger-side window, the glass missing.

No one else in the car.

"Hey, Harp. What the hell?" Reitano said. "You said there were two, right?"

Harper nodded as he approached the other side of the car. He stuck his head in the missing driver's window.

The car was old enough to have a radio with buttons, he noted.

He looked behind the front seats. No signs of a second person, but something about the backseat caught his eye. He grabbed the keys from the ignition so he could open the trunk.

"We'll start looking," said the second DPS trooper who'd pulled up. "And throwin' out flares."

He nodded, flipping through half a dozen keys on a keyring with a cheap metal, black and white skull and crossbones ornament. At the rear of the car, he tried the ignition key and several others without success.

Harper turned to the deputy who was still closest to his own car. "You got a crowbar?"

The deputy nodded and went to his trunk, grabbed the tool, then tossed it to Harper, who was waiting at the cable fence.

Harper walked around the car on the passenger side, noting that gasoline was dribbling from the fill spout. At the trunk, as he positioned the flat end to pry under the locking mechanism, a knocking sound came from inside, followed by a weak voice yelling for help.

"Someone's inside!" he called to the others.

The deputy and Trooper Reitano joined him and prepared to catch the trunk lid as Harper pried under the metal until it screeched then popped open. He dropped the bar and spread his arms to catch the person who fell toward him as the other men let the lid lower.

What tumbled out into Harper's arms were an armload of blankets and a child, blinded by the light for a moment, until she realized the man who held her was a police officer. She wiggled until she could wrap her arms around him in a hug so tight, he almost couldn't breathe.

"What's your name, Sweetie," he asked as he knelt to keep his balance, but she didn't let go.

"Don't let him hurt me anymore!" she yelled. "Make him stop!"

"You're safe now," Harper said in a calm voice. There were so many other questions he wanted to ask. "No one will hurt you again. How can we get you home?"

"No!" she screamed. "No no no!" She was crying so hard that sweat and tears soaked into Harper's shirt.

He looked at Reitano helplessly. He mouthed the words, "Is she injured?"

Reitano shrugged. "I'll call for a social worker to meet you at the hospital."

Harper tried again to talk to the child. "No one will hurt you. Can you tell me your name?"

She shook her head hard against his chest, still sobbing.

The other two officers had put flares on the shoulder of the road, and a highway department truck arrived to help push interstate traffic to the outside lane.

The ambulance had come the last half mile with the siren off and parked short of the crash scene.

A paramedic spoke to Reitano first, then approached where Harper had finally sat in the shorter grass near his car, holding the little girl who was still wrapped around his neck like a noose.

"I'm Tammy," she said softly to the child from behind him so she could see. "Would it be okay if Harp carried you to my ambulance so I could see if you got hurt in the accident? You took a real tumble in the trunk."

What could be seen of the dirty, tear-stained face shook hard.

"I know Tammy, and she wants to make sure you aren't hurt. Can I carry you over there? I won't let go," Harper said.

"He can make sure I don't do anything to hurt you, but you might need a bandage on your arm."

The child peeked out from her place snug against Harper's chest to look at Tammy, evaluating the woman, who didn't pull her from where she was. After a minute, the little girl bit her bottom lip and made a tiny nod.

"Let me help Harper to his feet, okay?" she said, offering a hand to him.

He carried the girl to the ambulance, stepping in through the side door and sitting in the captain's chair.

"Can you show me the scratch on your arm?" Tammy coaxed, starting with a minor injury.

The child twisted in Harper's lap so she could hold out her right elbow.

While the scrape needed cleaning, Tammy elected to not do anything that might hurt until she had built trust with the child. She took a non-stick bandage and placed it on the abrasion, then wrapped a stretchy gauze around her arm a few times, cutting it, and taping the end to keep it from unrolling. "Do you have a scratch on the other arm?"

The little girl leaned back and tried to look at the left elbow, then shook her head.

"How about on your knees?"

With one pale finger, she pointed to her right leg to a handprint-shaped bruise that wrapped around her thigh. It looked a few days old.

"Shall I put a bandage on it, too?" Tammy asked.

Again she gave a tiny nod, so Tammy bandaged that also, although it wasn't needed.

"Can we take you to the hospital so a nurse can see you?"

"No," the child said in a tinny voice.

"I can't leave you here," Tammy said. "I want to take you somewhere safe. Hospitals are safe places with safe people, like Harper. And me."

Harper tilted his head to look at her. "I want you to be safe, too. Tammy will take very good care of you."

Heartbroken, Harper realized that no matter who took her to the hospital, the little girl would think she was abandoned again when that person left. He hoped it wasn't him.

The little girl nodded, wiggled out of his lap, and went to stand in front of Tammy.

Harper got his first real look at the child, in dirty, torn clothes. Dark dried bloodstains on her shirt, as if it had been used to wipe up a spill.

Tammy was talking to the child in a calm, motherly voice, so Harper slipped out when the girl wasn't looking.

"Hey, Harp, did you know this vehicle was the Amber Alert from Flagstaff?" asked the deputy who'd provided the tool to access the truck. "It came out this morning."

"No, just a speeder who thought he could outrun the radio."

"Key wouldn't work on the trunk, eh, Harp?" Reitano asked, shaking his head. "You had to scratch the guy's car up?"

They all laughed.

"Your mess now," the other trooper said, and they both headed back to their units.

"Makes sense why I saw two occupants. I bet the driver told her to hide behind the back seat, 'cause there is no key. But I saw a strap hanging out of the cushions," Harper said, waving at the one trooper as he pulled away.

"Hope the girl's okay," the deputy said.

Harper handed the crowbar back and offered his hand to introduce himself. "Harper Sullivan, Benton County. Thanks for your help."

"You're welcome, nice to meet you," the deputy said, shaking his hand. "I'm Stephen Royce from Marshal County. I hear you're investigating me for the death of my ex-wife."

CHAPTER 48
Friday, November 13, 2009

Harper was working on paperwork in his office when he heard a female in the lobby, asking if he was in. He recognized the voice.

The phone on his desk trilled.

Harper knew who was looking for him. He suspected he knew why.

He did not want to talk to her while Stephen Royce clogged so much of his mind space, but the phone kept ringing. Instead of answering, he stood and walked down the hall. His footsteps gave him away as Ellanie Thomas pointed a finger at him and began a roaring tirade. He held up his hand to silence her. When she stopped yelling, he motioned for her to follow him back through the security door.

She did so, going straight to his office when he held the door open for her, so he followed her, and closed his office door behind them.

"You have some nerve, Harper Sullivan, insinuating my husband killed Lilah," she growled at him.

"I did not insinuate that he killed her. I point-blank accused him of screwing her. You must have known he was sleeping around because I overheard you telling Lilah," he retorted. "I went by the house one afternoon, and his car was there."

"It could have been me," she countered.

"No, I'd just left the ED, and you were at work." He turned away from her to the frosted window behind his desk, trying to remain calm.

"What'd you do? Stop and threaten him?"

"No, I was outraged, but I kept driving. I couldn't stand to find out the truth by confronting them. Why are you so pissed off at me?"

She slumped into the chair across the desk from his, so he also sat.

"At the barbeque at Ian's, I heard what you said to him. Everything began to make sense about him and her. I mean, I didn't want to believe it was her — she was my best friend," she said, looking at the floor. "After she died, Eddy changed. Like, drastically changed. He began begging me to have a baby, but he couldn't touch me without having two or three drinks."

When she looked up, Harper saw tears leaving a trail of black mascara on her pale skin. "Ah, Ell', I'm sorry. He keeps hounding me to come back to church like some sermon he gives is going to fix everything, but I can't stand the thought of listening to him preach his hypocrisy, especially forgiveness, when he was breaking half the Ten Commandments in my bed."

"I don't know what to do," she said as another tear dragging her makeup with it fell off her chin. "We had been going through a rough spell. He was depressed, then everything bloomed, like he was a teenager in love for the first time. Giddy, delirious. Even more than when we were dating. And I noticed a subtle change with her, too."

Harper said, trying to reason with her, "They probably had feelings for each other, so not only did he lose her, but he also couldn't tell anyone about her."

"That doesn't make it right!" she hissed in her tear-strained voice, then hung her head again. "He did. Have feelings, I mean, or whatever it was. He's changed again. Like I don't even exist. I'd been fighting off the suspicions, but after the barbeque, I knew I couldn't do it anymore. Last night, I finally shattered, I guess. I made him tell me the truth."

"No, Ellanie, what they were doing wasn't right. None of this has been right. But nothing I can do will change her being dead. I'm angry that he was sleeping with her, but I'm even angrier that someone killed her."

She chewed her bottom lip, trying to decide whether to say something, he thought.

Please don't ask me if I think Eddy killed her.

Nodding her head almost imperceptibly, she'd made up her mind.

"What are you going to do, Ell'?" he asked.

She rose and stepped around the desk toward him.

Out of habit, he stood.

She closed the distance in four more steps, leaving them a hand-width apart. She stared up at him a moment, then she leaned forward onto her toes and kissed him, softly. Enticingly.

Yet the kiss was an instant shy of invitation for more, he thought, not failing to respond to the kiss but not controlling it either. Knowing he could have. Knowing he wanted retribution for her husband's infidelity.

Knowing that another wrong would not make anything right.

The moment ended. She stepped back, thought another moment, then turned to leave. When she reached the door in slow steps, she stopped and looked back at him. "I don't know what I'll do, Harper. That's all the payback I can manage right now."

CHAPTER 49
Saturday, November 14, 2009

Without Paul, the endeavor seemed empty to Amber as she set up for an evening of computer contact with more perverts.

She and Kelly had decided that they could go on with the program and only seek the services from the cell company through Brady if they needed it. They had also decided it was too much to separate mentally by continuing to do it at her house, so they secured a room at the sheriff's department lab.

"Maybe we could dig further into your files from that computer you retrieved?" he asked. "We may have already crossed paths with some of those folks."

"I haven't had success getting names, but maybe you can see something I don't," she replied, turning her chair to get up when her computer pinged with a message.

"hey missy wybut?" the chat read in a program designed to provide a *dating* atmosphere to users of all ages. The keyboard shorthand meant "what you been up to?"

While Magnetism didn't tout itself as a pedophile shopping site, of course, it was not an age-limited platform, so whether you were eight or eighty, access to all was granted, divided only between those who used it for free, or for those who paid the $75 annual fee, which made for easy trolling.

"me?" Amber typed, pretending to be Amy for this session. Amy was an 11-year-old girl, a middle and thus invisible child, she complained to another girl chatting with her a while before this new person popped in. "do I know u"

"not yet. I'm Bret."

"m or f" Not using capital letters and other punctuation gnawed at Amber's command of English like a termite in a forest.

"M/14 U?"

"m2! I mean age, not the other" She smiled at what would have been a lie if anything about Amy was real.

"what brings you out tonight?"

"bitchin — grounded"

"Y?" meaning why?

"skipped school monday"

"Ya get caught?"

"my sister ratted"

"What were you doing?"

"riddin around NBD" Misspelling was even harder than the shorthand — No big deal. "what would u do?"

"Depends who was with me. if it was u, MB steal a bottle of booze from my dad's bar, go drink."

"yuck, i dont like alkahal taste"

"Not supposed to like it, just how u feel, gurl"

"whut else"

"I have a friend that might let us use his basement"

"pool table?"

"Yeah."

"i'm good at pool."

"MB we could play strip pool."

"yeh rite"

"you wouldn't fool around?"

"i have a boyfriend"

"ever do things w him?"

"like whut?"

"like play with his junk?"

"some"

"Liar what you do?"

"gotta go."

"chiken!"

"my dads home. grounded rember by"

Kelly leaned back in the chair so far his back popped. "Why'd you stop?"

"Watch this guy," she said, logging Amy out of the chat but watching the role-playing game she'd snooped around in but not engaged anyone. She had created a login that allowed her to invisibly watch others in the game, probably like that of the predators she was chasing. "I think this guy is prowling," she pointed to another user. "He isn't even pretending to be a kid."

"Wait a few minutes and log back into the game," Kelly said.

The game, a sideline to Magnetism's free chat, bragged it was a "zombie game" where players met and chatted while in a multi-role-player online contest in a fantasy maze that did not focus on combat as much as it did teamwork of players to collect points and rewards of extra lives, strength, intelligence, and appeal to your partner, whatever the hell that meant, Amber said.

"This seems weird inside an app to meet people. Why would an adult want to play this?"

"Most adults wouldn't," she said with a grin. "Just those who are shopping for children."

CHAPTER 50
Saturday, November 14, 2009

"I'll have to find a partner," Amber replied, clicking keys to log back in. "The character I'm using hasn't been here but once, and I haven't built much of a history for her." She tapped more keys, which allowed her to hack into the user data to find out about the adult she suspected.

His public profile showed him to be Adam Chaney, which she presumed was fake. He said he was 38, living in Mesquite, east of Dallas. What she read in his private data to get a paid account for access to all the sites of Magnetism, listed the same name but a date of birth that indicated he was 58, address the same. He had paid through a third-party service instead of using a credit card directly.

"No way he's using a cell phone for this," she said to herself. "Look him up."

"Good, make it look like you're trying to figure the game out, like maybe you've heard of it from a friend," he coached while browsing the user profiles.

"After you're done, log in. Let's play for a while. Then you can log off or get killed and leave me if we get him to bite," she said, flipping pages through her logbook. "Be Ferdinand, the elf. He's a thirteen-year-old named Jonathan who lives in Colorado."

Kelly logged in and entered the information necessary to become a member. "Okay. How do I catch up?"

"I'm not far. Take the trail left and watch for a tree with branches like arms," she said, watching his progress. "Yeah, that one. Stop and hug it."

"Hug it?"

"Yeah, hugging it earns you your first extra life," she said, laughing. "Kinda like the slot machines at the airport in Las Vegas. You win when you get to town, making you more likely to gamble if you're already winning."

"What if you bomb at the tables?" he asked, making his character wrap his arms around the trunk of the tree.

A magical *tada!* sound accompanied the appearance of a gold coin that then moved into a backpack-looking bag the character suddenly carried.

"Then you win on your way out of town, so your ego remembers that, not how much you lost," she replied. "Okay, take the next right. I won't be far."

In the game, a blue elf approached a witch wearing a dark purple gown carrying a crooked walking stick.

"Hi. I need a partner," she typed to his character. "Wanna join me?"

"Yeah, have you played this game? It's lame."

"No its not!" she typed, then muttered to herself, "Oh it is so lame."

"We'l see. I'm Fernando," he typed.

"I told you, it's Ferdinand!" Amber said, throwing a candy bar wrapper toward Kelly but missing.

"My real name is Chris," the elf character said.

She sighed and whispered. "Fine, then keep your own logs."

She typed, "I'm Wilda the Witch. Let's go this way."

"What's ur real name?"

"Brook. No jokes"

Brook would be a new character she'd make up as she went.

"What?" he said as Fernando brushed near a wildly gesticulating orange long-leafed plant, which wrapped tentacles around him and pulled him into a hole in the ground.

The computer let out a groaning sound followed by a low growling gulp.

"Swell," Amber said. "You're dead. Give it a second, you'll come back to the last turn."

His reappearance was announced with a tinkling sound.

"Ouch," his character said for itself, a programmed response.

"No kidding," Chris typed. "I'm back!"

"See? You needed that extra life already. We'll have to make sure you get the next one."

"Tnks. Brook is pretty."

"Sure, if you want people to make fun of you with water stuff. My best friend's brother calls me Lake, River, Creek, Ocean, Scumpond."

"yuk sorry. Wilda is cool 2"

A tall, armored character joined them from the left. "HiHo! I am Adam. You look lost. May I help guide you through a level or two?"

"Sure!" Kelly said first. "Where to? I need another life."

"You must have touched the Grr'orange plant," Adam said.

"Sweet!" Amber added. "I tried to tell him."

Over the next fifteen minutes, the game characters advanced through the fantasy forest, encountering colorful animated plants and odd creatures. In a place where the path got dark and narrow, a zabbon — a lion with the black and white stripes of a zebra and huge rabbit ears and white cottontail — lunged at Fernando, eating him on the spot. Chris lost his remaining life and would have to start over again.

"Ooh, sorry. I forgot the zabbons," Adam explained. "You two weren't friends, were you?"

"NBD we just met," she typed.

"Good. I guess it's us now. I can help you a lot as your partner if you'd like."

"I haven't played games like this before my friend Ashli showed me last weekend"

"Super! What character is she?"

"She's played enough to make her own character, so she's a green unicorn, kinda silly."

"And you are a witch. A good witch or a wicked witch?" He added, "Come this direction."

"I don't know, just a witch."

"What do you look like? Like your character?"

"No." Amber used one-word replies when she wanted to indicate she was uncomfortable.

"What color are your eyes?"

"My dad used to say they looked like chocolate kisses," Amber typed, then moved away from the desktop and rolled toward a trash can, pretending to gag.

Kelly laughed. "That was good, though. Flirty, but something she wouldn't think to say about herself."

Adam answered, "They sound beautiful. I love kisses."

Amber scooted back to the desk and connected her computer to the overhead projector so they could both see better. "I think their plain."

"Don't you believe your dad?"

"No."

"Why not?"

"He and my mom split a couple of years ago when he was having an affair."

"You don't see him now?"

"Only when I have to." She let her character stop walking.

"What do you mean?"

"Some judge makes us stay with him one weekend a month. It's stupid. He doesn't have a place for us because his new wife has kids too. We're supposed to sleep on the couch."

"I'm sorry, that sounds awful. I bet no one even asked you what you wanted to do." He typed, but he kept moving in the game, so she followed.

"No. I hate going," she stated. "And he doesn't want us there."

"You seem old enough to make decisions like that. You drive, right?"

"See? Why do I have to go?" She intentionally didn't answer his question about her age. "I'm sick of being treated like a little kid."

"You need a father who will help you grow up," he declared. "Someone who can provide you with exceptional opportunities to be independent."

Amber nodded, realizing she had a hungry fish circling the boat. "Yeah."

"What do you want to do when you graduate?"

"I love horses so I want to be a jockey," she said. "mom says I'm too tall."

"How tall are you?"

"Like 5-4 or so but I'm skinny and she makes me take ballet lesons, like I'd ever be good at it."

"That's not too tall to be a jockey if you're thin," Adam said. "I have a couple of horses."

"Really? What kind?"

"Actually, I have more than a couple. My brother and I breed Arabians."

If Amber could have made her character or her text squeal, she would have. Instead, she made the witch turn in circles. "I love Arabian horses! Theyr so beutiful!!"

"Arabians don't race, though. We raise them for the movies, so we have trainers and riders. Maybe you'd like to see them?"

"Absolutely! Could I maybe ride one?"

"Of course. You're welcome anytime."

She hesitated, trying to think out how this would go. "I don't have a car. mom can't afford it since my father left. She works 2 jobs. We have to walk to school."

"We'll work out something, I promise."

"i hope so im so sick of this shit"

"What's so bad? Sounds like your mom works hard."

"her boyfriend doesnt so he muches off us all the time"

"She doesn't leave you alone with him, does she?"

She hesitated for a count of ten. "sometimes"

"He hasn't ever hurt you, has he?"

Again, she hesitated. "usualy he peeks at me"

"What do you mean? When does he see you?"

Interesting. He ignores the innuendo the child's being hurt or molested.

"like getting dressed for school or when I'm in the bathroom, he opens the door like he doesn't know I'm there."

"Does he tell you that you're pretty?"

"no"

"Ever try to kiss you when your mom is gone?"

"yuck no!"

"Have you ever been kissed?"

"yah sure"

"Who have you kissed?"

"I have a boyfriend," Amber typed. "but mom doesn't know."

"Really? you kiss him sometimes?"

"yah"

"Do you like it?"

"sure"

"Does it make your chest tight? Or make you feel all tingly between your legs."

"I don't think so"

"Does he ever touch your breasts?"

"some."

"Do you have a picture you can send?"

"No." Amber was sitting straight, her brain working double as a child and as a cop. "This is gross," she whispered to Kelly, who nodded.

"Do you have a cell phone?"

"no, don't have one now. I only get to use the computer when no ones home cuz Gary is on it all the time when hes here."

"What's he do with it?"

"mom calls it lookin at his cuties"

"Women without clothes?"

"I guess IDK"

"Does it make him hard?"

"whaz that?"

"that tingly feeling women get, men get too. Their penises get hard."

"does it hurt?" Amber typed, setting Kelly into a fit of laughter.

"No, not really. Haven't you ever touched a penis when it's hard?"

"dont think so"

"Would you like to see it? When it's hard?"

"I guess."

"I'll send you a picture, but you have to do two things for me. First, after you look at it, you have to delete it so you won't get in trouble."

"okay"

"Second, send me a picture of you."

"no, I'm ugly"

"I think you're beautiful and smart and sexy. You make my penis hard. Maybe you'll get to touch it when you visit."

"no im not. your teasing me"

"Are you home alone now?"

"no, mom's sleep. works nights this week"

"What time does she leave? Maybe I could come visit you."

Kelly interrupted Amber's thoughts. "We don't have a safe house that would fit your description of a parent who has to work two jobs," Kelly said in a hoarse whisper as if he might be heard. "See if you can put him off till tomorrow."

Amber nodded but didn't look at him, afraid to break the spell of the conversation.

"Not tonite," she typed. "How about next wkd when I spose to go to dads?"

"That would be good. Are you ready for the picture?"

"sure"

Amber waited for the photo to load. Instead of one, it was a montage of a male in various states of erection and masturbation. No face. She waited, studying the hands in the images for distinctive characteristics that could be used to identify him as the subject.

"Did you get them?" Adam asked.

"yeh wow is that you?"

"Good wow?"

"its huge"

"Thank you. You make that happen. I would very much like to meet the woman who does this to me."

Amber did not answer.

"And I would love to teach you what to do to make it feel so good to you, too. Do you feel that tingling now?"

Still she hesitated a moment. "mabe"

"Why don't you touch yourself for me?"

"what if I get caught? Its almost time for mom to get up?"

Adam's reply, like a thousand needles sticking into her neck, said, "Trust me."

His words nauseated her to think of some pre-teenager, listening to maybe the first adult male who'd ever spoken to her with approval, with acceptance, with desire.

"gotta go mom tomro nite" she typed and logged off.

As she shoved her chair back from the desk, she realized she was shivering.

"Hey, Amber," Kelly said, holding out his hand but not touching her. "Let's go." He waited almost two minutes for her spell to break, wherever her brain had gone. He wouldn't ask what she'd been thinking. He was angry, enraged enough to go find the guy and leave him in pieces in the parent's basement he imagined the creep lived in; but he would never share that with Amber, either.

She finally blinked and took his hand. "I have to print the transcript first. I can't risk it being stored on a computer, even overnight." She stood, letting go of his hand to return to the keyboard, to tap in a series of keystrokes, setting the laser printer across the room on a 23-page job, followed by the shorter one that was only 14 pages.

They waited without speaking until the printer beeped its completion.

"I got it," Kelly said, going to get the pages, then following her to the lab's locked evidence locker. "Let's go find something pleasant."

She nodded, and they exited without seeing anyone else who wanted to do more than pass an evening greeting. Once outside, Amber stopped to inhale.

The air was cool, but Kelly could smell the exhaust on the breeze, though it was such an improvement over the room they'd left.

"Let's get something to eat on the way to your house?" he suggested, taking a step forward to see if she followed.

"Like what?" she asked, still moving on autopilot for a few steps as the ugly of the evening fell away.

"Let's get fajitas from Manuela's," he said, opening her car door for her.

"Sounds good."

He placed the order by phone, and she went in to pick it up.

Not until they were inside her house did she say anything else.

"I'm sorry," she said after she came back to the table and sat, helping to uncover the meal and its condiments.

Kelly had brought two bottles of beer for them from the fridge, and he opened hers. "No apology needed."

"I don't want you to think I'm taking out my frustration on you, but I'm furious that this problem is so damned easy for those monsters."

"And one by one, you are getting them out of the communities."

They each made and ate their first fajita, then after making herself a second, Amber got them both another beer.

"I'll call and get a suitable house to use in the morning," he said, getting ready to take a big bite.

"I think this guy — "

Kelly grabbed a napkin to cover his mouth. Coughed, making a weak, wet sound.

His face transformed — skin became pale, his lips blue. Panic glazed his eyes. One more attempt to cough yielded a napkin full of frothy blood.

Amber scrambled to his side in time to see his eyes roll upward as he passed out.

"Kelly?" Amber asked as she propped him against her from falling out of the chair. "Kelly!"

No way she could reach her phone on the foyer table, so she pulled him off the chair to the floor, rolled him to his side.

He groaned and coughed up more blood on the white tile.

Amber didn't understand what was wrong, but she was certain something *was* wrong. She grabbed her phone and dialed 911, gave her address and a brief report of what had happened. As directed, she left the line open. She unlocked and opened the front door, then went back and sat beside Kelly.

Eight minutes seemed like two hours to her as she waited to hear sirens.

She was scared, but she was not freaked out. She held his hand, telling him help was on the way.

Kelly stirred, grimacing and breathing hard, his other hand pressed against his chest.

When the loud sirens stopped, she got to her feet and hurried to the door.

In front of her house were a fire engine and ambulance, men and women pouring out onto the street from both vehicles, grabbing gear, then hurrying to where she stood. Two police cars came screeching to a stop behind them as well.

"He's in here. We were eating, then he coughed up blood and passed out. Last month, he was hit by a car, had to have surgery for a fractured femur," she offered to the woman kneeling next to Kelly.

Several others performed their tasks. Two brought in the stretcher to the foyer and lowered it. The paramedic, Amber saw on her badge, kept asking questions of her and a few of Kelly, who tried to answer.

The best he could do is shake his head or nod, but it seemed adequate.

Almost like magic, he had an oxygen mask, electrodes and wires to the EKG machine, and fluid flowing into his arm through an IV line.

"What's wrong with him," Amber asked the medic. "His mother's going to ask me."

"He's pretty young for a heart attack. Could be a bleeding ulcer, but based on his recent injury and surgery, my first hunch is a pulmonary embolism," the woman with a thick black bun told her as they rolled Kelly to a backboard. She told Amber which hospital they were taking him to so she could follow.

Kelly was lifted to the gurney, then wheeled outside and into the ambulance.

Before the last police officer left, he asked if she needed a ride.

"No, I'm fine, but why all the response for a medical call?" she asked.

He smiled. "The 911 center has this address tagged as a law enforcement residence. Is that him?"

"It's *my* house," she said. "We both work for Tarrant County S.O."

His brother-in-blue smile became a knowing grin. "I'll never tell."

That innuendo went right over her head after the day she'd had.

Amber dialed Dr. Goldsmith, hoping she could explain this to her boss without losing control. She felt frozen until she heard the diesel engines accelerate and the siren start again, which made her skin prickle.

"Hello?" Bonnie Goldsmith repeated, Amber finally aware that her call had connected.

"It's Amber," she said, struggling to find where to start. "Kelly's on his way to the hospital. We were having dinner and — "

"Which hospital?" Dr. Goldsmith demanded.

Amber answered the question, ready to explain more, but the call disconnected.

"All right, then. You're quite welcomed for the call, Dr. Goldsmith. I'll just sit here and have another fajita. Thanks," she said to no one, sinking to the floor. "So much for my job. I let my boss's son die at the dinner table."

CHAPTER 51
Saturday, November 14, 2009

While Harper felt the weight of his day float away on a glass of vodka, the only good news of recent days was that the girls were located and safe.

He got up to make a sandwich, remembering that bread was on his shopping list, so his bologna rested on one heel and a stale slice, scant mayonnaise, and a slice of some sort of cheese. A glass of milk would have made the meal complete, but the last inch in the half-gallon left a thick chunky film on the jug when it sloshed, indicating it was a week past sour.

Still, the sandwich was more than he'd had since someone had handed his breakfast out the drive-through of the donut shop at the edge of town. Two klobasneks, not kolaches, the clerk told him for the hundredth time, a chocolate glazed donut, and a giant cup of coffee, most of which was cold by the time he got to it two hours later.

He plopped into his recliner and balanced the paper plate on his lap so he could grab the sandwich in one hand and reach for the television remote with the other when someone knocked at the door.

Grumbling, he wiggled his butt on the fake suede far enough he could lean forward and stand without using his left hand, carrying his dinner with him to the door, leaning to check the peephole.

Outside stood someone he wouldn't have thought would visit him.

He sat the plate on the table where he usually dropped his keys, then unlocked the door.

"Sergeant Sullivan," Dierdra Preston said, "I need your help."

He stepped back, and she stepped inside without further invitation.

"Please, have a seat," he urged, eyeing the sandwich as he left it.

"I'm sorry to come to your home, but I wanted to talk to you off the record about your suspicion that Stephen was involved in the death of his wife."

"You *were* with him the night before the accident, right?"

"That's just it. He might have thought I'd be the perfect cover story. Now that I think more about it, I realize he was gone part of the night."

"I don't understand," Harper said, hoping the brain fog he felt wasn't from not eating. He wondered if it would be rude to take a bite in front of her as they sat.

"Yes, Stephen and I spent the night at the Royal Star Inn, like I told you. It was not hugely different from our other occasional nights together, except I fell asleep around midnight and slept hard, which has never happened. I never sleep well in a hotel; the pillows are too poofy or the room is too warm. Or he snores. Always something."

"I can relate."

"I remember that he got up around 4:30 or so, and I woke enough to hear him in the bathroom, but I could not stay awake. Next thing I knew, he was bringing in coffee and breakfast at quarter till seven."

"That doesn't clear up much."

"He brought in breakfast, from Hap's Deli out on Highway 70," she explained. "Nothing fancy, coffee and bagels. But he'd told me once how much he hates it because it was a dirty dive, he called it."

Harper's face must have communicated his inability to make any connections.

"I'm sorry, this sounds outrageous, but I really think it means something. When he left, he took my car, said his had a flat. I drive a '98 Pontiac Bonneville, and my gas gauge hasn't worked in a year, so I keep a note on the visor of what the mileage should be when I need to fill up next. I can't tell you how far he drove, but when I filled up, it took almost five gallons *less* than I expected it to need, based on how far past my reminder the mileage was. I figured I'd transposed a number last time."

"Wait, so the important parts are that he got up around 4:30 a.m., took your car and drove 60 miles or more, then probably put gas in your car, and he brought you breakfast from Hap's?"

"Yeah, crazy as it sounds, I think that's it."

"It's not proof that he did anything wrong, Dierdra, as much as I think he did."

She fell back against the sofa cushion, making the wood frame squeak. "I know he did it. I don't know how to prove it."

"Why do you think he did it?" he asked.

"Because he's an egotistical narcissistic ass who can't live with the fact that a judge in *his county* gave a woman who was divorcing him alimony or anything else."

"But that won't convict him of murder," Harper said. "Look, I haven't eaten all day. May I? Maybe I can think better if I have something besides liquor in my stomach."

"Oh, I'm sorry. Please, eat," she said, her voice sounding as exhausted as he felt. "Can I have a glass of whatever you're drinking?"

"It's vodka, but help yourself, if you don't mind. Glasses are left of the sink."

She got up, poured herself a few ounces of vodka, and came back to the sofa.

He chewed the first bite and swallowed. "I got to meet Prince Charming," he said as casually as if he'd seen a dead snake on the road. "He knows I'm investigating and that he's a suspect."

"Fabulous," she said, throwing back the rest of her liquor.

Harper scarfed the sandwich in four more bites, washing it down with vodka. "Thanks. So how do you think he did this?" He tossed his paper plate into a wastebasket beside his chair.

"I think he slipped something into the wine to make me sleep that night."

"Let me make a list," he suggested. "So we don't forget any details when we're putting together the case."

"You believe me?"

He smiled. "Oh, hell yes!"

With a sigh of relief, she said, "Thank you. Okay, first, I think he drugged me so I wouldn't know he left the hotel."

Harper wrote it on a notepad he found on the end table.

"He drove over 40 miles in my car, my best estimate of the mileage. Maybe more, but no less," she continued.

"Caitlyn lived in Harris, almost 30 miles from the hotel, so could he have gone that far?"

"Yeah, that would make sense. Sixty-some miles would be roughly five gallons. The damned thing only gets 12 miles per gallon with a strong tailwind."

"And he took your car because?"

"He said he had a flat."

"Did you see his car when you left?"

"I didn't see a flat tire on the side of his car closest to mine, but I was running late already, had to pick up my son at his friend's house to take them to school. I didn't think about any of these things that morning."

"He might have worried that someone would recognize his car in a different county, or that Caitlyn herself could have seen it. Or maybe it's an unmarked county vehicle with a locator device in it," he said, writing the idea down. "I'll check that."

"Nothing fancy like that in mine," she said.

"Did he tell you he took your car?"

"When he got back, yeah," she replied. "Why?"

"I'm wondering if that was his plan all along, or if he really had a flat. Or that he meant to use yours and not tell you, but something happened. Maybe someone recognized him at Hap's."

"Don't take this the wrong way, Harper," she said with a smile, "but you think the worst of people even better than I do."

"Compliment accepted. What's important about the deli?"

"Stephen told me before he wouldn't go there, but it's *where* the deli is that's important. Wouldn't you have to take Highway 70 to get to Harris? And Hap's is five or six miles from the hotel in that direction."

"Two points of coincidence. Go on."

"His favorite breakfast place is two miles in the opposite direction," she explained. "Why would he go to Hap's?"

"Reasonable question with no guess."

"Sometimes no answer is the best answer of all in court."

"How's he treated you since then?"

"He hasn't. Hasn't called, dropped by, emailed me. Nothing until maybe ten days ago, I can't remember the date."

"That a good thing or a bad thing?"

"I assume he was pissed off that I didn't go to San Antonio with him last month," she said, going to get the vodka bottle, then pouring them each another two fingers before sitting again. "Then he called, asked about having an overnight thing last weekend. I lied and said I had plans. When he got angry, I told him I didn't think we should see each other anymore."

"How'd he take that?"

"I'd pulled the phone away from my ear to disconnect, but I swear I heard him say, 'I do,'" she said, looking down.

"Are you afraid of him, Dierdra?"

"Yeah," she said, looking into her glass. "I am. I think he did what you said, and I'm not foolish enough to believe I couldn't be next."

The silence hung between them for a minute or two as each of them thought.

"He has a cell phone, right?"

She nodded.

"I have a friend who may be able to trace where it went that morning."

"He didn't take his cell phone with him," she replied. "I saw it on the table on his side of the bed when he came in."

"Damn."

"What should I do now?" Dierdra asked him. "Do I dare go to work?"

"Work would be a safe place, but I'm not sure about the drive, if you catch my drift," he said with a half-smile.

"Do you think we're in danger?"

"Doesn't matter what I think. Do you?"

"I'm terrified."

"You should consider going somewhere safe."

"I guess we could go to my ex-husband's. He's in Austin."

"I presume that's not something Royce would know, but he probably has connections that would make it easy to find out. Who else?"

"My brother lives in Oklahoma City. Maybe we can go see him."

"Is Preston your maiden name?"

"No, it was McFarland," she said. "I really can't leave. I've got a trial starting — "

"Tell your boss you've been threatened, that it comes from and about a person suspected of murder. If you don't leave, you may not finish the trial because you're dead. Simple as that."

CHAPTER 52
Saturday, November 14, 2009

Although Amber didn't think she'd really lose her job, she figured she'd lost Dr. Goldsmith's confidence regarding her son. She had gone to the hospital while Kelly was still in the emergency department, hoping to see how he was and what they were going to do for him, but his mother hadn't so much as spoken to her. Blatantly ignored her.

Amber left without seeing him, went home to clean up the kitchen. She'd put the leftovers in the refrigerator before leaving the house, but plates of food had sat untouched for hours. She picked up her warm beer and finished it.

Unsure what else to do, short of having another beer and a hard cry, she pulled her phone from her back pocket and dialed her father.

Zach didn't answer, so she dialed Julie's phone. She'd be better to discuss this with than her dad, she decided.

Julie picked up on the second ring. "Hey, Amber! What's up?"

The tears broke in the first syllable of her greeting.

"Honey, what's the matter?"

"Feels like everything's wrong. A man I work with was killed after he and his middle daughter were kidnapped last week. And an ambulance took the other team member out of my house a couple of hours ago."

"Oh no! What happened?"

"I don't know, Mom. We were eating dinner when he started coughing up blood, and I called 911. Then I called his mother, who's my boss, and — "

"Wait. Why is your boss's son eating supper at your house?"

"His name is Kelly Morgan," she began, explaining who he was and how she agreed to rent him a room in her house.

"Why with you?"

"I didn't want him to, but Dr. Goldsmith promised he wouldn't be an imposition, and she offered to pay, so I agreed. He's also on this child exploitation team with me, which is creepy."

"Him being on the team or what the team does is creepy? I thought you were working in the crime lab on computers," Julie said. "Sorry, I'm confused."

"Not him. I was working on a laptop that was used by traffickers, with a kind of a shopping list of children. Julie, I can't believe how vile these people are. Morgan, Paul, and I, we'd been engaging suspects online. I imitate a child to talk to until the suspect does something illegal."

"How do you do that?"

"My part has been hard to learn, but finding these predators is easy. Too easy. Perverts look for a child who needs attention, like from a single-parent household, or who is already suffering abuse. A child whose self-esteem is so low, he's willing to comply with anything from someone who seems to show him love, like providing nude photos. By earning trust, the pervert can lure a kid out of a home, either engaging in something sexual or outright selling to a life of prostitution, labor, even for organs."

"Organs?" Julie asked as if the word tasted like mud.

"Black market organs from healthy kids are worth a lot of money." Amber stopped to wipe her nose. "I don't think I can talk about it anymore. Thanks for listening. I hate being so far away."

"Never too far for a phone call."

"I know. I called Dad first. Do you know where he is?"

"He was in D.C. a week ago, but I don't remember where he was going next or what day he's coming home. He'll call when he sees your number," Julie said. "Anything I can do for you?"

"You've done it. I needed someone to listen. Thanks."

"You're welcome. I miss you. Can you get away to Albuquerque for Thanksgiving?"

"I hope so," Amber said.

"Bring your friend if he's okay."

"Kelly?" She didn't mean for her voice to sound like a croaking bullfrog when she realized how frightened she had been that he might not live, or that she liked him.

"You're obviously worried about him," Julie said. "Go check on him in the morning."

"I will." The investigator's curiosity tugged on her. "Kelly has a genetic condition, he's completely hairless. What's that called?"

"Alopecia. Completely?" Julie asked, trying not to sound too motherly.

"Everything not hidden by his swim trunks, Julie. His head and face are smooth as a baby's butt, assuming baby butts have no hair."

"It could be genetic or autoimmune," Julie replied. "Ask him, I can't imagine they haven't tested him. Why?"

"Wondering if he might have other genetic conditions besides that. Like, why did he develop a blood clot in his lungs?"

"You said he was injured a while back. Fractured bones and immobilization can both cause blood clots. Was he taking a blood thinner after he got hurt?"

"I don't know."

"It's not unusual for several auto-immune or genetic conditions to exist simultaneously, but not always."

"Great." Only it was anything but.

"Sounds like you saved this guy's life. His mother ought to be a little more grateful," Julie added. "What if it had happened when you were at work? He may not have been able to call for help alone."

"I know. But his mom went out of her way not to talk to me."

"Honey, you don't realize it yet, but mothers are just that way," Julie told her. "Let us know about the holidays. He's welcome if you want to bring him."

CHAPTER 53
Sunday, November 15, 2009

"I owe you a huge apology, Amber. I was out of my mind about Kelly being in the hospital again, and I was snippy with you when none of this was your fault. He's my only child, and it doesn't matter how old he gets, he's still my baby. I swear, he worries me more now than when he was learning to ride his bicycle," Dr. Goldsmith said. "He was four, by the way."

The paramedic had been right, she explained. Kelly had a large clot in the left lower lobe. Because he had arrived so quickly, they took him to the cath lab for a percutaneous thrombectomy, where the lung vessels are accessed to deliver medication directly to the clot to dissolve it.

"I've worried for a long time something else might be wrong," she said.

"What do you mean, wrong?"

"Kelly's blood clot was not your fault. Alopecia is the most obvious of the anomalies, but he also has several other rare conditions. One leaves him lacking an anxiety effect, like the one you're having right now." She gave a motherly smile. "He also has a congenital anesthesia mutation, so his pain responses are dulled but not absent. Thus, he may not have sensed any difficulty before the clot became a critical condition."

"I've heard of the second one. What is the first one?" Amber asked.

"How's your human physiology?" she answered, laughing. "It's an absence of the fatty acid amide hydrolase, which breaks down anandamide. Lacking this, the anandamide level can become unusually high. It fits into the cerebral cannabinoid receptors, like the ones affected by THC in marijuana."

"Like he's permanently stoned?" Amber blurted without thinking.

"I guess that's a pretty close description. He says it's more like a runner's high. At any rate, he's doing well now, but he must stay on a stronger blood thinner." She studied Amber. "He asked if he could still stay with you, but I understand if you would rather not."

Amber's shoulders dropped in relief. "I didn't think, well, that either of you would want to do that. I figured as mad as you were, you'd fire me today. I'm flattered Kelly still wants to stay at my house, then."

"Amber, it would be ludicrously wrong and extremely stupid to base your employment on a favor I asked you. In the meantime, he'll be off work until two weeks after the anticoagulants are done."

"Not even restricted duty?"

"Nope. That ought to make him cranky. You still want him at your house?" she asked with a smile.

"Sure, I could use more excitement." Amber rolled her eyes. "Honestly, other than needing an ambulance last night, he's been a perfect guest. I'd be happy for him to stay as long as he needs."

"I'm glad to hear that."

"Does he have any other autoimmune conditions? I've read some are more commonly associated than others."

"We don't know the extent of them. He was born with a full head of jet-black hair that fell out when he was three. The alopecia has been permanent since. Doctors believe his clot came from the knee injury, not from something autoimmune, if that is fortunate."

"How is he, Dr. Goldsmith? I worried all night."

"He's okay. He'll be ready to discharge tomorrow unless they agree the orthopedic surgeon should do the total knee replacement now, before Kelly has to start the drugs, rather than starting and stopping for the surgery, then starting again."

"Now? How much longer will he be in the hospital for that?"

"Only an extra few days," Dr. Goldsmith said. "Are you sure it's okay he stays with you?"

"I am. He can keep using the pool for therapy."

"He told me it's been a big help with his femur. That takes a load off my mind. Go see him. I was headed for a cup of coffee." She turned but stopped. "Amber, thank you for saving my son."

Amber nodded and smiled as she walked away.

In the ICU, she knocked softly on the glass door.

Kelly waved for her to enter. "I'm glad you got past Mom," he said, maybe kidding, she wasn't sure.

"She's better now that she knows you're going to be okay. She was scared for you."

"Like a lioness, I'm sure," he replied. "What about you?"

"I'm okay."

"No, I mean, were you scared?"

"Nah, you're too damned stubborn to die. I figured you just wanted to spend another month at my house to use the pool."

"Can I?"

"I'll think about it. You're kinda needy."

"But I can cook," he countered.

"That's one point in your favor. But I did have to clean up the blood all over my floor last night."

He smiled.

"What?" she asked, stepping back to sit in the room's single chair.

"Any other points I've earned?"

"You don't leave hair in the pool. That's a big plus."

Kelly laughed, making the heart monitor beep at the motion artifact. "You don't feel sorry for me. I like that about you."

"That's another point."

"That I like you?"

"No, that you like that I don't pity you. I worried I was supposed to, and that wasn't going to happen."

He took her hand. Only the ICU noises broke the silence between them until he spoke.

"I was scared, Amber. I've never been so afraid of dying before."

"All I could do was hold your hand," she said.

"Holding my hand meant everything to me."

CHAPTER 54
Sunday, November 15, 2009

"Mom, I *want* to help Amber," Mackenzie argued over dinner.

"Mac, it's ugly work. And it's so soon after what happened to your father," Vanessa replied.

Mackenzie dropped her fork on the plate with her meatloaf and green beans. "You act like Dad getting killed was the only disaster in this family. How about what happened to me?" She extended her arms as if it would make her less invisible. "Amber helped save me!"

"No, it's not, but I can't stand the thought of losing you again. You're only eleven."

"Let me help her keep someone else's mother from going through what you did. I owe it to Dad to at least try."

"Amber may not want you to get involved," Vanessa tried again to sway her daughter, who had returned from South Texas with a stronger will than ever. Mackenzie might have been born eleven years ago, but she had matured a decade in the days she was gone.

"Can't we ask her? Please, Mom. There has to be something I can do to help."

Vanessa nodded her surrender, aware that she could not win.

"We should call her tonight after dinner," Mac said, cutting off a bite of meatloaf with her fork.

"How's school going?" her mother asked, trying to change the subject and address both her daughters.

"Weird. Like people don't know what to say to me, so I get these super-friendly hello's or waves, but no one talks to me." She poked the green beans into parallel lines. "Even the teachers don't ask me questions or expect me to do my homework."

For the first time, Neela spoke. "Me either. Like I'm fragile, and everyone's afraid of breaking me."

"I'm sorry," their mother said, tears pooling in her eyes. "People treat me like that, too. I guess no one knows what to say."

"Don't they realize they make it harder?"

"And, like, no one comes to see us now. Funeral, then, poof! The Houdini Disappearing Act," Mac said.

They finished eating in silence, except for Calista, who babbled grand narration to her dinner.

When Vanessa finally reached for plates, Neela replied, "I'll get the dishes. You two call Amber."

Mackenzie grinned and pulled a piece of paper from her pocket. "I wrote down her number."

After taking a deep breath, Vanessa nodded.

Mac pulled out the cell phone that had been Neela's and her mom's before that, dialing without looking at the paper.

She hit send, then put the phone on speaker mode.

"Hello," Amber answered on the third ring.

"Amber, it's Mackenzie."

"Hey! How's everything going?"

"It's kinda strange, like we're expected to go back to normal."

"Hello, Amber, it's Vanessa, too."

"I'm happy to hear from you both."

Vanessa took the lead. "Mac would like to discuss helping with the project you and Paul were working on."

"Are you sure, Mac? It's really awful sometimes."

"I want to keep what happened to me from happening to someone else," she replied. "I know I could help."

"Sounds like you've put a lot of thought into it. What do you think, Vanessa?"

"I don't think I can change her mind. We've been arguing all weekend. I don't want to expose her to those nasty people, but she's got more experience now than most people who are fighting the perverts."

"That's true. Let me talk to Kelly about it and see what we can come up with. He's back in the hospital right now."

"Is he okay?" Vanessa and Mackenzie asked in unison.

"He had a blood clot in his lung. While he's here, they want to do his knee replacement, too," Amber explained. "He won't be back on duty for a while, so we'll have time to work something out. I'll get back to you in a few days."

"You aren't just saying that, are you? Do you really want me to help?"

"Mackenzie, your mother is right. It's revolting, but you understand it. I'd be happy to have your help to catch these monsters."

They said their goodbyes.

Mac beamed. "See?"

***

When Amber disconnected, she looked at Kelly, lying in the hospital bed.

"You can't let her see that shit," he said. "I'm almost 29, and I don't like to see it."

"Me either, but I think I understand why she wants to do it. She wants to have some control over it. To fix something she knows is wrong."

"That doesn't make it the right thing to do, Amber," he said then yawned. "She's a kid."

"She's a kid who has experienced first-hand what we're fighting. That's more than either of us can say. Paul told us how thrilled she was to teach me how to look and act like a kid online."

"I'm not sure Paul would think letting her close again is safe." He reached but couldn't touch the glass of water, so she scooted it closer for him.

"I'll go by in a few days and see what's really on her mind."

"You have such a good heart," he said, closing his eyes and drifting to sleep.

CHAPTER 55
Monday, November 16, 2009

"Son of a bitch!" Amber growled, tapping keys as fast as her fingers would move. Aggravated none of the files she'd tried to open today were readable.

The forty or so files she'd decrypted in the previous weeks had standard commercial encryption that only required her to figure out which program to use, hardly even a challenge. There were no more files saved in typical user folders. Each had been a piece to a jigsaw puzzle of child endangerment that felt like sand in her boots: the longer she walked, the deeper the skin rubbed raw.

Now she faced an unpleasant realization that the haystack of files where she searched for a needle wasn't a single bale but a whole field of them.

She'd found one similarly named file to one she had already opened, buried in a system program folder. One file might have been an accident, a drag and drop mistake, just like her finding it. But hidden files throughout the other thousands of system and program files might mean that the first files she'd found and decrypted were decoys.

That alone would make it necessary to go through every single folder and its subfolders, but at least one clue would be the date of creation.

The first hidden file she opened was a mix of letters and numbers with no obvious meaning to her. Not encrypted. Converted to a number-equivalent system. To be sure, she compared the text to several less-common programming or compiler languages without success. Nor was the text binary, which would yield only 0's and 1's. On closer scrutiny, the text was random numbers and, yep, letters only A through F.

That made the file contents hexadecimal.

Most English-speaking math uses a base of ten: **0, 1, 2, 3, 4, 5, 6, 7, 8, 9**, then starting over at **10** with a pair of digits, **100** with three digits, etc. The hexadecimal numbering system uses a base of 16, represented by the numbers 0 through 9 and the letters A through F. While using hex for numbers less than 100 doesn't reduce the number of characters, computers and other large digital systems use huge strings of binary numbers 0 and 1, which are difficult for humans to read and write without errors. Hex allows those to be written in a much shorter format than binary.

Amber searched until she found another file hidden where it shouldn't be. She found the same jumble of numerical and alphabetical characters that did not convert from hex to text.

She mumbled another string of profanity before realizing she was speaking out loud, looking around to make sure no one heard her.

Recalling a vague memory, a college professor had mentioned an encryption method he'd seen that worked by altering hexadecimal values with a simple search and replace. If you didn't know which characters had been replaced and with what, one failed trial could render the file irreversibly unusable. It wasn't uncrackable, but it had to have the substitutions undone correctly in the opposite order in which they were done.

The story seemed anecdotal at the time, and Amber hadn't tried to understand its importance.

She entered a string of numerals into the conversion program as **1234567890**, ten digits like a phone number would be. When she converted it to the hex format, it became **31323334353637383930**, exactly twice as many digits now. Simple enough, 3 preceded each original numeral in hex: 31. 32. 33. 34, etc.

Hex could also be used for text, so she entered: **The quick brown fox jumped over the lazy dogs.** This became the string:

54686520717569636b2062726f776e20666f78206a756d706564206f76657
220746865206c617a7920646f67732e

In hex, 16 characters could be used as a single digit or a pair, and pairs went no higher than the 70's. Therefore, if you didn't know what the text was, the first few digits of the string could have several options:

She took the first segment, knowing that the conversion was only letters:

54686520717569636b2062726f

In hex, each character could be a single digit or a pair, so taking just the first two characters: **5** could be *enquiry* and **4** *end of transmission*, which didn't make sense, or **54** could be the letter *T*.

54 68 65 20 71 75 69 63 6b 20 62 72 6f which equaled

```
The()quick()bro
```

Although it uses six letters, the conversion created both uppercase and lowercase letters, spaces and other characters for a total of 255 functions, 16 x 16, minus the 00 set. There is no number 20 as numbers are converted individually as two and zero, but in the table, 20 equaled a space in the text.

She made several copies of the file in case an attempt to unlock it made it worse.

She booted a converter program, typed part of the 23rd Psalms, the first lengthy quote that came to mind.

The LORD is my shepherd; I shall not want. He maketh me to lie down in green pastures: he leadeth me beside the still waters. He restoreth my soul: he leadeth me in the paths of righteousness for his name's sake.

Converted to hex:

546865204c4f5244206973206d79207368657068657264b2049207368
616c6c206e6f742077616e742e204865206d616b657468206d6520746f206
c696520646f776e20696e20677265656e2070617374757265733a20686520
6c656164657468206d6520626573696465207468652073746c6c2077617
46572732e2048652072657374746f72657468206d7920736f756c3a20686520
6c656164657468206d6520696e207468652070617468732036f66207269967
874656f75736e65737320666f7220686973206e616d6527732073616b652e

She made two substitutions, changing 6c6 to 4c857d21, and 8650 to 056b84a1

That became a jumbled but partially decipherable passage when changed back to text.

T`V◆JLORD is my shepherd; I shaL◆}!◆◆◆Bv◆B◆k◆◆◆◆WF◆◆RF◆◆g◆e down in green pastures: `V◆JL◆}!FWF◆◆R&W6◆FRFk◆◆7F◆◆g◆waters. @V◆Jrestoreth my soul: `V◆JL◆}!VFWF◆◆R◆◆Fk◆◆F◆2◆b&◆v◆FV◆W6◆W72f◆ "◆◆2◆◆Rw26◆R◆

Thirteen words remained in plain English and a few incomplete words, but there were too many characters that could not be reversed back to text as it was: these were the black diamond question marks.

Amber sat back, interlaced her fingers, and stretched her arms over her head, staring at the monitor screen. "How would you do it?" she said out loud.

"Do what?" Debby said, walking by.

Not answering with a snotty remark, although it came to mind, Amber decided that talking through her dilemma to someone who wasn't a computer nerd might be helpful.

"Got a minute?" she asked.

"Yeah, I guess," the other woman said, wondering what she'd stuck her nose in.

"I've been working on a laptop."

Debby pulled the rolling chair from the next cubicle over and sat down.

"Does it make sense to you to convert a file of some sort to hexadecimal — "

"Stop, you lost me after convert. I don't know anything about programming or encryption."

"That's a bonus," Amber said. She showed her the simple phone number change from 1234567890, how substituting one number failed, and how a pair or triple might not exist often enough to encrypt the list.

"First, how do you know what you have is phone numbers?" she asked.

"Every number is preceded by a 3. No letters in the original file."

"Why not just add numbers in the regular file?" Debby asked.

"You mean encrypt the text before you convert it instead of after?"

"I don't know what I meant, but it makes sense to alter what you can read first."

"Fair point." Amber scratched her chin. "Still, the user has to have a way to keep these substitutions straight."

"If all you are doing is number substitutions, why not put it in the file name?" Debby asked, leaving Amber's mind spinning with possibilities.

CHAPTER 56
Monday, November 16, 2009

"I told you to go pack, Blaine," she said when she found him sitting at his computer in his room. "I'd like to be on the road in half an hour."

"Why do we have to go?" he said without looking away from the monitor, where he manipulated a soldier shooting zombies in the digital streets of a war zone.

"Someone is threatening me, because of my job," she lied. "The police think it would be a good idea if we left town for a week."

"What about school?" he said in a voice that cracked.

"When have you ever cared that you'd miss school? I'll call your teacher and ask her to send your lessons, so you don't fall behind."

"That's crap, Mom!"

"One." She paused. "Two." She'd never reached a three with him, a bluff she didn't know how long she'd continue to have. He was too big to spank, and other than grounding him from his computer, she wasn't sure what else to do.

"All right, geez," he said, reaching to turn off the game. "You gonna tell your boyfriend where we're going so you can sneak off and — "

"Blaine Michael! I will not have you speak to me like that. Get your things packed or you'll do without."

He stood and faced her. "You do, though. You think I don't notice you aren't home some nights." When her face glowed crimson, he softened his voice. "I'm not a little kid anymore, so you don't have to keep secrets."

"What I do is none of your business," she said, just like her father would have said it, but she realized immediately it was the wrong thing.

"But it is my business, Mom. If someone else is going to be part of our family, at least show me the respect of meeting him."

"Blaine," she said, also ratcheting down her anger. "We can talk about this in the car, but it's really important right now that we — you and me — that we get going."

He nodded, but Dierdra couldn't help but see his father's posture when he turned and went to his closet.

"Can you at least tell me if I need winter clothes?"

"Probably," she said. "You never can tell what the weather will do in November."

The doorbell rang twice in rapid succession.

She hurried out of Blaine's room and closed the door behind her.

When she got to the kitchen, she looked out the window, relieved to see the lightbar of a patrol car above the shrubs that shielded her driveway.

The doorbell rang again, followed by a loud knock.

"I'm coming!" she yelled, her heels clicking as the flooring transitioned from the kitchen linoleum to the hardwood in the living room. In ten more steps, she reached the door, unlocked the deadbolt, and jerked it open.

She had been expecting Harper Sullivan.

Instead, she stood face to face with Stephen Royce, in full uniform. Dierdra was speechless.

"Ms. Preston, I'll need you to come with me." He pronounced her name in sarcastic elongated syllables like a snake: Mizzzzz Presssston.

Her brain was setting off expletives like cheap fireworks. "Ste — " she stammered. "I mean, excuse me, Officer?"

"That's *Captain* Royce, Ma'am. I need you to answer some questions about a criminal case you intend to prosecute. We have some questions for you to answer."

"Now is not a good time, *Captain*," she said, trying to hide her panic in similar sarcasm.

"And why is that, Ms. Preston? Are you *going* somewhere?" he said, pointing to a suitcase in the hallway behind her.

"Yes, we are," she said. "Blaine's father, he called to tell me his mother has had a heart attack. Grant says it's bad, so I'm taking Blaine to see her."

"Mom?" her son called from the hallway, much closer than she'd wanted him to be. "I'm packed. We need to get to the airport."

She turned to see him dragging a bag that had seen better trips. She had said nothing about where they were going, so how would Blaine have . . .

"Oh, sorry, I didn't know anyone was here," Blaine continued as he came to stand beside her at the door.

"Blaine's right. We've got to get going. I'll let you know when we return to town," she said, following her son's lead.

Stephen Royce looked at Blaine, frowning. A vein stood out on his temple. "That will be fine, Ms. Preston. Have a safe trip."

"Thank you."

She held her breath as she watched him turn and step off the porch, take a few steps then turn back to her, eyebrows furrowed in anger.

He got into his car and backed out of the drive before Dierdra exhaled.

"Mom, are you okay?"

"I am now, Blaine. Let's go. I have a lot of explaining to do."

CHAPTER 57
Monday, November 16, 2009

Harper watched the silver sedan pull into the service alley of the mechanic's shop. The rubber-chirping stop was an abrupt end to what had been a sharp corner and gravel-sliding approach, he thought, wondering why she was in such a hurry.

Strickland was already closing the overhead door behind her as planned.

The look on her face through the window told Harper she was upset, and he was reaching to open the door for her when she nearly knocked him down with it.

"I'm sorry, Harper," she said, trying to get her oversize tote under control. "Stephen came to the house. In uniform. Saying I needed to go with him!" Her voice got louder and higher with each word. "I told him Blaine's grandmother was dying, that I was taking him there. I shouldn't have said that. Now he'll — "

Harper tried to interrupt, but she kept going as she climbed out of the car.

"I mean, Blaine's grandmother isn't sick, and that wouldn't be hard to — "

Putting his hands on her shoulders, he finally squeezed hard enough to stop her panicked monologue.

"Calm. Down." He looked her in the eye until she closed her mouth, swallowed, and then took a breath. "If you don't go to Grant's, it's not a big deal. We've got a different car for you, and you can go anywhere you'd feel safe."

"I don't *know* where else to go," she said, voice quivering on the verge of a tearful breakdown.

"You and Blaine get your stuff moved to the other vehicle," he said, pointing to a beige nondescript SUV. "Let me make a call and see if I can help find a place that I have connections who can help you. Is that okay?"

She inhaled, held it longer than Harper thought possible, then sighed and nodded.

He pulled his cell phone from his pocket and dialed. No answer, so he dialed another number.

Blaine watched from the backseat of his mom's car as he rearranged stuff into a backpack to make it all fit.

"Hey, it's Harper Sullivan. Yeah, doing okay. You?" There was a long pause as he walked away, listening to the other party, then coming back before he spoke again. "I have a friend in need of a safe place. No, wait," he stopped. "Amber, I'm asking if you can meet with her and her son and help them find somewhere comfortable. I *did call* Brady, and that's where I think they should go, but he didn't answer. I want her to have a . . . yes, I understand. Great. I'll tell them," he said, writing an address on a scratch paper from Strickland's counter, then reading her a phone number. "Got it. What? Maybe four hours. After dark, anyway. Thanks! I owe you one."

Blaine stood when Harper pocketed his phone. "Who is she?"

Harper motioned him toward where his mother was putting stuff in the back of the SUV. "Amber Samualson is a Tarrant County Deputy. I recently met her while I was helping a friend when his coworker . . . geez, it's a long story that doesn't help. I can't reach Brady, my best friend, but Amber is going to meet you if I can't reach him tonight."

"You don't have to go to all this trouble," she began, but the timbre of her voice said she was grateful.

"It's not trouble. It's security. Leave your cell phones off." He squinted, remembering what Brady had told him about phones. "No, on second thought, take the batteries out now. Do not use them unless it's an emergency or until we've cleared this up. I have an unregistered phone for you. Amber's number is in the directory, as is Brady's and mine."

"You really think — " Dierdra stopped, then nodded.

"Yes, I think it's the right thing to do. Here's a road map, and directions to a truck stop where you'll meet Amber. You can follow her from there. She'll expect you around eight o'clock. If you get delayed, give her a call. She's a tough kid, Dierdra. Rock-solid. I've known her father for years."

"Blaine, you ready?" she asked, only to find him sitting in the front seat waiting on her. "Guess so. Thank you."

"Be careful."

She hesitated.

"I've had someone following Royce for the last hour, since he entered Benton County. He's back in Marshal County, so get going."

CHAPTER 58
Monday, November 16, 2009

The doctors had finally agreed that Elizabeth wasn't in critical condition as originally thought, but that a case of flu had triggered dehydration, culminating in her fainting when she got into the bathroom. When she fell, she hit her head on the edge of the tub and suffered a deep laceration to her upper forehead, which had bled significantly. Together with a mild concussion, she was incoherent when Brady found her.

"Brady, I'm really okay," Elizabeth told him as he sat beside her in a hospital room. "Go check on the kids."

"The kids are fine with Sandy." He wrapped his hand back around hers. "I'm not leaving you tonight."

He didn't have to act tough for her. Scared was drawn all over his face, but he didn't want to fall apart, either.

Elizabeth Cayson held his whole life together every day. Despite pregnancy difficulties, she'd brought three beautiful, smart children into their lives, doubling their love with every delivery. She fed and clothed them, taught them the finer skills of living that schools didn't touch, like how to write a budget, or the difference between cooking and making a sumptuous meal. And she provided them an example of how to be a good person, what love and forgiveness meant, and how to find the strength to take the next breath when it had been knocked out of them by fate or fight.

No other woman in the world could deal with Brady's chaos or mold it into charm. He would do anything for her because she was everything to him.

"What are you thinking," she asked.

"I was thinking that I don't buy you flowers often enough," he replied.

"Don't waste money on flowers," she said. "I could use a new vacuum cleaner."

"That's something you need. You deserve things that don't make you work. Things you want."

"I *wanted* to not come to the hospital," she said with a smile, "but that didn't work out for me, did it?"

"You're not supposed to be in a bloody heap on the bathroom floor. We've been over this before. That's *my* job."

True. He had been working on the plumbing under the bathroom sink when the cold-water line sprang a leak and sprayed his face. In the involuntary jerk, he'd bashed his head against the drain, cutting his head. That wasn't so bad, but when he wiggled free and got to his feet, he saw the blood running down his forehead in the mirror and passed out cold.

Elizabeth had heard him hit the floor upstairs and found him, sitting up, eyes squeezed shut, retching over the toilet.

His laceration wasn't as bad as hers, but he couldn't stand the sight of blood.

Well, most people's blood was fine. He didn't *like* seeing theirs. He fainted straight away when he saw his own. First, he fainted, then he puked. He'd proven his propensity to repeat this regimen several times throughout their relationship, starting on their first date when he opened the car door for her, then slammed it on his left thumb. Had she not opened the door before he passed out, some poor passerby would have found him, dangling by a bloody digit.

Elizabeth watched him rub his left hand against his pants, figuring that was going through his mind.

"If you stay, you'll get sick, too," she prodded. "Stress and sleep loss depress your immunity. Go home. Get a good night's rest."

"I never sleep when you're not next to me," he said, perfectly okay with how mushy that sounded. "And I had this ugly GI thing a week ago, so I'm safe."

"It was you! Thanks for sharing," she mumbled. "Please, Brady. Go home. I won't rest if you're breaking your neck in that chair all night."

He sighed. "I guess one of us should get some sleep then. If you're sure."

"Positive. And bring me a bagel for breakfast. You know, sesame seeds and — "

"Bacon and cheese," they finished together.

"And some clean clothes in case I get to go home."

CHAPTER 59
Monday, November 16, 2009

"Harper?" his daughter's lilting voice greeted him by name, which irritated him.

"I'm your father," he replied. "The least you can do — "

"Fine. *Dad*." The lilt was crushed by a mechanical sound. "I can't believe you called and upset my grandparents like that."

"Meredith, I called to speak to you. I had no intentions of upsetting them, but I love you and that entitles me to worry about you."

"Don't bother."

"If you're mad at me, you might as well say what's on your mind. What have or haven't I done this week for you?"

"This week? Geez, *Dad*! Ever since Mom died, you've acted like you're the only one who was hurt. Maybe if you weren't working 80 hours a week, you'd have been home to protect her! But then you began working more, so I was all alone. You couldn't be bothered then to do anything for me."

He took a breath to calm down so he could answer without screaming, wanting to list the things he *had* done for her. "You're right, and I'm sorry." When she didn't reply, he kept going. "I did work a lot before she died. And I worked more after. I didn't know how to help you, but I'm sorry I wasn't there enough to try harder."

The apology took her by surprise.

"When you wanted to go to your grandparents'," he continued, "I figured that was the best thing for you." He knew it wasn't worth arguing over how she ended up in Florida, that the decision to go had been hers, not his.

"It's a fricking geriatric ward now, Dad. I hate Florida."

"Then come home. Finish high school, get ready for college. I miss you."

She didn't bite, but she hadn't hung up on him, either.

"Why did you call the other day? What was so important?" she asked.

"Remember Brady? One of my friends from school? A guy he worked with was kidnapped from a mall. He was killed so they could take his daughter and several other young girls to Mexico *to sell them* for God-knows-what. I wanted to tell you to be careful. These monsters are everywhere."

He could hear her breathe.

"Okay, Dad. Thanks. I'll be careful." She paused. "And I'll think about coming back over Christmas, okay?"

"Absolutely okay. I'm sorry, Meredith. I wish we'd had this talk a long time ago."

"Yeah. Me, too. The grands are back. I better go. Wouldn't want another old-person-splattering-the-ceiling fit."

And she hung up.

"I love you, too, Meredith," he said to the phone.

Not a win for his side. Not yet. But it was a big score.

CHAPTER 60
Monday, November 16, 2009

"Hey, Dad!" Amber said as she was rolling the upright vacuum back to its place in a closet.

Kelly's apartment hadn't just been unused for weeks, it was bachelor-unkempt to start with, but fortunately not gross. In the last hour, she had pulled the sheets from his king-sized bed and found sheets for the daybed in the other room for one load of laundry and still had a load of towels to do because there weren't any clean, loaded the dishwasher with dishes stacked in and beside the sink, swept the kitchen and bathroom, and vacuumed.

I'll add this to the bill that somebody better pay! she'd thought more than once. *I don't have to work this damned hard at my own house.*

"Sorry I missed your call. I'm headed from Killeen back to Albuquerque tomorrow and thought maybe I could stop for lunch or supper on my way through," he said.

Amber crumpled into a fluffy chair. "I thought you were in D.C. I'd love that, but I think that supper would work better. I'll meet you at the house. You can let yourself in, take a nap, a swim, a shower. Then you can take me out to eat, stay the night."

Which meant another load of laundry when she got home.

"Sounds great. Did you need something the other night when you called?" he asked.

"No, I just wanted to talk. I've been working on a child predator team, and it's mind-blowing how evil people can be."

"That's no exaggeration. Are you okay?"

"Not so much. One of the team and his daughter were kidnapped by someone who traffics for a living, murdered Paul. We got his daughter and fifteen other girls back. I've concluded that the result is worth the ugliness," she said, "but it's like shoveling manure being the price you pay for steak."

"A criminal who targets children is the very worst. I hope there's a special circle of Hell reserved for them to endure everything bad they've ever done, repeatedly, for eternity."

"Me, too." She checked her watch. "I've gotta get going, but I'd like you to meet someone tomorrow while you're in town. Can you stay one more day?"

"Sure, but I don't want to impose if you already have company," Zach told her.

"Not now, but I have had. It's a long story I'll tell you over that steak."

"Would you rather I grilled?" he offered.

"I would rather, but I'd rather someone else wash the dishes," she kidded. "See ya around five. I love you!"

She pushed the button to disconnect and took another breath, but when she leaned forward to stand up, she glimpsed a sheet of paper under the television stand across the room.

Afraid it was something from his research into local kid predatory cases that neither Dierdra nor her son should see, she went to pull it out, only to find it was a picture.

The color image made her stomach churn, but it wasn't anything from Kelly's work.

It was an 8x10 picture of him and a woman, posed beside a beautiful little girl in a swing. Signed in the corner, "To my girls: All my love forever, Kelly."

CHAPTER 61
Monday, November 16, 2009

Following the directions Harper had given her, Dierdra had no trouble finding the travel station or the woman she was to meet. She found the vehicle Harper had described, parked away from the pumps and building at a typical truck stop and mega-convenience store on the outskirts of the city. Standing beside the driver's door was a woman wearing a snug long-sleeve shirt with reflective stripes on the arms and dark pants.

As soon as she parked nose to nose with the woman's car, Blaine bolted out the passenger door, headed for a restroom. First Dierdra had to find the cabin lights, then she had to look for the ignition of the strange vehicle.

By the time she stepped out, her hips and back slow to stretch, the younger woman came to the driver's side of her car.

"I'm Amber Samualson," she said, extending her hand, "Harper's second choice for hosting your stay."

Dierdra shook hands, noting that Amber stood at least six inches taller. "Dierdra Preston. I guess my son had passed the point of courtesy some miles back when I wouldn't stop. Honestly, I could use the facilities, too, but I'm too old to run," she said. "I apologize for being late. Traffic was heavier than I expected."

"Not a problem." Amber motioned toward the storefront where Blaine had disappeared moments before. "Harper and I agreed on an apartment of a friend who has been recovering from a leg injury, so it's been unused six weeks," she explained as they walked toward the building, too. "I had to do a little housekeeping. You know how men like to live, I'm sure."

"I don't mean to sound ungrateful, but are you sure it's safe?"

"Kelly and I are both Tarrant County Deputies," Amber replied. "The lease was in his mother's maiden name, so Kelly asked them to keep it for his protection as a cop. Making a connection from Harper to me to Bonnie and then to Kelly would be an astronomically wild guess. And it's gated."

"I'm sorry to imply that it's not secure," she said. "I don't mean to cause any trouble."

"Harper told me everything about the crash and how he thinks the ex-husband sabotaged the car, so I agree that it's only prudent to make sure you and your son are safe until he gets enough proof for an arrest."

"I guess he told you I am the ex-husband's supposed alibi?" Dierdra asked.

"That doesn't matter to me except that this guy has a nasty attitude about women who cross him. We'll keep you safe."

Inside, Dierdra introduced Blaine to Amber, then excused herself to the restroom.

"How was the ride?" Amber asked.

"Okay, I guess. This is really creepy. The cop Mom's been dating stopped by the house today and tried to get her to go with him, like she didn't have a choice," he said. "I guess he didn't think I was home, but I heard Mom telling him she was taking me to see Dad's mom, so I knew something was wrong."

Amber's head tilted as she processed the additional information, but Blaine interpreted it as her question about why he recognized it as trouble.

"Grandma Preston's been dead for most of my life," he explained. "I came out from my bedroom and told her we needed to get going to the airport."

"I see. Good thinking."

"He looked mad, like a rabid badger or something. And I could tell it scared Mom, but don't tell her I told you, okay? I don't want her to worry more."

Amber nodded as she saw Dierdra come out from the hallway where the restrooms were.

"Shall we get you on to your temporary quarters?" she asked, leading them back outside toward their cars.

Dierdra followed Amber's taillights closely until they got to the gated entry of the complex, and she waited while the deputy talked to the guard, who then walked back to Dierdra's vehicle.

He was a tall bulky man in his fifties, she guessed. He was professional and polite, but a significant enough mass to deter most problems.

"Ma'am?" he said, leaning to look in the driver's window and offering her an envelope. "Miss Samualson says you'll be staying for a week or two in Mr. Morgan's condo. I wanted to give you a quick overview of security, because it is meant to be strict. Here are the rules for the clubhouse, pool, and the gate. I've included a magnetic key card in case the guard is away for an emergency, you can still get in. You'll see when Miss Samualson goes in, the gate is a trap gate, so you tap the card on this side and in the middle. This also keeps someone from following you in."

"I appreciate that," she said, feeling a bit overwhelmed but liking it.

"The emergency number is on the card and the handout. We have the phone numbers to contact you if you have any visitors besides Deputy Samualson. I assure you that no one enters without clearance, and no one specifically for you unless you authorize it."

"Is this the only entrance?"

"A service entrance leads to the back of the clubhouse only," he said, pointing around to the left. "Entry is accessible by contracted vendors only, who must have a keycard and be verified on video, but the drive ends at the building. Residential traffic comes in exclusively through this gate, which is also video recorded. If this gate gets broken or the exit lanes, which are spiked, are compromised, we're armed and about four minutes from police response. Around the complex is a twelve-foot fence, either brick or steel."

"Thank you for explaining everything. I feel much better knowing about the security."

"My pleasure, Ma'am. Call anytime."

He went back to the brick office and closed the door before the gate began to operate.

"Do you really think he'd hurt you?" Blaine said casually, like the question hadn't been on his mind for the last four hours or more.

"Yeah, maybe," she said, trying to sound as nonchalant as he did. "But I'm more concerned he might try to hurt you."

CHAPTER 62
Monday, November 16, 2009

Blaine carried his and his mom's suitcases up the two flights of stairs to the bedrooms after Amber showed her the ground-level garage and got her parked.

"When you said a third-story apartment, I thought it was all on the third floor," Dierdra said, putting down her tote. "This is a condo."

"Earlier today was the first time I'd been here, so I was going off what Kelly had told me. Surprised me, too."

"You said he'd been injured?" Dierdra said, lowering her voice. "Was he shot?"

Amber smiled. "He's a crash investigator. He was working a big wreck on the freeway when a teenage driver plowed through it, hitting him. In his specialty, that must be the equivalent of being shot. He's in now for a knee replacement, which means more rehab and no stairs for a while yet."

Dierdra nodded, looking around.

"You should have most everything you'll need. Television is on satellite, but I saw he has a shelf full of DVDs. Feel free to eat or drink anything you find. I brought over a few days' groceries, the basics — milk, bread, coffee."

"Coffee? That's perfect!" Dierdra said, melting into the sofa. "What a day. Thank you."

"Mom! There's a sweet gaming system upstairs in the second bedroom!" Blaine yelled as he was coming down the stairs two at a time. "Maybe he'll let me play?"

Amber looked at Dierdra and shrugged. "I'll ask him tomorrow."

"He has a kid? I thought you said he was going in for a knee replacement. How old is he?" Dierdra asked.

Amber glanced back at the television stand where she'd found the photograph, not knowing if her answer was the truth. "The knee is from the accident, not his age, so apparently he's still young enough for video games."

She'd washed the sheets and made the bed in that room, too, but she hadn't paid attention to the computer set up, though she remembered her mental note to ask him about it. Her job involved computers, but he appeared to have a more elaborate system than she did. Hardware jealousy had been trampled by the rage she'd felt about the picture.

She blinked hard to refocus. "I'll let you get settled. I left directions to a nearby grocery store on the table. My father's going to be in town tomorrow evening if you'd like to join us for dinner."

"Oh, no, I wouldn't think of interfering with your family plans."

"I'll get Kelly to make a list of places of interest. Just because you're in Fort Worth doesn't mean you have to stay inside all the time."

"Amber, I appreciate you helping me. Helping us," she said when her son plopped onto the other end of the sofa.

"Happy to lend a hand. You have my number if you need anything." She turned toward the door but stopped when she put her hand in her pocket. "Guess you'll need these," she said, pulling out a keyring and the garage door opener.

CHAPTER 63
Tuesday, November 17, 2009

"We'll get you back to your room in a bit," the nurse in recovery told him, giving him a spoonful of ice chips. "Any pain?"

Kelly shook his head, which made the room waver slightly. He hated feeling he couldn't trust his senses.

"Your mother's out in the waiting room. Shall I bring her back?"

"Not yet," he replied. "I'm a little nauseated."

"No more ice for a bit then. I'll get you something for it."

"No. No more drugs," he insisted. "Let me close my eyes for a few minutes. I'll be okay."

She nodded and turned the overhead light in the little room off, leaving him in the curtain's shadow from the hall lights. "I'll get you a cool cloth."

Kelly closed his eyes, hoping sensory inputs would settle down. The nurse, a redhead. He couldn't remember her name. She was pretty. And attentive. Too attentive, even to a cop, he thought. He wasn't interested in starting another relationship with a nurse. The last one had smashed his heart to atoms.

Dammit! Leah was a ghost he couldn't escape.

Or maybe it wasn't her, but Aspen, her audacious daughter. A memory he refused to let go of.

The thought of the bouncy four-year-old with blond curls and big blue eyes, wise beyond her age. made his own eyes teary, even when closed. No matter what, Aspen would always have a big place in his heart.

Why? Why did he have to lose her? Anger surged through his gut, stirring the nausea.

"Here you go, Kelly," the nurse said as she came through the curtain, startling him with a blinding flash of light.

While his brain intended to loose a string of profanity at her, his body instead performed a set of improper functions simultaneously. His blood pressure dropped low enough he almost lost consciousness; he vomited thin yellowish bile, though there wasn't much in his stomach; and a thundering pain ripped through his back and legs.

The nurse, experienced enough to recognize something was wrong, took a step back into the hall and yelled for help. His heart hadn't stopped, but she'd need more hands to prevent that from happening.

CHAPTER 64
Tuesday, November 17, 2009

She knocked on his office door, waiting for him to look up. "Brady? Have you got a minute?"

"Sure. How're you doing?" He stood and waved her into a chair.

"I'm okay. Kelly's back in the hospital with a blood clot. They're doing his knee replacement while he's there."

"He's kinda young for that," Brady replied.

"He said it was really messed up in that crash. I think we all aged a decade in the last few weeks. That's sorta why I wanted to see you. Paul's daughter called me last evening. She and Vanessa together. Mac wants to help with what he had been doing. Legally, there's nothing she can do as far as our actions."

"Ahh, that's a tough one." He cleared his throat. "I don't know. Why does she want to do it?"

"Mac says she owes it to Paul, according to what Vanessa said this morning. She wanted to talk to me, to give her honest opinion without hurting Mac's feelings. Van is against it, only because of the magnitude of evil Paul'd told her about."

"I can't think of a word that describes how evil someone has to be to hurt or steal and sell a child. Most people don't want to think it exists, other than what you hear on the news occasionally about priests or teachers . . ." He let that thought go. "I worry a lot more about my kids now."

"I want to find something she can do to help without being face to face with this muck. I don't want to say no, but I can't see anything she can do."

"Maybe she needs to be your poster-child for public education, not a warrior."

CHAPTER 65
Tuesday, November 17, 2009

"Mom, I'd like to talk about what's going on," Blaine said as he sat at the kitchen table while she heated soup she found in the pantry.

"It's nothing for you to wor — " she replied without turning to face him.

"See? I knew you were gonna say that, but it's bullshit."

"Blaine!"

"See? That's not the truth, and you ought to know that I figured that out by now. What's happening affects me, too, or I wouldn't be here. That cop came to the house, but it wasn't police business, was it?"

She had been hoping he was oblivious to the threats, but Royce's stunt at the house had popped the balloon of childhood innocence, if nothing else.

"You're right. This affects you, and you deserve to know the truth." She turned the heat down on the stove and sat down. "The police officer who came to the house is Stephen Royce. Our jobs have crossed several times, and we've been seeing each other for a while, but we had no intentions of getting married."

"He's a jerk."

"Save your assessments for the rest of the story," she said with a half-smile. "He's divorced from a nurse who died in the hospital after a really bad car crash. The other cop you met when we traded cars, Harper Sullivan, is investigating the crash and believes someone sabotaged her car, causing the wreck. He suspects Royce, but because of the timing of the crash, well, he and I were together the night before the crash."

"Why is he so mad then?" Blaine asked. "If you were together, he couldn't have done it, right?"

"I'm not sure. We were in a hotel," she said, raising her eyebrows at her son to stop his reply about her behavior, "but he could have slipped something in the wine to make me sleep, and I know he took my car. I didn't wake until he came back to the room with breakfast."

"How can you prove it?"

"That's Sergeant Sullivan's job."

"He should check traffic cameras," the fan of crime shows announced.

CHAPTER 66
Tuesday, November 17, 2009

It would be a long day, she thought. Even after seeing Brady, yawns kept creeping up on her. She hadn't slept well the night before.

Thoughts of Kelly Morgan and the photo she'd found churned in her head long after she went to bed, then intruded into her dreams when she fell asleep. The woman in the picture appeared over and over, often laughing at her.

Kelly hadn't mentioned dating anyone when or since he came to stay in her house. That wasn't a romantic entanglement, at least to start with.

Was it now? What that woman why it hadn't become more serious?

Their time together had been pleasant. Meals, work, and one evening they'd debated being an actual date. She enjoyed spending time with him. He had a good feel for their work on the task force, even if she'd thought he wasn't much into computers.

He'd lied about that, too, she's thought, rolling over and punching her pillow.

Maybe he hadn't *lied* as much as not told her.

Why wouldn't she expect him to tell her things like that? He made a big production of unimportant things like wine.

By the time her alarm went off at 5:30, she felt like a muddy blanket dragged behind a sugar-rushed two-year-old for a week. What little sleep she'd gotten had been full of bad dreams.

She'd been stuck in a traffic jam for almost an hour on her way to Brady's office. Then on her way to work from there, she made an out-of-the-way stop at her favorite coffee shop for a giant cup of light roast with a liberal shot of sugar-free creamer, which settled into her stomach like battery acid.

Resisting the urge to pour the coffee down the drain when she finally got to work, she grabbed a protein bar from her locker, then went to her desk.

Several yellow message notes stuck to her blotter, a couple stuck on her monitor, perhaps indicating they were more urgent.

Buried under her stapler, written in Dr. Goldsmith's blocky backhand slant: K's surgery is this morning. Hope to see you after lunch?

Today's date.

She swiped up the square paper and crumpled it.

A color-printed ASCII conversion table lay next to her mouse. Trying to think how that encryption code might be hidden on the computer as well, she stifled a yawn that made her eyes water.

She believed Debby's suggestion that a simple character substitution made to a document's or spreadsheet's contents would be easier before than after conversion to hexadecimal format.

Digging through her hanging files, she found a folder, two inches of various reference papers of her work on this device, copies of originals kept with the working version of the laptop's hard drive. She thunked it on her desk and began flipping pages until she found a set of DVDs, one would have the list she wanted: The entire directory printout, over 180,000 files, sorted as a directory.

But Amber wanted to see how many individual files were named with numbers and what their dates of creation were. Finding them scattered throughout the drive would take too long. She booted the DVD and entered a DOS command to list all files with numbers in the name in numerical order, and then sent the request to print. Seventy pages sounded like a lot, but for roughly 2,000 files, she knew most were part of programs and ought to be easy to weed out.

After the first few pages had printed, she grabbed them and a highlighter, hoping to see a pattern and any outliers that might be encrypted files. But what she wanted to find was a relatively small text file that might be the key to correctly reversing the hex encryption. She highlighted those files she wished to take a second look at, eventually coming up with around 200.

Two hundred possible encrypted files on top of those she'd already decrypted. She hoped that the perverts involved didn't need that many files to hold all the information required to do their gruesome business.

As she skimmed the list, she found one ridiculously small file, 10 kilobytes, buried in a fifth-level folder by itself, named **2009_04_14.xls**

She opened it, revealing an unencrypted name and phone number: Monique Delacroix and a phone number with an Austin area code.

Couldn't be that easy, could it?

If she called the number from a work phone, it would appear to come from the sheriff's office. What the heck. She pulled out her cell phone and dialed.

This voice mailbox has not been set up and cannot accept messages.

At least it wasn't disconnected. She'd get the registration and account information later.

She went back to the list, but after a while, the text appeared to wobble on the page.

Moments passed before she recognized the throbbing headache accompanying her hunger. She'd lost track of time and worked through lunch. She fumbled open the drawer of her desk to get a tube of icing like Julie had shown her years ago. Three tries later, she got the twist-off safety seal off and squirted a stream of white cake frosting under her tongue. As it dissolved, she squeezed another teaspoon into her mouth.

Within a few minutes, the light-headedness decreased, and she dared to take a walk to the breakroom for a glass of orange juice she kept in the staff refrigerator. By the time she got there, her arms were trembling again, so she skipped looking for a cup or glass and turned the bottle up and guzzled a dozen gulps before moving to a chair to wait for the sugar to take full effect.

No question that it would screw up her blood sugar for the rest of the day. She'd have to be cautious with supper.

Supper!

She'd made plans with her father, who was probably already at the house.

She hurried back to her office and put all her work back into the evidence lockup, getting ready to go home.

Her cell phone rang in her pocket.

When she looked, it wasn't her dad. It was Dr. Goldsmith.

She'd forgotten about Kelly.

Crap on a cracker! she thought, pushing the button to answer.

"Amber?" the voice asked. "Are you okay?"

"Yeah, Dr. Goldsmith, I'm fine. I got into that laptop and lost track of time," Amber replied, still putting stuff away. "How's Kelly?"

"He's back in ICU. While he was in recovery, he had a bad reaction. His blood pressure tanked. His electrolytes are way out of whack."

"Oh no! I'm sorry I didn't come this afternoon."

"Wouldn't have mattered. He's been kinda out of his head, so they've sedated him."

"But I should have been with you."

"No, Amber. I'm fine. I'm waiting on the doctors to figure this out."

"Do they have any ideas?"

"Not that they've shared with me. I'm frustrated," she said.

Amber's forehead furrowed as she thought, though the low and now probably high blood sugar made her ideas a little unorganized. "We talked about whether the alopecia was genetic or auto-immune. Is this another auto-immune disease?"

"That's their focus. They've called in an endocrinology specialist who will be around soon, they say."

"Are you sure you don't want me to come stay so you can take a break?"

"No, but thank you. I'll go home later this evening and come back in the morning."

"My dad's in town tonight," Amber said. "We'll be out later. I could stop — "

"That's unnecessary," she said in a harsh motherly voice, but then her tone softened. "We should let him rest."

"Let me know if I can do anything, please. I feel bad I didn't — "

"Don't. I'm sure everything will be okay. You can come by tomorrow at lunch if you'd like. We ought to know something by then."

They said their goodbyes and disconnected.

The laptop's importance sank as she grabbed her bag and headed out the door to go see her father.

Traffic was crazy this time of day, and every stupid stunt some driver pulled to get a few car lengths ahead reminded her of how aggravating traveling with Kelly could be. How his attention diverted when he saw skid marks on the pavement or damage to a guardrail. That hyperattentive part of his brain didn't shut off any more than hers did when she was around something digital.

Finally, she pulled into the driveway next to what she presumed was her dad's rental car from the airport, a full-size sedan in a weird forest-green color.

Inside, Zach met her with a long hug.

"I'm so glad to see you," he said in a quiet voice. "It's always too long." Before breaking apart, he kissed the top of her head. "How are you?"

She knew he wanted a genuine answer, not a casual acquaintance answer.

"I got distracted today and didn't eat lunch, so my blood sugar crashed," she offered, not yet ready to discuss the bigger issues of her life.

"Then let's find the best steakhouse in town."

CHAPTER 67
Tuesday, November 17, 2009

They discussed possibilities of places to eat, then Amber went to change clothes, returning in a long blue skirt and ankle boots with heels that still didn't make her as tall as Zach.

"You didn't have to dress up for me," he told her as they walked out the door.

"I don't wear classy stuff to work, so it's a pleasant change."

They got into her vehicle, and again she faced the rush-hour traffic on the way to the restaurant.

Although others were waiting for tables, she and Zach were seated without delay.

"Must be the tie," he remarked after they were alone again.

"Um, no, Dad. It was the gun," she said with a laugh.

"Mine or yours?"

"No one can see mine," she replied.

"Women have the best options to carry," he whispered as the server placed two glasses of water and a carafe on the table.

The special of the night was described, including a 12-ounce ribeye topped with mushrooms and half a dozen blackened Cajan, barbequed, or garlic-grilled shrimp, and a choice of vegetable and salad was agreeable to both.

Steaks, Zach specified, his very rare, and hers medium. Garlic-grilled shrimp. Salads with the house Italian dressing. Baked and loaded potatoes.

Zach also ordered a beer for himself.

"I'll have water," Amber said, and the server left them alone again. "Still eating the barely-dead, I see," she said, as if to herself.

"Still ruining a good steak," he countered.

They laughed.

"We miss you," he said. "You look healthy."

She made a *Pfffft* sound. "Even swimming almost every day, I'm not in the shape I was before college when I worked with horses every day."

"You can always come back to the ranch," he offered. "We have two new colts this year."

"You don't pay as well as Tarrant County, and," she said with a smug smile, "I'm spoiled."

"Most women are," he said, stopping to take a sip. "I'll double your pay every month."

"I'm not mathematically challenged, Dad. Zero times two is still zero."

The server brought Zach's beer and a loaf of dark bread.

He held out the bottle for a casual toast, and she raised her glass of water. "Wish Julie was here, too." The glass clinked dully when they touched.

"What's she doing now?" Amber asked. "I called, but our conversation wasn't much about her."

"She's volunteering with the Bernalillo Sheriff's Department Mounted Patrol as a coordinator for scheduled events. Parades, crowd patrols, funerals."

"Funerals?"

"They almost always send four riders to law enforcement funerals within a day's drive," he explained. "Plus, she takes care of everything at the ranch when I'm gone."

"By herself? I can't imagine that."

"My mom helps a little, but for right now, we're leasing out grazing land, so all she deals with are the horses."

"And the house. Keeping a home is harder work than what they pay me to do every week."

"I don't doubt it. Especially with a guest," he said, intentionally changing the direction of the conversation. "I'm surprised we're having dinner alone."

Amber closed her eyes a moment and sighed, knowing this story would take longer to finish than the steaks. She reached and sliced the bread into several chunks, then slathered hers in the soft butter.

Screw the blood sugar.

Zach sipped his beer and waited.

"There's this guy," she began.

"On the official list of every father's least favorite words," he said. "Go on."

She explained that Kelly was also a deputy, half-expecting another sarcastic response from her father. "He was working as a crash investigator at a train versus car incident the first time we met. Not long after, he was severely injured on a freeway crash when a car hit him, plowing into the whole mess of cars, from what I heard."

"That's living a little close to one's profession, I'd say."

She nodded. "Come to find out, his mother is my boss, and she asked if he could stay with me a few weeks while his fractured femur, kinda like mine, healed so he wouldn't have to climb the stairs at his condo. Reluctantly I said yes."

"So why didn't you invite him to dinner tonight?"

"Wow, that's even more complicated. He had a blood clot in his lungs that put him back in the hospital, and they decided to do his knee replacement while he was there before they started all the anticoagulant medication."

"A knee? How old is this guy, Amber?" Zach said with a frown.

"He's 29, Dad. You don't have to be old to need a joint replacement," she said, leaning to her right and looking under the table to indicate his.

"Thank you, I think."

"The knee was part of the injuries from being hit by a car, but they needed his femur to heal first." She took a drink of water then played with her bread without taking another bite. "The surgery was this morning."

"As good an excuse as any to miss dinner," he replied. "Is he renting a room from you, or is there something more to this?"

The server, rescuing Amber from having to answer, presented the salads and offered fresh ground pepper and parmesan cheese before disappearing again. She happily dug in to put something of substance in her grumbly stomach.

"Amber?" Zach pressed.

She put down her fork. "I'm not sure, Dad. I like him. He's smart. He's funny, like you."

"But?"

"Always a 'but,' isn't there?" She thought about Kelly, trying to decide how to explain what made her question her feelings. "When I was at his condo cleaning last evening, which is another story altogether, I found a photo of him and a woman and little girl. He's never mentioned them."

"Is he supposed to have?" Zach took another drink, ignoring the bread and salad, waiting. "I mean, is your relationship to that point?"

"I don't know. He signed the picture 'Love always' or something gooshy like that."

"Is it framed and on his bedside table?"

She pursed her lips. "No, I found the photo — no frame — under the television stand."

"Then it must not mean much to him, Amber. Why don't you ask him? Or does he not know you were in his condo?"

"We're using it as a safe house," she was trying to explain when the server brought steaks. "He knew. He offered to let me use it."

"If you could cut into these and make sure they are done enough," the guy asked, pointedly looking at Zach.

Zach picked up his fork and stabbed the slice of meat. "Didn't make a sound. Looks perfect."

Amber wasn't sure the server didn't gag just a little.

"Mine is fine, thank you," she said, trying to save the poor guy more torture. "Could I get a little buttermilk dressing to go with my potato, please?"

Probably fearing Zach might ask for a side of raw penguin eggs or something, the server nodded and fled their table.

"You were saying," Zach prompted as he cut the first bite of his steak, letting the red juice pool on his plate.

While she was fixing her baked potato, she continued talking. "So, Harper Sullivan, remember him?"

"Of course. I talked with him a week or so ago while he was on his way down here."

"Oh, yeah. I'll get to that case, which is how I met him," she said, making a face. "They're intertwined. Before that, Harper responded to a single-car rollover with ejection, the driver with critical injuries. She woke up, and he went to interview her. She said something to the effect that her 'ex-husband did this.'" Amber stopped and looked around to make sure their conversation wasn't being overheard. "Then she died."

Zach was chewing, so he nodded.

Amber stared a moment at the steak as he sliced off another bite, hoping she was imagining the smell of raw beef in a butcher shop. She doubted the meat was warm all the way through.

"As he started investigating, he found evidence that someone had sabotaged the car. Going on her dying statement, he began looking at how the ex-husband could have done it. The window of opportunity was 14 hours, and the ex- had an airtight alibi — he'd spent the night with — Drumroll, please? — the prosecuting attorney."

Zach's eyes widened when his eyebrows rose.

"When the investigation circled the rumor mill, this guy threatened the attorney, so Harper was going to send her here to a friend's house for safety, but *his* wife is in the hospital. I was Harper's next choice to help, and since Kelly's apartment has been empty for a while, everyone agreed it would be a suitable place for Dierdra and her son to hide."

"I see." Zach emptied his beer and looked around for the server, caught his eye, and wiggled the bottle to indicate he wanted another. "Actually, I don't."

"Dierdra, the prosecutor, believes he might have drugged her to sleep through him leaving the hotel, taking her car, driving to the ex-wife's house. The car was in the driveway. All he had to do is squat down, pull the cotter pin from the passenger-side tie rod nut, and walk away. The nut would work its way off eventually, though he wouldn't know when. Maybe he loosened it some, too. Dierdra says he stopped at a breakfast place to get coffee and bagels as an excuse why he was out. She said he'd never done that before."

"Charming guy." Another bite.

"From what I gather, he's a freaking narcissistic bully." She cut into her steak, happy to find it barely pink, took a bite. The meat was juicy, well-seasoned, and tender. She stabbed a couple of mushrooms for her next bite.

She pointed to her plate with her fork. "This is fabulous, but it's not as good as yours, Dad. I miss you both, too."

"I miss you, though I have to say that dinner with you has become more like eating when Julie's talking about dead bodies."

The server exchanged the empty beer bottle for a full one and hurried away.

"The attorney? She's staying until Harper can zip up an arrest?"

"Yeah. He told me that this guy, who is also a cop, stopped at her house and found Dierdra and Blaine, her son, getting ready to come here yesterday. Told her she had to 'go with him to the station' regarding some case. She said she couldn't, they were going to see her mother-in-law, who'd had a stroke or something. Blaine said he knew something was wrong when she said that. His grandmother's been dead a long time. But Royce let them go."

"Okay. Meanwhile, back to, what's his name? Kelly?" Zach asked, smearing a piece of the bread with a glob of butter.

"Kelly Morgan, yeah." She emptied her water, but Zach picked up the carafe for her and filled her glass then took a drink from his fresh beer. "I told you he had surgery this morning, right? His mom called before I left work. Something happened while he was in recovery, and he's back in ICU now."

"Is he okay?"

She shrugged. "Dr. Goldsmith didn't know what was wrong yet. She said his blood pressure dropped."

"Would you rather be there with him?"

"No, I wanted to see you tonight," she said. "I'd intended to go after lunch, but I got distracted at work. He's sedated now."

"I appreciate that. You could drop by and see him after we eat," Zach suggested.

"Visiting times are limited," she said, taking another bite.

"In case you think that the badge and gun are only useful at restaurants, they work well in hospitals, too."

CHAPTER 68
Tuesday, November 17, 2009

"Deputy Sullivan," Dierdra said into the cellular phone he'd given her. "Blaine said something tonight that made me wonder. You asked if Stephen had taken his phone when he left the hotel."

"Yeah, I've recently learned how much some phones communicate with their networks, so I'd hoped it could be tracked."

"When I picked up my son the next morning, he'd dropped his phone in the car. It was there overnight. Does that help?"

"Maybe," he said, his voice giving away his interest.

"The phone was a recent gift from Blaine's father, who still tries to be the cool parent. After an injury at work, he lives on a generous annuity from the company and disability. Other than groceries and child support, he spends money on things for Blaine," she explained. "Blaine tells me his phone has some sort of GPS on it."

"I'll get with Amber about it in the morning. That may be the key to the puzzle. Thanks!"

He dialed Amber's cell. No way was he waiting all night.

"Hey, it's Harper," he said when the call connected. "Dierdra remembered something that may be the most important piece of this case."

Amber and Zach had finished dessert and were waiting on the check.

"I can hardly hear you," she said. "I'm in a restaurant. Give me a few minutes, and I'll call you back so I can hear."

They disconnected.

"Speaking of Harper Sullivan," she said. "He has information about his investigation."

"Let's go find out what he has," Zach said, waving over the server who'd delivered salads to a nearby table. "Check, please? You go on out and call him."

"No, I'll wait so you can hear it, too. Fresh ears might help."

The server took his time to bring their ticket to the table, which irritated Amber.

"Good thing he doesn't do my job," she grumbled as they got up from the table.

"I don't think you could do his, either," Zach said with a wry smile. "You'd have poured that second beer in my lap after bringing me that steak."

"Yes. Yes, I would have," she agreed.

Finally in her car, she dialed Harper's number and put the call on speaker so they could both hear.

"Harper, thanks for waiting. My dad's with me. Is it okay if he listens?"

"Yeah, of course. Hey, Zach."

"Harp, how's it going?" Zach replied.

"Have you told him about the crash and all?"

"Most of it," Amber said. "Not a straight line to follow, you know."

"No kidding. So Dierdra called me tonight. She and Blaine had been talking about the night at the hotel. She said that Blain remembered that his phone had fallen out under the passenger seat that night, found it when she picked him up for school the next morning from a friend's house," Harper explained. "Royce didn't know it was there. Fortunately, Blaine's dad buys him all the latest gadgets to make up for not being around."

"Can Brady help like he did with Paul's phone?" she asked.

"I hope so, but I'll leave getting Blaine's phone to Brady when he's back to work. With Elizabeth still being sick, he won't want to leave the kids home."

"Hey Harp?" Zach said.

"Yeah?"

"If what Amber told me about the cotter pin being missing is true, he'd have to have pliers or something to pull it. The tie rod assembly isn't hard to see if the wheel is turned, but it could be a twisty reach. Have you looked at where her car was parked when the pin was most likely removed? You might find it and be able to match it to a tool this guy has."

"Fantastic idea, Z'."

"Or match the grease," Amber added. "If he used his own pliers or something, he might not get rid of them."

"Thanks! I appreciate the help. I'll let you know tomorrow if Brady needs you to pick up the kid's phone."

They hung up again, and she started the car.

"That sounded positive," Zach said. "I guess phones have come a long way since I was looking to find yours."

She backed out and headed from the parking lot onto the feeder. "You wouldn't believe how far." She accelerated onto the freeway toward her house. "Paul Keegan worked with Brady. After he and his daughter were kidnapped, she had managed to hide the brand-new phone Paul had purchased for his wife. We were able to trace it when she turned it on."

"Smart kid. Tell me more about this predator task force."

Amber spent the next fifteen minutes explaining how the process worked, how she pretended to be a kid and played into the perpetrator's trust until a crime was committed or a meeting was arranged.

"How can you tell what the perpetrator wants with the child?" he asked.

"We play that based on his feedback in the conversations, but our first bust was for someone who probably started with child porn, then arranged to meet a girl. He also invited a photographer who evidently specialized in sexual assault. He had hidden a huge collection of stuff. We don't know whether it will be sexual assault, kidnapping and sale to some trafficking purpose like sex or prostitution, or even murder."

"Depressing."

"That's why I called, just to talk to you or Julie. To say thanks for keeping me safe."

"With one exception, you made it pretty easy, I recall."

"It could have been different if I'd stayed in Albuquerque. Mom worked every day but Sundays, so I spent a lot of afternoons and Saturdays alone. And summers, geesh. I used to walk to her shop, to the mall or the movies."

"Good kids aren't excluded from this threat," he said. "I've been glad you're in my life since the moment I saw you."

She smiled.

"Anything I can do to help?" he asked. "The FBI has been involved in missing or kidnapped children since the disappearance of Charles Lindbergh's son in 1932."

"Don't they have to be missing 24 hours, or evidence that the child crossed state lines for the FBI to act?" she asked.

"No, the FBI can activate a team as soon as a child, especially one younger than 12, is reported missing to a field office or the National Center for Missing and Exploited Children. They can deploy the Child Abduction Rapid Deployment teams for any case the FBI determines an investigation is indicated or that local authorities need more assistance."

"Have you ever dealt with a child abduction?"

"No, thankfully."

"It's hard to think about," she said, so soft he almost didn't hear. "I can imagine what's happening to them."

"Plenty of people are trying to save those children. I'm sure some days, each one of them goes home and cries."

CHAPTER 69
Tuesday, November 17, 2009

"Sorry I didn't call you sooner, Harp. I got Elizabeth home this morning and had to get her settled and go buy her medicines," Brady said into the phone, out of breath. "I ran a preliminary check on the phone number I got from Amber. Looks like it was active the morning on the date you gave me. Otherwise, I have to have the subpoena to provide you any official documentation."

"Sure. I'll go straight to the judge," Harper replied. "I hope this is the piece of the puzzle we need."

"This can be quite damaging evidence when it supports a solid case, but it's not a solo gig."

"I think we'll have a strong case if this can provide the glue to hold it together. Thanks, man. Talk to you soon."

Brady leaned back in his chair, realizing he'd forgotten to ask about the woman Harper had wanted to send to Dallas for her safety. She must be okay if Amber got the kid's phone.

Meanwhile, Harper stood and headed for the door to go meet with the judge for the subpoena.

"Sullivan," his boss yelled from a back room.

Harper tried to hide rolling his eyes, but the clerk in the front office had turned to see what the noise was about.

She smiled and shook her head; Harper shrugged and turned around to go find Ian Molina in the storage area of the office.

"Yes, sir?" he said.

"I heard you on the phone, something about getting Judge Taylor to sign a subpoena," Ian said, on a stepstool, searching on a top shelf for something. "Is this about Royce's wife?"

"Ex-wife, sir. Yes. Dierdra Preston's son's phone was in her car the night that he allegedly took it to his ex-wife's house. The contact I have with the cellular company says the phone was working that night, but that's all he could say without the legal stuff."

"So, you have the attorney's word that he left the hotel, and a server at the diner drive-through who can identify him getting breakfast for two that morning?" Ian stepped down, putting the men within arm's reach.

"Yes. She knew him from when she worked at Franco's, chatted with him a few minutes while fresh coffee was brewing. There's video."

"Now you believe we will get evidence of the path he drove?" Ian asked, trying to not sound excited. "Any chance he got a speeding ticket?"

"No sir, but I also found video footage of him putting five bucks' of gas in Ms. Preston's car a bit after 6 a.m."

"Any other surprises I should know about?"

"Ian, is any of this a surprise?" Harper asked.

"No, not really. Good job, Harper."

"Gee, thanks, *Sheriff*. Glad I could reach the bar for good."

"What is up your butt today, *Sergeant*?" Ian retorted with the same sarcastic emphasis on rank.

"Honestly, sir, I'm disappointed that my commitment to this case has only gone from your refusal to let me do my job because I might damage someone's ego to barely tolerated before I developed so much definitive evidence. And all I get's a 'good job' that I did it without causing an intra-agency war from day one."

Ian's face deepened from hot pink to crimson as Harper spoke.

"I hope someday I get a little higher on your performance scale than merely good."

Molina pointed to his office. "Sit."

Harper ignored the command, about to say that he wasn't a damned dog.

"I'm sorry, Harper. It's time we called a truce."

Harper followed him into the office but would not take a seat, so Ian continued anyway.

"I wouldn't be surprised if you think I'm a lazy cop and politician, and I guess that's true. But I'm not too bad at the politics this job requires. If you were sheriff, I promise you, you'd hate every minute."

Harper still stood, leaning his shoulder on the doorframe. "True. No interest in being the sheriff, sir."

"But you're right. I don't give you the credit you deserve for the job you do, and I should. Breaking the professional courtesy rule to solve a crime was the right thing to do, even if it wasn't the politically correct or easy thing to do, Harper. I admire that. I admire you standing up for a victim."

Ian's cell phone buzzed, but he reached to silence it.

"I know I'm late offering, and I'm sorry, but how can I help you with this case?"

CHAPTER 70
Wednesday, November 18, 2009

"I hoped I'd see you today," Dr. Goldsmith said from a chair in the waiting room. "Things have stabilized."

"Do they know what happened?" Amber said, taking a seat.

"You were more correct than you thought. Along with the genetic cause of his alopecia and the other issues I'd told you about, he's developed adrenal insufficiency that's probably worsened since the accident. The orthopedic surgery set it off like a wildfire. By the time he was in recovery, his sodium had dropped, and potassium had spiked, both critically."

Amber found no words.

"All quite manageable now that they've diagnosed it. Like your diabetes, it took a critical incident for it to be recognized."

"How'd you know I'm a diabetic?"

"It's in your file. Never had to be a secret, but you must manage it well."

"Except yesterday. I got so wrapped up in the encryption, I lost track of time and didn't eat lunch. By four, I was shaky."

"At least you can identify your issue now," the woman said. "It's possible that Kelly's Addison's disease will have to be medicated by circumstances that cause a crisis rather than just symptoms, because he has little recognition of the distress."

"I don't know anything about it."

"That's okay. If you're interested, you'll become well-versed in the details, like everything else you've learned."

Amber nodded, not sure exactly why she would want to learn more.

"Go see Kelly. He's looking forward to talking to you." She looked in her bag for a tube of lip moisturizer. "He likes you, you know. That's something I wasn't sure I'd see again in him."

"Why? I don't understand."

"He'll tell you when he's ready. Be honest with him if you don't see a future together." Dr. Goldsmith stood. "I'm going to work. Stay as long as you wish. I'll talk to your boss about letting you have the afternoon off," she kidded.

"I've got to get back to that encryption problem today," Amber replied. "If I can crack these files, I might get a list of people involved. Waiting could put more kids in jeopardy."

"Amber, I understand your drive. Remember that you are now in possession of the computer, so no one else can access its contents."

Dr. Goldsmith's statement rattled something in Amber's brain, but the idea didn't take shape.

"Later. See Kelly first."

CHAPTER 71
Wednesday, November 18, 2009

"Where is she, Sullivan?" Stephen Royce bellowed from the lobby of the Benton Sheriff's Department. "I know you helped her leave town!"

Ian Molina walked past Harper's empty office, thankful he wouldn't have to separate the two men. "May I help you, Captain Royce?" he asked as he came around the corner as Royce raised his hands to pound on the counter.

The clerk rolled backward in her chair, fear in her eyes when she caught sight of Molina, who nodded for her to go into the back offices.

"Where's Sullivan?" Royce demanded again.

"I don't keep tabs on my officers doing their jobs."

"He's not doing his job. He's harassing me, and I want it to stop!" he bellowed. "Dierdra told me she and her kid were leaving town. I want to know where they are!"

Ian crossed his arms, satisfied that the man's anger had clouded his brain's ability to concoct an infallible lie. Through the windows to the parking lot, he saw two patrol cars roll up, lightbars on, but no sirens. As the officers began approaching the front door, he heard the back door open and close, too.

"For the record, Royce, you won't find Mrs. Preston and her son, and she is no longer your alibi. My deputies have collected video evidence of you in Mrs. Preston's car, getting gasoline as well as getting breakfast at Hap's on the morning your ex-wife Caitlyn Parker was involved in what became a fatal crash."

Royce's face blotched bright red as a sneer twitched his left nostril. He did not hear the door open behind him nor the officers' entrance, guns drawn.

He barely heard Ian Molina's voice; his blood pressure was so high he heard a pulsating whoosh in his ears.

Sullivan came around the corner behind Molina.

"And we know you were at Caitlyn's house at 5:48 a.m. for seven minutes," Harper added.

"You can't prove that!" Royce looked one sane thought away from crawling over the counter to get at Harper, who looked as nonchalant as Ian.

"We'll see," Ian said, nodding to the officers behind Royce, who put up a pathetic struggle against being handcuffed. "Arrest him for the murder of his ex-wife."

"I'll have your jobs!" he screamed.

Harper laughed. "You can have mine if you think you can do it, but you're not much of a detective."

CHAPTER 72
Wednesday, November 18, 2009

"Don't you look like crap today," Amber remarked from the doorway of the ICU room.

"Is my hair messed up?" he replied with a smile, rubbing his head.

"Sorry I didn't come see you yesterday. I found a new cypher pattern on that laptop and completely lost track of time."

"I'm told I wasn't taking visitors yesterday anyway," he said, scooting his hips over on the bed, patting a spot she could sit and not interfere with the machine bending and straightening his leg. "What d'you find?"

She looked at the bed. "I can't sit there and face you," she said, pulling the room's only chair closer to the bed.

Before she sat, however, he took her hand and pulled her close enough for a kiss.

Not a brief social kiss.

Not a long, romantic kiss.

But it lingered somewhere between.

She finally stepped back and sat, breaking eye contact. The only sounds around them were hospital noises.

"I've finally left a woman speechless with a kiss. I can die a happy man now." He leaned back with his fingers laced above his head.

"You die, I promise you won't be happy."

"Would you miss me?" he said, with enough hint of teasing she wasn't sure if he meant it.

She didn't answer.

"Wow. I'm sorry," he said. "I don't know what you're mad — "

Before she replied, she took a deep breath and held it for a count of ten. "Who is the woman and little girl in the photo I found in your living room?"

His eyes opened wide. "The little girl on the swing?"

"How many other photos of women and toddlers do you have, Kelly?" Amber stood to leave.

"Please. I'll tell you. It's not a secret, it's a nightmare from my past." He reached out and took her hand again. "Please?"

She sat, but he didn't let go, though she tried to tug her hand away.

"When I lived in Abilene, I began dating a woman, a nurse. Everyone said cops shouldn't date nurses, that it was an armed bomb. We got pretty serious but not quite to living together. Leah had a four-year-old named Aspen I adored. Curly blond hair, big blue eyes. A whole lot of smart sass. She was going to be a real heart-breaker." He blinked hard. "One fall afternoon, Aspen was in the apartment playground area. Leah said she'd run back to her place to get a sweater, but Aspen was gone when she got back. Just a few minutes, she said."

Amber clamped her free hand over her mouth.

"We — the police — they did everything I could imagine to find her. I did everything I could think of. Double shifts, search parties. Leah blamed *me* for not finding Aspen, like I'd failed her. Then the truth came out that Leah had been on the phone in the apartment, maybe fifteen minutes. With her ex-boyfriend. My sympathy for her died," he said, his voice getting quieter with each word.

In a voice that sounded crinkling rice paper, Amber asked, "Did they . . . I mean, was Aspen ever . . ."

"Found?" Kelly shook his head. "No. Not knowing feels worse than finding her dead. I learned a lot about trafficking and other crimes against children during that. No way I could ever look at Leah again, acknowledging her negligence had made snatching Aspen in broad daylight so damned easy."

"I'm sorry, Kelly."

"I couldn't stay and get my head straight, so I applied a half dozen places across the state. I accepted the crash investigation job here because I had the creds. Moved into Mom's condo and she got a smaller place, in case you wonder how I got a place like that. But after a while, I started spending an hour or so a week, checking the cases of missing children in the state, hoping I'd find some little piece to lead me to who took her. That's why I wanted on this task force team. I don't think I'll ever find out what happened to Aspen, but maybe I could save someone else's little girl."

"And the photo?"

"I keep it for two reasons. One, to remember Aspen. It's the only thing I have. Two, to remember why I left."

"What happened to the woman?" Amber asked, not wanting to say the name.

"I don't know. Or care."

"Did you love her?"

Kelly tilted his head back onto the pillow to look at the ceiling before answering. "Here's my philosophical outlook: love and hate are at opposite ends of a long rope. But sometimes the ends get tied together, so they are right next to each other, and moving from one to the other is easy. I loved her. I hated her. Then I threw away the rope."

"Does that mean you don't feel either for her anymore?"

"Not her. Waste of energy."

"Me?" Amber whispered.

"I like you. A lottle," he said, "which is like a little, only more." He lifted his hand to stop her. "We have something to build on. We're not a blazing fire of lust, we're friends, Amber. We fit together well, but we're two whole people. I can talk to you."

"You didn't talk about her."

"I try my damnedest not to think of her. Or the photo. I haven't seen it in months. Where'd you find it?"

"Under the television stand."

"Sounds right. Every fall on the day Aspen went missing, I swear I won't, but I spend the night, drunk, on the floor, crying."

"Kelly, I'm sorry I got mad. I feel stupid not asking," she said. "I was cleaning before the attorney and her son arrived."

"Sorry, I'm not a good housekeeper."

"I'll send you the bill," Amber said, smiling. "Oh, by the way, Blaine wanted me to ask if he could play your video games."

"Sure."

"He'll be thrilled. He says you have quite a setup."

"Have you heard how the case is coming that made them come to Dallas?"

"Yes. Brady was able to track Blaine's phone in her car that night. And some other things."

"I hope I get to meet them before they leave."

"Really? Why?"

"Just to find out who got you to clean my condo. You were going to tell me about the computer files?"

"The files! Oh my God! I forgot. Listen, so I started finding hidden files, stuck into places the system doesn't save personal files, right? But they're encrypted in a really weird way," she began, explaining the text substitution and conversion to hexadecimal. "To decrypt, you convert back to text by reversing the substitution exactly in the reverse order."

"What do you think the file you found is supposed to be?"

"A list of phone numbers and initials. When I convert it from hex back to text, some numbers are ten digits, but they vary from eight to thirteen. Looks like the list is about 75 entries long." She stood and picked up a pen from his tray table and wrote an example on his napkin:

ABC 2345678910

Then she explained how the substitution had to work to get the variation of the number sets, for example swapping a two-digit set with five digits, then taking two of those digits and changing them to four digits, then taking any set of five digits and substituting them with only two. "Or by some other algorithmic pattern," she said. "By doing this several times, it alters more than half of the phone numbers, leaving me to guess which ones. And if I don't have the right numbers in the right sequence to reverse, I'll never know if I got it right."

"And the other files you decrypted?"

"Commercial encryption. Some are spreadsheets of names, maybe even matches to these initials, but most are groups of children with certain characteristics checked, like age, or whether one has blue eyes or brown, blond hair or black." She sat back down. "The damned shopping lists I told you about. The worst thing is that now I'm second-guessing whether the information is real or if it's a decoy. Decoding them was easy."

"Decoys," he repeated.

"I'd bet that none of the numbers go to a landline, so unregistered cell phones would be the most likely."

"If you were operating this, how would you do it?" he asked.

She smiled. "I'm not the best person to ask how to do it, but I know who is."

CHAPTER 73
Wednesday, November 18, 2009

"This is a slow process, making all the court documents," Brady told Harper on the phone. "I suspect I won't finish for a week."

"A week is fine. That's not why I called." Harper hesitated. "How's Liz?"

Brady knew his friend was stalling, but he went along. "She's much better. Her mom is still staying with us to keep the kids fed and transported, which lifts an enormous burden I couldn't have accomplished. I don't know how Liz does it."

"Women are simply better at family stuff, I guess. Like with Meredith. She called the other day and said she might come home."

"That's excellent news, Harp. I hope you guys get things worked out now that you've had a little space and time. Did she say when?"

"No, but maybe Christmas. She's had enough grandparenting. Must be something like parents, only squared, pardon the pun."

"Few of us would enjoy living with family two generations back these days."

"Sorta brings me to my reason for calling. You mentioned it might be too late to search the records for a phone in the area when Lilah was shot. I was thinking I could talk to the sheriff and have him follow up if it still exists in your system."

"I saved an enormous chunk of data for later review. It's safe and waiting on a subpoena."

"How did you know you'd ever need it?" Harper asked, almost in grateful tears.

"I didn't know, and company policy says I can't volunteer this stuff, so it's been on hold. I hoped maybe your supervisors would think of it without you, but no one asked."

"Thanks, Brady."

"Don't thank me until you see the reports."

"Why?" Harper asked, panic tightening his throat. "Did you — "

"I haven't looked, interpreted, nothing. Don't get your hopes up too high."

Harper sighed. "I've waited this long."

"Off the record, you'll be pleased with the results of Preston's phone data. I'll be skippy to explain this one to a jury."

CHAPTER 74
Wednesday, November 18, 2009

Getting through the family greetings and catching up on events finally leveled out so Amber could explain her question.

"I told you about our team, but now I have a question. Without telling you anything else, tell me how you'd set up and encrypt sensitive files in a buyer-seller business," she explained.

"Okay," Julie said. "A few parameters. How sensitive is the information?"

"Very. A list of buyers or sellers of stolen merchandise. Illegal stuff."

"You don't want the legitimate method?"

"Probably not."

"There must be dozens of encryption programs for files of data. Are any of them suitable for the operation?"

"What I've found so far is 40-some files using various commercially available cyphers. The biggest challenge was finding which one for which file, which I can do in my sleep. Mostly three programs, but no more than seven or eight altogether. All are document or spreadsheet files in the typical locations for saving them. Then I started finding other files," she said. "Inside system folders, named with numbers and letters in a random format."

"Encoded?" Julie asked.

"Big-time, but in a strange way. In a nutshell, one is a long list of what I think are initials and phone numbers that appear to've had multiple sets of substitutions made, and then files were converted to hexadecimal to make them look like nonsense if opened by mistake," Amber said. "If the process is not undone in the correct order, the file is hopelessly scrambled."

"Not quite brilliant, but effective if not cumbersome."

"Has to have a key. Where would you save it?" she asked. "There are thousands of files, and short of opening each one of them to see if it's bogus or not, I can't undo this."

"Sounds like an egg you can't unscramble."

"Exactly."

"Your question is, where would I put the key to decrypt this text. Does it have to be on the same computer?"

"Yeah, I guess. You?"

"On first thought, I would not. Tell me about the machine."

"The laptop stays locked in evidence, of course. I've been working with a copy of the hard drive," Amber said. "Pretty standard commercial laptop. Nothing unusual as far as hardware or software."

"If I were personally carrying the data around on the laptop, I'd use some sort of code built with a long string of numbers, like the serial number of the device itself."

"That's not helping."

"Oh, you wanted me to *help* you?" Julie said with a laugh. "If absolute security is the goal, I wouldn't record that key on that machine."

"Where would you put it?"

"Maybe it's on a floppy drive. Or it gets emailed to the user. Could be someone's driver's license number. The possibilities are infinite," Julie said. "Sorry."

"Worth asking. Thanks."

"Sure. Is Zach still there today?"

"Yeah, he's going to spend the night again and leave tomorrow. I was hoping to introduce him to Kelly tonight."

"You still can, can't you?"

"That's the thing. Kelly's still in the hospital after his knee replacement. Remember we talked about his auto-immune disease? He had a horrible complication after surgery with adrenal insufficiency he didn't know he had. He's awake and everything now, but I don't know whether I should . . . "

"Should do what, Amber?"

"I'm afraid they'll keep diagnosing more auto-immune diseases." She sniffed. "I like him, but I'm scared. What if . . . what if he dies?"

"Amber, no matter who you fall in love with, death is inevitable. We all die. You and I both understand how grieving can nearly break those of us left. The risk exists every future moment that death will separate you. And it will, the question is when. Take the moments you are given. Enjoy them, don't fear the future."

"That sounds so easy," Amber said. "That's not how it felt when we thought Dad was dead."

"No, it's not, but even if it had been real, my biggest regret was not having had more time together when he was alive. I wouldn't have wanted anything less than what we had. Don't fear death so much you don't enjoy living. Grief is the cost of love."

CHAPTER 75
Wednesday, November 18, 2009

"Thanks for meeting me," Amber said as they walked toward the hospital.

"Are you going to tell me who this guy is?" Zach asked.

"He's a deputy who's been working with me on — "

"No, Amber, who is he to *you*?" He motioned for her to go before him through the automatic sliding glass doors.

"I'm not exactly sure right now. We're friends, and he'd been staying at the house because of his leg, which was weird in the beginning. We've gone out on one date, but the rest of it is crazy. I like him. I want to see where it goes."

They made it to the elevator, and she pushed the up button.

"Okay."

"Just okay?" she echoed. "You've threatened a dozen guys I've dated. One of them I never heard from again."

"The difference is, Amber, you thought you were in love with every one of them. You didn't say that about Kelly. You said you're friends. That's the right start."

The doors opened. Inside, she pushed the button for the 4th floor.

"I'm not surprised you like him because you have things in common, but he is a cop. That makes things a bit more complicated, you realize," he said as the doors closed. "Riskier."

"But so am I." She smiled. "And come to think of it, both our parents are in law enforcement, too."

On the fourth floor, Amber led the way to the intensive care unit and to Kelly's room.

"You missed my mom," Kelly said. "And you almost missed me. I'm being moved to the orthopedic wing as soon as they clean a room. Two more days."

"Do you need anything?" Amber asked, taking the chair.

"No, but I'm so ready to get out of this place," Kelly replied, turning to Zach. "I understand you are with the FBI now, Sir."

"Terrorism task force in Albuquerque," Zach answered.

"What's your thought about what happened at Fort Hood?" Kelly asked.

"I've wondered a long time why people do such horrific things to each other, and I still don't have a clue," Zach said. "Humans aren't the only animals who kill for reasons other than survival, but I suspect they are the only ones who like it enough to plan ways of doing it in massive numbers."

"Yes, sir."

"I'm going to go get something to drink," Amber interrupted. "Either of you need anything?"

"I could use some water," Zach said.

"No, I'm fine."

And she winked at Kelly on her way out the door.

"She's . . . I don't know, she's everything. She's smart, beautiful. Did she get that wicked sense of humor from you?"

Zach raised an eyebrow. "You presume I have a sense of humor?"

"Yep, that's the one. She's magic with a computer, my mom said. This child exploitation team we've been working on, she's sensitive to it, but she won't give up."

"Amber's not one to walk away from people or causes she believes in."

"She says you taught her to ride horses."

Zach nodded. "She took to it like she'd started when she was four. She's terrific with horses."

"And people. It's weird. She hates crowds, but she is pretty good with people."

"That probably comes from her teen years in a rural area instead of a big city."

"She told me her mother was murdered, but she didn't elaborate."

"I think that's a story better left for her to tell. But afterward, my wife and I invited her to live with us, and we'd recently moved to Washington."

"You spent time in the DEA, right? Not my mug of tea," Kelly said, reaching for his plastic cup for a drink.

"Not mine anymore either or I'd still be there. I enjoyed doing the job. I hated being a pawn when one of my team killed two others and tried to kill me."

"I'd walk away, too. Was Amber really in New York City on 9/11?"

"She was. Another story for her to share, but she got hit by a car and had a fractured leg almost like yours, she said."

"Which is a cosmic coincidence," Kelly said. "But letting me stay where I don't have stairs to climb has been an immense help, as is the pool."

"I'm sure it has."

"She ought to be back by now," the younger man said. "The machine isn't that far away."

"Maybe she went to the cafeteria," Zach suggested.

They both looked at the clock, then each other again.

"I'll go look. Excuse me."

Part IV

CHAPTER 76
Wednesday, November 18, 2009

Zach had been gone less than fifteen minutes when Kelly heard an overhead page, something uncommon in the hospital, asking Amber Samualson to please call the operator.

He hasn't found her, Kelly thought. Where could she have gone?

Panic swirled in his stomach, throbbing with the same intensity his knee did on the machine that bent it.

He needed to help find her, but reaching the straps on his leg was impossible, so he was stuck until someone freed him. But he could reach his phone, the logical part of his brain prodded.

Use your resources.

First, he called Brady Cayson.

"I'm already doing it, Kelly," the voice on the other end said. "I'll call you back."

Okay, next?

He called the sheriff's department dispatcher. "Reyna, it's Kelly Morgan. I need you to put out a BOLO on Deputy Samualson." He gave her specifics for her physical appearance, the clothes he'd just seen her in, although it was a memory test because who pays attention? He was trying to remember the plate number on her vehicle when Zach came back into the room.

"Car's still in the lot," he said, interrupting the description.

Kelly canceled that part, finished the call and disconnected.

"You'd already called Brady, I learned," Kelly said, pressing the heels of his palms to his eyes. "What, you have him on speed dial?"

"As a matter of fact, I do," Zach said, taking a seat. "Where would she go?"

"I can't think of anywhere she would go and not tell one of us. Theoretically, if the car is still here, she should be."

"But you don't believe that?"

"No, sir, I don't. And I don't like the reason." He dropped his hands to his lap.

Zach nodded for him to go on.

"She's told you what we've been working on, right?"

Another nod.

"These people, they kidnapped our partner and his daughter, at a mall. Made it look like Paul was helping a stranded nurse."

"A nurse?"

"Someone wearing scrubs, it looked like. We were able to see the mall's security footage. They, whoever *they* were, killed Paul then took Mackenzie and several other girls. From what they learned when they captured the men transporting them, which was damned little, they were headed toward Del Rio to the border."

"You think someone grabbed Amber?"

Kelly shrugged. "Honestly, sir, it's the worst-case scenario I can think of, and the most likely."

Zach took a breath to answer but an imposing woman entered the room, so he stood, purely out of habit.

"Mom. Jeez," Kelly said. "Have you seen Amber? Like, did you two stop to gab in the women's restroom?"

"No, Kel, I haven't seen her today," she said, looking from her son to the tall man on the other side of the bed. "What's wrong?"

"They came — " he turned to Zach. "This is Zach Samualson, Amber's father. Zach, my mother, Bonnie Goldsmith."

The parents shook hands across the bed, but Kelly continued talking.

"They dropped by less than half an hour ago, and we chatted a bit, then Amber said she was going for something to drink. She hasn't returned."

"This hospital is huge, maybe she took a wrong turn somewhere going to the cafeteria," Dr. Goldsmith offered.

"Zach looked, had her paged. Her car is still in the parking lot."

"Surely it's nothing to be concerned with," she said. "And you need to take a moment and calm down."

"Mother, I'm extremely concerned, and if I could get out of the damned contraption by myself, I'd go walk the halls looking for her."

"You might as well tell the nurse you need more steroids because you're certainly using any reserve you have," she said to him, looking back at Zach. "He suffered an adrenal crisis coming out of this surgery. Stress like this is dangerous."

"Walking the halls isn't the answer," Dr. Goldsmith and Zach said together.

"I'll go call Brady, see where he's at with pinging her phone," he said. "You stay in that bed. I'll leave you to her."

He walked out, lifting his phone just as it rang.

"Her phone is, well, was in the trashcan on the main floor. I called it when it appeared to still be in the building. Some maintenance guy dug it out and answered it."

"Which side of the building was that closest to?" Zach asked, hurrying toward the elevators. "I may lose you in the elevator. If so, I'll call back."

The doors opened, Zach stepped inside, joining two nurses. Out of habit, he reached for the button panel, only to see that the main floor was already lit.

Going down seemed to take minutes, and Zach could feel his nerves ratchet tighter. Finally, the bell chimed, and the doors opened.

"Still there?" he asked.

"Yep. The corridor is behind the emergency room. Looks like an exit passes around the back toward the east side of the building."

"Floor plans?" Zach said, curious where the information came from as he followed the signs toward the emergency department.

"Yeah, we did an install for a cellular wi-fi system in the new wing last year."

"Are you sure the exit's still here? It wasn't temporary, right?"

"Not according to my records. Should be a double door, opening outward into this hall. Probably alarmed," he was saying when a wailing siren sound filled his ear. "Yeah, that's it. I won't bother calling security. They'll be right along."

"Thanks," Zach said. "They can follow me."

Brady could hear footfalls echoing in the empty hall followed by the push-bar crashing open a metal door.

"Should be ambulances to the right. No nearby cars or even places to park," he said, "unless you were driving something that looked like a police car. Call ya back."

Brady put his phone down, wondering what Zach was doing.

Zach saw an EMS crew walking toward the ambulance closest to the door he'd just exited. "Hey, excuse me!"

One looked over at him and stopped.

Zach pulled out his identification for the paramedic and introduced himself.

"We believe a Tarrant County deputy was abducted from the hospital. They found her cell phone inside near this exit hallway. When you pulled up, did you see any law enforcement vehicles parked over here?"

"No, but we were kinda busy with the patient," he said.

His EMT partner joined them from the passenger side.

"Did you notice any cars here?" Zach said, not wanting to repeat the whole spiel.

"Yeah. A county car, but it wasn't Tarrant's colors. Had a dark green broken stripe on a white four-door sedan," she said.

Both men looked at her in surprise.

She gave a half-shrug. "I drove and backed in, so I saw it when I got out."

"Thanks. Anything else you remember?"

"Getting ready to leave, I assumed. Two male deputies," she said. "One female prisoner."

CHAPTER 77
Wednesday, November 18, 2009

"Amber?" he asked, the voice sounding odd, hoarse.

"No, it's still Lyle, the maintenance man. How many times do I have to answer her phone till you come get it?"

"I beg your pardon?"

"You're not that FBI guy I'm supposed to wait for, are you?"

"I'm Sergeant Harper Sullivan," he said, confused. The only FBI guy he knew in person was Zach, which started a chain of mental connections that led him to no conclusion. "Tell him when he finds you to call me."

"Yeah, sure. I'm not someone's damned answering service," he muttered and hung up.

Harper was confused. What started as an easy call to find out the phone number at Kelly's place so he could call Dierdra left him baffled. He sat at his desk, holding the receiver until he heard the signal it was off the hook. He looked at it again before replacing it in the cradle.

Why did a maintenance guy have Amber's phone? If she lost it, sure, but an FBI agent? Where was Zach and was it really him who would retrieve her phone?

He thought about calling Zach but hesitated. What would he say?

Calling Dierdra would have to wait.

CHAPTER 78
Wednesday, November 18, 2009

Dark. Moving.

Squinting open her eyes produced no light. Amber realized her head was covered with something snug, clingy, with a dusty, sour odor. The heat from her breath magnified the smell and made her nose burn.

Slowly, she took inventory: A gag smashed her lips against her teeth, bulky enough her jaws ached. Arms tied or maybe handcuffed behind her back, lying on her left side. Left hand numb and cold against the other. Knees and ankles tied together.

Her head bounced hard on the cold bare metal floor, causing bright lights to flash through her vision.

Thoughts jumbled. Every heartbeat pounded her brain against her skull.

Some strange music increased in volume.

Most of Fort Worth could probably hear it, she thought, feeling the bass rumble from the metal through her bones.

She had to clear her mind. The cover on her head might be thick enough she wasn't getting enough oxygen. Or she might have been drugged.

Trying to take a deeper breath made her cough. She tried to turn her head, to pull away from what stuck to her face. Based on the sound, she feared it was plastic.

Alarmed that she could suffocate, her lungs tried again to expand, against her will.

A longer coughing fit.

Where am I? How'd I get here?

Blurred memories. Didn't matter. Only the present and future were important now.

Moving. Had to be a vehicle. Something large enough for her to be on a bare floor.

Van. Truck.

Not a pickup. She couldn't feel wind.

Unless it had a cover.

Have to free myself.

She straightened her legs slowly until she met something firm but not rigid. A thigh? Shoulder?

The effort was answered with a nudge.

Trying to respond, she barely made a sound. Her throat was dry.

She pushed slightly against the body, she presumed, realizing she still had on her boots. She tapped her toes against it a couple of times to indicate she was awake.

The reply was a series of nudges against her feet.

Amber wasn't in good shape, but at least she wasn't alone.

That meant something, didn't it?

Her thoughts faded into a hazy world of her past, a few days after her mother had gone missing, when Julie had taken her out of Albuquerque into Colorado before stopping to eat. She'd asked Julie why someone would kidnap her mother.

"People are kidnapped for several reasons. Threats to a hostage are to make someone else comply with demands, such as ransom. Kidnapping may be used to move someone to finish the crime or elicit information. For payback."

The words didn't sound like Julie's, so maybe Amber's brain was making it up.

She'd been kidnapped, at gunpoint. And after more dreams, one name came up until she understood why.

Monica Delacroix.

The name in the tiny file with a phone number she'd dialed just once.

Had to be a warning system. If someone dialed that number, it would indicate to someone that the whole computer was in jeopardy of being read.

Why hadn't I realized that? I should have recognized the name!

Monica Delacroix Bond was the mother of the fictional character who Ian Fleming had named James.

CHAPTER 79 – Wednesday, November 18, 2009

Two broad-chested security officers from the hospital approached Zach as he bid the EMS crew goodbye.

"Sir, you exited through a fire escape, setting off alarms," the younger man said. "We'll need you to come with us."

"My daughter has been taken from this building against her will," he said. "I need to meet with maintenance staff to get her cell phone. Then I'd like to see — "

The younger man's hand grasped Zach's upper arm, without coming close to wrapping around it. "I said you need to come with me," the man repeated.

Shaking the man's grip off like shooing a fly, Zach flipped open his credentials for them. "And I'm telling you, that's not going to happen."

The younger officer reached toward him.

"If you grab me again, I'll arrest you for battery on a federal officer," Zach said, raising his eyebrows in a warning. "I don't have time for that, but it will get you out of my way."

The older officer stepped forward, holding out a hand. "Darrin Shorter," he said. "How can we help you?"

They shook.

Zach explained as they walked toward the emergency department what he believed had happened to Amber.

They found Lyle, who relinquished the cell phone and the message to call the last person who called.

"Did someone else call besides me?"

"Twice, yeah. One hung up when I answered."

There was a number between his own and the one he recognized as Sullivan's.

Why would Harper have called Amber, he wondered, then realized their conversation likely was about the case Amber had explained. Who else? Probably Kelly.

He turned back to Darrin. "Another deputy's in ICU. You should post a guard on him until we get this figured out."

The suggestion was answered with a nod of acknowledgment to Zach, and a nod of assignment to the younger man, who balked.

"Go," Darrin said. "Two officers. Now."

The younger man slunk away, muttering to himself.

"Kids," Darrin offered, rolling his eyes. "Plenty of brawn, not much brains. No respect."

Zach thanked the maintenance man, who grabbed his black and yellow cart and walked away, unphased by the situation except for its interruption of his tasks.

"Can we check surveillance?" Zach suggested. "From what the EMS crew told me, she might have been taken out the alarmed door and put directly into a vehicle. The EMT said she thought it was a patrol car from another county she didn't recognize, had two officers and a female in the back. Green stripe except for the driver's door."

"Easy enough to wrangle that footage, but we'd been helping with a mental case in the emergency department who was taken out by deputies from Cooke County. Sounds like their vehicle," Darrin replied, turning to lead through several turns from the main hallway, finally to the security office. "Carl, send me the last," he looked at his watch, "the last hour of the video feed from ICU, elevators, cafeteria, ED, and all exits to my computer. Keep watch for, well," he turned to Zach. "You describe her."

Zach squeezed his eyes shut to remember what Amber'd been wearing. Not a uniform. Not the skirt from dinner. Finally, the image came into focus in his head, and he gave Carl the information, then followed Darrin to an office.

"Let's follow her from ICU," Darrin said. "We ought to be able to keep her in view of cameras throughout the hospital. Ever since we had a baby nabbed a year ago, ain't no limit on how much I can spend on security equipment."

"Wouldn't Carl or someone have noticed her being dragged out? I can't imagine she'd be quiet."

"Maybe she was drugged," Darrin suggested, manipulating images on a computer screen, then using a remote to turn on a nearby big-screen television. "I'll send the image over there, so you can get a better look. I'm sure I don't have to tell you, but with enough time, you can change the appearance of everything but someone's eyes."

"Doubt they had time to do anything fancy," Zach said, pulling a chair around to watch the screen.

A few minutes later, Darrin had found the point Zach and Amber had come out of the elevator on the ICU floor until they entered the patient room. He zipped forward again until Amber came out of the room, headed for the elevator.

Darrin switched views to the correct camera for the elevator car. She was alone, down to the main floor, where she exited and turned left. Again, Darrin switched views as she walked toward the cafeteria. She wandered through the refrigerator units stocked with drinks, finally choosing what Zach thought looked like apple juice and a bottle of water. She paid at the register and appeared to be walking back the way she'd come until a nurse who wasn't facing the camera approached her.

"What I'd give to hear that," Zach grumbled to himself.

"I wish. You keep watching that, and I'll follow the nurse backward and see where she came from," Darrin said, pushing more keys.

Zach watched the woman in plain dark scrubs, carrying a large tote bag, pointing vaguely outside as she talked to Amber.

From that point in time, Zach watched forward and Darrin watched backward to find out if this encounter was what they were searching for. Zach had to interrupt and have Darrin switch views again as Amber walked beside the nurse toward the emergency department.

"The nurse came in through the main doors," Darrin said. "I'll see which parking lot she came from, but it's not an employee entrance."

"I doubt she works here," Zach replied on autopilot, watching his daughter chatting with the stranger, laughing once even. "Amber has no idea. Or maybe she does." He thought maybe she was looking around for cameras.

He was so intent on the screen, Darrin tossed a stress ball at him to answer his cell phone.

Not his, Zach noted.

Amber's.

CHAPTER 80
Wednesday, November 18, 2009

Amber's dreams continued to be about Julie, talking to her. Telling her of the man who fell in his living room and couldn't get up, eventually dying because lying in one position had damaged his muscles, which caused his kidneys to fail.

This dream startled her awake, understanding its significance. She needed to move.

The body part she was touching continued to shift occasionally, so as Amber became more coherent, she thought perhaps it meant the other person could not get free either.

Her left shoulder and hip ached. She had no idea how long she'd been in that position, but without being able to see, she wasn't sure how or even if she could move without, well, the list of bad things that could happen seemed daunting. She might get partway over and get stuck, unable to move at all. Changing positions could alert the driver she was awake, which might cause her to be drugged again. Or worse.

Without a sense of time, she could only tell that the pain increased until repositioning became mandatory.

If she could get circulation and sensation back in her left hand, she knew she was limber enough to wiggle her arms down over her buttocks in cuffs.

She wiggled her toes, pulled her legs away, trying to stretch out to roll over.

The same body she'd bumped into before twitched against her in rapid succession when Amber tried to roll to her stomach, which she interpreted as *No no no.*

Could the other person see? Apparently so.

The more difficult maneuver, rolling over onto her arms, must make more sense somehow.

Amber inhaled and rolled onto her back, felt more warm body parts on her right shoulder, scooted her hips and shoulders left, and rolled again onto her right side. She had to bend her hips to bring her legs forward so she wouldn't roll back as the vehicle slowed, but it told her which way she was facing.

Someone else, Amber thought, wiggled around, bumping into her until she felt fingers against her head.

Fingers that tried several times to get a grip on the stretchy hood over Amber's face.

CHAPTER 81
Wednesday, November 18, 2009

Zach answered Amber's phone when he recognized the number.

"Amber?" a male voice said, sounding vaguely familiar to him.

"Harper? It's Zach."

"What the hell is going on there?" Harper asked. "I was trying to reach Amber to get a phone number to Kelly's apartment."

"What the hell isn't even close," Zach said, more to himself than Harper, still watching the video. "I'll give Kelly your message if you don't need it right away."

"I wanted to tell the attorney she could come back home. We arrested the cop who had threatened her." He paused but Zach didn't answer. "It can wait."

"Amber and I came to the hospital to see Kelly, but she vanished."

"What's Kelly . . . ah never mind. That's not the point. Kidnapped?" he asked.

"We're reviewing hospital security footage now. I'll call you later."

Darrin had stopped both videos.

"The woman, she parked in Lot B," he said. "I've sent someone to watch the car."

"Okay. Move this one forward again," Zach said. "They are coming to the same-day surgery unit."

"That's odd. It's closed this time of day." Darrin gasped as they watched the stranger pull the door open. "That door should be locked."

The woman entered, and Amber followed, though Zach couldn't imagine why.

Inside, the video was limited to one view, and as the women walked past it, Amber looked straight at it, neither smiling nor giving any other sign of duress.

"There," he said, pointing at her. "I bet the woman threatened either me or Kelly if Amber didn't follow her."

Moments before they disappeared, Amber appeared to scratch the back of her head but flipped her middle finger at the camera. In a few more steps, they turned the corner and were out of sight.

"Did she just . . ." Darrin said, half smiling.

"Yep, that's my girl. She'd have been a rabid grizzly bear if she thought she was alone with that woman."

"Carl, dispatch all available officers to the Same-Day Surgery Unit," Darrin yelled out the office door.

"Any other exit from that unit?" Zach asked.

"Two. Staff elevators, so they can take patients to a room without coming out of the unit," he said, "and the other is to a limited-access corridor straight to the morgue."

While that thought wasn't comforting, Zach kept on point. "The morgue has an exit, of course. Cameras?"

"Working on it." He had to have more video directed to his station, but within a minute, they were watching surveillance through the morgue, advancing at double speed until Amber came around a corner into view, now beside a man dressed in dark clothes and a cap, guiding her by the elbow toward the exit doors to the loading bay. As they turned, Zach glimpsed a gun being pressed against her ribs.

"Damn it!" he bellowed. "Tell me there's a camera outside."

"Of course," Darrin replied, hitting the keys harder as he tried to hurry.

The screen changed, but there was no image. The recording was static.

"What the hell?" Darrin yelled at Carl to make sure he'd gotten the right stream. "Carl, send two men around south to the morgue dock."

The other man dispatched the new assignment. "We don't normally monitor the morgue, sir, unless we know there's a pickup.

Looks like the video has been static for a couple of days but no one noticed," Carl replied while searching through camera feeds.

"Some guy with a gun marched her out the back door of a hospital, and no one has a picture of what happened after that?"

Darrin answered his phone instead of answering the demanding but valid question of an increasingly distraught father with a gun. He listened, said he'd be right there, and hung up. "I understand you need to find your daughter, sir, which is still the highest priority. Carl will call the police and get everyone involved. Maybe if he finds the vehicle leaving that side of the building, they can follow it on street cams. Meanwhile, my officers found the nurse, dead. Shot twice."

CHAPTER 82
Wednesday, November 18, 2009

Once the hood was off, Amber expected to be able to breathe. The smell wasn't the mask. The air was stifling hot and smelled of . . . dead bodies. Her eyes, after she tried blinking away the initial nausea, were well adjusted for the dim area. One hole in the back door of the container occasionally letting in a beam light. Not sunshine, she thought.

Around her sat six younger girls, teens, no older. They sat between her and what looked like a rolling loading door. When she turned to see why rolling the other way had been wrong, she barely made out the shape of a body. In a pool of blood.

Explains the smell.

She exercised her hands, but the return of circulation caused more pain and a cramp of her biceps, but she could feel the hard metal of handcuffs. That was good.

Wiggling to get her hands in front of her had to be her next action now that the hood was off. Once her hands were in front of her, she could reach the handcuff key her dad had once suggested she glue inside her belt.

Thanks, Dad!

She opened and closed her fists for a few more minutes while she thought through her plan: Hands free, gag off, untie the rest of her restraints. Then help the others.

Two teenage girls sat facing each other on each side, not quite foot to foot again now that the one had scooted back against the wall after pulling off Amber's hood. Sweaty and grimy. Wide-eyed, like an injured horse, Amber thought, and likely as apt to hurt her as help her.

She smiled and said, "Thank you," and the panicked look from the girl across from her eased a bit.

Amber didn't set a personal best time in getting her handcuffed wrists squirmed around her butt and legs, but she did it.

The next thing she did was yank the dirty gag out of her mouth and wipe her lower lip. The blood on her fingers was dark. Her jaw and cheek hurt, so someone had probably belted her for fighting before they got her drugged enough to throw into the truck. Must have been a hell of a punch — her lip was split, and the inside of her cheek was cut where it had mashed against her teeth. Having the gag out was a vast improvement.

The girl opposite her stared in awe and nodded her head with approval.

Amber noted that the six girls all had similar gags, but their hands were tied in front of them. Why were their gags still in place if they could remove them? she wondered. Maybe the dead body beside her had been a sufficient reason.

Unbuckling her belt, she reached the spot inside near the buckle where she'd used a clear silicone adhesive to attach a handcuff key. After peeling it from the leather, the flexible glob proved harder to tear apart to get to the key than she expected. She finally bit the rubbery material to split it, but the difficulty reinforced her confidence it had been secure and more than worth the effort. Finally, the key was out, and she unlocked her left cuff.

Her left hand alternated between numb and the pins and needles of blood flow, so holding the small key was impossible yet.

The truck slowed, made a left turn, then came to a lurching stop.

She popped the key into her cheek, then grabbed the hood and dragged it back on her head and laid down where she'd been, only on her right side with that arm under her, so if someone opened the door, she would still appear restrained. She put her finger to her covered lips, hoping her fellow captives would stay quiet, especially about her in-progress escape, and then draped her left arm behind her out of sight.

CHAPTER 83
Wednesday, November 18, 2009

Cellular calls had made a crazy zigzag in the panic of Amber's disappearance. Zach had called the police department. They were dispatching units to the area, reviewing signal light camera footage starting as close to the hospital as possible. His call to the local FBI office had yielded an immediate assignment of a unit for Amber's kidnapping and the murder of the woman at the hospital.

Short of calling Julie and breaking down, Zach had mobilized the connections he had. He should call her, he thought, but he needed to stay focused.

Instead, he returned to Kelly's hospital room, now guarded by two uniformed security officers who addressed Zach with the respect an FBI agent in a suit would likely get instead of a tall man in faded blue jeans and a black long-sleeve T-shirt. One opened the door for him, closed it behind him.

"I'll tell him. He just came in. Yep, thanks." Kelly hung up. "That was Harper."

"Yeah, he asked me to have you call him about the attorney," Zach said, though it had slipped his mind. "Said he needed your number."

"I've lost track of who's called whom, but anyway, the problem is that Dierdra isn't answering either my house phone or the cell Harper gave her for emergencies."

"Not my priority at the moment." Zach felt like a jerk for saying it, but it was true.

"No, of course not. But Harper's concerned. Hell, I'm concerned. I had the security guy go look, and their car is in the garage, but no one's there."

"Amber said a cop this woman had been dating threatened her because she's the prosecutor and that she supported the investigation into whether he sabotaged his ex-wife's car. Harper told me they'd arrested the guy."

"Exactly. And it could be as simple as the two of them going for a walk around the complex. But he's been trying for hours."

"What am I supposed to do about it?"

"Every cop in six counties is searching for Amber," Kelly said. "As soon as they get something — "

"I know how this works, Kelly," Zach responded with a deepening scowl. "What do you want from me?"

"Could you please go over, look around for me. Maybe they're home now. The cell's dead, the kid unplugged the phone to play games. Just see what you find."

"I don't know my way around this mess of a town — "

"I'll take you," Bonnie said, standing and reaching for her purse.

Zach shrugged in surrender. "Fine. But you stay in touch."

CHAPTER 84
Wednesday, November 18, 2009

Sounds from outside were muffled, but she could hear the voices of at least three different men. They moved around the back of the truck, and someone rattled the mechanism holding the door closed. In the dim light, she hadn't had a good look at it, but she doubted they could open it from the inside.

"Get rid of the two women," one said. "There's a place outside of — "

He was interrupted by a long string of Spanglish that Amber wasn't quite able to translate, but it referred to someone's mother's heritage and bestiality, best she could tell.

She almost smiled until a gunshot and thud struck the back door of the cargo box, making her jump, interrupting the speaker mid-word. Apparently permanently.

"Now, anyone else want to argue about my orders or discuss my mother?" he asked, acting as if he expected an answer. "I didn't think so. You, drive. I'll meet you at the airfield in Oklahoma."

Oklahoma? she thought. Not Mexico?

The driver's door opened and slammed shut again, and the truck started. No passenger. In seconds, the truck was rolling again.

Amber could tell it was a different driver. Someone who maybe didn't have experience driving a larger vehicle. Or who didn't care what happened to the cargo.

Now that they were moving and safe from entry again, confidence in her plan ballooned, but she needed to help the girls first.

Amber sat up and yanked the hood off her head again, feeling the static crackle through her hair. She slipped the key from her mouth and unlocked the right cuff, wanting to throw them across the truck until she realized she might need them. Before she stuck them in her hip pocket, she examined them more closely. The Smith & Wesson Model 100 nickel cuffs, she realized, were hers.

Bastards. . .

She wiggled on her butt and scooted until her back against the wall of the cargo area.

"Are you all okay?" she asked in a low voice.

Several girls exchanged looks, and the one across from her nodded.

"I'll get you loose after I get us some help."

The girl sitting closest to the door crumpled toward the girl beside her like a rag doll, revealing a spreading stain on the front of a dirty green shirt.

Panic spread to the others as Amber figured out the bullet must have passed through the man and into the cargo area, striking the girl.

After a wide-eyed look of confusion spread among them, she realized they didn't speak English. But none of them, despite being dirty, looked Hispanic, so her limited Spanish wouldn't help.

"Press on it," she said, mimicking the motion until the one beside the injured girl understood.

Amber reached to pull up the right leg of her jeans, revealing a high-top dress boot with an elaborate pink and purple stitched flower design. Inside the boot, she wiggled her fingers into a pocket to retrieve a small cell phone.

The girl beside her inhaled hard, but Amber wasn't sure if it was the phone or the pocket of the boot. Not standard footwear design, but the other boot had a larger pocket with an even better surprise she didn't need yet.

Short of fancy features, the phone had one that was crucial — GPS location.

Amber wasn't sure the metal box would strangle any signal for telephone or GPS signal, but she pushed the power button and waited.

Turning her head to the girl sitting next to her, she smiled. "Getting us help."

The girl's eyes lit up.

Amber reached to help work the gag out of the girl's mouth, curious why none of them had removed theirs.

Her lips looked much like Amber's felt, raw and swollen. She puckered and licked them, then smiled at Amber and nodded.

"Do you speak English?" Amber asked.

With her fingers held flat, she touched her lips and ears.

"You're deaf?"

Another nod.

"Read lips?" Amber asked, making a circle, pointing to her mouth.

The girl pointed to herself and the girl opposite them and nodded.

Amber nodded, then made a motion of pulling something from her mouth, then pointed from the one whose gag she'd removed to the others.

Not American Sign Language, to be sure, it was clear enough. Amber gave a thumbs-up to them all, then turned her attention to the phone.

While calling 911 would make the most sense to most people, not knowing where she was would make that a long process, even if the phone could reach a signal.

As her finger perched over the number pad, she realized she didn't remember the number she wished to text. She'd never copied her contact list to this phone.

Damn it!

Made sense to try a number she knew by heart.

She dialed.

CHAPTER 85 — Wednesday, November 18, 2009

Irritated that he was being sent on a rookie errand, Zach followed Dr. Goldsmith to the elevator and through the lobby to the main doors. Outside, however, she veered toward parking that was off-limits to the public.

"I'm sure my car is closer, and no one will ask me a dozen questions at the gate."

Her car was a county supervisor full-size SUV with a lightbar mounted on the roof.

"Bet you don't get to drive one of these," she quipped, hitting the remote to unlock the doors.

"True, but the FBI lets me cross state lines," he replied. "You are not what I imagined, Dr. Goldsmith."

"Did Amber tell you I was a gruff, fat old lady with no sense of humor?"

"No. She used none of those words," Zach said, trying hard to hide his smile as they climbed in. "But she respects you."

"She's an incredibly smart tech. I'd trade kids with you if that were possible. Kelly's bright, but she has an edge over him I haven't put my finger on yet. She's driven to learn more."

"Wouldn't trade, sorry."

Bonnie took off out of the parking space reserved for law enforcement like she was driving the pace car at Texas Motor Speedway.

With her driving, the trip took less than twenty minutes.

The guard at the gate asked for her identification, checked it, and nodded. "Thank you, Dr. Goldsmith." And the gates did their open and close procedure.

Inside, she didn't bother to stop at the first intersection and accelerated through the turn left. After several turns, Zach's sense of direction was useless, not that he had much of an idea where they were. She whipped into a short driveway and shut off the vehicle.

"Let me see if I have this straight," he said before he opened his door. "This attorney and her son are supposed to be hiding here, which is your son's home, right? And Harper called to tell them they could go home, but she didn't answer the cell phone he gave her or his home phone."

"That's it."

"What are the possibilities? Any other ways out? Any chance they went for a walk and got lost, because I can see how that would happen."

"One other way out," she said. "An exit-only gate on the far east side of the subdivision, a half-mile drive. But they didn't take their car."

"Cab?"

"All vehicles have to enter where we did, even if they might exit elsewhere. No record of any strange vehicles entering. Kelly checked."

Zach nodded, and they got out of the vehicle, Bonnie sliding off the seat and her heels clicking loudly on the concrete.

"Any chance someone murdered them in their sleep?" he mumbled as she stuck her key into the lock.

"Hasn't been a violent crime in this place for sixteen years that I'm aware of. Because it's gated, maybe a few cases of vandalism, theft from cars, that sort of thing."

"First time for everything."

"You're quite the optimist," she said, shaking her head, pushing the door open.

The entry split, straight leading up a flight of steps, or left through a door to the garage.

"Anyone home?" she yelled in a voice that made Zach think she must have had half a dozen children instead of one. "Yoo-hoo! Dierdra? Blaine? We're coming to the living room."

No answer.

Reaching the top of the stairs and turning left, the room opened to a large living area and a kitchen big enough to make Zach more than a little jealous.

Bonnie stepped into it to make sure no one was hiding. Or dead.

They froze when they heard a noise from the third story. This time Zach led up the stairs, hand on his gun, flipping the strap that secured it, though he did not remove it from the holster under his T-shirt.

At the top of this flight of stairs, a hallway split toward two bedrooms. The noise, now clearer, came from the second bedroom. The door was open, but the lights were off, and the shades were drawn.

Carpeting muted Zach's steps as he passed a bathroom, lights also off. Then at the doorway to the room, he stopped with his back to the door jamb, easing his gun out of its holster to a ready position.

As he swung around to draw down on the source of the noise, the phone in his pocket rang.

CHAPTER 86
Wednesday, November 18, 2009

Surprise approach blown by a call that made only one ring, Zach continued his pivot around to a bank of computer equipment on black shelving, a leather gaming chair sat facing it.

"FBI! Hands up!" Zach announced.

Nothing happened. Except the second ring of his phone.

All sorts of curse words ran through Zach's head.

He couldn't *see* a person, but he presumed someone was sitting among the electronics, playing the video game he saw on the monitor. Someone who ignored his command but kept pushing buttons, ducking and dodging in miniature movements that mimicked the video character's.

No third ring.

"FBI!" he yelled this time, an arm's length from the chair.

He got a glimpse of dark brown hair just before the chair swiveled left hard, leaving Zach looking at a young teenage boy with a gaming controller in his hands, eyes bugged as he looked at a .45 caliber barrel. The scream he made had no sound, but air hissed out his throat.

"Whoa! Everybody. Are you Blaine?" Bonnie asked from behind Zach, who'd lowered his gun and was breathing as hard as the boy, who yanked the earphones down around his neck.

Blaine nodded aggressively.

Zach stepped back and holstered his pistol.

"Blaine, where's your mother?" she asked, trying to reorient the kid who'd just had three years' growth scared from him.

Blaine's eyes cut to a dusty wall clock, which probably hadn't had working batteries for two years. He shrugged.

"Sorry," Zach said. "You didn't answer when we came in."

Blaine glanced over his shoulder as noises from the headphones indicated his character had been blown up or something equally as computer-dead. "I didn't hear you. I'm sorry! Amber said Kelly told her I could play. I'd never gotten this far at home."

"Where's your mother," she repeated.

"She went for a walk with the lady next door."

"How long have they been gone, Blaine?" Zach asked.

"A while, I guess. I dunno," he said, then added, "sir."

"Any idea how long? Like was she here at lunch?" Zach asked, agitation barely in control.

"Yeah, lunch. We had sandwiches," he said. "Then she was going to a store for a phone charger. The one Sergeant Sullivan sent quit working."

Bonnie and Zach exchanged looks. "Can you show us which neighbor?"

"I wasn't watching."

"Could you come downstairs with us, please?" Bonnie asked.

Though watching Blaine unfold his crossed legs made Zach's artificial knee ache, the kid carefully took the headphones from around his neck and placed them back where he'd found them.

When he stood, several joints popped as he stretched.

Bonnie led the trio down the steps to the living room, coming face to face with Dierdra Preston and her gun leveled at Bonnie's chest.

"Who are you?" Dierdra demanded. "Blaine, get over here."

The boy skirted around the intruders in the house to where his mother stood.

"I'm Bonnie Goldsmith, Kelly's mother," Bonnie said. "We came looking for you when you didn't answer the phones this afternoon."

"How do I know that's the truth?"

"He didn't kill me, Mom. He could have," her son said.

"I'm Zach Samualson," he said, stepping forward past Dr. Goldsmith, "Amber's father. I'm also an FBI agent, if you'll allow me to get my ID. Harper has – Harper Sullivan, I mean – he's been trying to reach you all day." He tossed his credential wallet to Blaine to show Dierdra.

She lowered the gun. "I'm sorry. The phone was dead, and we didn't find the right charging cord here. I met Carol, who lives in the units across the way, while I was taking out the trash, and we chatted. When I asked her for directions to an electronics store so I could buy a new charger, she offered to drive if I was interested in stopping for a coffee along the way."

"And I didn't hear the phone because I was wearing headphones," Blaine added.

"What did Harper say?" she asked.

"He said they arrested the cop for murder, so you can go home," Zach replied.

CHAPTER 87
Wednesday, November 18, 2009

The call might have made a brief connection but cut off before being answered.

Her father would not have recognized the number, even if it connected long enough to display, but she could not remember Brady's number.

Dad. In cargo truck going into Oklahoma, unknown route. Have Brady track this number. 143

The numbers stood for the number of letters in *I love you.* Verification the message was from her, she hoped.

She hit the send button.

The girls were ungagged now, and they were working on untying each other. The one was still bleeding, so Amber crawled to check on her.

Blood flowed through the fingers of the girl holding pressure.

Amber waved for the girl who could read lips. "She's hurt really bad. I've called for help, but it may not be soon enough."

The girl signed this to the others, then held up one finger on each hand and then moved them to be side by side.

Amber frowned. "Sisters?"

The girl nodded.

Amber made a circle in the air around them. "All sisters?"

Shook her head, pointed at the one who'd been shot and the one holding her.

CHAPTER 88
Wednesday, November 18, 2009

Zach's phone beeped three times.

When he looked, it was a text from the same number as the call a few minutes ago. He opened it.

"Thank you, God!" he said. "Where's the phone in the house?"

"In the kitchen," Dierdra said.

Zach rushed to it, replying to the text: **Received. Help on the way. Copy?**

"Geez, what's wrong with him?"

Bonnie shrugged.

Zach pulled a card from his wallet and picked up the receiver to dial.

One ring.

Two rings.

Brady answered.

"It's Zach. Amber texted my phone. She needs you to track this number," he said, reading it from his cell phone. "She's in a truck of some kind going north into Oklahoma."

"Oklahoma?" Brady replied, confused. "That's not the direction they went when we tracked Mackenzie."

"I don't know or care what that means, but track it, then get with FBI Agent O'Banion," he said, reading off a phone number on another card. "He can coordinate a rescue." The cell phone on the counter beeped again.

Copy. Thx.

Confirmation that she could receive text messages, too.

"Okay, let me see if I can get a general location before you go," Brady said, typing on a keyboard so hard Zach could hear.

Eternal seconds passed. Zach turned to see Bonnie, Dierdra and Blaine looking at him like he'd lost his mind.

Covering the mouthpiece of the handset, he explained. "Amber has access to a cell phone that they think they can trace to find her."

This left the two women exchanging information about what had happened, how they each knew Amber, and whether they could help.

"Got it!" Brady exclaimed. "Let me call law enforcement."

The line went dead.

CHAPTER 89
Wednesday, November 18, 2009

Zach's message gave her goosebumps of relief. She responded so he'd know she got his message, too.

The girl who'd been shot was fading fast.

Will need medical evac. One hostage shot. Bleeding badly. She sent the message to Zach.

Within seconds, she received another text.

Amber, it's Brady. Got your location. Will request medevac ASAP, which popped up on her phone before Zach's message, **Copy that.**

Help might not be too far away now, but how could she increase the odds of them surviving if one man shot another already? Although she hadn't pulled it out yet, she had a small pistol in the other boot, holding seven shots. Could she make all seven count?

The driver was someone different. Had he seen where the girls had been? Amber didn't remember being put in the truck, so she didn't know if she was in the truck first. They were closer to the door, so probably not.

She looked around the cargo area. In the dim light, she found the best likely answer.

Accomplishing her goal took longer to explain than it did to implement, but they were ready when Amber heard the first siren in the distance.

She checked the time on the phone. Eight minutes had passed.

By the time a second siren was audible, she felt the truck speed up and then swerve.

In the dark, the swaying and bumps intensified until she was sliding several inches on the metal floor each direction change the driver made.

Amber felt impending doom for the occupants she'd shared the last few hours with. The weaving was getting worse. She'd lost count of the number of sirens after five, but she doubted this was a high-speed chase in a truck designed to barely meet the speed limit. She was sure she'd made the right decision for the girls, getting them into the small section over the cab once she realized it was a rental-type moving van, and she'd tucked them in with a dozen shipping blankets stashed there. They wouldn't have far to slide in a deceleration, which was the most likely predictable force. With the rope she'd pieced together and tied across the opening, she hoped it was enough to keep them from falling out if the truck rolled.

When the truck rolled.

On the other hand, she was a marble in a shoebox, waiting for the inevitable. The only padding she might have was the dead body.

Although Amber had considered using her handcuffs to attach her belt to one of the tie-down rings, the thought of a fire she couldn't escape nixed the idea. Plus, no matter where she attached herself, she could end up hanging by her belt in the air.

Time to do that, even if she wanted to, vanished as she heard the truck crunch into something, probably another vehicle, on the driver's side. Acceleration had probably reached top end, she thought. No way this vehicle could outrun police vehicles.

Just one more thing she could do to help them stop this nightmare.

She slid to the driver's side of the cargo box, facing forward, her feet against the front wall. Making a guess where the driver sat in relation to her, she pulled the compact .45 caliber pistol from her boot and leaned back almost flat before she fired all seven shots through the metal into the cab.

Her ears rang with the enclosed shots, making her head feel like pudding sloshing when the truck began to weave, somewhere around shot three or four.

Based on how the truck jerked and then rocked, she must have hit him.

Calculating the odds of which direction the truck would overturn, Amber tucked into a ball before the impact against the rear wheels pitched the truck sideways. The driver must have hit the brakes, so the momentum was enough to tip it, first skipping on the passenger-side wheels then toppling on over, slamming onto the pavement, throwing Amber to the right wall. The truck slid for what seemed like minutes as the scraping sound echoed inside the cargo area, adding to the ringing in her ears.

The stiff body she'd dragged toward the door when she moved the girls had also tumbled forward into her back, creating a pile that looked more like a bundle of mannequin parts than humans.

When the sliding stopped, Amber jumped up and reached into the area over the cab where she'd had the girls hide, helping lift out the one who'd been shot first, then the others.

"Go bang on the door," Amber said to one who could read lips. She tried to make a gesture of hitting something with her fist high in the air, but her hand wouldn't work, and the first zap of burning pain ran from her neck to her fingertips.

The girl understood and grabbed another to help her.

Amber took over holding pressure on the injured girl, but the effort made her dizzy.

The deaf girls could not hear the voices outside, the prying of a lock, or the attempts to open the door, now a sideways slide.

The first crack of headlights and flashers was blinding.

"We need an ambulance!" Amber yelled. "Gunshot wound!"

CHAPTER 90
Wednesday, November 18, 2009

"We need to go," Zach announced. "Brady has a location for Amber."

"Please contact Sergeant Sullivan so you can get back to your lives," Bonnie said, shaking hands with Dierdra. "But if you have time, Kelly mentioned he'd like to meet you."

"I'd like that," Dierdra said. "We'll drop by tomorrow before we leave. And I hope your daughter is okay, Mr. Samualson."

Zach shook hands with Dierdra and Blaine. "Sorry I scared you. Both of you."

Apologies for the phone issues began, but Bonnie could tell if she didn't go with Zach right now, he'd hot wire her car and leave without her.

"All right," she said, following him down the stairs. "Where are we going?"

"Brady says they are on Highway 77 toward Denison."

"Let's go find your girl."

Without needing directions, Bonnie backed out and drove to the back exit she'd mentioned, then out through side streets to a major street, and on until she made the entrance to U.S. Highway 77 northbound.

Traffic was light, and again, Zach was sure Bonnie'd learned to drive on a racetrack somewhere, but this time, he appreciated every second.

"See if you can find out how far past Denison they are now," she said as the city thinned out.

Zach picked up his phone and texted Brady.

His phone rang instead.

"The moving truck they were in crashed during the chase north of Denison before the bridge," Brady said. "Amber was banged up, but they say it's nothing critical. Ambulances will go back to Denison. Meet them there."

"Ambulances?"

"Several girls were in the truck with her."

"You're sure she's okay?" Zach asked, his heart racing.

"Only what I was told. How far away are you from Denison? The hospital's on the south side of town."

"Denison?" Zach asked Bonnie.

"Twenty, probably."

"I heard. Should be there about the same time."

"Thanks, Brady. I owe you."

CHAPTER 91
Wednesday, November 18, 2009

A blur of activity whirled around her blurred as Texas Department of Public Safety troopers and Grayson County deputies and EMS personnel performed their duties.

Someone in a uniform told her to let go.

For the first time, Amber looked at the girl she'd been holding in her lap as the paramedics prepared to move her to a gurney.

Tiny, she thought. She's so small. Please don't let her die. I don't even know her name. Any of their names.

"You must be Amber Samualson," a trooper said, helping her to her feet. "Are you hurt?"

"I'm okay," she said. "Did you catch anyone besides the driver?"

"He's dead, so we won't be getting anything from him."

"Gee, that's too bad," she said, looking at her hands and jeans at the blood of a little girl.

"Two other men in a car got stopped in Oklahoma. Drugs, weapons. Not sure we can positively connect them to this."

"Match the ballistics to the bullet from the girl and one of the drivers back wherever we'd stopped before. That should be enough," she said, feeling woozy. "I need to sit."

"Medic!" the trooper yelled as Amber slid down the metal of the truck roof to a crouching position.

CHAPTER 92
Wednesday, November 18, 2009

Bonnie pulled up to the hospital where the ambulances had brought the victims.

Zach left her sitting in the truck as he was out and moving before she'd put it in park.

She couldn't blame him. Some of her recent trips to hospitals for her son had been similar walks into the unknown. She gathered her bag and followed through the door where he'd gone.

Hectic was an adequate description of the ED, but not chaotic. She knew the difference. Still, her help was not needed, so she followed the signs out to the waiting room.

A nurse had pointed Zach to Amber's room, and he burst through the door like a center linebacker, almost running over the nurse between him and the gurney.

Seeing Amber on the backboard shocked him.

She still wore a hard collar on her neck and tightly rolled blankets beside her head, taped so she couldn't move. A purple bruise stained the skin of her cheek, and her mouth was bloody.

"Amber?" he said, trying to step around the nurse, who mirrored his movements until it looked like they were dancing.

"Dad! You found me!"

"I will always find you," he said, a tear sliding over his cheek as he touched her hair. "But you led us to you. How'd you do it? Whose phone did you use?"

"Mine. Since Paul was murdered, I've carried a spare phone in my boot, just in case. And my off-duty gun."

A nurse and radiology tech came to take Amber to CT scan, leaving Zach alone in the room, saying a silent prayer of thanks. He considered calling Julie, but before he could decide what to tell her, Amber's gurney was rolled back into the room.

"That was quick," he said.

"The MRI will take a lot longer," she said. "That's next."

The ER tech brought a pan of soapy water and a stack of washcloths to her bedside table. "I thought we could get you cleaned up a bit while you're waiting for the MRI." she began.

"I bet you're busy," Zach said, pushing up his sleeves. "I've got this."

"Sure?" she asked, giving him a nod then excusing herself.

"Most of the blood on me is from one of the girls. Someone got shot near the truck and the bullet came through the door and struck her," she said.

Zach tossed a handful of washcloths into the pan, swished them around in the hot sudsy water and pulled one free, and squeezed water from it. He gently wiped grime, first from her eyes, then her uninjured cheek, folding the cloth as he went.

"You're pretty good at that," she mused.

"Julie taught me all about it after my knee surgery."

"Knee? Oh shit!"

"Remember, I was working a horse who went down with me." He tossed the bloodied rag into a nearby sink and got another from the water.

"No, I remember that. I meant Kelly. His knee surgery. Is he okay?"

"Yes. Bonnie's out in the waiting room and has probably already called him."

"Why is she here?"

"Honey, it's a long story with a lot of missing pieces. We'll get it all straight later." He picked up her right hand, but it felt limp, and he was afraid he'd hurt her. "Something wrong with your arm?"

Tears welled in her eyes. "Not just my arm, Dad. I can't move. I mean, I can still feel, and the doctor said that was a good sign, and the CT scan didn't show any broken bones in my neck, but I'm headed for an MRI next."

"Brady said they told him you were okay," he said, focusing on scrubbing the dried blood from her fingers, afraid now to touch her head.

"I zinged my head and neck when the truck rolled. I was walking at first."

Zach's heart skipped a beat then did a triple thump.

What little he knew about medicine was based on horses, and a horse that couldn't move . . . Well, no jumping to conclusions, he told himself.

He cleared his throat. "We'll see after the MRI then. Shall I call Julie while you're getting scanned?"

"Yeah, maybe you could call Dr. Katz and see what he says. I'd feel better if he said I won't be in a wheelchair the rest of my life. They won't tell me anything."

"Perhaps I could help with that," a woman said from behind Zach.

"Dr. Goldsmith! Dad said you were here, too. Is Kelly okay?"

"He's fine. Would you like me to speak with the physician?" she said, going to the opposite side of the gurney from Zach. "I am a medical doctor."

"Oh my gosh, I didn't realize that!" Amber exclaimed.

"I didn't either, Dr. Goldsmith," Zach said. "My apologies."

"It's true, so let me go see if I can learn anything useful," she said. "With your permission, of course."

"Absolutely. I'd love a long lesson on neurobiology today."

"Next order of business between us? My name is Bonnie. Please use it. We've gone through too much to continue being so formal."

"Yes, Ma'am," Amber said, earning her a stern look.

"Dad? The little girl who was shot. I don't know if she's alive. The other girls tried. I tried to stop the bleeding." Tears rolled toward her ears. "Can you check on her and the others? Please?"

"When I'm finished," he said, wiping her eyes.

"I'm scared, Dad." She reached and squeezed his arm.

CHAPTER 93
Wednesday, November 18, 2009

Neither of them gave her grasp a second thought for a full five seconds as Zach continued to wipe away the grime on her face.

Amber's brow would have furrowed, had it not been covered in tape to hold the head blocks in place.

Zach saw her expression and was about to ask if he'd hurt her. His attention moved from her chin where he'd been washing to the fingers wrapped around his right forearm.

"You moved," he whispered, not trusting his voice. "Your arm moved."

"I know," she replied. "I thought I was dreaming."

"Move the other hand."

Amber closed her fingers into a loose fist, but it was slow and still weak.

"That's fantastic!" he said, looking around when he heard the door open.

Dr. Goldsmith and a tall, gangly man in scrubs came in the door.

"She moved her hands!"

Trying not to be the dad who jumps up and down at his child's first word or first step, he stepped back and let the two doctors discuss the improvement with Amber.

"I wasn't thinking about doing it," she said. "I bent my elbow and touched his arm."

"That's the progression I'd been hoping for," the doctor said. He looked like a human equivalent to Walt Disney's Goofy. "We'll still get the MRI, but I believe you're suffering a type of temporary spinal shock with edema around the injured area, which is responding to the steroids we've given you."

"I'll be okay?" she asked.

He moved toward her feet. "Wiggle your toes."

While the action took a little concentration and was feeble, he felt it. "I can't predict the future, but spinal cord injuries receiving treatment within four hours have an excellent prognosis."

CHAPTER 94
Thursday, November 19, 2009

Little arm-twisting was necessary to convince Dr. Howell to transfer Amber to a larger hospital. Some might think it was a coincidence that the receiving facility happened to be where Kelly Morgan was still a patient.

"I don't want to go by helicopter, Dad," she argued. "I'm perfectly stable and improving."

"I've done it. Wasn't all that fun, but there are worse things. Besides, I saw the sticker on the back of the pilot's helmet that says, 'Stop screaming! I'm terrified, too!'"

"Tell me you're kidding," she said, rolling her eyes.

"Nope. At least Craig hasn't tried to convince you he just got his license last week," the flight nurse said. "Always makes a big commotion when he says sometimes he can't remember how to get it started, so he keeps pushing buttons till the whirly parts move."

"Fabulous," Amber groaned. "Real comedians."

"Thanks!" a tall stocky guy said proudly. "I checked the Jesus nut on pre-flight this time. Sometimes it comes loose."

"Jesus nut?"

"You know, the one nut that holds the rotors onto the helicopter? And if it fails, you talk to Jesus before you crash?"

"Dad! I'll go, all right? Please make them stop."

"You guys are a riot," Zach said. "How often do you get to practice this routine?"

The pilot, flight nurse, and medic, in unison replied, "Every flight, every night!"

Zach thought they must have done mental high-five's all around for that.

The flight itself didn't take as long as the loading and unloading.

At the receiving hospital, Amber was rolled directly to an intensive care cubicle, lifted to the bed by a scoop stretcher to keep her spine straight, and made as comfortable as a human can be in an ICU bed.

"Thanks for making this trip less scary for me," she said as they gathered gear to leave. "Hearing you make fun of yourselves while doing your jobs was comforting."

"Not all of our patients are in shape to appreciate our jokes," the flight nurse said. "We wish you the best."

That Amber could shake hands was a satisfying accomplishment.

Once the ICU nurse finished getting Amber hooked to every device in the room, she rolled in a computer and began asking the thousand-question admit information. Questions about her diabetes were the most relevant to her treatment, Tana said. Otherwise, Amber's past medical history was boring other than her femur fracture.

"No MRIs," Tana said to herself as she typed.

"No, the hardware is all titanium," Amber answered.

"You can't put metal through the machine, Sweetie; it's a big magnet."

"Then I should be stuck inside the one in Denison, because I had an MRI about two hours ago."

Snit seemed to be a kind word for Tana's reaction, but to her credit, she tried to hide her ire at being corrected by a patient.

An hour later, Amber was alone in a room, listening to the sounds of devices that monitored her vital signs. No way she could sleep with the cacophony of hers and the other patients' machines. No television. No telephone. Not even a clock within her field of vision, though she could hear one ticking. Like a damned bass drum, barely enough strength in her muscles to try rolling over or covering her head with the pillow.

She'd been hospitalized before, but she didn't remember being so sensitive to sound.

Closing her eyes made the volume seem louder, but the room lacked anything of interest. The nurse would also be returning to get her blood sugar reading, check the IV, do hourly neuro checks to see how her strength was increasing.

Wait, she hadn't even thought to ask anyone what day it was. She was hungry, but she hadn't had any insulin. How long had she been unconscious in the truck? Was it all from being drugged or did she have a head injury, too?

The heart rate alarm beeped, and though she realized it was probably high because of her anxiety, hearing it unnerved her even more.

She wanted to cry.

Until she heard her father beyond the curtain meant to provide her privacy.

"I don't care if it's past visiting hours," he said in a calm voice. "I don't mean to be difficult, but . . . "

Amber imagined him presenting his FBI badge with a glimpse of his holstered weapon.

Nurse Snit must have relented, but she was probably unhappy about it.

The curtain fluttered, and there he stood, backlit by bright hallway lights.

"I see the helicopter crew managed," he said. "Jokes all the way?"

"Right up till they walked out."

"That's good." He kissed her forehead now that they had removed the tape and headblocks. "How's the muscles?"

"I won't be in a weight-lifting contest anytime soon, but hopefully I'll walk tomorrow," she said. "Did Dr. Goldsmith go back to Kelly's room?"

Zach nodded. "She'll bring him to see you in the morning. We can answer each other's questions about this mess after you get some rest."

"I don't think I can sleep with all the noise."

"When I talked to Julie, she recommended I stop and get these for you," he said, pulling a small box from his jean jacket pocket.

"Earplugs? That's perfect. Tell her thanks."

"You can tell her tomorrow. She'll be here before lunch."

"She didn't need to come for me," Amber said.

Zach laughed. "Are you kidding? She's coming for me, silly girl. You guys have worn me out!"

CHAPTER 95
Monday, November 23, 2009

"I get it," Amber said. "Having a driver is kinda fun."

"I'm a little tired of it," Kelly countered. "But at least he doesn't look for potholes to hit."

"Is that an insinuation I did?"

"No, not at all."

The car stopped in front of the Keegan house.

Mackenzie came running out to greet them. "I've been so worried!" she said, trying not to dance, looking like a tethered balloon in a strong breeze. "I wanted to visit you in the hospital, but Mom said I should wait. Have you heard anything about me helping?"

Vanessa stepped out on the porch. "Mac! Let them get inside." She greeted them with a hug. "Glad to see you're both on your feet. Come in. Can I get you something to drink?"

Kelly and Amber had discussed beforehand that this would probably be a long visit.

"I'll have water, please," Amber said.

"If you have a soft drink, that would be fine," Kelly added.

"So you were kidnapped, too?" Mackenzie asked, sitting opposite them.

"Yes, I was, along with six teens from the Dallas School for the Hearing Impaired. We were in a small rental moving van, headed to an airport in Oklahoma, although I believe I was not supposed to make the flight."

"Why you?" she asked as Vanessa brought in drinks for them all. "Was it the same people who got me and Dad?"

"Actually, it was. I had been working on the files on a laptop recovered from a car crash. I came across a small file with a phone number in it," Amber explained, "and I was dumb enough to dial it on my personal phone. It was nothing more than a warning to these people that the files were being decrypted, but because that phone registered my number, they were able to track me down. The same woman in scrubs who tricked you and Paul found me in the hospital, threatened to harm Kelly if I didn't come with her."

"That's so scary," Vanessa said. "Like you can't trust anyone."

"Who wouldn't trust a nurse, right?" Kelly replied. "But Amber was carrying an extra phone in her boot."

"Since what happened to you, I thought it was a great idea. Worth every penny I spent on it. They didn't think to look in my boots."

Mac jumped up and plopped down beside Amber, wrapping her arms around her. "I'm so glad we're okay."

Amber hugged her back. "I learned a lot from you. This brings us to what you asked me about helping us. The law says only members of the police force may participate in such activities," she said, "but the sheriff and police chief have approved an alternate program you can help with. He wants us, you and me, to write and produce a 30-minute television program on how to help kids and their parents identify these creeps, and to explain the consequences from our first-hand experiences."

"A television program?" Mac looked back and forth from Amber to her mom and back. "Really?"

"Yes. And we'll be working with other law enforcement agents, including the FBI."

The balloon tether seemed to come loose as she danced around the room.

Amber looked at Vanessa. "With your approval?"

"Oh yes! That's such a relief."

"We'll want your story, too," Kelly said. "About how you almost lost Mac."

PART V

CHAPTER 96
Friday, November 27, 2009

Ian Molina answered his private line, an extension number few people had, so he knew the caller had to be someone important to him.

"Sheriff Molina," he said.

"Sheriff? Brady Cayson. I have finished both cases I've been working on for you."

"That's good news, Mr. Cayson."

Brady cared little for the formality, but he hadn't been asked to call the sheriff by his first name, either.

"As far as the crash involving Caitlyn Parker, records show that Blaine Preston's phone was stationary in the hotel area, as his mother had indicated, and in proximity to Mr. Royce's until approximately 5:10 a.m. on September 30. From that location, it traveled to the tower connection at Harris in Frederick County, where only one cell tower services the area. It appears at the same direction from the tower for approximately seven minutes, then begins a return route to Lake Marshal, and back in the proximity of his own phone again at approximately 6:45 a.m."

"That's not conclusive," Molina replied. "I thought this technology would — "

"Sir, I'm not finished. While the cellular signals themselves are not detailed locations, the GPS signal recorded by the phone is, and I've plotted points for every minute between the times of the cell signal estimates. That mapping shows that Blaine's phone went from 3885

North Highway 70 in Lake Marshal at 5:10 a.m. to 1718 Merritt Street in Harris at 5:48 a.m. That's three houses from Miss Parker's house at 1704 Merritt. The phone was there eight minutes and change, then returned to Lake Marshal via Highway 70, showing stops at a convenience store at 5106 and a restaurant at 5509 North Highway 70, before returning to the original location."

"Damn! I'm sure Mr. Blaunshine will be happy to hear that."

"He was, sir. I personally delivered the documents to him this morning," Brady said. "Which leads me to the other project I've been working on."

"Go on."

"In this case, we weren't looking at where one particular phone went on the day in question, but whether we could identify *any* cellular activity in the area around Harper and Lilah Sullivan's house on the day she died. This location is served by two towers owned by StarData Cellular, with a small ellipse of overlap in coverage. What we found, at the time of Mrs. Sullivan's death, which was noon to 2 p.m., were three cellular phones."

"Okay, whose?"

"I think you and the prosecuting attorney need to see the other details in person if you intend to make an arrest or follow through with indictment."

"The case is that strong?"

"Sir, that's not for me to say. I only produce the reports. Would you meet him and me in an hour at his office?"

CHAPTER 97
Friday, November 27, 2009

"I've never fixed a meal for so many people before," Vera Katz told Julie and the few guests who'd already arrived the night before. She kneaded dough.

Julie peeled sweet potatoes.

Kayleigh was stirring ingredients together for pecan pies. "Why would you design a kitchen this size?" Kayleigh asked. "It's bigger than my first apartment."

The kitchen was huge, with dozens of cabinets. An island the size of a car sat surrounded on three sides by deep counters and oversized appliances much too large for the two people who lived in the house. A breakfast bar seated five with ease, possibly six within elbow distance of each other. In an adjoining room sat a formal dining table set for twelve.

"Zach does everything his size, and this is his kingdom, not mine," Julie said, laughing.

"You'd think we were feeding forty people," Kayleigh said.

"I don't doubt that we couldn't," Julie replied. "Or that we aren't. I'm not sure who all will be here."

"I can't wait to see Amber," Vera said, forming the dough into balls that would become dinner rolls. "And to meet her new boyfriend."

"Zach left for the airport to get them less than an hour ago. She's going to be so surprised. Zach's got her convinced you and Gerald went back to Michigan for Thanksgiving," Julie said. "She has no idea you all are here."

"Did someone say my name?" Gerald asked, with both of Kayleigh's twin daughters hanging on him like monkeys, Kimber on his back, and Amalie wrapped around his leg.

"We decided not to tell Amber everyone was coming," Julie explained, "because she might not have brought Kelly with her."

"I hope we don't scare him too badly," Kayleigh said. "I wish Reese could have come. Maybe everyone can come to Michigan for Christmas."

"I'm glad you postponed the big dinner so we could all be here to help," Vera added.

"Thus, the ginormous kitchen," Julie said, spreading her arms to exaggerate it. "I know who you named Kimber after, but how did you pick Amalie?"

Kayleigh named one daughter after her sister, Kimberly. "Amalie was Reese's grandmother's name. I like the way it sounds when it's pronounced right, but I'm afraid we've cursed her to correcting people for life. For two years, I've told people it's pronounced *ah-ma-lee* and not a misspelling for Emily."

Gerald grabbed carrot sticks for himself and his clingers, ambling back to the den.

"He loves those girls!" Julie remarked, putting the sweet potato chunks into the casserole dish.

"They can't wait to go horseback riding. That's all Amalie talked about while they were in the bath last night," Kayleigh said. "Do you stir in your pecans or sprinkle them on top?"

In unison, Julie and Vera each answered. Differently.

They all laughed.

"I've never made a Southern Pecan Pie before, and you two aren't helping!"

"It doesn't matter much in the end as the pecans float over the liquid as it gels," Vera explained. "Kai hated pecans, so I made a Mock

Pecan Pie for him one holiday season. It's made with oatmeal instead of nuts."

"How'd that work out?" Julie asked.

"He informed me it was worse than the pecans, so I might as well make it right."

"I hadn't heard that one. Zach doesn't talk much about his dad," Julie said.

"He's not still mad that I wanted to move to town when Gerald and I got married, is he?"

Shortly after Zach and Julie's cabin in Washington had burned to the ground, they moved back to Albuquerque. Vera and Gerald were going to get married and decided he would move to New Mexico, too. They sat together at Vera's kitchen table one evening, discussing the temporary options, but the most reasonable decision was for Vera and Gerald to stay in Vera's house on the ranch, and for Julie and Zach to live in Dagmar's house in town until a new house could be built for them on the ranch, too.

"No. I think he was overwhelmed with the idea that my previous boss was going to be his new stepfather," Julie said. "I thought it was a great idea, personally."

"Me, too!" Kayleigh added. "You guys have made my side of the family so much nicer to be around than Reese's."

Knowing nods passed around the room.

Pies went in the upper oven, the sweet potato casserole into the lower oven.

The smell of turkey and dressing drifted through the house.

"Rolls in half an hour," Vera announced. "The green bean casserole is in the warming oven along with the gravy and white cheddar baked corn. Pumpkin pie, pineapple cream pie, and chocolate pudding for the kids, all in the fridge. And the wine's chilling!"

"I think that's everything," Julie agreed.

The ladies were headed for the den to rest when Julie heard a vehicle. She checked out the kitchen window and saw a strange pickup park in front of their house, and a tall man reached for flowers and stepped out into a bright New Mexico day.

Julie opened the door as he stepped onto the porch. "You must be Harper! I'm so glad you could come." She greeted him with a big hug, waved him inside. "Zach's on his way back with Amber and Kelly from the airport. Let me introduce you to everyone. Did you find the place without any trouble?"

CHAPTER 98
Friday, November 27, 2009

"Thanks for coming over today, Sheriff," Brady said, extending his hand.

"I'd have invited Harper, but he's taken a holiday weekend for the first time since his wife died, and I wasn't about to say no," Molina replied.

Ronald Blaunshine, the Benton County Prosecuting Attorney, invited the two men into his office, though the courthouse was empty on the day after Thanksgiving.

They took seats at a conference table that Brady was sure had to be older than his grandfather. He made a mental note to ask his dad while he and his family were visiting for the holiday weekend in Brighton.

"I think the documents you brought for the Royce case make it an unbeatable prosecution," Blaunshine told Brady for the third time. "So, what about Deputy Sullivan's wife?"

Brady took a deep breath. "This is probably not what anyone expected. One of the cell signals in the area was a propane delivery guy. The other two phones belonged to the account of Edward Thomas."

"The pastor?" Blaunshine asked, unsure he could believe.

"His wife is one of the ER nurses," Molina added. "Go on."

"The phones appear to be independent, not arriving in the area at the same time by about fifteen minutes, but departing within about eight minutes of each other. I have gathered phone logs that show conversations between Mrs. Sullivan's and these two phones. I have also created text logs between all three phones."

"Do we know what the texts say?" Molina asked.

"No sir. Just that they do exist. There are 40% more texts between Mrs. Sullivan and the number I believe to be Mr. Thomas's than between the two Thomas phones or Mrs. Sullivan and Mrs. Thomas."

"What does that indicate?"

"Interpretation is not my job. I'm only providing the summary of the data in a user-friendly format," Brady said.

"Which one arrived first?" Blaunshine asked.

"Again, presuming I have users correctly assigned, Mr. Thomas arrived first to the area."

CHAPTER 99
Friday, November 27, 2009

Zach stood outside the security zone at Albuquerque International Sunport, waiting on Amber and Kelly. Thanksgiving travel was bustling, but the general mood was better inside than it had been on the interstate getting there.

He hadn't seen his daughter since a few days after the kidnapping, though he would have stayed longer if asked. Julie, who had flown to DFW, stayed two days longer to help get Amber settled at home.

Amber's recovery had plateaued once after she was walking, but for several days she had not seen muscle strength improvement. Bonnie had arranged an in-home physical therapy assessment for Amber and Kelly before they were to use the pool, and a second visit had added a few exercises Amber found helpful.

Zach wasn't sure what to expect, except he hoped for the best. He checked his watch again. Several aircraft had landed since he arrived. He paced the hall.

Flashing his credentials would get him past the checkpoint, but he wasn't willing to misuse his job to get closer. Much as he disliked it, he waited with the small crowd.

Five minutes passed before the deplaning passengers began to come through.

Standing gave him an easy view above most in the gathering throngs by at least six inches, but he moved closer as others drifted toward the baggage claim areas.

Finally, he saw Amber, using a cane and walking slowly, accompanied by Kelly, who had a slight limp but was pulling a rolling suitcase, followed by Bonnie Goldsmith, unexpected but welcome.

Clear of the security area, one of the major changes since the 9/11 attacks, Zach hugged Amber and shook hands with Kelly and Bonnie.

"I hope it's not a terrible inconvenience that I came," Bonnie said as they headed straight to the parking structure, not needing to wait for baggage. "Amber insisted."

"That's my girl!" Zach said, patting her on the back. "Always room for more."

Zach loaded the 40-pound bag Kelly had been dragging.

"That's a change of shorts and two pairs of socks for me," Kelly explained. "The rest belongs to them."

"Welcome to my world," Zach said. "I've had to move Amber several times. One suitcase for two women? You got off easy."

After exiting and leaving the mobs around the airport, the ride was smooth.

"It's really beautiful, with the city against the mountains," Bonnie said.

"Sunset is even better when the mountains get this dusty pink glow," Amber explained. "And the Sandia Tram to the top is the second-longest in the world."

Zach let Amber tour guide her guests as they turned north on I-25, then west on I-40. He enjoyed hearing what she found interesting after having been away so long. The city gave way to wide open range, then he exited and took the road to the ranch, still with occasional commentary from the backseat.

Kelly had paid attention to Amber's points of interest and trivia, but he and Zach exchanged a glance and smile about her excitement. "Just wait," Zach had whispered.

He parked in front of the house, got out and helped Amber from her seat.

No one had come out the door, so he assumed they would all be ready to jump out and surprise her inside.

"Isn't that Harper Sullivan's truck?" Kelly asked.

"Uh, yeah. I'd invited him, but I didn't think he'd come," Zach said.

Up four steps to a wrap-around porch, Amber turned to gawk. "Dad, the porch is fabulous! I haven't been home since you finished it."

Zach opened the door and held it, and Amber went in first to what looked like a surprise party. Introductions were made all around, with special attention to Kimber and Amalie, whom Amber had never seen in person.

Last-minute details to their Thanksgiving meal in motion, Julie took her place beside Zach, snuggling under his arm. "This is perfect."

He smiled and nodded.

After getting everyone seated and a lengthy prayer of thanks that each adult added to, the huge turkey and ham were presented. Gerald was asked to slice turkey, Zach the ham. Dishes went around the table.

"I can't believe you didn't tell me they would all be here," Amber chastised her parents.

"We were afraid Kelly and Bonnie wouldn't come," Julie said, passing another dish.

"So long as there's no test on names after dessert," Kelly replied. "This is fantastic."

Side conversations began as connections were explained, how who knew who. Even Harper, who'd come alone, was catching up with Zach and Kelly when his cell phone rang in his coat pocket. He didn't answer it, and as desserts were selected, he forgot about it.

CHAPTER 100
Friday, November 27, 2009

Ian Molina spent two hours reviewing the case and evidence before he asked that the two suspects be brought in individually for questioning and kept in separate rooms.

Ellanie Thomas had been at work at the hospital.

Eddy was at home, working on the Sunday sermon.

In tears, Ellanie explained that she had been at work when Eddy called her, horrified because he'd arrived to find Lilah dead. Ellanie drove there, certain that Eddy was wrong. Seeing her best friend dead, a gun on the floor beside the bed, she was in shock herself, she said, but she decided that neither of them should be involved, so they both left. It was wrong, she admitted, but she'd panicked. It wasn't till later, she said, that she figured out Eddy had killed Lilah.

In another room, Eddy confessed that he was there and that they had been in bed. He stated he was in the bathroom washing up, when Ellanie came in and confronted Lilah, still in bed, then shot her. Ellanie threatened to kill him as well if he talked to the police. He said he didn't know where Ellanie got the gun but stated that she left it on the floor, hoping Lilah's death would look enough like suicide that the case would be closed. He left the area a few minutes before his wife.

The interrogations both confirmed the cell phone documentation that they were at Sullivan's house, but each had incriminated the other. Worse, they both mentioned a gun on the floor when they left. No gun was present when police searched the scene.

Harper Sullivan's statement said he found no gun.

Ian was frustrated.

The autopsy summary reported Lilah Dawn Gentry Sullivan was killed by a brass-jacketed round-nose 95-grain bullet, most consistent with a .380 caliber, fired from a six-groove right-hand-twist barrel weapon. No manufacturer had been identified. Entry was through the right temporal region within a few degrees of perpendicular, but the barrel was not directly in contact with the skin. The exit wound was present on the left pre-auricular area. Brain death had been instantaneous; cardiac death took approximately four minutes, causing substantial bleeding from both wounds.

The medical examiner had collected samples for DNA analysis, finding mostly saliva, one with seminal fluid without sperm. Results had been ready and waiting for a comparison for sixteen months. Edward Thomas willingly gave a specimen, already acknowledging he was there and had been engaged in sexual activity with the victim.

Inventory of Sullivan's centerfire handguns, totaling eight, included 9 mm, .40 caliber, .357 caliber, and .45 caliber. He did not own or have ammunition for .380 auto, and none of the bullets weighed less than 115 grains. Criminal history was negative. All but the duty weapon on his person at the time of the call were locked in a gun safe with other rifles and shotguns, all accounted for matching a handwritten inventory.

Ian Molina called Harper's phone a second time later that afternoon.

"You know I'm on vacation, right?" he answered.

"Harper, I need to ask you something about Lilah's death. Are you sure you didn't find a weapon?"

"What's this about?"

"Did you?"

"No, sir," Harper answered. "No gun, no brass."

"You were upset that day. Do you have any other weapons that weren't locked in the gun safe?"

He hesitated a moment. "Yeah, when I sold the house, I came across a pistol my father had given me."

Before. After. Would that ever end?

"Was it there when Lilah was killed?"

"I'm sure it was, but I didn't think about it. I don't even remember where I found it when I packed. I just threw stuff in boxes and crates."

"We'll need to see it, Harper. Mr. Cayson delivered his reports to the prosecutor and me today."

"Sure. I'm in Albuquerque. I'll be home Sunday afternoon."

Molina said nothing.

"Did the cell report show anything?"

"I probably shouldn't tell you, but yeah." More silence. "His reports show that both Edward and Ellanie Thomas were at your house about one o'clock that day."

"Ellanie?"

"Why does that surprise you about her but not Edward?"

"Ellanie was Lilah's best friend. It's hard to wrap my head around that."

"You aren't friends with Eddy?" Molina asked.

"No, sir. I can't say I am. He's always been a little too much Bible-in-your-face for me."

"Do you think either of them could have killed your wife?"

Harper did not want to speak, fearing he'd say something wrong. "I've seen people do some really warped things, but I can't imagine why them."

"You think about it. I'll see you Sunday. Call me before you get to town, I'll meet you and get the gun."

"Yes, sir. Thanks for letting me know."

Harper disconnected, sat on the porch, watching Zach and Julie walk one horse, Gerald and Vera another, each couple holding a bouncy twin on a horse's back.

Kelly came out to the porch as Harper finished his call. "Those are some happy kiddos," Kelly said, sitting in a chair close by. "You look like that was bad news."

"I'm not really sure. The sheriff has two suspects in my wife's death, having used the technology Brady has," he said. "It's hard to believe."

"Because it might finally be solved?"

"Because the two people identified were her best friend Ellanie and her husband Eddy."

"Whoa, that's not what I expected, either."

"Nope." Harper's gaze was out toward the Sandia Crest, but that's not what he saw. "I guess I'd given up on the case."

Amber and Kayleigh came out of the house, Kayleigh with her camera, which she pointed toward the men and clicked without aiming. They were laughing about something, but Amber said she was staying while Kayleigh went to take more pictures of the kids' first ride.

"They think they solved Harper's wife's murder," Kelly told her as she sat.

Harper didn't speak.

Kelly gave Amber a slight shrug. "Look at them," he said, nodding toward the barn and the girls, whose squeals could be heard. "Wish you could be out riding?"

"You just want to see me on a horse, don't you." Not a question.

"Yep!"

"Have to wait."

Harper stood abruptly. "I'm gonna go crash for a while." He went into the house.

"Doesn't appear too excited about it," she whispered.

"How long ago was she killed?" he asked.

"Never heard anything about it. Maybe Dad knows."

CHAPTER 101
Friday, November 27, 2009

When it came time to make sleeping arrangements for their guests, Amber said she'd like to stay at Vera's to catch up with Kayleigh and play with the kids.

"She's in one bedroom, so we have space for Amber and Kelly," Vera said.

"We've got room for both Bonnie and Harper, so it's all good," Zach replied.

Amber almost panicked as Zach drove her and Kelly the half-mile to the original ranch house he'd grown up in.

Kelly grabbed the bag and went inside, but Amber dallied, waiting to be alone with Zach.

"I can't believe you're okay with this," she hissed.

"With what?"

"Putting us in the same bedroom!"

"I thought since he was living with you — "

"He's staying at my house, Dad. We're not living together. We're not sleeping together."

"I'm sorry. We have an extra bedroom at our house. I can — "

"No, do *not* embarrass me by trying to fix this." She turned away and walked to the house.

Kelly met her at the door and held it open, waved to Zach.

"I think I like him," Zach said to himself, getting back in the vehicle.

"Everything okay?" Kelly asked as he followed Amber down the stairs, finding a large bedroom, a bathroom, and the laundry room. "Um, where am I going to sleep?"

"See? That's what I was asking Dad. Everyone assumes we're sharing a bed."

"Because I'm staying at your house," he finished. "I'll go sleep on a couch upstairs."

"We need to talk."

Kelly swallowed hard and sat on the edge of the chair. "Okay."

She bit her bottom lip, wanting to say something, not sure what. "I'm scared."

"Of me?"

She frowned. "No, *about* you. Your auto-immune problems. What if you have more?"

"I can't say I won't, Amber. I'm sorry."

"I was terrified you were dying that night you had the blood clot."

"So was I. Honestly, I've lived on the edge for a few years because I didn't care about anyone, even me. Especially me. Now all this medical stuff terrifies me, too, because of you," he said. "Are you that afraid of my future?"

She looked down and nodded. "And your past."

"I can't change any of that stuff, but I will take the best care of me I can. For us." He smiled. "I've been afraid of 'us' because we've been stuck together by other people, like tonight. Not that I wouldn't be happy cuddled next to you, but I was afraid you'd resent how we got there. That it was everyone else's expectation, but not our idea."

"Does feel like we didn't choose much of it."

"Let's choose. Will you take the chance to be with me, knowing I'm broken?"

Amber nodded.

"I love you, Amber. I have, since, I don't know, since our first kiss. Since before. Like, maybe forever." He stood and wrapped his arms around her, moving back and forth slightly in a dance to unheard music.

"I love you, too." She snuggled against his shoulder, feeling the warmth of his body against her. Amazed at how good they felt together.

"Maybe I should move out so we can date?" he asked.

"I was thinking maybe you should stay, so we don't have to."

CHAPTER 102
Monday, November 30, 2009

Ellanie sat in the interrogation room next to a bland-looking man in a dark suit, presumably her lawyer.

Harper watched them for a short time through the one-way glass, wishing it were a large picture window like television crime shows used. Instead, this was about a hand-spread tall and two across.

Ian Molina and a department detective as well as the prosecutor entered and sat across from them. Ian slid a microcassette recorder to the middle of the table. "This interview is being recorded on November 30, 2009, at 0914. Present are Ellanie Noel Thomas and her attorney Mr. William Archer; myself, Sheriff Ian Molina, and Deputy Detective Dennis Caldwell. Also present is Benton County Prosecuting Attorney Ronald Blaunshine. Do you consent to this session being recorded, Mr. Archer?"

Mr. Archer said yes.

Dennis opened a folder he'd brought to the table, appeared to read from the top page. "Mrs. Thomas, you understand you will be charged with the shooting death of Lilah Sullivan on April 5, 2007. You have been read your rights. With your attorney present, do you have any questions about those rights?" Dennis Caldwell asked.

Ellanie shook her head.

"Please answer verbally," Dennis coached.

"No questions." She appeared irritable, but she'd been in the county jail over the weekend, in solitude only because there were no other females. Wearing a jumpsuit from the jail, she looked pale against the bright pink. She'd had a shower this morning, but she wore no makeup, making her look less cheerful.

"I understand that you wish to make a statement this morning?" Ian asked. "Go on."

"Eddy called and told me she'd killed herself."

"And the weapon?"

"Was on the floor." She wiggled in the seat. "I went to the house, but I told Eddy we should just leave."

"I see. That's not the truth, Ellanie, and I can prove it. Don't you think Harper deserves to know what happened to his wife?" Ian said. "Tell me the truth."

She stared at him.

"Would you like to know the evidence we have against you, what will convict you of first-degree homicide?" Ian asked. "I'll tell you if you'll tell me the truth of what happened."

"Since you have proof," she said, sounding bored, "I'll tell you."

Her attorney whispered in her ear, advising her, begging her not to say anything else.

Ellanie turned to him and told him to go to hell.

"I'd like it noted for the record that I advised her not to speak to you."

"So noted," Blaunshine said.

Three men waited almost four minutes for Ellanie Thomas to speak.

"My intention wasn't to kill Lilah. Maybe Eddy, but not her. I did, though. I was so angry. I don't know the details of when or why the affair began, and I told Eddy I didn't want to hear it.

"We'd had a patient brought to the emergency department a few days before I shot her. He'd been assaulted, was unconscious, died. When I was removing his clothes, I pulled off his boots and found a small pistol. While I was cleaning up, I hid the gun in my cargo pocket, then my bag in the break room without anyone noticing that it existed. It was fate.

"The day I shot her, I'd called Eddy to ask him some insurance question, but he told me he wasn't home, that he was having lunch with a parishioner, which wasn't unusual, except I suspected he was lying.

"I told Lisa I had to go change my scrubs, that I'd had an accident, my period, you know. I drove to Lilah's house. Eddy's car was in the driveway. I took that gun out of my bag, stuck it in my pocket, and went in through the front door. I could hear them in the bedroom, giggling like teenagers. I knew what to expect when I got to the bedroom, except they were moving around, covered by the sheet. They didn't see me.

"Standing beside the bed, I watched, maybe a minute, as they writhed under the satin sheets. Honestly, even that pissed me off. Satin. I'd offered to buy satin sheets, but Eddy told me they were slutty. Slutty indeed." She took a moment to regain her train of thought. "I made a polite cough, to make them stop. Lilah pulled the sheets down from her head, with this happy-to-horrified transition on her face when she saw me. I didn't think about it. I pulled out the gun and pointed it at her, waiting for Eddy to poke his head out, too.

"The gun fired. I didn't intend to pull the trigger, barely touched it, I think. The sound made my ears ring, but I saw her body tighten up like a seizure, then relax. Eddy had piled out the other side of the bed by then. I thought it was funny because the prim and proper preacher kept yelling, over and over, 'What the fuck!' I laughed, wondering what his God would think of him.

"Then he looked at her and changed to 'You shot her!' I stopped laughing. I pointed the gun at him, told him that if he ever told a soul, which is pretty funny, too, that I'd kill him."

"Told him to get dressed and leave. He did. Probably took him a full minute to get out the door to his car. I wondered how I could solve this *problem*. I don't know why I even looked, but I pulled open the bedside table drawer, and there sat Harper's gun. More fate, I figured. I took it out the back door and fired a round into the ground," she shrugged. "I wanted to make it look like she'd used his gun, so I removed six of his bullets, then loaded the six remaining bullets from my gun in the clip, so the medical examiner would see that they matched the bullet and the casing. Before I wiped my prints and put the gun in her hand to get her prints on it, I touched the barrel to the blood on her temple, and then dropped it on the floor."

Dennis nodded. "Do you think your husband went back to the house after you left?"

"No."

"Did you go home?"

"Nah, I changed scrubs in the car. I always have an extra set. Then I went back to work."

"How do you explain Deputy Sullivan not finding a weapon on the floor as you describe?" Ian asked.

"That's not my job. Did you find the brass under the bed?"

"Yes. One."

"What did you do with the gun you used?" Caldwell asked. "And the bullets."

"I threw it out in some pasture south of town." She shrugged again. "Your turn."

Ian opened a folder. "With cell phone records, we can prove you and Eddy were both at the house during the window of her time of death. We can prove that Lilah was not shot with the gun from Harper's bedside table, because it is a 9 mm. The bullet that killed Lilah was a .380, which matches the brass casing found in the bedroom."

"They're the same."

"No," Ian said, a flash expression of a smile twitched the right side of his mouth. "A .380 can be considered a 9 mm short, but they are not the same."

Her lips tightened.

"And we've recovered the missing 9 mm Smith & Wesson weapon that you fired outside and say that you dropped on the floor. The six shells you put in the magazine from your gun were indeed .380, a match to the bullet that killed Lilah and to the cartridge casing found on the floor. Your fingerprints were on the brass and the magazine."

"Circumstantial," she said. "None of that proves I killed her."

"Oh, except for your confession."

"You said you had proof I killed her," she argued.

"No, I asked if you wished to hear the evidence against you, in exchange for telling us the truth."

"You lied!"

Ian smiled. "No. I didn't."

CHAPTER 103
Wednesday, December 16, 2009

Kelly knocked, waiting for Amber to look up from her computer. She was behind a real desk in her new office, the recently named Supervisor of the Crimes Against Children Task Force. The position was so new that the office still smelled of drying paint in the mornings when she unlocked the door.

"Hey there!" she said.

"Ready for lunch?" They were scheduled for a group meeting with the Tarrant County prosecutors at one o'clock.

"Almost. I'm finishing the request for a cell company to provide a history on the cell phone from another investigation. I wish it were with Brady's company. Maybe with its history, we can track where it went."

Kelly nodded his approval. He'd had returned this morning from Benton County where he was the expert witness on crash investigation for the first-degree homicide prosecution of Stephen Royce, who'd thought his record as a peace officer would secure an acquittal. Dierdra, although recused from the case, had dinner with Kelly after his testimony. She didn't think the defense could make Royce likable enough for the jury to believe.

"Almost," Amber said. "Let me finish this paragraph. I spent last evening with Mac, writing the introduction for the video," she said, fingers continuing to type as if they were not connected to her brain. "She's such a smart kid!"

"I'm glad she's involved. Makes it credible, and kids can relate to her."

Amber nodded, hit a few more keys to save her work, then closed her laptop.

"You need a plant or something," he observed. "Get your jacket. We're going to Pandora's."

"We'll never get out in time for the meeting."

"They called and canceled. But they also informed me that they have confessions and convictions for all three of the guys in your first two cases. Two for ten years. One for twenty with no parole. No trials. No media. At least one divorce. Probably new cars for defense attorneys paid to make this go away quietly."

"That's a shame. It should be headline news for a week."

"They have forwarded a new website to troll, pardon the pun, called 'The Ocean' because there's always more fish in the sea. We should be able to get in early. It just started up a few weeks ago."

She stood and grabbed her coat from the rack. "In that case, Pandora's it is, and you can buy!"

CONCLUSION – 10/10/2010

Zach Samualson stuck the pin of the American flag into the lapel of the dark suit coat. As much as he hated wearing a suit, he hadn't worn a uniform since his last day as a police officer in Houston in 1991. Carrying a badge wasn't wholly synonymous with a uniform: His earlier years in DEA had been mostly undercover or at least in business-casual clothes.

"You're so handsome in a suit," Julie said.

"And I can't wait to dance with you in that dress. I'd have forgotten you have such a nice —"

"Zach!" She tried to interrupt what she thought would surely be some remark about sex.

" — pair of legs if you didn't look so damned good in jeans," he finished.

She reached to brush a stray piece of lint from the shoulder of his shirt, remembering the first time he'd dressed for his current job, in a suit, pressed shirt, tie, and polished shoes.

"I've almost gotten used to the jacket now, but I don't ever think I'll like the tie. Promise not to bury me in one." He didn't think he'd ever overcome the sensation of feeling two threads away from suffocation.

"Honey, I promise. If you die before me, a tie will be the least of your concerns," she said in a sweet tone, batting her eyes.

While a suit offered a professional image, he thought as he knotted the silk tie around his neck and imagined his face bulging, it would never be functional as a cop. Though fitted by a tailor, his shirts and coats felt like a shrinking neoprene wetsuit, squeezing him until he could barely breathe. He missed the extra space of his home clothes, as he thought of them now. Room to move. He enviously eyed the full-quill ostrich boots sitting next to the dresser.

Julie had always helped him choose suits. She and the salesperson at some big-man's formalwear store had argued over fit versus function. They both had insisted on white shirts, but Zach had stood firm in getting several shades of grays and one dark purple, which had turned out to be his favorite.

And Amber's, which is why he wore it today.

He hated white shirts, starched stiff enough to stand on their own, snug across his shoulders, all cotton. He'd found in his first months of work, he couldn't raise his arm far enough to reach his gun in a belt holster without ripping out the seams, so he'd opted for a shoulder holster. And looser shirts, style be damned.

What the hell was I thinking, taking a job where I have to wear a suit and I'm away from home so much?

He'd asked himself that question every morning he dressed for work for the last six years of the eight they'd been back in New Mexico. In the first two years, he'd been too busy for a job, what with overseeing the house build, running the ranch, and learning to accept Gerald Katz as his stepfather when Vera remarried.

The greatest difficulty he'd faced was leaving Amber in Washington to complete her undergraduate degree in Seattle. In Julie-fashion, she finished a year early despite having to repeat her first semester because of injuries she'd sustained in New York City. And she'd graduated with top one-percent grades. She'd been looking for a first-time career in criminal forensics but had considered going on for a doctorate at the University of North Texas Health Science Center in Dallas/Fort Worth. She spent a year's internship with the Tarrant County Sheriff's Department before being offered a position as a deputy working with its computer and cyber-crimes division of the crime lab.

"The apple didn't fall far from the tree, did it, Amber?" he muttered to himself in the mirror. Secretly he always hoped she'd go on for a doctorate and get a lab job, where it was far less likely she'd be shot. And he liked the sound of it: Dr. Amber Samualson.

Now that wasn't going to happen.

Reflecting on his own job, he *was* likely to get shot, working in a task force branch under the counterterrorism division. The goal was to identify and break up criminal activity related to gangs or other groups whose operations pose a significant national security risk. As much as he liked parts of the job, being an FBI special agent had required he attain then maintain his fitness. He'd been in good shape, considering ranching didn't require him to run much. Training for the physical agility test had taken serious focus after he'd wrecked his knee while trying to work a green horse for his mother. Since then, he was as fit as he'd ever been, running five miles without stopping.

He slid on the shoulder holster and smoothed the crisp dark purple fabric of his shirt beneath it. Kevlar was not in his wardrobe today. Nodding in satisfaction to himself in the dresser mirror, he adjusted the tie — almost black with tiny gray horses — dots unless you looked closely — and shrugged on the jacket.

Yesterday, he'd chased monsters. Next week, he would think about retiring. Again.

But today? Today he would walk his lovely daughter Amber Marie down the aisle of an old church in the Old Town area of Albuquerque to give her away to Kelly Morgan.

Zach actually liked the young man, but he would slip him a note when he gave Amber's hand to him.

If you break her heart, remember, I still have a gun, a shovel, and an airtight alibi.

If you are a victim of human trafficking or child exploitation, please reach out for help. Many men and women work to help those taken advantage of or even kidnapped from their homes and other places.

Parents, pay attention to who you and your children talk to electronically. Unmonitored internet access can invite criminals of all types into your home. Seemingly harmless comments about going shopping for the day and a picture of you and a friend could indicate to someone your child could be home alone. Complaints from your unhappy child, grounded for reasonable punishment, could catch the attention of a predator. Predators promise greener grass to entice a child or teenager out the door to become a victim of sexual assault or other forms of human trafficking, including forced labor such as prostitution, a donor for healthy organ sales, or even murder.

Report suspicion of child sexual exploitation to your local police, your ICAC Task Force, or the National Center for Missing and Exploited Children CyberTipline (www.cybertipline.com or 1-800-843-5678).

About the Author

Val Conrad has two passions she's found a way to mix: writing and medicine. As a nurse practitioner with years before as a paramedic and nurse, she has plenty of experience to blend with real pieces of history that touch those affected. She does both in the flatlands of West Texas.

She is the author of the *Julie Madigan Thriller* series.

Note from the Author

Word-of-mouth is crucial for any author to succeed. If you enjoyed *Signal of Guilt*, please leave a review online—anywhere you are able. Even if it's just a sentence or two. It would make all the difference and would be very much appreciated.

Thanks!
Val Conrad

Thank you so much for reading one of Val Conrad's novels.
If you enjoyed the experience, please check out our recommended
title for your next great read!

Blood of Like Souls

"An addictive first entry in the *Julie Madigan Thriller* series...
fortunately for us, a second *Julie Madigan* book awaits."
–BEST THRILLERS

www.ingramcontent.com/pod-product-compliance
Lightning Source LLC
Chambersburg PA
CBHW010726100726
47899CB00009B/2941